BEASTS OF CARNAVAL

BEASTS OF CARNAVAL

ROSÁLIA RODRIGO

/11 MIRA

ISBN-13: 978-0-7783-8723-7

Recycling programs for this product may not exist in your area.

Beasts of Carnaval

Copyright © 2025 by Rosália Rodrigo

All rights reserved. No part of this book may be used or reproduced in any manner whatsoever without written permission.

Without limiting the author's and publisher's exclusive rights, any unauthorized use of this publication to train generative artificial intelligence (AI) technologies is expressly prohibited.

This is a work of fiction. Names, characters, places and incidents are either the product of the author's imagination or are used fictitiously. Any resemblance to actual persons, living or dead, businesses, companies, events or locales is entirely coincidental.

For questions and comments about the quality of this book, please contact us at CustomerService@Harlequin.com.

TM is a trademark of Harlequin Enterprises ULC.

Image: Scene break icon © Bricklay/iStock/Getty Images

Mira
22 Adelaide St. West, 41st Floor
Toronto, Ontario M5H 4E3, Canada
MIRABooks.com

Printed in U.S.A.

To my mother and her mother
Mami, teller of bedtime stories
Abu, keeper of the earth
Gracias por la magia, el jardín y los cuentos

Content Warning

Dear reader, note that this story touches on themes related to colonialism, slavery, and war, including discrimination, forced assimilation, and native land theft. It also includes mentions or descriptions of natural disasters, such as hurricanes. While I made an effort to approach these topics with care, I understand this content may be triggering for some readers. A full list of content warnings may be found on my website, rosaliarodrigo.com, or the Trigger Warning Database.

ACTO I

Before

THE MONSTER ARRIVED as night descended.

At the knock on the door, the boy's knife stilled. He'd not been expecting his visitor for another hour at least.

With calloused hands, he brushed the wood shavings from his trousers and placed the carving on the side table. It was a small thing, half the length of his thumb and just now taking shape: there, the sweep of a wing, poised for flight; here, the sharp point of a beak, ready to slice and crack and carve out its burrow. To make, for itself, a place of its own. Somewhere hidden. Safe.

With the whittling knife pressed flat to his side, the boy went to the door of his suite, and though it was inevitable what awaited on the other side of it, he allowed himself to fantasize a different fate: the edge of his blade scoring the wood, cleaving out of it a portal to elsewhere. To a new beginning molded from an ending, a tragedy rewritten in steel and sawdust.

A key slid in, unlocking the door from the outside. *Click.*

There, in the amber lantern light of the hallway, stood a monster.

And it was not the one he had been expecting.

This one was garbed in silken frills and a mask of forest green ending in horns dipped in gilt—six of them, arranged from forehead to cheek. Jagged teeth lined a smiling mouth, and darkness shadowed the wide skeletal pits of its eyes.

Before the boy could speak, the monster handed him a letter.

With a surprisingly steady hand, the boy broke the golden wax and removed a slip of cream paper. It bore a single word. He read it slowly, sounding out each letter in his mind the way his sister had taught him.

Sígueme.

The boy glanced up. "Where to? Who's sent you?"

The monster said nothing. Monsters of this kind never did. Instead, they turned, moving in the manner of someone expecting to be followed.

He could have refused, locked the door, relegated himself to the fate he knew rather than chance it all on a destination yet unknown. But that barely registered as an option. Already, the boy was across the threshold, trailing the monster's footsteps, taking with him only the tool in his pocket. He had better ones, sure. Chisels of tempered steel and knives that cut through salmwood like it was coconut meat, but he'd learned such finery came with a debt owed, and he was done paying it.

Together, they descended toward the distant sounds of laughter and the rhythmic *ba-bong, ba-bong* of drums. The air was sweet there, fragrant with yellow and pink alhelí, and the lingering scent of coffee and spices. Another time, the boy's stomach would have grumbled with hunger. As it was, it knotted tighter.

Head down, he forged ahead until they came to a nondescript door. It opened with a groan into a spiraling stairwell, lit only by the flickering lantern swinging from the monster's hand and echoing with the distinct sound of rushing water.

The boy hesitated. "Where are we?"

Again, the monster said nothing, treading deeper into the dark and taking the light down with them.

Cursing, the boy considered turning back, finding a path that did not end in shadowed cellars or shadowed rooms, but who was he trying to fool? No such fate existed for those like him. Drawing courage, he walked into the gloom.

The stone was slippery beneath the worn soles of his boots, the iron rough with rust against his palm. As he journeyed deeper, the burble and hiss of water grew louder, and just beyond it lay another sound. A soft humming resonating like a ghost's lament.

It became clearer as he neared the bottom of the stairs, its strange words more pronounced. The voice lacked polish, and there was a deep, gravelly harshness to it. No one would ever have described it as beautiful, yet it held the boy's ear better than any songstress's dulcet tones.

When he finally reached the bottom step and squinted into the dark, he saw her, standing alone in the cavernous chamber. Her hair was a curtain of sable silk, and her eyes the black of volcanic stones. They mirrored the fae glow of the lantern, reflecting veins of red and amber like magma flowing from the earth. Dangling from her fingers was an obsidian mask. It cast winglike shadows onto the wall at her back, rendering her a creature of elsewhere. A thing that dwelled in nightmares and the dark of the caves.

There, at her side, a river ran, and on it bobbed a small canoe.

The corner of the woman's mouth crooked upward as she turned to the boy and said, "Get in."

CHAPTER 1

When night descends, Carnaval rises.

—Chronicler

AN EBONY WING kissed the curve of Sofía's cheek.

In a flurry of feathers, the bird pitched sharply skyward, abandoning its perch on the hanging planter by the balcony door. But not before she caught the flash of scarlet along its throat.

A woodpecker.

Instinctively, she reached for its likeness. The figurine rested against her breastbone, underneath the scooped collar of her cotton dress. Her fingers felt along its shape, the black beads of its eyes, the splatter of red at its neck, worn smooth and faded from how often she sought the tiny creature's comfort. More with each day its maker remained gone.

Above, the feather-and-flesh woodpecker gave an indignant screech before swooping off the veranda and into the fields of sugarcane below. Sofía followed its path over the reeds, their ribbony leaves long and vivid green against the blue of midday. Near a hundred men and women toiled there under the harsh sun of Etérea, hacking away at the crop with quick, practiced swings of their machetes. Others prepared the cane for transfer, hefting the bundles onto ox-drawn carts.

Thirteen years it'd been since Sofía herself had sweated over the fields of Hacienda Esperanza, yet it was as if no time at all had passed. Standing there, she was seven again, her bony fingers knotting the cane into bundles, tying as fast as others could cut them down. She could feel, still, the chafe of unwashed cotton on her sunburnt skin, the bite of gravel against her bare soles. She could hear the rasp of sugarcane stalks dragging across the ground behind her, their jagged ends forming thin tracks along the earth.

"*Oye!*" called a gruff voice from down below. "Got another of them machines here for the lady!"

Sofía leaned over the veranda to see near a dozen field hands lugging a metal contraption. It was enormous, with rear side wheels that dwarfed even the tallest among the men. The main body was built like a cannon, and at the front end of it was a smokestack, longer and narrower than that of the cargo train that passed by once a fortnight.

"If you don't mind me asking," called up one of the younger men, a lanky lad, recently hired. Ernesto, Sofía thought was his name. "What is it . . . exactly?"

"That," Sofía said, her tone droll, "is the future."

"Whatever it is, this's as close as I'm getting to it," grumbled another of the workers, wiping at the sweat beneath his straw hat. "Last time the lady made us try one of her machines, I nearly lost my toes."

A slight exaggeration, but Sofía kept the thought to herself. "I'll be sure to pass your concerns along, Mateo."

Seemingly satisfied by the response, the workers took one last look at the monstrosity, and scattered—some to the field, others to the mill where the cane was processed and refined. Sofía lingered on the veranda for several heartbeats longer in defiance of the drilled-in urge to go inside and seek shelter from the sun, to safeguard her skin's near-respectable pallor.

Her fingers curled, stubbornly gripping the balustrade. For once, when the sun hit the backs of her hands, each veined with a network of old scar tissue, she did not pull back into the shadows. She leaned into the heat of day, reveling in the knowledge that soon there would be no one demanding she seek shade, or cake on layers of too-pale powder, or brave the sting of whitening soaps.

When Sofía finally stepped back inside the manor she'd served almost all her life, she did so with the straight-backed confidence of someone who had never been owned. Never been bartered for. Never known their worth in coin. She walked . . . like a Hisperian, imagining, as she had long ago, that all this was hers. The courtyards teeming with orchids, lotus, and passion-fruit flowers, the opulent rooms with their endless treasures, the clay-tiled ceilings that neither leaked nor bent under the brute strength of Etérea's autumnal storms. To a child born to die for a master's harvest, this place had seemed a sanctuary, its orderly adobe halls a reprive from the unstructured, unpredictable world beyond it.

The illusion, of course, had broken as swiftly as it'd swept her away.

Perhaps if she'd been endowed with a healthier imagination, she might unsee the bars beneath the elegance and glamor—if only for today. Today, she'd have liked to lose herself in it. To conceive one last perfect, sparkling memory, bright enough to paint over the shadows of this place.

The door to the study opened with a push, revealing floor-to-ceiling shelves packed to bursting with encyclopedias and maps and leather-bound tomes. With the histories of places far and near, and a rich body of the latest scholarly work in politics, philosophy, scien—

She caught the whiff of smoke before she saw it.

At the far end of the study, the young lady of the manor was frantically trying to stamp out a fire with her heeled boot.

"Mother of Waters." Sofía rushed forward at once. "What've you done now, you fiend?" She reached her just as the last of the flames were smothered, and all that remained were the charred pages of a book entitled *The Right to Govern: A Treatise on Hisperia's Colonial Rule*.

Not a terrible loss then, she thought. The library could certainly do without this particular piece of literature.

"There." Her lady, the indomitable Adelina de Esperanza Montañez, smiled up at her with a charming, albeit slightly chagrined, expression. "Another crisis successfully averted."

Sofía shot her a mirthless look and snatched up a folded newspaper from under a pile of notepads, loose scribbles, and precariously stacked books. "Get those windows opened up. Quickly now." She was already unlocking the double doors to the balcony and fanning out the smoke with the day's copy of *La Gaceta*.

"I nearly had it, Sofía. Got through a whole line of stitches before the blowback. I think I might've added too much heat to the engine, or maybe the smokestack got clogged up with debris . . ."

Sofía eyed her lady's latest undertaking, a sewing machine rigged to a system of belts and wheels all connecting to a small boiler, light and compact enough to sit on one corner of the desk. "Perhaps next time, run your tests somewhere less . . . flammable?"

Adelina paused as though only just noticing the room's many incendiary hazards. It was just like her to home in on a project with such focused precision, all else fell away.

Within a few minutes of frantically airing out the room, the stench started to clear, bringing with it the syrupy scent of boiled sugar from the mill outside. Tired and lightheaded from the smoke, Sofía melted down into the leather armchair across from Adelina. Up close, the lady's cerulean eyes were watery and bloodshot from the fumes, and spots of pink tinged the alabaster of her cheeks. A few wisps of bronze hair had come loose from their elaborate coiffure, framing her heart-shaped face. She rubbed a hand across it, smudging ash over the button of her nose, the dimple above her cupid's bow. As she leaned her elbows onto the desk, she said, "You're on page three," with a nudge toward the newspaper on Sofía's lap.

"Truly?" Sofía could not open *La Gaceta* fast enough. "Who'd you have to bribe to get . . . *No*. Tell me, please, you've not gone and accepted Francisco's hand."

"Saints above, no, can you imagine? I would be a nightmare of a wife to him. No, no. Francisco needs someone who is much more . . ." Adelina paused, considering. "Traditional," she decided. "You know, the kind less likely to set accidental fires in a room full of kindling."

"Or premeditated ones?"

"For the thousandth time, it was a tightly controlled conflagration," she protested. "Look, that is all to say that as hopelessly smitten as he may be—and let's be honest, why wouldn't he be?—I had nothing to do with this. Francisco is, by his own admission, a rabid fan of your essays. He could hardly contain his excitement when he heard you'd written something new. Tore the envelope right out of my hand, he did."

Sofía flipped through the rumpled newspaper until she found it—her critique of the civil rights reform, which succinctly described the ways it had failed to extend proper protections to the islands' freed people. Most of whom were still living on the outskirts of Etérea's society two years after the Emancipation. Despite it being signed *Anonymous*, something in her came alive at seeing her words in print. To someone used to being erased, dismissed, always dangling in the empty space between two categories, being read meant being seen. *I am here*, she thought, and felt herself resolve into something . . . *more*. That different state of matter she became when her words were laid out in front of her.

The page was her anchor, absorbing her as it would ink. Rendering her solid after years spent compressing and contorting herself to fit whatever vessel her masters poured her into, no matter how small or narrow the shape. It was as she squeezed herself into those too-tight spaces that she thought, and she read, and she wrote. And she realized she could write herself into existence. That the words of a nameless slave could seed more words, propagating across the islands like weeds. That the winds could catch them and carry them to the heart of an empire all the way across the sea, where they would take root, and spread, and grow so large that even the newly crowned king would hear of them as he settled into his throne.

When Sofía wrote those first words at fourteen, she had no idea they would tangle in those of others like her, helping to catalyze a movement. One that would earn her her freedom. Her right to exist.

She brushed her fingers across the ink, lingering on what might be the last time she saw her words in print, and right as she was about to fold the page closed, she caught a glimpse of the article beside hers.

Postmortem Examination Inconclusive

Capitán José Laureano of the civil guard tells the press the unidentified deceased discovered off the coast of León bore "no evidence to suggest a violent or unnatural death." The coroner's report concludes that the manner of death is consistent with symptoms of malnourishment. Authorities have issued a closure of the investigation but continue their search for the deceased's next of kin.

"They're closing the investigation?" Sofía laid the paper down firmly across Adelina's desk. "The body was found in costume. A *carnaval* costume. And . . . what? That's not at all suspicious to them?"

Adelina busied herself with her machine, hoping, perhaps, that Sofía would move on to a more pleasant topic of conversation.

"Well?"

"Well," Adelina conceded. "It's all there. Officially, the prevailing theory is that the man was an itinerant performer, some poor sod down on his luck. A sensible conclusion, wouldn't you say? Given the sorry state he was found in."

"And is that what Francisco thinks?"

"Gods, if only. He's as obsessed with this case as you are. Thinks the civil guard has some sort of 'arrangement' with the owners of Isla Bestia." The island south of mainland Etérea where the elite went to imbibe and indulge and leave behind the mundanities of life. Adelina leaned in conspiratorially. "All very hush-hush, of course. His source claims the guard's sent out several investigators to the island since this whole mess started, and all have come back jaunty and blithe, singing Carnaval's praises."

Sofía muttered beneath her breath, "At least *they* have come back," because it was the kind of thing neither she nor Adelina ever said above a whisper. That way, the other could pretend not to have heard, and both could go on playing make-believe another day. Carrying on as though they'd lost nothing to that island. As though that place hadn't stolen from them both.

Sofía occupied herself folding the paper into uniform pleats, half wishing Adelina would acknowledge the remark, and half dreading she would. What terrible secrets could burst forth from them once that door was opened? How long before Sofía was confessing, *I've done enough waiting, and this is goodbye?*

"Your new toy's arrived," she found herself saying instead, trying not to think of the boarding pass tucked into the apron of her dress. Of where it would take her once this day was done.

"What, the tractor? So soon?"

Sofía nodded, regaining her grip on her composure. Not that it showed; her thoughts so rarely made it onto her expression. "The boys hauled it in just a minute ago." A brief pause, then she added, "It's hideous."

Adelina beamed, unbothered. Surely, she'd take one look at the metal mammoth and think it the most beautiful thing in all the world. "Can you believe this is finally happening, Sofía? Sage above, by this time next year half the hacienda's labor will be done by machine." Not only would it improve conditions massively for the field hands, but if her numbers were correct—and they always were—mechanizing the hacienda would more than double its current sugar production. Surplus revenue would be reinvested into those in its employ in fairer wages and better living conditions, even sponsored schooling if all went to plan.

If being the operative word there.

Assuming Doña Elena remained oblivious to her daughter's flagrant philanthropy, it was still a decidedly lofty plan, and an expensive one to boot. Should the master of the house ever return from his overlong holiday, one glance at the ledgers would surely render him catatonic.

Sofía watched Adelina for a moment, this bold, enterprising version of the girl she'd grown up with. While her lady had certainly never lacked for confidence, this focused purpose was a more recent development. *This* Adelina did not need waiting on or tending to.

She was self-sufficient. A woman of business, her life too crowded with numbers and ideas and ambition to make room for loneliness. That was what Sofía told herself. What she'd been telling herself for months now. Only then did the guilt roiling in her belly ease.

IT ALWAYS SURPRISED SOFÍA, the myriad of ways her new freedom came with qualifiers. The unwritten clauses in the laws that two years ago relinquished their claim over her body, but not the ties that bound her. Tonight, freedom meant buying passage on the trolley, but being charged twice the coin. Having the liberty of traveling without a master's company, but fearing the dangers that could befall a mestiza alone.

It was reckless of her to not have at least tried to mask the sandy brown of her complexion. She ought to have done her hair up in fashionable curls or worn something that did not so clearly mark her as a servant. It would have been the smart thing to do, the *safe* thing to do, but salt and seas, she was tired of it. Tired of the pins pulling at her scalp. Of the hand-me-down gowns she'd wear when Adelina wanted a friend, not a criada. Of erasing her mother from her skin, extracting the brown from it like molasses out of sugar.

What energy Sofía had she'd exhausted convincing herself to abandon the one place that, while certainly not a home, was familiar. Predictable. Such a fixture of her life, she kept glancing over her shoulder, expecting to see the fields of sugarcane behind her, the outline of the manor limned in a sunset glow. As though it might have crossed the distance with her, hounding her steps like a vengeful spirit.

To distract herself from that unhelpful train of thought, she studied her journal's contents under the fluctuating light of the streetlamps. For years, she'd been building a repository of all things related to el Carnaval de Bestias. Notes, rumors, and magazine clippings, torn right off Adelina's society periodicals in the hopes of wringing something factual out of all that sensationalist nonsense. Pages upon pages of gossip columns, essays, and pretentious exposés, and looking at it now, it amounted to nothing more than crumbs. Her research, if one could be so generous as to call it that, painted an abstract picture of the infamous Carnaval, rendering a paradise of myth more so than a place within this earthly realm.

"Plaza las Delicias!" yelled the trolley driver over the blast of the engine.

When the vehicle slowed to a stop, Sofía clutched her luggage firmly between both hands and stepped onto the cobblestoned street of the southern port town. The plaza she disembarked onto was a square of blocky, pastel-colored buildings with arched balconies and narrow windows set around a place of Hisperian worship that boasted an obscene amount of sculpted details. A hulking bust of the Three-Headed Gods loomed over the door, depicting the Youth, the Father, and the Sage with their necks joined together at the shoulders.

It was an eyesore. Almost as much as the stone fountain at the plaza's center, which featured statues of renowned Hisperian conquerors posing victoriously with rifles and swords. Light from a nearby gas lamp illuminated the inscription below the lip of the fountain—*Los Exploradores*.

Sofía snorted. Leave it to Hisperians to conflate exploration with domination.

Oh, it was a clever narrative, she had to admit . . . a romanticized pseudohistory in which brave heroes rescued an unenlightened world from the dangers of incivility. In that version, it was a peaceful, even welcome, transition, not the near extinction of a people.

It was exactly three centuries ago that Hisperian ships first arrived on Etérea's shores, bringing with them pestilence, gunfire, and a hunger for gold. The history books marked that day as one of discovery. New lands had been found—*what a triumph!* Never mind the fact that those lands already belonged to another, the ones scholars called "savages," but whose descendants knew as the Taike'ri.

The island natives who did not fall to violence or disease were forced to labor in the fields, and in the mines, and in the beds of foreign men. Over the years, their blood mixed with that of their conquerors, and their stories, words, and ways were laid down like bodies in a grave. What Sofía knew of her ancestors was diluted through the diaries of Hisperian chroniclers, the mouths of her elders, the songs whose meanings were lost along with those who sang them.

Metal rattled as the trolley started down the rail.

Sofía noticed the other passengers had begun dispersing and thought it best not to linger there alone in the dark. After taking a quick moment to orient herself, she started down the tree-lined path, following the telltale brine of the sea. She kept out of the shadows and moved with purposeful haste, remaining vigilant until the port appeared.

All the planning in the world could not have prepared her for the sight of the steamer bobbing in the Gilded Sea, waiting for her to board it.

There, in the distance, lay her destination . . .

Isla Bestia.

The small island had been home to el Carnaval de Bestias—some iteration of it or another—for decades now. Initially, a secretive, invitation-only kind of affair, and now the premier tropical getaway of the beau monde. Wealthy visitors came from all across the Gilded Islands to attend, as did plenty of travelers from Hisperia and its allied nations on the Continent.

It was there Adelina's father, Don Reynaldo de Esperanza, had gone five years ago, bringing with him Sofía's twin brother, Sol, as his personal valet.

Neither one had been heard from since.

As it often did these days, Sofía's head swam with visions of a body floating in the very waters she was now set to sail, a fanciful costume the only clue to its demise. There was no taming the images that came to her. When she closed her eyes, all she could see was her twin, his sweet face superimposed upon the dead's. The lanky length of him gone still and bloated with seawater.

It wasn't Sol, she told herself. *You know it wasn't him.*

She'd read what was in *La Gaceta*, studied it line by line until she could recite the report by memory. It was not his eyes they'd described, not the black silk of his hair or the golden brown of his skin. That a report existed at all should have told her all she needed. Dead men who looked like her brother did not get investigations, and they certainly did not get to headline the front page of the news. At best, someone might give him an unmarked grave somewhere afield if he was lucky, and Sol had never been lucky.

That realization had been the clarion call she'd so desperately needed to finally disrupt the life she knew, the only one she thought she'd ever know. And so it was, that with her arms bearing all her brother left behind, she resolved to go find him. No longer could she idle away her days waiting for his overdue return. Daring to hope he *would* return.

Taking a deep breath of briny air, Sofía hugged her luggage close, squared her shoulders, and marched onward. The steady clip of her steps against the cobblestones gave way to the clack of wood beneath her heels as she reached the boardwalk.

A small crowd was already forming there, distinguished-looking men in their finest formal wear, flaunting top hats, silk cravats, and tailcoats cut long in the latest fashion. The women at their arms were just as extravagantly dressed in brightly colored fabrics that hugged their hips and tied into generous bustles at the back, ending in impractically long trains.

Sofía bowed her head low and skirted along the edges of the crowd. She knew she looked out of place among the passengers, her cacao-dark hair scandalously unbound and rumpled from the tight braided knot she had combed it back into every day since girlhood. Instead of an evening gown, she wore a sensible garb of lightweight ivory cotton, easy to move in and blessedly breathable. She could not imagine traveling through this hot, humid weather wearing such heavy layers.

Thankfully, her fellow passengers paid her no heed. If they thought anything of her at all, they probably assumed her yet another lady's criada—she spotted a few along the fringes, guarding travel trunks or holding their ladies' trains. Here, the role afforded Sofía a certain degree of invisibility, and most importantly, protection. The ton might not have much in the way of goodwill for one another, but they at least respected each other's property.

Relaxing a fraction, Sofía leaned against the handrail and turned her sights to the steamer. It was a decently sized vessel with two covered decks and an ample viewing area atop. The exterior was made of glossy red-tinted wood, paired with gilded accents, and at the very center of the bow stood a flagpole, flying the gold and crimson of Hisperia.

"What do you mean I cannot carry my own luggage?"

Sofía's head jerked in the direction of that voice, her eyes squinting through the thick cloud of tobacco smoke. It sounded like . . . *No*. It couldn't be.

She pushed her way through the gathering to where a line of horse-drawn carriages had formed. The area was in a frenzy with dock workers transporting food supplies, shovelers scraping horse muck off the cobbles, handsomely attired ladies and lords pouring out of the carriages, and bulky travel trunks being unloaded onto the boardwalk.

Sofía stilled.

Standing there, with hands braced against generous hips, was none other than Adelina de Esperanza. She wore a long lace mantilla over her hair, pinned in place with a pearl comb, and a bustled gown made of the same blue as her eyes. One cream satin slipper tapped impatiently as a nervous young man assured her that her luggage would be well taken care of.

As if sensing her presence, Adelina paused midargument, and turned.

Their gazes locked across the short distance, but neither of them moved.

"Señorita?" The young porter's hands hovered uncertainly above the trunk, unclear as to how he was expected to proceed.

Adelina recovered first, stepping forward. She cleared her throat and flicked open her folding fan, feigning an ease that did not quite match her expression. "There you are, cariño. Can you believe they refuse to let me carry my own luggage? Is the female form so fragile that even this I cannot accomplish on my own?"

Sofía stared flatly at her, one eyebrow cocked. To the porter, she said, "Please pardon my lady, she appears to have misconstrued your crew's safety protocols as a direct affront to her gender." While Adelina was prone to brandishing her independence often and boisterously, she was never quite so unreasonable. Then again, this irascibleness likely had very little to do with the *actual* luggage. The unfortunate lad had simply been the one to bear the brunt of her misdirected frustrations. "I'm certain she will compensate you properly for your troubles."

Adelina had the decency to look contrite as she reached into her reticule and pulled out two copper reales.

The porter pocketed the coins, tipped his hat, and hurried off with her trunk before she could change her mind. Meanwhile, people continued spilling out of carriages, clinking crates full of bottled wines were hefted onto the ferry, horses whinnied, crewmen shouted, and laughter broke out from somewhere behind Sofía.

Despite the noise all around them, silence had lodged itself into the space between the two. And not the companionable silence of a lifelong friendship. This silence had teeth.

"Why are you here, Adelina?" Sofía *knew* why—she had slinked away like a thief in the night, leaving behind a lousy letter in place of a goodbye.

"For the same reason we're all here, of course. Why, you didn't think I'd miss out on this grand adventure, did you?" Her tone was level, playful even, but the swift flutters of her fan were giving way to something verging on violent. "Surely, there exists no scenario in which you just . . . walk off, ending thirteen years of friendship in half a page's worth of words. Which, if

I'm being candid, was not your best work. For a person with your linguistic talent, I'd have expected something with a little more . . . flair. Or at least, some variation in your sentence structure."

"Adelina." Sofía pressed her eyes closed. "I need to find Sol."

"Lucky then that I'm an excellent sleuth."

"That's not what I— I need to do this on my own."

"Nonsense." The grin she plastered on could not distract from the tremble in her voice. "We're a team, you and I, always have been. How could I stand by as you crawl into the jaws of high society? Besides . . . seems a right good time someone tells Papá to come home."

Something she could have easily done at any time in the past five years. She had, after all, the resources and the status to go where she pleased. What stopped her was likely the same fear that kept Sofía awake at night. That she'd get to the island and find her loved one had moved on from loving *her*. Chosen endless revelry over family. Or worse, that she would travel all the way there, and there'd be no one for her to find. Neither had ever given voice to that very real possibility, yet it made itself known in the way they both went about their days in a permanent state of suspended mourning. In the way they talked *around* the issue of the dead man in the water, unwilling to admit what passed through their minds as they read the news.

"If you truly mean to go without me," said Adelina, reading Sofía's silence, "then at least have the decency to say goodbye."

It had taken all her strength just to walk out of the hacienda earlier that day. She had not been brave enough to say it then, and she knew she was not brave enough to say it now. Adelina was kin, dear to her as her own blood. Yet, she was also a constant reminder of what Sofía once was and would forever be so long as they were together.

At seven years old, she had been gifted to this girl. To mend her clothes, and set her curls, and pour her tea. And though what she found was a friend instead of a mistress, she could never forget that this girl she loved as a sister had once owned her. Not that she would ever dare say those words out loud. This thing between them was too precious, too fragile, to fracture with the truth.

A bell clanged, and they both looked toward the ship.

"Boarding passes at the ready!" shouted one of the crewmen. "Any luggage not already aboard will be collected upon entry!" A strong jet of steam blew out from the stacks then, and everyone moved as one, shuffling toward the gate.

Adelina reached for Sofía's hand, clutching it between both of hers. "Tell me to stay behind," she said, voice rising with an edge of desperation. "Tell me to stay and I will let you go."

They stood there as the crowd swelled, then thinned, and in her mind's eye Sofía saw her path branch in two directions. In one, she pulled her hand free, boarded the steamer, and braved her tenuous future on her own. Over time, the years would dampen the loss, draw out the bitter poison from the memories until only the sweetness was left. And Adelina . . . she would remain like a heartbeat, vital, but unnoticed, a constant pulse in the background. Now and then, Sofía's thoughts would wander to her childhood friend. Had she finally settled down? Allowed a wealthy man to make a wife of her, and traded her toolbox for a child at her hip? Her eyes would search for her, in the streets, and in the market, and in the papers, until one day—

Sofía could make it no further into that story. She had tried, salt and seas, she had tried, but a life without Adelina in it had always seemed so utterly, acutely, viscerally *wrong*.

Before she could rethink her decision, tell herself they were delaying the heartbreak by a mere matter of days, she squeezed Adelina's fingers and led her down the pier to the steamer.

CHAPTER 2

*They come chasing paradise,
and within its shores, they find it.*

—Chronicler

THE SWEET CROON of a guitar greeted them as they set foot upon the deck of the steamer.

A covered salon with large glass windows dominated the space. Chandeliers dangled from its ceiling, swaying to the ocean's gentle current. The light cast the room in ripples of soft warm gold as it danced over the fashionable gathering, catching on the bright jewels the women wore like dewdrops on their hair, or draped delicately around slender necks and dainty wrists.

"Come now." Adelina linked arms with Sofía, pulling her toward the salon. "Let's see what we can gather from that gossiping lot." From the way she carried on, it was as if all was well again between them. An obvious farce, but one Sofía was well acquainted with—and grateful to go along with.

"I'll wait here," she said. "I've no interest in mingling."

She had been Adelina's companion long enough to have occasionally grazed her social circles, passing by like a tourist on holiday. Her brief forays into the world of the highborn had been educational. Illuminating, even—in the same manner stool samples could be illuminating. All to say, neither was the kind of thing you messed with if you fancied keeping your hands clean.

"Mingle or perish, cariño. We're about to march into the most secretive soiree in all the Gilded Sea, and you expect to survive it without first arming yourself with knowledge? Honestly, what do you even know of Carnaval?"

As much as your tabloids would tell me. "It's a party, Adelina. Not a war."

"And to win at either requires cunning and calculation."

The ship let out a violent jet of steam, the only warning they got before the vessel cast off from the dock toward their destination. Sofía threw her arms out for balance, teetering a little on her feet.

Adelina, to her credit, did not miss a step. "Think of it as practice." She continued down the deck with a steady stride, undeterred. "I'll even do all the talking. You just stand there and strive not to look like someone witnessing an execution— *Oh*."

"My apologies, señorita." A wiry, bespectacled man with a drooping mustache blocked the entrance to the salon. "I'm afraid criadas must remain on the deck," he said, not sounding apologetic at all. "The salon is for *paying* passengers only. Surely, you understand."

Adelina's chest puffed. *"Excuse—"*

"How fortunate then—" Sofía placed a hand on her friend's shoulder "—that I have paid my fare in full and with my own hard-earned coin." A full year's salary, in fact. Though, granted, she hadn't exactly been forthcoming when she purchased passage. With Carnaval being a highly exclusive affair, when the ticket clerk assumed she was there on behalf of a mistress, she hadn't bothered to correct him. "It is thus my lawful right to be among other patrons, as abhorrent as I may find their company. Now, please do me the favor of stepping aside. These legs of mine are not, it would seem, cut out for an adventurous life of seafaring, and I would like to find a nice wall, or even a sturdy piece of furniture, to latch on to for the remainder of this miserable journey."

With that, she slipped past the man, exercising as much grace and dignity as one could reasonably manage while wobbling like a newborn calf.

Adelina joined her soon after, eyes shining with mirth. "That was brilliant."

Foolhardy was a more accurate term. In protecting her pride, Sofía had been careless with her safety—and not for the first time either. Her recalcitrant nature had landed her in trouble more times than she could count. "No doubt I looked ridiculous," she said blithely, as though that were the extent of her worries.

"That's half the reason why it was so brilliant. Confidence in the face of bigotry is, of course, commendable, but paired with a comedic lack of coordination it becomes a weapon unlike any the world has ever seen. Now wait here, I am going to see a server about some celebratory wine."

Sofia watched Adelina until she disappeared behind the bulk of a graying man arguing passionately about Imperial taxes. The other men in his group nodded their agreement from a tactful distance, avoiding the wild slosh of his champagne. Nearby, a gaggle of women in their middle years were exclaiming over some scandal or another, while another traded whispers behind folding fans, throwing the occasional glance Sofia's way.

Sofia leaned back, resting her cheek against the cool window glass and staring out into the dark vastness of the sea. Perhaps she'd been a little too hasty in agreeing to mingle . . . The salon was uncomfortably warm, the air thick with a pungent mix of rose perfume, sweat, and tobacco smoke that made her head throb. The rambunctious chatter, the press of the crowd, and the floor swaying underneath certainly did not help matters any.

She attempted to distract herself with gentle, grounding thoughts of the scholastic variety, mentally reviewing her latest reading material: some fascinating news on the first formally recognized oceanographic expedition, a dry but informative guide on the entomological classification of aphids, and an incisive retrospective on the role of the so-called "Women of Letters" in the abolitionist movement.

Sofia sighed. It didn't bode well for the remainder of her evening that she had yet to start a conversation and already was in such a sorry state. She anchored herself firmly to the knowledge that, in a few short hours at least, she and her brother would share the same shores again. *Just a little longer, Sol . . .*

Her storm-gray eyes drifted closed, and when they reopened, it was to the sight of Adelina holding two glasses of wine. Her brow creased in concern.

"Headache?"

Sofía accepted the wine with a grim nod, but did not drink it. She found it tended to aggravate her ailment. "Just a small one this time."

"Hmm." Adelina worried her nail against the stem of the glass. "You let me know if we need to get you out of here, alright?"

"Of course," Sofía responded, waving her hand in a non-committal gesture. It was the kind of dismissive response that would normally have invited an onslaught of well-meaning smothering.

Thankfully, Adelina's attention was fixed elsewhere. *"Demonios,"* she hissed, downing her drink. "It's the condesa and her ogre of a husband."

"Ah, so it is," Sofía observed as the lady approached.

"Palomita! How long it has been." The condesa leaned over to kiss Adelina lightly on both cheeks. "You are an absolute vision in that dress, and look at that, not a single spot of engine grease in sight. I always did tell your mamá you'd grow out of that ghastly pastime."

"A reassurance I am sure she still treasures to this day." Adelina continued to smile beatifically, but Sofía could tell she was seconds away from stuffing the woman's mouth with her own head plumage.

"I take it Elena's not here then? Oh, my dear, I do trust you are not traveling without a chaperone?"

Adelina affected shock. "I would not dare, Condesa. Papá's waiting for me in Isla Bestia. He went there to celebrate his recovery, and as luck would have it, has befriended a young gentleman from the Northern Colonies. An entrepreneur of distinct renown, and a promising match, I am told."

The lie came easily to her, Sofía could tell. She had always been a competent dissembler, but since taking over the management of the hacienda, she'd been sharpening those skills to a dangerous degree. A year spent impersonating her father in all correspondence, overseeing his estate, and standing in for him at social events had elevated her from a tinkerer to a formidable industrialist in her own right.

"How wonderful for you," exclaimed the condesa. "A Northerner would make an excellent husband. They are less fussy about pedigree, and I am sure they would not mind a wife with your . . . unique upbringing, rabble-rousers that they are." She glanced quickly in the direction of Sofía, one side of her mouth curling in distaste. "I must say, it is quite the unusual choice, having one's criada mingling freely among the proper classes, but I suppose as long as she's here, we might as well put her to good use. Girl." She snapped her fingers at Sofía. "Go fetch me a red one."

Sofía straightened to her full height, but did not move from her spot. Though the condesa was tall, Sofía was taller, and she leveraged her advantage now. "I do not fetch," she said plainly, as if it were a factual limitation of her biology. Up there with limb regrowth and contortionism.

The woman balked. "Beg your pardon?"

"I do not fetch," she repeated, her tone flat. Then, as an afterthought, added, "Condesa." Sofía turned toward the musicians then, purposely facing away from the irate noble and her lackluster abuses. Being well acquainted with this particular brand of entitled outrage, she did not even have to feign disinterest.

Beyond Sofía's periphery, the condesa continued her tirade. "Well?" she asked, turning her unacknowledged ire on Adelina. "Are you not going to reprimand her?"

When Adelina barked out a laugh at the suggestion, the condesa grabbed her husband and left in a huff—albeit not without a thinly veiled threat to ruin both her and her family's reputation. "I thought we would never be rid of her," Adelina said, seemingly unfazed. "Let's try to find a less odious conversation partner, shall we?"

Sofía pointed to the opposite end of the salon, where a young woman in an orange evening gown stood by the corner wall. Prominent freckles dusted her cheeks, and her curly auburn fringe sat so low over her brow it nearly brushed her lashes. She'd been fidgeting with the golden band on her wedding finger since Sofía first noticed her.

"That one. She's eager for company."

Adelina shook her head. "Much too young. She will know less about Carnaval than we do."

"Yes, she's young, but somewhere here is likely a husband that's much older and better traveled. Perhaps, even one who's a repeat visitor of Carnaval?"

Adelina tapped a slipper, nodding slowly. "Oh, what've we got to lose? Let's go mingle with the doe-eyed child."

The two worked their way toward the back of the salon, dodging elbows, clumsy feet, and overly emphatic gestures. Adelina sidled up to the girl, and because she liked to envision herself as this modern heroine, chafing against societal conventions and whatnot, she skipped right past introductions and opened with, "Handsome devil, isn't he?"

The girl, who until that moment had been admiring the guitarist, blinked wide hazel eyes at them. "Sorry?"

"No need to be shy, he's objectively gorgeous. Isn't that right, Sofía?"

Sofía offered a neutral shrug. Physical beauty simply held no allure for her. She understood it only as a concept, in terms of facial symmetry, health signaling, and reproductive fitness. But a face, no matter how conventionally attractive, stirred nothing in her.

"Oh, I—I don't really have an opinion either." The girl held her ringed hand up by way of explanation. "Though, I do suppose he bears, um, some resemblance to my Felipe . . ."

"That accent . . ." Adelina angled herself toward the girl, in that way that suggested nothing in the world was more important. "You're from the Continent. Southern Hisperia, if I have to guess, am I right? What brings you all the way to the Gilded Sea?"

"Honeymoon." She tucked a curl behind her ear, beginning to brighten under the attention. "My husband and I, we've been touring the islands. This will be our, hmm, sixth—no . . . seventh stop? Oh, we were expected home ages ago, but then this couple at our inn told us the most wonderful tales about their stay in Isla Bestia and we simply knew we had to revise our itinerary."

"And a good thing you did. Rumor has it the spectacles are absolutely to die for—you cannot possibly come all this way and *not* take part in Etérea's preeminent social event. Why, I hear revelers journey from all across the Gilded Islands and beyond for this purpose alone, you know." Voice dropping to a conspiratorial whisper, she said, "Well, those who can afford it. But oh, how gauche of me, gossiping on when we've yet to do proper introductions. Please, call me Adelina."

"Fátima." The young woman shook her proffered hand with a predictably starstruck expression, one Sofía had observed plenty on the faces of shopgirls, maidservants, and ladies alike. Beyond being beautiful by Hisperian standards, Adelina was also aggressively charming, with the confidence of a seasoned torero stepping out into the bullring.

Eager to impress, Fátima was quick to divulge everything she knew about Carnaval, echoing many of the stories that'd been circulating among the upper classes for years: the sumptuous feasts, the bottomless wine, the celebrations that ran from sundown to sunrise.

As the evening went on, others shared vague iterations of the same. El Carnaval de Bestias, to hear them tell it, was less an experience than a mood. A chimera of hyperbolic adjectives—*dazzling! Magical! Thrilling!*—the whole affair described with the hazy whimsy of someone recounting a vivid daydream. Even second-time visitors offered little that was concrete, resorting to unhelpful banalities in the vein of "words could not possibly do it justice" and "it can't be explained, only *experienced*."

Sometime past the halfway point of their voyage, following yet another futile conversation, Sofía and Adelina finally abandoned the endeavor and retreated to the observation deck for some fresh air and quiet.

They watched, with a shared sense of dread and anticipation, as the island grew bigger and bigger. In something of a daze, fueled by giddiness and fear and a good dash of motion sickness, Sofía traced the shape of the island with a finger, following its contours from head to tail. It was clear from that distance how Isla Bestia had gotten its name. It was a mountainous land, broad on one side and long and tapering on the other, giving it the appearance of a beast floating amid the star-speckled waters.

The impression lingered even as they crossed into the shallows of that sea . . . As they pulled into the dock. As they were invited to disembark. Time contracted and stretched, hours folding into minutes and seconds lengthening into hours. And all Sofía could do was stare as the passengers hurried off, imagining the island opening its maw wide, swallowing her as it had done her brother. Vanishing her in a single bite.

Her hands were locked tight around the railing, her feet anchored to the steamer. Her every fear was a stone, weighing her down, keeping her rooted. Years of waiting and planning, missing and worrying, and now . . .

Here she was.

She felt a hand settle lightly against her wrist.

"Come on," Adelina coaxed gently. "Let's go find them."

THE SOUND OF distant music and revelry welcomed them as they walked along the wooden pier and up the cobblestone steps, toward Isla Bestia's legendary hotel.

The Flor de Lis sat on a tall outcrop of rock at the island's tail, surrounded by starry waters, pale sand, and tufts of bright green vegetation. It was the grandest thing Sofía had ever laid eyes upon. The hotel rose five stories into the air and extended far beyond the evening's shadows, wrapping around the soft curve of the island. It was built in the traditional style of the colonies, with salt-white stucco walls that gave way to tall rounded towers, terracotta roofs, and wrought-iron balconies. The asymmetry of the architecture would have bothered Sofía, except there was a clear sense of intentionality, cohesion even, that belied its apparent arbitrariness.

"Well," Adelina grimaced, coming to an abrupt stop in front of Sofía. "This is certainly a . . . unique version of hospitality."

Sofía followed her gaze up to the hotel gate, where masked attendants waited to welcome guests. They were all dressed as vejigantes, monstrous tricksters from Etérea's folklore, notoriously prone to all manners of mischief and mayhem. Though they originally represented demons in the fight of good versus evil, the vejigantes had taken a new form here on the archipelago. Sculpted by the hodgepodge of local cultures, they had become caricatures. More inclined to boorish satire than true devilry.

Their face masks were crafted out of coconut husks, painted in a bright palette of colors and adorned with long, pointed horns that protruded from the sides like tentacles. Their features were ghoulish, with dark hollow pits for eyes and mouths that stretched wide in exaggerated grins, revealing rows of pointed teeth. To complete the bizarre look, the performers wore a head-to-toe ensemble of bright ruffled silks, layered with capes cut into bat-like wings.

"Sage above," Adelina hissed. "We've been spotted. Quick, back to the steamer."

"Oh, come now." Sofía blocked her path. "You're not still scared of them, are you?"

The vejigantes had been a recurring source of Adelina's childhood nightmares ever since she first encountered one at a town festival. Sofía, to her friend's chagrin, had failed to sympathize. Despite their startling appearance, she found the unfortunate-looking creatures surprisingly . . . whimsical. The thought that something so disturbing could also be so garishly unfashionable had always struck her as amusing.

"Scared? Please, Sofía, do refrain from making such wild accusations. I simply find their wardrobe choices offensive to the eye."

"Good. Because a particularly toothy one is heading this way." Sofía pushed her up the last few steps.

The toothy vejigante graced them with a sweeping bow and bid them to follow, and as was tradition, did so without uttering a word. Together, they continued up the seemingly infinite set of steps to the hotel gate, an impressive stone archway wrapped in flowering vines. Beyond it sprawled a massive courtyard, lush with rare blooms and towering flamboyán trees—a local favorite, nicknamed "the flame of the forest" for their crimson leaves. Their canopies grew wide and dense, stretching across the garden like fiery parasols. Moonbeams pierced through the breaks in the foliage and glittered against the nighttime dew coating every leaf, petal, and blade of grass.

Footpaths extended outward from a grand fountain at the center of the courtyard, winding in intricate patterns along the ground. Open archways lined every wall beyond the entry, and suspended above them were several tiers of narrow balconies. There were flowers twined through the gaps between the railings, overflowing from clay pots, and spilling down the walls like drips of paint.

A breeze blew through, bringing with it the scent of sea salt, spring blooms, and—curiously—the acrid burn of kerosene from the nearby lamps. Sofía would have thought a place of such renown would be employing the latest technologies, rather than still relying on oil for lighting. Then again, what did she know?

Sofía heard Adelina's intake of breath beside her and knew she was not the only one struck by the sight of it all. The garden was nothing short of a masterpiece, and if their guide had not been gesturing insistently at them to move, they would have likely kept on gawking. Sofía, ever the pragmatist, was the first to recover.

They were soon ushered into a lobby with plush seating, glazed adobe walls, and thick embroidered rugs spread across the terracotta floor. To the left, a grand piano rested under a blanket of enchantress flowers—blossoms red as rubies, with overlapping petals that formed a teacup shape. They'd been her mamá's favorite, once.

"Welcome, esteemed guests, to Isla Bestia," said a voice near the back of the lobby. A tall fellow stood behind an ornate desk of glossy rosewood, wearing a finely tailored suit, white gloves, and a feathered crow mask. It hid his features from forehead to cheek. Off to the side stood a second figure, slighter in build and just as impeccably dressed. Like the concierge, he wore a mask, solid black with glassy bat wings that extended over the crown of his hair—sable and sleek, worn long and tied at the nape of his neck. Unlike the concierge, he made no move to welcome them.

The concierge nodded at the vejigante, who bowed deeply and swept out of the room at his signal. The second man continued his solemn vigil. Perhaps he was a guard, Sofía thought, or a manager. Someone far too important to bother ingratiating himself with them.

"I trust your experience thus far has been to your liking?" said the concierge.

"Quite." Adelina stepped up to the desk with confidence, slipping into the genteel role she had been groomed for. "Two rooms, please."

"Certainly, Señorita. Would they be under the same account?"

Sofía rushed to object. "No—"

"Yes," her friend insisted. "Please add them to Don Reynaldo de Esperanza's existing account. I am his daughter."

The concierge scanned his books. "My apologies, Señorita de Esperanza, but . . . it appears there is no guest here by that name."

A wave of dread washed over Sofía.

"That can't be right. Do please check again," said Adelina.

He did. "It appears the last guest we had by that name checked out of the Flor de Lis nearly four years ago . . . Perhaps he is lodging alongside another guest? We offer a few apartment suites, and there are, on occasion, those who opt to share these accommodations under a single account."

Adelina's shoulders stiffened under their puffed blue sleeves. "Yes . . ." She cleared her throat. "That must be it." *It had to be*, echoed a voice in Sofía's head, the same one that for years insisted, *he's alive; you will find him* . . .

One signature and a hefty deposit later, they had their keys, ornate things of cast iron, each molded in the image of a flor de lis. Right below it, an engraving on Sofía's key read Moriviví, referring to the extraordinary little plant whose foliage retracts when touched. It was, the concierge explained, the name of her assigned room.

"Your luggage will be brought to your suites shortly, Señorita de Esperanza. Now, if you will step this way, we can get you two all set for Carnaval." With a sweeping gesture, he parted one of the velvet curtains behind him to reveal a room.

Inside, the walls were covered floor to ceiling with gilded mirrors and rows upon rows of masks in all shapes, colors, and sizes. Not the kind the townspeople wore to the local carnavales, those flimsy things of pulped paper and rice flour paste. There was nothing charmingly homemade about *these* masks. They were works of art, every one of them, sculpted of ceramic, glass, and hammered brass. Shaped into the faces of beasts from air and land and sea, creatures of legend and lore, and every manner of earthly and celestial element. Sunbursts and clouds. Molten rock and ocean waves.

"As part of our services, we offer complimentary masks for guests to wear in the common areas. We at the Flor de Lis pride ourselves in our ability to create a climate of . . . discretion. I am sure you, as well as our other distinguished patrons, will appreciate the value of such anonymity."

Adelina glanced meaningfully at Sofía, and with every ounce of diplomatic restraint said, "I've no doubt we will."

The curtain closed behind them.

Sofía angled an eyebrow at her.

"Oh, don't go giving me that look. It is not as if *I'm* to blame for all the crimes of my fellow countrymen. Personally, I find this all just as suspect as you do. I mean, 'a climate of discretion'—who actually says that?"

Muffled voices bled in from the adjacent room then, and Sofía angled herself to listen.

"The party before us," Adelina explained, lifting a jeweled mask from its pegs to inspect it. "I saw them getting escorted in as we rounded the corner."

"Ah." The establishment's attention to detail was nothing short of impressive. The well-rehearsed speech, these private chambers . . . it was all part of a carefully staged illusion of anonymity. No doubt many were taken in by it. She'd have been too, had life not hammered into her a deep sense of distrust for all that glittered.

When she glanced sidelong at Adelina, she caught her friend gazing listlessly down at a mask, cradling it like it was an injured bird. "You're worried."

"Aren't *you*?" Her voice came out strangled. "You heard what he said. Papá hasn't been here in years."

"That doesn't mean he's left the island." *That* possibility was not one Sofía was willing to entertain, not when her search had only just begun.

Adelina averted her gaze. "No . . . but what if it means something worse?"

THEY WERE GIVEN adjoining rooms on the fifth level of the Flor de Lis, with balconies that faced out into the Gilded Sea. The suites were laid out identically, with matching furniture carved from gleaming walnut wood. Both had the same ornate wardrobes. The same canopied beds. The same settees in wine-red damask.

Distantly, Sofía was aware of Adelina rummaging through a travel trunk. Her attention, though, was on the room itself. At first glance, Adelina's appeared a mirror image of hers. A reality so improbable that rather than accept it, Sofía was bending over backward to try and disprove it.

Since stepping through the door, she had been scouring that space for something . . . more. Something *better*. The discrepancy she was entirely certain had to be there. Adelina may have thought Sofía her equal, but the world had certainly never treated her as such. Why should it start now?

Is it the vanity? No . . . Perhaps the writing desk? That's not it either . . . Surely this room is bigger then? She had started counting the tiles—hexagon by hexagon—when Adelina stepped into her line of sight.

Sofía's eyes slowly traveled up from the floor and over the evening gown of vibrant scarlet silk Adelina held in her arms.

"I ordered this made for the gazette's anniversary ball. Francisco insisted you attend and be recognized for your contributions. I, of course, told him you abhor that sort of pageantry, but I hoped perhaps . . ." She trailed off, looking uncertain. "I'm sure you think it quite frivolous."

The dress was cut in the emerging fashion among Etérea's freedwomen, a unique, vibrant fusion of the island's native and foreign styles. The flowing skirts cascaded down in three overlapping layers, each one longer than the previous and softly ruffled at the trim with delicate lace. The bodice was bolder, with short sleeves that rested off the shoulders, leaving the collarbone exposed.

"It's . . ." Sofía struggled to decipher what precisely it was she was feeling. Emotions were such fickle, abstract things. She longed for the tidiness of scholarship, the quiet comfort of existing solely as an observer to mysteries outside herself. She could spend forever teasing meaning out of *those* without tiring. "I do not hate it . . . I think."

"I should hope not. Red silk is outrageously expensive."

"That being said," she soldiered on, "I've no need for such finery. You must know I never intended to come here as a patron, surely? I was to apply to be a maid or a seamstress—figured a place this big could use the help. But now you expect me to not only be a guest, but to prance around in some lavish dress, and this one no less. Adelina, this is a symbol. I put this on, and I broadcast to everyone I do not belong here." *Or anywhere else.* At least in her current garb, she had a place. In *that* dress, she was . . . unclassifiable. Was that to be her fate? Always too little of this, too much of that, forever a paradox to be unraveled.

Adelina brought the gown to Sofía, held the sleeves to her shoulders so it draped over her white servant's dress. "They'll say you don't belong no matter what you wear, Sofía." She spoke without malice, simply . . . resignation. "With this on, at least, you've beaten them to it. Claimed the words before they can claim *you*."

CHAPTER 3

*The stage was their altar, and decadence their rite.
Devout they came . . . yet traded in their saints
and gods for wine at eventide.*

—Chronicler

THE FRANTIC BEAT of drums led them down the corridors of the Flor de Lis. The building shook with the infectious music, and the air thrummed with the wild sounds of celebration. Sofía could feel the rhythm climbing up the soles of her feet as her heels *click-click-clicked* a brisk staccato against the terracotta floors.

Adelina led Sofía down through the moonlit passages at a lively pace, her lace mantilla fluttering behind her. It did not matter that Adelina was a full head shorter than Sofía. What the young lady lacked in height, she more than made up for in motivation—not all of which, Sofía sensed, had to do with finding her papá.

She could not entirely fault Adelina for it. Despite a genuine desire to do away with the trappings of Hisperian society, the allure of the mysterious Carnaval de Bestias was one few could resist.

They passed another courtyard, set up as an outdoor dining area, and a shaded oasis with small pools of steaming hot springs. Water cascaded down from a ridged wall of moss-covered rock and gently poured into the sparkling pools below. Plumes of steam curled up from the surface, toward the starry night above.

Golden light spilled in from the opening up ahead, and with it, a rush of sounds Sofía had not heard since childhood. The quick rasp of güiros, the rhythmic rattle of dried calabash fruit, and the pulsating beat of drums. Voices rose above the music, chanting in what sounded strangely, impossibly, like the islands' native tongue.

A language that lived only in nooks, hastily stashed into the cracks of history and left to gather dust. The language was folded, like a secret, into nighttime songs, preserved in prayers whispered to zemís, and quietly stitched into another people's stories, another people's words.

It did not belong *here*, in this temple of small gods. Like her, it survived by keeping to the shadows, by shedding pieces of itself, taking up less space than it needed.

It was what the naturalists would have called an adaptation.

The passage emptied into the main entrance of the hotel, an elevated terrace that wrapped across the front of the building. Sofía and Adelina made their way to the curving balustrade and stared, wonderstruck.

A labyrinth stretched over acres of land.

The complex latticework of hedges encased the venue like an enormous green spiderweb, drawing intricate spirals around the gardens below. Weaving through and around it all was a great river extending far beyond the grounds of the Flor de Lis, toward the chain of shadowy mountains in the distance. And looming over the entrance of that labyrinth, her head cresting above the terrace, was the immense topiary of a woman carved from the earth.

The giantess emerged from it like a siren surfacing above the ocean's waves, a being of elsewhere momentarily caught at the boundary between two worlds. Her skin was made of tightly woven laurel leaves, and her delicate features were framed by a wild mass of locks sculpted from moss and summer blooms. It spilled outward, absorbing back into the earth and surrounding hedges.

Any moment now, it seemed she would climb out from the land to rise above the Flor de Lis like a god of old. Vast and unfathomable. The raw might of mountains compressed into a woman's form. Her delicate hands were spread wide, palms up, and on each lay the head of a serpent with scales made of mirrored glass, iridescent as the skin of a rainbow boa. Their sinuous bodies faded into the labyrinth. Or rather, they *became* it—every bend, every loop, every dead end.

"How . . . how is this real?" Adelina's cerulean eyes were wide beneath her mask, the irises shining with the honeyed warmth of lantern light.

As much as Sofía hated to admit it, she was equally impressed. Oh, she had expected Carnaval to dazzle, of course, all legends were born from some small kernel of truth, after all. But she could not have imagined the sheer scale of the event. The dozens of vejigantes bearing platters of the finest food and wine. The garden sculptures that must have cost a king's fortune to create. The domed solarium at the heart of the labyrinth that appeared to have been framed in *actual* gold.

Awe and repulsion warred within her.

While Sofía may not have had her brother's keen eye for the arts, nor his passion, she found comfort in balance and precision. There was a discipline to art that soothed her, and yet . . . the part of her that grew up on so painfully little was disgusted by Carnaval's extravagance. How beautiful, and how wasteful all this was.

Sofía scoured the sea of masked faces below, anxious to catch the familiar slant of her brother's smile, the dark buzz of his hair, shaved ever too close to the scalp. She trained her ears, thinking that if she concentrated, she might hear the gentle rumble of his laughter. That incongruous sound that had always seemed so jarringly out of place, a softness unfit for the unkindness of their reality.

Standing there, amid all that noise, the flash and glitz that fought for her attention, the strange faces made stranger by those masks, it hit her. The full magnitude of what she'd undertaken, how utterly unprepared and ill-suited she was to that task. Did she really believe that armed with an arsenal of research, she might contend with the likes of Carnaval? A journal's worth of words could not help here, no more than reading about wings could help her take flight. But how was she to know? Having explored so little of the world beyond the hacienda, she had neither the experience nor the requisite imagination to envision such a grand affair.

She had never even been among a crowd this large. To think, she'd been intending to waltz into this island and just . . . find him. The presumption struck her as laughable now. Almost arrogant, the notion that all she had to do was *look*.

"Come on," With a firm tug, Adelina towed Sofía at a brisk pace down one of two massive staircases.

"Slow down, you infernal woman," Sofía protested, grasping onto the banister. "I can barely see through this blasted mask." And that was despite having chosen the one with the fewest embellishments. It was a simple domino of glossy black glass, painted with a small silver crescent below each eye, like a teardrop. A stark contrast to Adelina's—a delicate thing of bone-pale porcelain shaped into dove-like wings.

At the base of the stairs, beneath the giantess's left hand, they were greeted by a vejigante carrying an ornate tray of pearlescent goblets. Adelina was so enthralled that not even the presence of her bogeyman gave her pause. She reached a hand out distractedly to swipe a goblet up from the tray.

When it was Sofía's turn, she waved away the offer. "I've no need. Thank you." Her gaze was so busy sweeping the crowd, she failed to notice the vejigante moving to block her path. With a low, theatrical bow, they picked up a goblet and presented it to her with a small flourish.

She was about to decline again when she caught sight of a familiar bat-winged mask. It was the sable-haired gentleman from the lobby, the one who'd stood rigid and broodingly silent as the concierge checked them in.

"Oh, very well then. I'll take it if it keeps *that* one off your hair." She swiped the glass from the server's gloved hand, splashing a few drops of the wine in her haste. "I know enough to recognize the management here has a very . . . unique set of expectations." Honestly, she would not have been surprised if the vejigantes were under strict orders to promote an atmosphere of blissful overindulgence. This, according to the tabloids, was a place where you could *be* anyone. *Do* anything. Excess and secrecy were the only price of participation.

Sofía forced her grip to relinquish the woodpecker dangling from her neck, hoping that the little carving, shaped by her brother's own hands, would not be her sole connection to him much longer. Her palm, dented red where the birdling's beak had pressed into the skin, joined the other, locking around the goblet's delicate stem. It was good, having something else to hold. With her headache now but a soft pressure on her temples, she even dared a sip of the wine to quiet her nerves.

At the mouth of the labyrinth, two figures waited to welcome her in: a mestiza somewhere around Sofía's age, and an older man with umber skin. They stood one to each side, adorned in lush greenery and each bearing a large serpent with scales that shone yellow and blue under the light. Sofía mistook the serpents for props before noticing the slow twist and slither of their bodies.

"Come," said the carnavalero to her right.

"Step inside," said the other.

"Who knows where the paths may lead you . . ."

As one, they made a sweeping gesture, ushering her through. She entered the labyrinth, and their voices came with her.

"What will be found . . . ?"

"What will be lost . . . ?"

"Who will you be in the end?"

The path before her was lit only by moonlight. Braids of brilliant green were threaded through it all, adorning the walls and ground like snakeskin. Mirrors were embedded in the hedges, each shining with a subtle iridescence and tall enough to show Sofía in her full stature.

Her gaze skimmed right past her reflection, vision softening to a vague focus. Avoiding her own image was a reflex at that point. Once, she might have found precious traces of her mother there, but the years had long stripped away what little of her mamá there was, whittling down the roundness of her face, diluting the black of her hair, fading her skin to the tawny brown of sand after a wave has rolled in. Now when Sofía looked in the mirror, she saw not her mother, but the face of the man who forced her twin and her into this world. A face she saw only once, the day he sold them for a handful of coins.

No. Sofía caught herself. *You look to the past only for what it can teach you, and there is no lesson there you have not already learned.*

In the path ahead, Adelina bounced eagerly from foot to foot, affecting the demeanor of someone whose sole purpose, at present, was to gambol and frolic. Sofía did not doubt Carnaval's draw was strong enough to quell most worries, but this degree of enthusiasm could not have been entirely genuine, considering that not an hour ago she'd learned the hotel had no official record of her father.

"Gods, look at this place," Adelina remarked. "No wonder Papá never came home, I'm half considering moving here myself."

However feigned or not, Sofía needed that. That rosy outlook that transcended objectivity, that casual, easy confidence that made her believe her brother was right around the corner. When her hope had worn down to the quick, and the facts she so relied upon were painting a bleak picture, it was Adelina's sunny disposition that always propelled her one step further.

It was, Sofía thought, what made the two of them work despite how fundamentally opposite they were.

"Hold on," Sofía said, pulling her to the side as a group walked past. "Let's stop and think for a moment. How precisely do we go about finding someone if we ourselves don't know where we are?" The irony of the situation did not escape her in the least.

"What do you propose we do, come back once we've plotted out a map?—Never mind, that's exactly what you're suggesting." Adelina gazed skyward with a sigh, as though consulting her saints on how to broach the matter delicately. "Look, we have but a few hours until sunrise. Either we spend that time planning, or we spend it looking."

Sofía chewed on her bottom lip. "Fine. *Fine.* We do it your way." She was out of her depth here anyway. How much wiser would it be to try and cobble together a plan when she could barely grasp what she'd walked into? "No maps. No strategy. Just our treacherous human whims and gut instincts . . . may your saints save us all." Before she could change her mind, she dragged them down the path on the right.

Adelina laughed. "I thought you refuted the existence of those, and I quote, *incorporeal warmongers*."

"Well, yes, but if I'm to give in to the trappings of intuition, I may as well tackle other phenomena with scant empirical evidence. Get them all in one fell swoop, for efficiency, if nothing else." Sofía turned sharply to the right, surprising more laughter out of Adelina. "And in the meantime, perhaps *you* may even begin to see the value of a nice well-plotted map. There is beauty in reliability, Adelina, you need only open your eyes to it."

"Devils take me if I ever dare approximate such a degree of sound judgment."

The two meandered down the twisting passages, slowing whenever they crossed paths with other patrons. Eyeing their masked faces for far longer than was polite, trying to discern the features hidden underneath.

Are you here, Sol?

Her twin could be anywhere, patiently attending to the mercurial Don Reynaldo's every selfish whim, and in between, he would be drinking in the sights, marveling at the wonders all around him.

Sofía had always admired the way her brother chased beauty, dredging art out of the ugliness when all she could think of was survival. Even after she was drawn into a life of relative comfort, it was he who left her small treasures beneath shrubs of pink hibiscus: a dappled stone he'd found by the river, a shard of tinted glass that made light refract into rainbows, the glossy feather of a colibrí. For as long as there had been breath within them, he had been the clear skies to her somber storms, the heart to her logic. Without him, her life was thrust violently out of equilibrium.

As they searched, they passed settees upholstered with moss, secret doorways cut into hedges, and an entire menagerie of topiaries. Among them, a hummingbird with wings spread midflight, a trio of coquí frogs stacked one atop another, and an explosion of multicolored fish arching gracefully over the pathway. They ducked through tunnels that opened into hidden alcoves, peered through windows that shone like kaleidoscopes, and detoured down paths that appeared, at first glance, to lead nowhere—until you looked closer.

That was how they found the door.

Its leaves were a brighter green than the surrounding hedge, and on it grew delicate white flowers, small as the bumblebee fluttering above them. Adelina tugged the knob of twisted bramble and opened it.

It led into a closed circuit of hedges, a maze within a maze spiraling like the shell of a nautilus. Or a knotted snake's tail, if one were keeping with the evening's theme.

Stepping inside felt like crossing a threshold, a distinct quality of transitioning from *here* to *there*, in the way of storybook children stumbling into elsewhere.

It was the play of light that set the space apart, elevated that secret alcove into the realm of the surreal. The mirrors, curved and smooth as mercury, caught the moon just so, diffusing its shine into a spectral mist.

As Adelina moved, her reflections moved with her, the mirrors creating an illusion of an infinite passage swarmed by masked figures in sky blue silk. The effect might have been stunning if it weren't also so disorienting.

Sofía, following her friend along the circuit, was losing track of which Adelina was real and which was the echo. There was something off about the reflections. An asynchrony, as though each was on a slight delay. Or was it her eyes that were deceiving her?

"We should turn back," she called, feeling disconcerted in a way she could not translate into words.

Adelina's response was unintelligible, a muffled distortion, like her voice too was being mirrored, replicated many times over in a senseless, overlapping tangle. Sofía hurried to catch up, but instead of finding Adelina, there were only her reflections. And then, merely fractions of the whole. The trim of her skirt . . . the wing of her mask . . . the corner of her mantilla, floating behind her on a breeze.

The maze devoured her in pieces. Every turn revealing a little less, until Sofía was alone with her own reflections, her own unanswered calls.

"Adelina?" That slightly off feeling was devolving rapidly into concern, and while Sofía was not wont to indulge in such unhelpful emotions, she also did not typically find herself trapped in some illusionist's box, subjected to manipulations of sight and sound that others labeled entertainment. Under normal conditions, she could rely on her keen eyes and ears to tell the monsters from the shadows, yet here, they seemed but one and the same.

It was not a fate she was prepared for, this betrayal of her once-trustworthy senses, and thus, her mind. Another fresh terror for her to catalog then, and here she thought she knew them all already, *had* known them since long before she knew her letters—the shape and sound of them, their respective order along her internal alphabetization.

Sofía had just rounded another circle when she heard the crunch of glass beneath her feet.

The shattered remains of a wine goblet.

She swung around, casting her gaze left, right, and back again, feeling the weight of Adelina's absence with every stilted breath. Her attention went to the scatter of shining shards again, reading the scene before her with the untrained eye of a fledgling detective, following the trail of glass and white wine all the way to the edge of the mirror. No . . . *under* the mirror?

"Quit fooling around already, Adelina. Where the devils are you?"

A part of her urged her to be calm, reasonable, to not extrapolate danger out of so little evidence. Adelina had a penchant for wanderlust, it insisted. A place like this, well, it would drive her to distraction, lure her away with the promise of something extraordinary. She'd merely strayed too far, gotten lost. Or perhaps this was all a game. Yes, a game, and soon she would—

The mirror swung open with a push, revealing a secret path where the trail of wine ended. And Adelina was nowhere in sight.

Sofía was still trying to process what she was seeing—and not seeing—when her body chose to move, for it bore in its cells the knowledge her memory could not. Of the vanished girls, the stolen ones, their absences tattooed to the soft flesh of membrane, dormant until it was time to remember. To feel. To *run*.

She bolted down the path, pulse hammering against her throat as she yelled Adelina's name. All the while, her mind, normally so disciplined, so unwaveringly dependable, conjured ghastly scenarios, collaging the present and the past into a frightful picture. Sofía cursed their ignorance, their baseless confidence. Did they think Carnaval a sanctuary? A place so joyous, so liberating, that a woman could exist in it without looking over her shoulder? This was not a woman's world, no matter how far removed from reality Isla Bestia seemed.

With her hands pressed against the mirrors, she moved. Unlocking twisting pathways that branched off into yet more twisting pathways, like a nesting doll of mazes drawing her deeper the harder she fought to escape. She was halfway through another opening when, from the corner of her eye, she saw a shadow move across the mirrors.

Sofía froze.

The reflection showed a young man standing at the other end of the passage. Tall, with a wiry frame, wearing a slate gray jacket that was two sizes too large. Dark hair cropped close to the scalp accentuated the thick arch of his eyebrows, the jut of high cheekbones. Though her own complexion paled under the moonlight, his skin glowed a warm brown with deep ochre undertones, as if lit by a fire from within.

Sofía did not see his eyes, but she knew they would be the same coppery gold of her mother's.

She twisted on her heel. *"Sol?"*

Her brother was already gone.

Or . . . almost gone. In the mirror opposite her, she caught the reflection of a coattail as he vanished down the next passageway.

She stepped stumblingly after her twin, one foot after the other, feeling as if she were trudging up a violent river, pushing against the current with all her strength. The shock gradually loosened its grip on her body, making way for something else to take hold. A desperation that sapped her mind of everything else. The fears that had led her on a mad dash down the labyrinth dissipated like smoke, and in that moment, all Sofía knew was that her brother was somewhere in that treacherous maze. Alive.

She could not lose him again.

Sweat poured down her neck as she ran, trailing the shadows of a boy who had not seemed capable of casting one. In the mirrors, she found traces of him that the rest of the labyrinth hid. A shoulder here. The flap of a coattail there. The silhouette of her brother's back as he turned away from her. She was *so* close. If she were just a little faster, she could—

Sofía burst through yet another opening. And startled backward.

She was back in the main labyrinth, where the paths were greener, more open, and the moonlight less unnatural. There, sitting on a divan pillowed with rainbow blooms and soft moss, was Adelina.

Her eyes were fixed on the mirror across from her, and she wore an expression Sofía had never seen on her, something halfway between longing and grief. A few of her curls had come loose from their intricate bronze updo, and her arm bled from a thin gash, the red seeping into the white silk of her glove. She did not seem to notice it. She did not seem to notice anything beyond her own reflection.

Relief flooded Sofía in a rush at the sight of her friend, and just behind it came the memory of fear, the gut-wrenching knife of not knowing where she'd gone. It powered her into motion, mutating into something darker. Harsher.

"*What happened to you?*" She jerked Adelina up by the arm—the uninjured one—forcing her off the divan.

Adelina blinked up at Sofía, appearing surprised to find her there. "I . . ." Her eyes traveled over her surroundings, slow and unfocused. "I thought . . . I thought I saw . . ."

Sofía came alert at her words.

"Sol?" She looked around, like he might be there, waiting. "Adelina, did you see Sol?"

"What? No . . ." Her eyes widened, understanding. "Did *you* see Sol?"

"I . . ." Had Sofía truly seen her brother, or were her eyes playing tricks on her, showing her Sol as she last remembered him—in that baggy suit with the hastily patched elbows? She had sewn them in herself, and would have taken the sleeves in too had he not been forced to leave so abruptly. No one knew of Don Reynaldo's travel plans until the night before he was set to depart. He, of course, must have known for weeks, if not months, but that was the kind of man he was. The kind that made a sport of testing his household, throwing a wrench in their routine, if for no other reason than to gauge their response time.

Adelina blamed it on his military past. Sofía, knowing better, blamed it on his parentage. There must have been a chupacabra or two somewhere in that man's lineage.

"No . . . I suppose it must've been someone else, or . . ." She swallowed. "Whoever it was fled at the sight of me. Sol, he . . . he wouldn't have done that."

"Never." Adelina rushed to assure her, taking her hand and cradling it between both of hers. "Your brother adores you. Truly. The way he talked about you—oh, you should have heard him . . . one would think you put the moon in the sky."

It surprised Sofía to hear her speak of Sol. For the most part, Adelina mentioned him only in the vaguest of terms, as though he hadn't been a fixture of her youth. As though the years he'd orbited around them, coming and going like a planet around a star, had unhappened the moment he vanished. As though by avoiding any mention of him she might also avoid the guilt.

It was her personal endorsement, and high praise of his artistic potential, that'd gotten Sol promoted from a field hand to Don Reynaldo's personal attendant. A victory at the time, to be sure. A chance at a more comfortable life, and later down the line, maybe even the prospect of buying his freedom—*if* he did his job right, and Don Reynaldo was feeling magnanimous.

In the end, it was that same promotion, that sparkling promise of a better, distant *something*, that tore him away from Sofía's life.

The line of blood dripping down Adelina's arm pulled Sofía out of her thoughts. She hissed a curse. "Salt and seas, what did you do to yourself?"

Adelina glanced down at her arm and frowned. "Must have snagged it on some bramble."

"Well, take off the glove. It's ruined now, may as well use it to staunch the bleeding." Adelina did as she was told, and Sofía rolled up the white silk and pressed it to the cut. Blood soaked into the fabric, forming a gradient from deep red to petal-pink at the edges.

"What's the verdict, Doctor?" she asked in a droll tone. "Am I dying?"

"Hard to say without knowing the source of the incision. Sepsis is always a possibility, and there are accounts of open wounds leading to a flesh-eating disease. Necrotizing fasciitis, I believe it's called." Sofía hunched down to inspect the cut. "That's unlikely to be the case here, it's only been recorded in soldiers and navy men. To date, at least."

"How . . . reassuring."

"Shift a little more toward the light for me? There." She cleaned around the cut as best she could then disposed of the glove, burying it in the nearest hedge. When she looked back, Adelina was plucking a fresh pair from her pearl-studded reticule.

"Of course you'd keep an extra pair of gloves on you."

"Cariño, they are *white* gloves." She tugged at the thick cord of her reticule, drawing it shut, but not before Sofía glimpsed what was inside.

"Was that . . . a pistol?"

"Nicked it from Papá's safety box. I'd have liked to take the bigger one, but alas, it wouldn't fit." Adelina clipped the purse onto the back of her chatelaine belt, on which also hung an enamel pocket watch, a miniature screwdriver, and a silver telescope ring. "Saints, how I miss pockets . . ." She patted her hips, sighing yearningly. "What good is a dress that cannot hide a woman's secrets? Her Majesty must be a forthcoming lady to pioneer such a trend."

"Ah, yes. The volume of a woman's garments is how I personally ascertain her candor." Rattled though she was, Sofía took comfort in the easy ebb and flow of their banter. It was familiar. Something she could rely upon when nothing else, least of all her mind, was making sense.

Adelina, nodding without a hint of irony, wiggled her fingers as she slipped on the new gloves. She paused suddenly, glancing down. "Sofía, dear heart, where in the world are your shoes?"

Sofía lifted her skirts to see her toes peeking through the rips in her black stockings. She must have lost her slippers when she ran, chasing after Adelina, then the apparition of her brother.

That was how she chose to think about the situation. The alternative, that Sol *had* been there and fled at the sight of her, was not a reality she was ready to contemplate. It was far simpler to believe her eyes had played her for a fool. That the face she'd seen was a trick, an optical phenomenon, no more tangible than the colors diffracted over those mirrors.

She thought about the illusionists and their clever deceptions—acts of science disguised as sorcery. They were all the rage on the Continent, their stunts often spectacular enough to warrant a full spread in Etérea's gazette, the reports claiming that with just lights and mirrors, these men could make objects, and even people, appear and disappear as if by magic.

Surely, this maze was no different. Just a cunning ruse meant to confuse and mislead the unsuspecting.

"They hurt my feet," Sofía said finally. It was not a lie, exactly. The slippers were half a size too small, taken from a box of personal artifacts Doña Elena had given to her to discard. Though her wages since Adelina took over the business were generous enough that she could have commissioned herself a pair of sturdy boots, wasting coin on comfort felt . . . irresponsible. If she found

Sol—and she had to believe she would—they might be living off her savings for some time. It could be weeks, maybe months, before they found new work.

"Let's walk," she said, drawing Adelina down the passage in an attempt to distract herself from her meager finances and the daunting prospect of new footwear. "I hear voices nearby. Might be wiser to travel with a group."

As they turned the corner, they crossed paths with the party, most of whom sported nautically themed masks. Wasting no time, Adelina insinuated herself into their group with something pithy and delightful, and they welcomed her into the fold as if she were a longtime friend. Watching her, energized by these strangers' attention, Sofia knew that what she'd glimpsed of her friend earlier, that hopeless anguish, was no more real than the sight of her brother in his hand-me-down suit.

This was the real Adelina, quick with a wisecrack, quicker with a smile. Her heart a steady, impermeable force. Sadness might occasionally brush its surface, like water rolling off a pane of glass, but it could not stick to it. There were not enough holes in her life for it to get a good grip.

Sofia breathed easier, comforted by the knowledge that her friend would never need to know that brand of pain, the kind that lingered. Her own light might have blown out at its first flicker, but Adelina's was still alive and brilliant, shielded as it was within a childhood of safety. Stability. Abundance. Sofia had basked vicariously in that warmth for years, borrowed its glow like the moon does the sun's, and it had been strong enough for both of them. Strong enough that when Sofia finally walked away, Adelina would come out the other side unscathed. *She may mourn you when you leave, but she will move on . . .*

She always moved on.

CHAPTER 4

*Drink and dine, wonder-seeker.
Yield to it your troubles, your darkness, your shame.*

—Chronicler

THAT NIGHT, a woman fell from the sky.

And as she fell, she transformed.

Sofia watched, neck craned backward, as the woman's muscled brown arms stretched, her sleeves unfurling into plumed folds of gauzy iridescent green. The fabric billowed in the air, forming the shape of wings. Starlight shone on her face, a masterpiece of shimmering paint, framed by a mask of shining emerald feathers with a nose that tapered down to a point—in the suggestion of a hummingbird's beak.

She dropped to the sound of gasps, plummeting five feet. Ten. Twenty. Sofia shielded her eyes, and then . . .

Laughter. Hoots and hollers. Raucous applause.

The woman hung above the gleaming ebony floors of the solarium, her body suspended on flowing swaths of night-black silk, her dark gaze roving over the stunned audience with cool confidence.

Here was a woman who had never known the ground. Sofia could almost believe her a creature born to the skies, for who else could hover there with such formidable certainty, daring the world to bring her down?

She was still reeling from the stunt, when the woman vaulted off the stage in a spinning leap, tangling her legs and arms around the flowing fabric and climbing it with swift, graceful tugs and twists. She was nearly to the top, high above them all, when her hands released the silks and her body plunged once more, legs fanning out in a blur of rapid spirals, as if to simulate the speed of a hummingbird in flight.

Sofía followed Adelina through the crowd, clapping dazedly against her fresh goblet of wine, which one of the servers, spying her woefully empty hands, must have given her during a moment of distraction.

Back on the ground, the hummingbird lady's feet propelled her into the air and beyond the circle of the stage with one powerful leap. Wings outstretched, she glided above the audience on silk ropes, zooming in and out between them with a kind of desperate fervor, as though she were reaching for something vital. Wherever she went, cheers followed, and arms lifted eagerly, hoping for the brush of her silks, the graze of her fingertips.

Music dipped and soared along with her, matching her urgent movements beat by beat, as if it were the rhythm of her flight. Arising *from* her. Had Sofía not been watching the musicians playing right there on the stage, she might have let herself imagine that was true, that this woman's dance needed no accompaniment, that it could give rise to its own music.

Below her, the orchestra moved with a languid rhythm, circling the outer rim of the stage. Massive contraptions of red crêpe, bent into the shape of enchantress flowers, were fitted to their backs, matching their sleek red ensembles. The aerialist dove over them, reaching with arms extended, hands straining, ready to touch, lock tight, and never let go. But every time she drew near, the silks pulled at her. Reeled her back to the heights where she belonged.

It was then, as Sofía's gaze drew skyward, that the evening brightened into a summer blue, and where the woman had been, now flew a tiny thing of a bird with radiant wings. The vision bled in so seamlessly that the shift in reality hardly registered as she tracked the colibrí's flight in and between the branches of an enchantress tree, its needle-fine beak brushing the waxy red skin of its flowers, the black marble of its eye wide and searching.

Music wrenched Sofía from her strange daydream, and she blinked herself back into the present, tried to untangle the swift beat of wings from the strum of strings.

The cuatristas' fingers were quick and light on their instruments, the tune of the cuatro crisper and more acute than that of a guitar. Yet while the song itself was lively, almost upbeat, it stirred a pang of wistfulness in Sofía.

The last time she heard the cuatro, her mamá had been there holding her hand, trying her hardest to get Sofía to dance. *Baila, mi cielo*, her mother cajoled as she swayed to the cuatrista's tune, showing her how. The steps had come naturally to Sol, but Sofía did not feel the music of the mountains move her as it moved him. As it moved her mother—tall, full-figured, with ochre skin that gleamed in the firelight. Her head tilted back to the sky, her eyes fluttered closed, and the thick tumble of her silken hair swished against the curve of her hips. Sofía's mother was unpredictable. Chaotic. Burning bright as the bonfire beside them.

It almost hurt to look at her. And yet . . .

She was beautiful. More beautiful than words, those perfect words that wrangled the messy abstractness of Sofía's thoughts into blissful order.

I should have danced for you . . . Grief pulsed dully inside Sofía. Its edge, though worn, could still cut her ragged even after all these years. She welcomed the sensation, the reminder of why she was there.

It was *not* to gawk at the entertainment.

Shame overtook her grief at the realization she had allowed herself to be distracted, to get drawn into the pomp and glitz of Carnaval as if she had not spent an entire life scoffing at such frivolousness. It was unnerving how easily it claimed her focus, tugging at those bittersweet memories of a childhood lost, severed roughly at the roots.

Her eyes swept the crowd with renewed determination, and she pushed deeper into the domed solarium, towing Adelina after her. She squinted into the masked crowd, elbowing her way between strangers as she searched for the face she once knew.

Would she recognize him, that scrawny boy of fifteen, now a man grown? Would he recognize her, in her black mask and crimson gown, her dark hair freed from its pins and braids? She kept expecting to find at least one woman in a homespun dress or a man in a patched suit, tending to their employers. She had counted over a dozen criados and criadas on the steamboat, and assumed there must be hundreds more on the property. Perhaps they were barred from the festivities, consigned to serve their employers within the confines of their suites?

Even if that proved true, and Sol was sequestered away in some room where he could not compromise the fine-tuned operation that was Carnaval, perhaps not all hope was lost. Don Reynaldo could very well be among them, drinking the same wine, watching the same performance.

"Any sign of your father?" Sofía spoke over the music.

"No." Adelina's mouth twisted like she'd tasted something sour. "But then . . . it's dark and everyone's wearing a mask."

"You'd recognize him though?"

"I . . . Yes, of course. I'd know him anywhere."

Sofía did not think she imagined the note of uncertainty in Adelina's voice.

They kept on looking, seeking those they'd lost as the crowd cheered, and the music played, and the aerialist contorted her limbs into impossible shapes. Had Sol been there, he would have translated for Sofía the subtle language of Carnaval. Filled the gaps like he did when they were children, explaining, in that gentle way of his, the nuances she often missed—the many shades of meaning between two absolutes.

She knew how to take the art apart, color by color, line by line, but he . . . He knew how to piece it together, finding poetry where she only heard semantics. If only she could see Carnaval through his eyes, see beyond the talent to the wonder, the magic. The many reasons why she should not only be impressed, but *moved*.

Applause rang all around Sofía, but to her ears it sounded muffled. It was his voice she heard most vividly, describing to her a spectrum of beauty she knew only through him. As if the two were one mind, split down the middle, each given what the other lacked.

Distantly, she was aware of the performance coming to a close, of the hummingbird lady fading into the dark, her black silks drifting behind her.

The crowd began to disperse, gathering in gossiping clusters around the banquet tables and lounge areas with plates laden with seasoned fish, saffron rice, fried plantains, and decadent cakes soaked in coconut milk or infused with rum. The rich scents of garlic, oregano, and turmeric wafted through the solarium, reminding Sofía she hadn't eaten since breakfast. Her hunger stirred, but her stormy gaze remained trained on the ceiling, staring after a woman long gone.

Adelina stepped beside Sofía, leaning her head lightly against her shoulder.

"Sol would know," Sofía told her.

"Know what?"

"Why it mattered . . . Adelina, what do I do if I never find him?"

"You will. *We* will. Your brother is out there, cariño. He has to be." She made it sound like an inevitability—an object thrown, bound by nature's laws to return to the ground eventually. But Sofía had never inhabited that world where good things simply . . . *happened*. The physics that governed it did not extend to her own realm of existence. In her world, the things you failed to keep ahold of did not just find their way back.

The two stood there, watching the cuatristas roam the stage in their elaborate costumes, their music now more of a light breeze than a colibrí's frenzied flight. Eventually, Sofía let herself get drawn to the banquet table, and when Adelina bade her to eat something, she grudgingly obliged. Without looking, she reached for the nearest platter and ladled onto her plate a generous scoop of whatever was inside. Boiled octopus, she realized belatedly, set in a marinade of salt and vinegar, cooked onions, and green olives sliced into rings. She pierced the pieces with an impractically tiny fork and tried not to dwell too much on the knobby texture of the tentacles. It was not entirely unappetizing, though she had certainly eaten plenty that toed the line of inedible.

She chewed thoughtfully on her octopus, and as she went to turn, drawn to a steaming dish of paella, a hand came down over her shoulder. Sofía traced the gloved hand to a woman in sunflower yellow. Mint green eyes, veined red from drink, peered at Sofía through a mask of lace-fine filigree. "Let me guess . . . a vocalist?"

Sofía cocked her head to the side.

"No?" The woman, losing her balance, tightened her grip on Sofía's shoulder. "*Ah*, I know." She snapped her fingers. "A diviner. Oh, thank the saints. The other one's grown incompetent. Told me just the other night that my philandering husband has forgotten my name, as if that's news."

The woman prattled on, oblivious to Sofía's discomfiture.

"An hour-long wait, just to hear something I already know. Is it not bad enough she makes us track her down like hounds sniffing out quarry? She must think herself quite the enigma, that Madame Anani, having us chase after her every night. Bothersome girl."

Finally, it clicked for Sofía. *She thinks I'm part of the entertainment . . .* The concept was almost laughable. She had zero talent for the stage, unless reciting encyclopedic facts from memory counted as one. Yet, here was this woman, presuming her artfully inclined, all because she looked more like the performers than she did the patrons.

"Do you do palms?" The woman began tugging off her glove, seeming to interpret Sofía's silence as confirmation.

Her eyes flicked toward the offered hand. The fingers were delicate, the nails buffed and polished, the skin unmarked by labor. This woman's hand had never scrubbed a floor, never felt the stinging burn of lye that kept her gowns fresh and cottons bright.

"Well?" she said impatiently, wagging her hand for Sofía to take it.

Sofía, instead, set her empty plate on the proffered palm.

The lady gaped at the dish, probably wondering if this was part of her divination technique. When she finally did register the insult, Sofía was already well on her way.

"What was that about?" Adelina approached with a fresh glass of wine in each hand.

"Information." She accepted the drink, mind buzzing with a renewed spark of determination. "I may have found us someone who can help."

"A FORTUNE TELLER?" Adelina hissed as she followed Sofía through the labyrinth. "What in the bleeding saints could you possibly want with a fortune teller? You think weather forecasting is a hoax."

"Not a hoax, just more an aspiration than a science." Sofía nudged her head left, beckoning Adelina down the next passageway. "And obviously," she went on, "it's not her mystical abilities I'm after, but her keen powers of perception. I may not believe her eyes can see into the future, but I do believe they see a great deal others fail to notice. What is a diviner, after all, if not an expert observer?"

"Um, a *fraud*?"

"Well, yes, that's a given. Look, hoping we might come upon Sol or your father while wandering aimlessly through a crowd of hundreds is profoundly impractical. But if there's anyone that can give us a nudge in the right direction, I'd bet good coin it's the one person here that deals in information." They dove through an arched hedge, and as they emerged, Sofía caught the sound of running water.

"Fine. Let's say you're right, and this 'Madame Anani' is not just a common charlatan or—gods forbid—a practitioner of the unholy arts. Even if she *could* help, we are in a maze the size of a small town, have only a handful of hours until sunrise, and your bit of reconnaissance back at the solarium told you nothing about her whereabouts, other than they are as cryptic as her fortunes. Honestly, what are the odds we will . . ." Adelina came to an abrupt stop behind Sofía.

"You tell me." Sofía's mouth twitched into a small smile. "Odds are more your area of expertise than mine."

A narrow opening in the wall revealed a hidden alcove, shaped around a section of the river bordering Carnaval. There were creatures of vine and bramble recessed into the hedges, echoing the motif of serpents, fish, coquís, and hummingbirds reflected throughout the labyrinth. At the center, right above the river, floated a small round tent draped in the greens of earth and canopied with a latticework of coconut palm leaves. Whatever held it aloft must have been concealed under the water's surface, creating the impression of a floating structure. Flickering lanterns ensconced within glass cast their light upon the river, rippling sinuously across its dark surface.

"Come on." Sofía marched to the river's edge, hiked her skirts up over her ankles, and dipped a foot in experimentally. As she'd suspected, her toes came upon something solid. She set her heel down and tested her weight on it before stepping in fully. The water cooled her skin, soothing the scrapes and blisters she had been collecting since before she lost her shoes.

With an unintelligible grumble, Adelina slipped out of her pearl slippers and waded through the water after her.

The gentle clack of wooden wind chimes welcomed them as they drew closer to the tent. Sofía attuned her ears, listening for any signs that the diviner had company. "Hello?" She inched open the curtain with one hand. "Madame Anani?" When no response came, she ducked her head inside and stepped through.

A woman sat behind a round wooden table, shuffling a set of flat stones across its surface. Her hair was a glossy veil of black, flowing in loose strands past her hips. She wore a long sleeveless tunic of white cotton, cinched at the waist with a braided belt inlaid with slivers of seashells. On her neck lay a wide collar of jasper and guanín, a composite of gold, silver, and copper that glimmered with a reddish sheen. Matching bands encircled her upper arms and wrists, and charcoal framed the coals of her eyes like a mask. Black paint adorned her brown skin, drawn across it in lines and geometric symbols.

"What you skulking over there for?" Without looking up from the table, Madame Anani waved an arm toward the open seat. "Sit. I ain't got all night."

Sofía exchanged a glance with Adelina, then splashed across the short distance, settling down on the cushioned seat opposite the diviner. Adelina lingered uncomfortably by the tent's opening with her skirts bundled in one hand and her slippers dangling from the other. She shifted from foot to foot, scanning their surroundings with unease. Sofía did the same, cataloging what little ornamentation the tent had: a small cabinet overgrown with leaf and moss, a pair of hanging lanterns, and a brass holder swinging from a hook on the ceiling, burning an herb that filled the tent with a strong, earthy smoke. To her surprise, there was nothing overtly theatrical about the decor—apart from the structure being embedded in water, that is.

"First reading?" Madame Anani moved without hurry, scooping the stones into a black pouch, each one clinking as it joined the others.

"Yes," Sofía said. "Last one as well, if I can help it."

That caught the diviner's attention. Dark eyes narrowed on Sofía, studying her with the quiet intensity of a crow. "You're younger than my usuals," she noted, though she herself could not have been much older. Or . . . was she? Her skin was unlined, her features youthful, but there was a quality about her, a gravitas that made her seem far older than her years.

"Hmm, I take it you've been here for a while then, to already expect a certain type of . . . clientele?"

The diviner snorted in a most unladylike fashion. "A lifetime, it seems." She reached into her cabinet for a small lidded coin pot and slid it across the table. "Love readings are three reales each."

Behind Sofía, Adelina broke into a fit of coughs, though it did little to conceal her laughter.

"How does this work?" Ignoring her friend, Sofía reached into the pocket of her skirts and dropped the coins in with a clink. "Do I . . . drink some tea? Pick a card?"

Madame Anani snorted. "Please. Tea's revolting, and cards are for amateurs." She set a candle dripping in wax on the table and pinched the wick between two fingers. "*I* prefer fire."

Instantly, the candle sparked.

Sofía blinked at the flame. A sleight of hand? Some chemical reaction triggered by the contact? Whatever the trick was, it was frustratingly clever.

Madame Anani set a shallow bowl of clay on the table next, poured the bag of stones in, then bent down to cup water from the stream. She dripped it over the stones, then sprinkled it with a fine ash-colored powder. As she did, she intoned in a language meant for the staccato of a drum. The words did not mean a thing to Sofía, but their rhythm . . . *Skies and stars above.* That rhythm felt achingly familiar, reminding her of the songs her mamá used to croon for them at night, when she returned from the kiln house, weary and stinking of smoke and cured tobacco.

Sofía wanted to ask the woman what the words meant, how she'd come upon them. Had they been passed down to her by a knowing elder? Were there places on Etérea's islands where their ancestral tongue was kept alive?

"Think of a question," instructed Madame Anani, handing Sofía the burning candle. "*One* question. Hold it in your mind as you bring the flame over the stones."

She rolled the candlestick between her fingers, considering. She could stop there, expose this ritual for the ruse it was, but she was admittedly intrigued by the surly diviner, and more than a little curious to see where all this led.

Right then.

She touched the fire to the stones, and the bowl went up in flames.

Curls of fire rose, and the stones steamed and popped. Sofía pressed herself back into her chair, away from the scalding heat, but Madame Anani leaned closer, eager eyes watching the flames. The glow lit her skin and dusted her irises with sparks, like embers on a dying hearth. Sweat poured down Sofía's temples as the fire peaked, then receded into a silvery haze of steam.

When only three stones were left burning, the diviner plucked them—still hot—from the clay bowl and placed them on the table, glyph side up.

Sofía recognized none of the symbols. Each stone bore a different one carved onto the surface. The one at the center showed two interlocking spirals that never touched, but melded as if they were one. The glyph on its right resembled a child's drawing of a flower, and on the left, the stone was etched with a half-moon shape, reminiscent of a carnaval mask.

The scholar in Sofía itched to study them, ask questions, record her findings . . .

Madame Anani crossed her arms over her chest, and frowned. "You're not here for a love reading."

Sofía raised an eyebrow in challenge. "Then what am I here for?"

"Closure." She angled her head at the stones, her expression intent, as though she could indeed read the truth in them. "You're looking for someone. Someone you're not so sure you'll find."

Sofía sneaked a glance at Adelina, sensing her discomfort. Though plenty of devotees of the Hisperian faith made a pastime of the occult, Adelina, for all her daredevilry, drew a hard line at heresy. She might not have been as devout as Doña Elena would have wanted her to be, but she was more gods-fearing than she'd ever admit. As Sofía herself believed in neither the divine nor the supernatural, her wet stockings were the extent of her personal discomfort.

"My brother," she replied. "And her father."

Madame Anani tapped a finger against the edge of the table. "How fortuitous then, that you should seek me on this night."

"How do you mean?"

"Haven't you caught on yet? This night . . . it is one of transformation." She smiled with all her teeth, and there was nothing sweet, or soft, or even particularly joyful about it. "And is transformation not, at its core, something that is lost, and another that is found?"

Sofía thought about it. "In a way," she concluded. "Might I take this to mean you will help us?"

"That, I'll leave to the stones."

"*Or* . . . we can move past this farce. Truthfully, I've come to you for information, not fortunes. You may, of course, keep my coin."

The diviner barked out a laugh that was half amusement, half disbelief. "A farce, you say. How arrogant can you be to insult my work, yet expect my aid?"

"On the contrary, Madame Anani, I am a fan of your work. You watch and you listen, and you catch what others don't. The world would be a richer place if others were half as observant."

"Ahh, you're one of those grounded sorts. The kind that don't trust nothing they can't see or touch or measure. Don't get many of you lot around here, for obvious reasons. My art doesn't exactly appeal to skeptics."

Sofia laced her fingers over the table. "Irrespective of what I am or am not, I believe you may be able to point us in the right direction. It was a little over five years ago that the two arrived on this island. Perhaps your paths crossed? The man we're looking for, his name is Reynaldo, Don Reynaldo de Esperanza. My twin brother, Sol, was with him—fifteen at the time. Tall, close-cropped hair, coppery-gold eyes. He's—"

"I can't help you." Madame Anani began gathering the stones back into the pouch.

"Pardon?"

She pushed the coin pot back across the table. "Take your payment. I charge for readings, not conversations."

"But—"

"We can pay more." Adelina stepped forward, clutching her reticule in the hand that'd been, until that moment, holding up the train of her dress. The fine silk floated above the water, drenched through. "Name your price."

The diviner tipped the coins onto the table, and Sofia watched as one rolled off the edge. She was too distracted to catch it before the current pulled it under.

"We're done here," said Madame Anani, dismissing them both. "Shut the curtain on your way out." They plodded back out of the river, wet and shivering and *miserable*.

"A simple no would have sufficed," Adelina argued as she wrung water out of her skirts. "*Really, it . . . inexcusable manners . . . even if . . . not a reason to . . .*"

Sofía found herself tuning in and out of her friend's lengthy tirade, unexpectedly preoccupied with the small sculpture on the nearby hedge. It was of a woodpecker, its mighty beak held high, its beady black eye focused and watchful. There was a quality to the way it perched there, a sort of haughty affectation that had Sofía reaching for the pendant at her neck. Visually, it bore little resemblance to the one across from her. For one, it was in an entirely different medium, and not even the design could be said to match, with hers favoring a kind of playful stylization over the other's hyperrealism.

And yet, it was so much like her brother's in the way it seemed, more than a sculpture, a *character*. A unique entity, imbued with its own mind and spirit.

Before Sofía could grasp what she meant to do, she was already turning, splashing back across the river and through the flap on the tent.

The diviner raised her head as she entered.

"Guak mun aní," Sofía said, chest rising and falling as though she had run a mighty distance.

". . . Sorry?"

"Guak mun aní," she repeated, her voice louder and clearer now. "We are *here* . . . It's something my mamá used to say . . . 'We are here, do not forget. We are here, though they'll tell you we're gone. We are here, and we're not alone.'"

Though the diviner did not respond, she appeared to regard Sofía more closely.

"You . . . you speak the old tongue," Sofía explained, her confidence beginning to waver. "I thought perhaps—"

"That we might bond over our shared displacement?" Despite her words, the diviner's expression *did* soften. She bent forward, elbows coming to rest over the small table, her fingers dancing absently over the fire—leisurely touching the flame without it burning her. "Taroo," she said, "ceded his humanity, let the zemís make of him a hummingbird so that one day, he might find his lost love among the flowers . . ."

The diviner, indifferent to Sofía's confusion, forged ahead before she could get a word in edgewise. "Yayael, son of Yaya, gave his bones so that we would have our oceans, and all that dwells within them. And to become a hero, Guaguyona first had to make himself a monster."

Sofía remained silent for a beat before venturing, "Madame Anani, at the risk of sounding rude, what is this about, exactly?" She had completely lost the thread of the conversation.

"It's about you," said the diviner. "What is *your* search worth?" Her dark eyes flicked up, peering at Sofía over the flame. "To find what you seek, what will you sacrifice?" A pause. "What will *you* become?"

ACTO II

WE WAKE.

We roam the halls as others sleep, warm in their sunlit beds, dreaming of the world we'll make for them. It is only when the breeze cools and the shadows grow and deepen that their doors will open. Until then, we ready their meals . . . rake the leaves . . . sweep away the evening's dust and debris . . .

They will not see us when they walk among us. Will not know us beyond the faces we show them. But *we* see *them*. We *know* them. The selves they've unmade, and the ones they've created. We were there when the mask first slid over their skin, when the lies they told became their story.

For the latest arrivals, it will be no different.

They will have a taste of all this life can be, know its sweetness on their lips, the snap and crunch of it between their teeth, and they will gorge themselves on it.

And there we'll be, serving them joy upon a platter. There is no appetite we cannot satisfy, no craving we cannot ease. That is why they seek us, all who step through our doors—who want better. *More.* Here, they'll not suffer reality.

Here, they'll have it all.

CHAPTER 5

*Youth, god of passion. Father, god of war.
Sage, god of mastery. Their eyes watch all.*

—Chronicler

AT THE FLOR DE LIS, breakfast was served at sunset.

Sofía leaned tiredly against her chair, nursing a cup of strong black coffee and a throbbing headache. Behind the long layers of her crimson gown, her feet lay bare, toes curling around the manicured grass of the courtyard. She closed her eyes against the fading light above and breathed deeply.

Around her, the courtyard was abuzz with excitement. Patrons lauded the previous night's events and tried to predict what wonders this new evening would hold. Carnaval was not a static experience, to Sofía's great dismay. It was constantly evolving, teasing revelers with a steady stream of mystery. No wonder so few ever left. It fed the very thing that had lured so many to abandon the comfortable and predictable, and embark toward an uncertain destination across the sea.

"Are you going to finish that?"

Sofía dragged her eyes down from the twilight sky to Adelina. She sat primly in her cushioned garden chair, wearing a gown of champagne silk and sipping her dainty cup of overly sweetened café con leche, an abomination of a beverage she insisted on calling coffee. Sofía stared at the crumbs of pastry on Adelina's plate and pushed her own plate across the wrought-iron table.

Adelina dug happily into the remnants of the meal—a dish of poached eggs, heavily spiced with rosemary and thyme, and a small plate of half-moon empanadas, stuffed with yuca and fried to a golden crisp. Sofía kept only her bowl of fruit, unable to stomach anything else.

"You—" Sofía said, stabbing her fork through a slice of guayaba "—are an opportunist. I've met beggars with more restraint."

Adelina rolled her eyes. "Please, it would have just sat there," she mumbled through a mouthful of food, "and you hate waste."

"Ah . . . so it was a selfless act, entirely devoid of ulterior motive."

"Precisely."

"Then you wouldn't mind me beckoning our server for another round of coffee."

Adelina caught her hand before she could signal for a vejigante.

Sofía leveled her a look. "It will be a month before the next steamer arrives. Do you propose we avoid them until then?" Not that they *could* elude them with any semblance of success. The vejigantes were posted at every corner, their silent, watchful presence inescapable.

It was part of what so intrigued Sofía. The things they must know on account of both their station and collective guise. A shield of invisibility for those who already were largely invisible. Overlooked like some ornament on a wall when secrets were traded and confidences shared. At least one of the vejigantes would know where her brother was, or where he'd gone. They might have seen him, even known him. Might have shared a meal at his table or passed him in the halls.

If only they would speak to her.

"I'm giving it another go," she decided, her sights set on the vejigante farthest from the breakfast tables. "The one over there." She pointed with her fork. "Alone, on that corner, far from prying ears. They might be more inclined to break character."

"Hmm, you reckon?" Adelina bridled her optimism. "None of the others would risk it."

So far, every staff member Sofía had approached had deflected her attempts at conversation. If she was not ordering a meal or asking for directions, their response was, unfailingly, a protracted silence.

"There'll be no one around to overhear us this time. If I've any chance of getting them to bend the rules, this might be it." She gulped back the last of her coffee. "Back soon."

Sofía strode across the courtyard, past the fountain at its center, and around the bend of a flamboyán tree, only belatedly thinking she ought to slow her stride, affect a look that was not so suspiciously purposeful. The vejigante might not be so keen to talk if there were eyes on them. Not that anyone was likely to pay her any mind—or to care what she was up to, for that matter. Still, she thought it prudent to be cautious, if not for her sake, then theirs. She'd witnessed plenty of servants punished for pettier transgressions.

"Buenas tardes," she said in a low voice, facing discretely away from the object of her interrogation. "Worked here awhile, have you?" Though they said nothing, she persisted. "Might you have come across a criado by the name of Sol in your time here? Arrived five summers ago. He's a sculptor, makes the most magnificent things out of stone and wood. Hums a little ditty when he's lost himself inside his work. The same one too, drives all around him mad."

From the corner of her vision, Sofía watched the vejigante turn their head toward her. There was an uncanny intensity to their observation, and for a moment, she could appreciate what it was that so unsettled Adelina. The monstrous horns, the hungry grin, the inscrutable depths of their eyes. It was so easy to forget there was a person underneath it all.

"We'll not be overheard here," she promised, still facing away from them, pretending to be admiring the scenery. "Or keep your silence if you must. I'd make do with nod, or a shake of your head if that's all you can spare me." A pleading note crept into her voice. "Please . . . ? I just . . . I just want to know he's well."

The silence dragged, and it was clear that it was not a pause, but an ending. If she wanted answers, she would have to search for them elsewhere. "Forgive me for asking . . . I really don't mean to make trouble for you." Nor did she have a right to. She, with her fine dress and luxurious bedsheets, and a well-to-do friend bankrolling her expenses.

I am like you, she wanted to say. But were that true, she wouldn't be there, dining on coffee and pastries. She'd be the one serving the meal.

Though she'd only picked at her breakfast, she felt it sour in her belly as she walked away.

The last rays of orange-gold bled out of the sky. Strange to think her day was only just beginning . . . She'd stayed up until sunrise, and somehow slept away the afternoon. Fortunately, so had all the other patrons.

It was the way of Carnaval, it seemed.

Around her, the courtyard had gone completely silent. Masked faces were turned upward, eyes eager, waiting for the dark to fully settle over Isla Bestia, for nightfall to usher in the glorious start of the festivities. It dawdled, timid, taking the sky back inch by inch. Was it normally *this* slow? Night had always caught her unaware, seeming to descend abruptly.

But perhaps she had simply never stopped to watch its arrival. Sunset views were meant for those with time to spare. For her, a blackening sky was not something to gawk at, it was a cue. A reminder that she had gowns to press, iron to polish, and a meal tray to prepare for a temperamental Doña Elena.

The world went dark at last—the kind of dark that had a weight to it, a thickness. Sofía felt it pressing in, dripping over her like oil paint, and then . . . the lamps came alive. One sconce after the other in quick succession.

In the distance, a sound rose: the pulse of a drum. An invitation.

Carnaval had begun.

SOFÍA REJOINED ADELINA at the table as patrons flooded the corridors.

"You have that gleam in your eye," her friend noted. "What are you up to, cariño?"

Instead of answering, Sofía drummed her fingers against her knee, lost in contemplation. "That door there," she said, nudging her chin in its general direction. "I think it leads to the servants' quarters."

"Let me guess—you want me to wait here as you skulk around belowstairs?"

Sofía winced an apology. "Would you mind? It's just—"

"That I'd stand out like a sore thumb? Trust me, I'm keenly aware my presence there would only complicate matters." She dipped a miniature churro into a mug of thick hot chocolate. "Go on then." She shooed Sofía away. "I'll be here, indulging in fried dough until I expire."

Sofía slipped out of the courtyard, making for the door she had seen the vejigantes carrying breakfast trays in and out of all evening. It opened with a groan into a dim spiraling stairway. Narrow, in a way that made her gulp for breath before slipping inside.

As she made her way belowstairs, she listened closely for approaching footsteps, but the stairway was quiet save for the creak of wood, the brush of her skirts along the steps, the distant clatter of pots and pans. She wondered if she ought to have changed into her work dress first. How would it look, a patron of presumable wealth waltzing in to ask after a servant? Would anyone believe her when she told them of her missing brother or would they dismiss her story? Refuse to speak to her?

Were the roles reversed, she knew she'd be wary of her too.

In the end, she settled on removing her mask, and hoped that would be enough.

At the bottom of the stairwell, Sofía paused and craned her neck to look. A vejigante was disappearing down a long corridor. Dimly lit and windowless, with plain stucco walls that had not known a good scrub or coat of paint in many years. She lingered there awhile, making sure the hall was well and truly empty before slipping inside.

Up ahead and to the right was an open doorway leading to the kitchens. It was a familiar scene, complete with the smoky, mouth-watering aroma of spices, the muggy heat of steaming cauldrons, the crackle of oil sizzling on pans. What was missing was the friendly chatter, the barked orders from the head cook, the dishwasher's absentminded humming . . .

A quick survey of the kitchen told Sofía why. Everyone on staff, from the bakers to the dishwashers to the cooks, was dressed head to toe in the attire of vejigantes.

How stringent must the Flor de Lis's management be, if the staff had to remain in character even behind closed doors? Wearing all those layers in the heat of the kitchens must have been grueling.

She debated approaching them, but ultimately decided the smarter thing would be to canvas the area first, gather what information she could before someone banished her back abovestairs.

With a last look at those unnervingly silent kitchens, Sofía continued down the corridor. The doors on her left opened to a pantry, a supply closet, and a wine cellar. After a quick peek inside, she locked each quietly into place and went to scout out the next hallway. It branched into two paths, each lined with another dozen doors on either side. She inched open the nearest one. Behind it lay a room with two cots and a stout wooden table lodged between them. Though the cots were draped in perfectly starched sheets, the room itself was shrouded in a thick layer of dust and bare of personal articles.

The next room was the same, as was the one after. Room after room, all unlived in.

Where in the world were they housing the servants? With the number of staff and personal attendants on the property, every single one of those beds should have been occupied. Questions flitted through Sofía's mind as she turned back into the corridor. And froze.

Eyes like dark pits looked back at her.

She jerked backward instinctively, then tried, unsuccessfully, to mask her alarm with laughter. The sound ground against her ears—surely, the vejigante could hear how forced it was.

"Perdone, señor—eh . . . señora? Did not see you there." She bobbed her head in a quick apology, apparently having decided she should act and sound like someone else entirely. Of all the possible times to dabble in the art of improvisation, what could have possessed Sofía to do so now? It was by no means the best way she could have managed that situation, which led her to conclude this was a rare, emotional response.

Why? What danger had her subconscious arrived at that hadn't yet made its way to her conscious calculations?

She mulled it over. Getting caught likely meant being redirected—politely—back abovestairs. At worst, she might be reported to the Flor de Lis's management, assuming they gave a damn about patrons wandering off into restricted areas. At Hacienda Esperanza at least, when houseguests occasionally wormed their way into the servants' hall, neither Don Reynaldo nor Doña Elena ever bothered to interfere. All in all, being caught should no more than inconvenience her search.

And yet . . . if that was really all she had to worry about, why was she going out of her way to avoid suspicion? Why was her impulse to put on an act rather than enlist the vejigante's help? "Doubt you get that often, huh?" She prattled on uneasily. "With all the . . . teeth . . . and the . . . uh . . . horns."

It was the silence. That was the reason.

The empty rooms.

The dust coating every surface.

The vejigante only stared, head angled in question.

She felt the wild urge to shake them, pry their mask off, prove to herself there was indeed a person underneath the monster. Instead, she said, "I should be off now," and made a hasty retreat.

Again, she passed the empty rooms . . . the wine cellar . . . the supply closet . . . the pantry . . . When she reached the kitchens, she stopped to look back, and though it was unlike her to trust such a feeling, she could not shake the sensation of eyes on her. Watching until she vanished up the stairs.

CARNAVAL WAS ALREADY in full swing by the time Sofía made it outside.

Hundreds of masked patrons mingled among musicians costumed in spectacular garments of glittering gold, and stilt walkers donning towering headdresses—gilded and bladed like giant sunbursts.

The focal point was the parade floats, a ring of tiered platforms of polished ore, tall as the Flor de Lis itself and mechanized to move in seamless synchronization. A cavalcade of entertainers occupied each step, organized into tapering rows of drummers, dancers, and vocalists, and atop each of the highest tiers stood a lone figure wearing an extravagant backpiece of goldwork, wire frame, and embroidered silk. A mind-boggling feat of engineering, to be sure, fanning out high and wide behind them like a peacock's plumage. The backpieces moved with the dancers, rocking to the sultry shimmy of hips, the flutter of naked arms, and rhythmic tap of bare feet.

"There you are!" Adelina wove through the crowd, wine goblet in hand. "Isn't this just grand?"

Sofía drew her friend by the elbow, and raised her voice above the music. "What happened? You said you would wai—"

Movement drew her eye. Up ahead, performers spun flaming metal rods. Fire dancers stirred to the music's hard, frantic rhythm, stepping, spinning, and leaping to the quickening beat of conga drums, their skin glistening with sweat, gold leaf, and firelight. As they moved, their flames lingered in the air like glowing lengths of thread.

From Sofía's vantage point, they all seemed a single organism, one heart beating in flawless coordination. They dove in and out between the rotating parade floats, coming together and apart, drawing patterns with their movements, telling a story in a language of twirls and kicks and fire.

Sofía shook herself, jerking her attention back to Adelina. "You said you would wait," she persisted, practically shouting to be heard over the hubbub. "Must you always be so reckless? Wandering off on your own and without even a—"

"What?"

This was obviously neither the time nor place for this conversation. Sofía waved in the universal sign for *never mind* and

Adelina was only too eager to move on. Her gaze was already straying elsewhere, catching on some fresh novelty—of which there was no apparent shortage.

As vexing as it was to admit, the night was truly something to behold, and Sofía found her own focus lapsing as she guided them through the masses. She swept her gaze over that crowd of strangers, extrapolating the faces behind the masks, the voices beneath the music, trying to match them to the memory of her erstwhile master. Like she was playing a game of Patience. Each patron a card face down upon the board, each new draw a test of luck and observation.

One man had a similar build to Don Reynaldo's, but his hair was a few shades darker. Another had eyes the same rich azure as Adelina's, but he was laughing, and Don Reynaldo never laughed. And that one there looked exactly like him from afar, but the similarities faded upon closer inspection.

Sofía had taken two steps toward her latest target when a flash of light flooded her vision. Nearby, carnavaleros in gilded headdresses exchanged flaming wands, tossing them across the air in brilliant arcs. In one fluid motion, their bodies took to the air, like they too were an instrument, launched skyward by an unseen hand. Gravity, to them, was not a force to obey, but one to be conquered.

Everywhere Sofía looked, fire and steel flew, slashing across the dark, scarring it with streaks of hot luminescence. The warmth pressed against her skin, and the heavy smoke filled her lungs, but she did not pull away.

Rods were thrown, twirled, and passed from hand to hand. Others were balanced on the curve of a forehead, the crook of a shoulder, or the tip of an index finger. Some carnavaleros swung lengths of dark rope with flaming wicks, winding them around their wrists. Their ankles. Their necks.

They rejoiced in their daring, smiling with a wild glee even as they flirted with death.

Hours passed in that way, measured not in minutes, but in drumbeats, in emptied goblets, in the thickening haze of smoke. Sofía roamed in aimless circles, looking and looking and *looking*.

Cycling through the motions, the pure mechanics of it, like this hopeless search was a script she'd learned the lines of. Her one-woman play with herself as the audience.

Murmurs from the crowd alerted her to the newest development in the night's performance, and though she had no intention of stopping to watch, her steps slowed, her head tilted back, and her eyes trailed up, up, up.

The topmost step of each parade float was opening via a hand crank, the floor gaping like the mouth of a clam. From it unfolded a series of tubes and steel wires. When bolted down and connected across all six moving floats, it formed a triple tightrope high above all.

And below, cast in its shadows, a shape Sofía recognized. She had seen it the night before, etched into a stone still warm from the diviner's flames, a flowerlike symbol drawn in bold lines, and on its center, circles creating the impression of a gaping mouth and eyes wide-open. Seeing it stamped onto the earth in darkness and firelight, she couldn't rationalize ever comparing it to a child's drawing.

Here, it felt like a warning.

"What is—" Adelina started to ask, just as two performers peeled off from the crowd and began climbing up the floats. They were clad in bold costumes and heavy jewelry, and every inch of skin left exposed was painted with shimmering gold. Over her beaded braids, the woman wore a metal headdress in the shape of a sunburst. The man wore only a golden mask, tied over a long tail of jet-black hair. *"Oh."* Adelina breathed out excitedly, apparently realizing what they meant to do.

The music slowed and quieted to an ominous beat, and as the suspense thickened, the raucous shouts and applause that had punctuated the performance before gave way to shocked gasps and tense whispers. When the performers finally crested the tightwire's ladder, a hush fell over the crowd, heavy with anticipation.

Suddenly, the music stopped altogether and the lights of Carnaval winked out, plunging everything into pitch-black darkness. The only sound was the nearby crash of waves, the rustle of leaves, the anxious breathing of all who watched. Then, from above, a flame sparked to life. Followed by another. And another, as the slow, powerful strike of a drum rose above the silence, pulsing like a heartbeat. The island's heartbeat. The man and the woman took their first steps, twirling a flaming staff in each hand. Their bare feet glided gracefully across the wire, carrying them closer to the center, and to each other.

Sofía tipped back her wine.

Their twisting fires were the sole source of light; their steady, determined stride across that needle-thin terrain the only motion. Everyone else stood still, not just the observers—paralyzed with awe and terror as they were—but the carnavaleros as well. They posed in place, still as statues, their dark silhouettes lined in an ember glow, their arms raised toward the night as though in worship.

Another few steps and the aerialists reached the center of the tightwire. The metal bent beneath their combined weight, and their flames blurred into one, so bright against the gloom, they left imprints behind Sofía's eyelids the few times she dared close them.

The woman backed away then, and Sofía thought she would retreat to her edge of the wire. But instead . . . she leapt.

Beside Sofía, Adelina yelped, grabbing for her wrist just as the man crouched down on the wire, one fire staff held out before him, another gripped between his teeth. The woman vaulted onto the staff poised in his hand, and he lurched, heaving her skyward. She spun in the air and landed on the other side, fire staffs twirling.

Sofía had only a second to feel relieved before the whole wire went up in flames.

The crowd screamed as the pair raced to opposite ends of the burning structure, their feet taking off at a solid run. Below, patrons' panicked shouts urged them to hurry, but instead of escaping, they ground to a halt, stopping just before they reached the ladders.

They turned to face one another.

"What are they doing?"

"This is madness."

"They'll burn."

The music built in tempo, the floats resumed their clockwise rotation, and the stone-still dancers came to life, moving with even more vigor than before. Atop the flaming wire, the gilded aerialists continued their routine, and others soon joined them. Between them, they juggled several dozen flaming batons, tossing them back and forth across the overlapping wires.

Despite the obvious dangers they faced, they looked . . . euphoric.

"Bleeding saints . . ." Adelina whispered as one of the female aerialists ran across the high wire and flung herself into the air. Her partner caught her with a single hand, lifting her as far as his arm would go. The woman rose on one foot, spinning her batons and laughing as if she hadn't a care in the world. Behind her, the first rays of dawn sliced through the night, and the spiked ends of her headdress ignited.

Oh.

Light glinted off it, rendering her a myth. A goddess ablaze. And behind her, sunlight broke across the sky, ushering in the morning, and with it, a sense of rightness. Of peace. As though Sofia was exactly where she was meant to be.

CHAPTER 6

Each full moon night, the island chooses one.
Anoints them in her rivers, and garbs them in her ore.

—Chronicler

"IT MAKES NO SENSE," Sofía told Adelina as she paced the length of her suite some nights later, back and forth along the same narrow stretch of space she had been stomping through for the past half hour.

"That there's still a floor for you to walk on? I am as shocked as you are. Would have expected you to wear through it ages ago."

Sofía spun on her heel. How could she be so blasé about it all? Her increasing avoidance of anything to do with Sol or her father—the *only* reason they were there—was devolving into something akin to indifference. "I'm serious, Adelina."

"Dearest heart, that's not exactly the revelation you think it is." She leaned over her vanity to blend a hint of rouge onto her cheeks. Then, catching her friend's scowl in the mirror, loosed a long-suffering sigh. "You're absolutely certain they're not below-stairs?"

"I am. I've gone back twice more just to confirm my eyes weren't deceiving me."

In fact, Sofía had spent the last few evenings inspecting every guest hall, room, and facility. There was a place for every vice and recreation. Smoking parlors. Music rooms. Thermal baths. Libraries. Even an indoor court for games of boliche. Outside the main building, there were gardens, and greenhouses, and gazebos from which one could watch the sun set over the sea.

Yet, no matter how long she looked or how many halls she wandered down, there was no other logical place to house the servants. Much less the hundreds of performers that brought Carnaval alive each night.

"And beyognd tzee pwopetee?" Adelina mumbled through a mouthful of hairpins as she unsuccessfully tried wrangling a defiant curl into position. *"Blashted har."* The curl slipped, and she fired an impressive round of profanity.

Sofía moved without thinking. "You've seen it, Adelina. There's nothing beyond the property but acres of untamed wilderness." Past the river bordering the Flor de Lis, the land was overgrown with vegetation so dense the only way to travel through it would have been by foot. A challenging undertaking when sensibly attired, and nearly impossible when wearing soaring headdresses and backpieces that protruded like wings. If indeed there were lodgings beyond the hotel property, there would have at least been a clear footpath, and more realistically, a road for wagons to load props and set pieces in and out each night.

Sofía's mind was contorting itself trying to work out the logistics of it all.

Lost in thought, she snatched the pin from Adelina's hand and secured the wayward curl in one practiced motion, then proceeded on to the next out of habit. It had been a long time since she had dressed Adelina's hair, and yet the steps came naturally . . .

Serving came naturally.

Sofía's fingers went still.

Hundreds of days and a dozen leagues from that life, and she still defaulted to servitude. It mattered not that two years ago the law had pronounced her free, her body knew what it did not. That there were no words, written or said, spoken by gods or inked by kings, that could undo the harsh lessons she learned under the crack of a master's whip.

Adelina's hand came down over hers. Gentle but firm. "Not your job anymore. Remember?"

Sofía stepped back from the vanity, hugging her arms tightly to her waist. *This is why*, she thought, hot with shame. *This is why I left you behind.*

"Tell you what." Adelina pinned the last few curls into place and stood, hands on hips. "You follow my lead tonight—hush now, I'm not finished. This whole time, you've been going off on your little sleuthing missions and we're still no closer to finding them. Frankly, you've hit a wall, and so either we change tactics, or we might as well sit here, twiddling our fingers. And yes, I know you hate being out there, mingling with the ton and listening to their endless gossip, but right now, we need that. We need *them*. They can tell us things you wouldn't get from your jaunts through the dark."

It was the next logical step, but it still rankled Sofía. Not even a week into Carnaval and she was already exhausted of the high borns' petty games: the coded gestures, the veiled slights, and double entendres. The perversion of meaning when the words themselves mattered less than the context, the tone of voice, the precisely timed flutter of a fan. She had no idea how anyone got anything done when they were so busy outmaneuvering each other.

Sofía would much rather continue pursuing her more direct investigative approach, but she had to admit it had taken her as far as it could for now. Moreover, this was the most initiative Adelina had shown in days. The past few nights, any concern Sofía brought to her had been met with trite optimism, if not an outright redirection, and her moments of vulnerability—of *anything* befitting the gravity of their situation—had become few and farther between.

"Fine," Sofía relented. "I'll follow your lead."

"Excellent."

"*But*, you have to keep your wits about you. No more wandering off, no more distractions."

Adelina placed a hand solemnly above her heart. "Consider my wits kept." Then, in a quiet, earnest tone, added, "I—I want to find them too, find *him* too. Your brother, he deserves to come home."

A feeling like a rope knotted around Sofía's throat. "Right. Yes, well." She turned toward their suites' connecting door and said, "I ought to get dressed then. Let's meet downstairs at our usual table," as she closed it behind her.

As the despair at last eased its strangling hold on her, she unhooked her gown from the dresser and was just pulling the soft silk over her worn linen corset when she heard a shout.

It had come from outside, and it was so incongruent with the festive soundscape of Carnaval that she rushed out onto the balcony, her arms the only thing pinning her bodice in place.

Below, a man stood upon the rocks. He perched there precariously, his back to the sea and his arms held out as though to ward off some dangerous beast. The sun was setting, and even limned in darkness, the alabaster of his suit and the silver of his mask shone like a beacon.

"Don't come any closer!" he warned the figures in the shadows, and as they stepped out of the dark and into the bands of moonlight, Sofía noticed the horns, the jagged mouths etched into permanent smiles.

Waves pounded at the rocks, breaking around him with enough force that he had to fight to keep his balance. "I know what you've done," he said, as even more vejigantes peeled out of the gloom. "I won't be a part of this anymore."

"You're unwell," replied a voice from somewhere beyond Sofía's line of sight. Smokey and feminine. Composed despite the circumstances. "Let us help you."

The man's answering laugh had a wild edge to it. "I've had quite enough of your '*help*.'" He looked over his shoulder at the roiling water, and Sofía understood what he meant to do. "This is the only way."

Another wave surged, and when it fell, he was gone. Like a magic trick, a curtain dropping to reveal empty space where once was a person.

Sofía stared at where he'd been standing, unable to reconcile what she'd witnessed with the calm and silence that followed.

No one cried out or rushed to help him. No one dove in after him.

They only watched as he vanished beneath the swell of the sea.

"Mierda," Sofía swore. What were they waiting for?

She made a split-second decision and raced out of her suite, sprinting across the hall and down five stories, taking the stairs two at a time, all while holding the blasted gown in place. By the time she made it out of the building, to the spot where the man was lost to the waves, not a single soul stood upon that shoreline.

She peered through the twilight, refusing to believe they could have just left the man to his fate. It was here, wasn't it? This was where it had happened. Her legs carried her along the water's edge, up and down and up again, as close to the lip of the rocks as she dared. She searched the darkening sea, certain that the next wave would reveal a hand, reaching for salvation, or the white of an evening coat, the polished silver of a mask. How long did it take a drowned man to float to the surface?

Barely any daylight remained when Sofía at last gave up looking.

She gazed vacantly at the water, turning what she witnessed over in her mind like a puzzle she had only to examine from the proper angle. Clearly, she'd misheard, or misperceived, or misconstrued the situation. It had been dark, she told herself. It had all unfolded from a distance. The waves had been too loud, their voices too soft. She was going nearsighted from so much reading. She'd been tired. Confused.

And then she thought of a different man, his lifeless body washing onto the shores of the mainland. Would this one make the papers as the last one had? Would they send investigators to Isla Bestia who would leave with fewer questions than when they came, and no answers? Just a head full of dreams and an insatiable wanderlust.

"You're not going to jump, are you?"

Sofía turned at the voice. The young freckled face looking back at her, though partially obscured by the mask of a red stag, was instantly familiar. It was the girl from the steamboat. Fátima, Sofía thought was her name.

"What makes you say that?"

The girl tipped her head to the side in a contemplative gesture. She seemed . . . different. Subdued, where just nights before she'd been all blushing, nervous mannerisms and eager smiles. "It happened earlier," she said slowly, laboriously. "Not an hour ago, in fact. There was a man here."

"You saw it too?"

Fátima pointed to a balcony on the second story. "That's my suite right there," she said by way of explanation. "He must have been quite deep in his cups, poor man. Thank the Sage that swim woke him right good."

Sofía pored over her words, parsing out the implication. ". . . He came back?"

"Of course." Fátima stared off into the horizon with a wistful smile. "Why would anyone want to leave?"

THE QUESTION STAYED with Sofía, relentless as an itch she couldn't scratch. A phantom sneeze. A word trapped at the tip of her tongue.

What *was* it about it that nagged at her so?

"—absolutely dying to hear more. Aren't we, Sofía?"

She stared blankly at Adelina, then at the two fashionably pale women watching her expectantly from across the banquet table. "Mm-hmm," she lied, having checked out of the conversation a good while back. "I can hardly contain myself."

With a look that said, *Dodged that one, didn't you?* Adelina returned her attention to their companions.

"Do go on then, you must not keep us in such suspense. He's the heir, is he? The standoffish fellow in the bat mask? Rather lacking in manners he was, couldn't even be bothered to greet us when we arrived."

"Alas, a family trait." The woman in the lion mask nodded in commiseration. "The founder of the Flor de Lis famously disdained most of Eteréan society. Only the crème de la crème were ever permitted onto this pretty little island of his. A superiority complex his progeny seems to have inherited, along with everything else."

"The stories are true then. A family of reclusive hoteliers who never venture outside their remote palace . . ." Adelina mused, delighting in the gossip. "How scandalously unconventional."

The other lady—Margarita? Camélia? Some kind of floral name—chimed in with, "And frankly, who could blame them? They built themselves a paradise." She made a sweeping gesture with her fan, encompassing the whole of Carnaval. "What beyond these shores could ever tempt them to leave?"

Why would anyone want to leave?

A half-eaten croquette was still clutched between Sofía's fingers when she jolted to her feet. "That . . . that's it."

Spurred by the realization, she hefted her skirts and took off at a run.

"Cariño, what's gotten— *Sofía?*"

All of Sofía's focus now converged around a single objective, and anything outside the pinpoint scope of her fixation fell to the wayside. Nothing could break through that state of hyper-concentration. Not Adelina calling for her to stop, nor the patrons blocking the door, nor the vejigante offering her more tapas and wine. She powered ahead with single-minded purpose.

Back in the Moriviví suite, she flipped through the pages of her Carnaval journal. Sifting through years of sketches, and headlines, and article clippings taken from Adelina's society magazines.

And there it was.

. . . From the moment we stepped onto that island, we knew in our hearts we would never want to leave.

. . . "We could stay here for years," they jested. "We could stay for a lifetime. What is there to return to? What could ever make us leave?"

". . . and I danced, oh, how I danced! From moonrise to moonfall, praying I'd never leave."

". . . why would we leave?"

". . . could not imagine leaving . . ."

". . . dreading the day they'd have to leave . . ."

Sofía dropped the journal like it'd burned her.

THE FOLLOWING EVENING, a box waited outside her door. Tucked within were the slippers Sofía had lost the night she'd arrived at the island.

The dirt had been scrubbed clean, the short heels waxed to a shine, and each shoe arranged delicately over a soft, velvet lining.

She may have been one patron among hundreds, but someone, somewhere, had been watching her. Closely enough to know the shoes she'd worn under layers of red silk. Was it common to be so diligently attended to in places this grand? Even in her finest moments, Sofía had certainly never served her household with half that degree of zeal.

Perhaps she ought to have been grateful.

Instead, she felt unsettled.

"Oh good, they found your slippers."

Sofía slammed the lid over the box. A knee-jerk reaction, as if rather than footwear, a venomous creature lurked within.

Adelina's eyebrows shot up.

"I . . . You startled me," Sofía explained, attempting to downplay her reaction. "I gather this is your doing then?" She pried the lid back open. "Told the staff I'd lost them, did you?"

"Oh, hmm, did I? I mean . . . *yeees*? Possibly?" The answer inspired little confidence, yet the fact remained it was the most reasonable explanation. Adelina, her head clouded with wonders and wine, had reported the shoes missing, only to then forget she'd done so.

That had to be it. There was, objectively, nothing inherently sinister about a shoebox.

Sofía was overthinking it, distorting yet another innocuous occurrence with her paranoid suspicion, reading patterns where there was only coincidence—like with the journal, and the man by the water. Her mind, unable to fathom the radiant utopia she suddenly found herself living in, couldn't resist conjuring villains from its every shadow.

Get ahold of yourself, you're no good to anyone this way.

"Well," Adelina said, "aren't you going to put them on?"

Banishing the last hints of uncertainty from her mind, Sofía slid her feet into the too-small slippers. Settling into the discomfort.

AT THE SIGHT of the glittering crown, the crowd erupted into cheers. It was a massive thing of brilliant gold, studded with fat jewels and so garish it was almost a parody of itself.

They laid it upon the woman's platinum curls with all the pomp and ceremony of a true kingmaking rite.

Her head canted under its impressive weight.

Though the woman wore a different mask tonight, Sofía immediately recognized the mocking edge to her lips, the proud way she carried herself despite the burden of her oversized crown—as if her spine were precious metal, a substance not designed to bend. It was the woman from the solarium, the one who'd wanted Sofía to divine for her a fortune.

Flanking her were two carnavaleros costumed in iridescent scales, their dark tresses adorned with stunning headpieces crafted to look like fish fins. The taller of the two cued a multitude into silence with a single motion of his tattooed hand.

"Honored guests." His baritone voice smacked the air with the force of thunder. "We present to you . . . the King of Carnaval!"

He bestowed the newly dubbed "king" with an ornate gourd, which she raised high, like an offering to the heavens, and drank deeply from. All around, people joined their new king, raising their goblets high and knocking back drinks in single gulps.

Sofía and Adelina did the same, caught in the whirlwind of celebration. And as their glasses came down, the lights turned on, revealing a sight that left them gaping.

Mist blanketed the ground, moving as though it were alive. Not a weather phenomenon, but a creature, shrouding Carnaval like it would devour it whole. A thousand flames burned blue inside crystal globes, painting the mist the deep indigo of an evening sea. Above it floated a chain of platforms, tufted in green and edged in pale sand, like islands amid a starry ocean.

Rippling waves of glass held each enormous platform aloft, concealing whatever mechanized them into motion. They moved at an easy pace, like a barge drifting along the water's current. It brought to mind the steam-powered parade floats that graced the town center's cobbled streets every year during the Saints' Eve festival. Those were far simpler constructions of lightweight timber and papier-mâché, bedecked with religious motifs: the Triple Eye of the gods, the thorn-rimmed chalice of saints. Next to these marvels, those floats would have looked like a child's craft project.

The misty air glittered with trapeze artists in rainbow-hued scales trailing long trains of gauzy opalescent fabric behind them. They swam through the night as if it were their ocean, and their bodies were windbound, and there were no wires holding them aloft. Sofia craned her neck as they zoomed past the terrace to land on the clay-tiled roof of the Flor de Lis. Shimmering dust rained down from their elaborate garments, alighting feather soft on her cheek.

With an excited sound, Adelina plowed her way through the crowd, dragging Sofia down with her.

Sofia yanked back at her elbow. "Wait—*look.*"

A shadow moved through the mist, growing larger the closer it came.

What is—

I don't know—

A sea monster—

Theories and questions transformed into gasps of delight as an enormous creature punctured the midnight veil. Azure firelight glinted off the sea turtle's solemn eyes—twin rounds of gold, each the size of a dinner platter. Its shell, large enough to comfortably fit forty patrons, was sculpted from bark, unpolished and ridged with the tree's natural grooves, as if it had not been carved, but molded. Moss grew over the plates, tracing the shape of the bark, ridge by ridge. Most remarkable of all was the ceiba tree growing from the turtle's back; tall with gnarled, spiny branches and roots vaster than a court lady's hoop skirt.

There had been one just like it behind the fields Sofía's mother had worked from dawn to dusk. *"Es un árbol sagrado,"* she told Sofía and Sol on one of those rare evenings when they would gather by the old ceiba tree for dancing and music. *"Long, long ago, our ancestors believed it was the sacred bridge between the realms of the living, the dead, and the divine. Its branches connect to an island beyond ours, where the zemís live."* Sofía had frowned up at its branches. It was not *that* tall of a tree.

"And its roots, you see how big they are? They reach aaall the way to Coaybay, where the spirits of the dead roam until moonrise, when they fly into our world as bats to dance, and sing, and eat guava fruit."

She had tickled Sol's belly, which made him giggle. He loved guayaba too.

"That's why we always stop at the edge of the ceiba's shadow and ask it permission to come near."

"But it's a tree, Mamá," Sofía had said, small fingers tracing the furrows in its bark. *"It won't answer."*

Her mother had smiled and tucked a lock behind Sofía's ear. *"It will, mija. If you learn how to listen . . ."*

Despite not sharing her mamá's belief, despite knowing the ceiba was as likely to be real as the sea turtle beneath it, Sofía still bowed her head as it drew near.

When the turtle's back flipper dropped, anchoring to the ground, patrons wasted no time racing up the ladderlike contraption. Adelina was the only one among them who made straight for the undercarriage instead. "Remarkable." She held an ear to the waves of sculpted glass propping up the sea turtle. "I cannot hear the engine rumbling at all. Have you ever seen anything quite like it, Sof—"

Sofía hauled her up the laddered flipper before they lost their spot.

Aboard, they elbowed their way onto the upper edge of the shell and there, as the turtle staggered into motion, Adelina resumed her investigation. She folded herself over the makeshift guardrail, shaped from the ceiba's overlarge roots, and peered down. "Is this beast even on wheels? I must say, I cannot feel the engine at all."

Sofía pulled her back by the collar of her dress, like a mother cat plucking up a wayward kitten. "You're going to fall."

"Down an eight-foot drop, you worrywart. The worst that can happen is I scuff up a knee or two."

It was not the fall that worried Sofía most, it was losing her in the mist. Already, the Flor de Lis was a blurry silhouette in the haze. The people in it indistinguishable, save for the dark outlines of their masks. Her gaze caught on one in particular: flared wings, its surface a black so deep it reflected moonlight.

She got the feeling that the wearer of that mask had been watching her long before she started watching them.

The sensation, bizarre as it was, lingered even after the mist descended in earnest, obscuring her view. The platform islands alone stood out then, points of warmth in a strange sea of flickering blue flames. One in particular loomed high above the rest: an isle detached, small enough to discourage visitation. It had room for only the throne and the woman upon it. She sat tall, drinking from her gourd, finger tapping to the distant rhythm of rattles and drums.

"Looks smug," Sofía mused. "You'd think she's *actually* a king."

"A baroness, in fact," said a portly man with more gray than black in the sweep of his hair. He wore a silver mask lined with the body of a serpent, its tail curling over his cheek and its mouth open wide over the curve of his left brow, revealing sharp metal incisors. On its own, it might have seemed intimidating, but paired with a ruffled tailcoat in powder blue, the overall effect was a rather bit more amusing than sinister. And not by accident either, a combination that incongruous *had* to be intentional.

The man struck Sofía as vaguely familiar. Perhaps they'd crossed paths in the corridors or sat near each other at breakfast . . . "You know her?"

"As much as you can know anyone at Carnaval," he said, blowing a cloud of strong, woodsy tobacco smoke. "She's been vying for that crown since she first set foot on this island. All them gentle folk here have, I s'pose, it don't matter how many estates they own or how fancy their titles are." He leaned forward, like he was letting Sofía in on a dangerous secret. "See, a king's crown can be won by blood or by sword, but this crown . . . this one you have to *earn*. Makes it all the more irresistible."

"Earn how, exactly? By flaunting how much they can imbibe and how profligately they can live? You will excuse me, señor, if I fail to see how anyone here could truly earn anything."

Sofía had not meant to share her opinion aloud, but the wine had loosened her tongue.

The man bellowed a raucous laugh. "Right you are, Señorita . . . ?"

"Sofía. Just . . . Sofía."

"Ah, from the Old Helas root meaning *wisdom*. Fitting name." He offered his hand, sun-spotted, ungloved, and stained with violet ink. The skin of his palm was puckered white with an old burn scar, sweeping up from the base of his thumb to the tip of his index finger. "Vicente Gallardo."

She shook his hand firmly. "You're a businessman, Señor Gallardo."

"And what makes you say that?"

"Your hands."

"Hmm, what about them?"

"You can tell a lot by a person's hands . . ." Sofía absently brushed the scars along her own. "Clearly, yours have known hard labor, and yet you don't hide them away under gloves. You bear your marks as a sign of pride. Is that not the hallmark of the scrappy, entrepreneurial spirit?"

He puffed his pipe. "Maybe I just don't like gloves."

"No one *actually* likes gloves. They're impossible to keep clean, make simple tasks harder than they ought to be, and are much too warm for the tropics. People wear them because it's proper."

"Then I'm a bit of a scallywag, of ill repute among my blue-blooded fellows."

"Your 'fellows' is it now? Not 'them gentle folk'?"

A slow grin unfurled across Vicente's features. "Remind me never to play liar's dice against you." He seemed entirely too amused to actually mean it. "Do share your secret, now. Why, of all plausible vocations, presume me a man of business? It's not just the gloves and the . . ." He wiggled his fingers. "I have to imagine I project a strong mien of unscrupulousness."

"I made an educated guess." Sofía waved her hand in a dismissive gesture. "You have been here for at least a month and are obviously prepared to splurge on room and board for several more weeks. It stands to reason that you are in possession of a fortune substantial enough to squander on leisure, and what trade, aside from industry, would propel a man of common birth to such prosperity?"

He angled his head in thought, and the light caught on the silver snake's jade eyes. "And how would you know how long I've been here?"

"The steamer runs on a monthly schedule. If you'd been aboard the last one, I would have remembered."

Vicente had a laugh that could be generously likened to the blast of an air horn. "Either you've got the brains of the Sage himself, or I've made an impression. Is it my striking good looks? My avant-garde sense of fashion?"

"Your tobacco," she told him. "That strain . . . My mamá would come home reeking of it every night. I'd have recognized its stench immediately."

There was a question in his gaze, but before he could ask it, Adelina barged into the conversation, practically bouncing with excitement. "It has to be an electric motor. The journals implied those were still experimental. I thought it would be years before they were ready for commercial use!"

Sofía considered this. "Surely your bookman's not selling you outdated copies again?"

"Nonsense. He wouldn't dare such foolishness twice . . . would he?" Her brow drew together with dawning suspicion. "That *scheming* swindler," she hissed.

Vicente smiled dotingly and extended a hand in greeting. "And who's this charmer with venom on her tongue?" Coming from him, it genuinely sounded like a compliment. "I don't believe we've met. Vicente Gallardo."

In a blink, Adelina composed herself into the very picture of decorum. "Excuse my uncharacteristic vitriol, Señor Gallardo. I've just discovered a man has been running his business dishonestly." She placed her hand daintily in his. "Adelina de Esperanza Montañez. Pleased to make your acquaintance."

"No disrespect to you, señorita, but seeking honesty in commerce is like looking for fresh water in a bog." His eyes went to the mist then. They were approaching one of the artificial islands. Or perhaps, it was approaching *them*. "De Esperanza . . . any relation to Reynaldo de Esperanza?"

"You know my father?" The mere mention of his name seemed to jolt her, as though she'd already forgotten the promise she made Sofía. *So much for keeping your wits about you . . .*

"You could say that. We haunt the same circles, he and I—from a distance, of course. Never could hold a conversation with the man that didn't end in a fierce hankering for violence. No offense, I'm sure he's a delight of a father." His expression lacked conviction. "Where's he been hiding you though?"

". . . Pardon?"

"It's always the little one he parades around at parties. What's her name again? Ana . . . something? My niece, the little shit's about her age, never shuts up about her damn dresses. *'But they're so lovely, Tío Vicente!'* Humph. She'll run me broke trying to copy your sister's wardrobe, just you wait and see."

Adelina smiled politely. "Could you be mistaking my papá for someone else? I am his only child, and I can assure you I have never missed a party."

The floor suddenly lurched as the turtle docked beside the island. A flipper connected to the edge of the land, serving as a gangplank. Patrons crowded to that side, jostling each other out of the way, racing to be the first to disembark. Adelina walked on with Vicente, but Sofía remained behind long enough to place her hand on the ceiba tree. Its trunk felt sun-warmed against her skin, its bark rough and furrowed and as real as the one from her memory.

If not for the creak that warned of the gangplank's imminent retreat, she would have lingered there a little longer, safe under the tree's canopy.

She gathered her skirts into her hands and crossed onto the floating island. The heels of her slippers dug into pale sand as she made her way up the slope and through a boundary of bloodwood trees, their roots thick and bent like arthritic knees. Every detail, down to the crimson resin dripping off their bark, the marshy grasses at their base, and the fresh dew on the leaves, was remarkably realistic. Sofía ducked beneath the trees' tangled limbs, through the door-shaped hollow where two trunks met like lovers in an embrace. For a moment, she could see nothing beyond the azure mist.

When it did finally clear, she was . . . elsewhere, transported someplace far from her plane of existence.

By some trick of light or mist or shadow, the rainforest surrounding her appeared to stretch farther than was physically possible, even if one were to disregard its architectural constraints. It was rendered all the more otherworldly by the brightness and color. All was aglow with bioluminescence—species of flowers Sofía had neither seen nor read about, trails of cocuyos lighting up the dark with their shining eyes, spikes of colored crystals growing from the ground like small shrubs. Had Sofía not known any better—and she did, didn't she?—she might truly believe she had stepped beyond her earthly realm, into one where myths were born and marvels made reality.

"There you are."

Sofía's gaze drifted over to the voice. In her daze, it took her a moment to react. "What happened to Vicente?" she asked, noting his absence.

"Got swept up in the crowd," Adelina said with nonchalance. She was tracing the radiant crags along the bark of a tree, gliding her fingertip along a zigzagging vein of blue crystals. "Interesting man, that one."

"Not a promising lead though, I take it. Despite knowing your father by name?"

"Please, everyone and their abuela knows his name, he owns the largest sugar mill in all of Etérea. Vicente may run in the same circles as Papá, but he clearly has him confused for someone else."

Her arm hooked around Sofía's. "No matter. The night is young and there is hope for us yet."

Her unflinching optimism, though frustrating at times, was an antidote to Sofía's disappointment.

Together, they started down the footpath of glowing stones, breathing in the scent of petrichor that clung to the air as though that mock island was subject to a different weather. Cocuyos flitted about, lighting the dark like stardust, and owls with tawny down tracked their progress, their pupils dilated and liquid with eyeshine. They perched high in the trees, where the branches grew knotted. Sofía could glimpse nothing of the night beyond that canopy. There was only the mist, rippling, inexplicably, with the blue cast of witchflames, as if the forest were underwater.

Voices up ahead drew her gaze back down. Just in time to see the faces of her fellow patrons go slack with stupefaction. A great shadow moved over them, the form of a creature with long legs and long arms and a spine rounded in a deep arch. Sofía turned to look at what manner of beast loomed behind her, and what she found did not disappoint.

To call what the carnavalero wore a costume seemed an oversimplification. It was more of a sculpture, a masterwork of raw wood and gnarled bramble chiseled over a living, breathing body. The carnavalero stood, arms and legs upon stilts molded in bark, looking every inch as though they had sprouted right off a tree and kept on walking. Nothing human remained beneath their vesture and makeup. Even their eyes looked unnatural in the ghostly glow of that synthetic forest.

A short distance away was another. A female figure, trailing a flowing dress of fresh-grown earth that hid the stilts beneath her. Moss masked her skin in green, and grasses wild and long spilled from the crown of her head. There was a lightness to her pace, a weightlessness to the way she glided that made her appear to be floating. She paused, reached her arms toward the ground, and from it rose another like her. The newcomer emerged with a satisfying yawn, and it was like watching the earth awaken in humanoid form. She peeled herself off the forest bed and came to a stand, moving with the same quiet serenity as her counterpart.

Little by little, the forest came alive, unleashing its sentinels from the rocks, and the thickets, and the hollows within trees. The longer Sofía watched, the more she had to remind herself, *this isn't real*, even as her eyes insisted it was. Blurring fact and fiction as the unnatural figures emerged like spirits from the land. Where were the seams that would unstitch them back into mere women and men? The cracks baring the skin beneath the paint? The lines where their masks met flesh? If there was any trickery there, Sofía could not find it, rationalize it into the actuality of her vision.

But she could deny it, quash the magic with the mallet of her truth.

She and Adelina kept pace with their party, startling every time a pile of leaves rattled, and from it surfaced another specter. Some seemed made of crumbling stone, others were painted in waxy amphibian skin—multicolored and slick with moisture, like a frog fresh out of water. One was sculpted in coarse blackened earth and pulsing arteries of hot, flaming red, their body rendered a volcanic eruption.

All towered, ethereal and strange.

By the time Sofía managed to peel her gaze from the spectacle—for it was, she repeated to herself, a spectacle—Adelina was standing several yards ahead, coaxing out secrets, just as she'd said she would.

When Sofía joined her, Adelina paused to slide her arm through Sofía's in a conspicuous show of camaraderie, shielding her, as always, from any potential antagonism. Unnecessary though it was—for Sofía's heart was inured to barbs and slights—she appreciated the effort.

There were the usual looks of polite confusion, the discrete scrutiny as they attempted to decipher what box she belonged in. They probably assumed that whatever gentleman had sired her illegitimately had allowed her to be raised as a proper daughter of his household. It was not unheard of, and it was certainly more believable than their actual story.

A few among the group, Adelina had apparently met in passing over the years. They were the sons and daughters of wealthy gentrymen from Etérea and its neighboring colonies along the Gilded Sea. Like Adelina, their mothers were from minor noble families blessed with a few too many daughters, or too down on their luck to afford proper dowries. She whispered this into Sofía's ear as the others commiserated over the Empire's supposedly dwindling coffers, family feuds over inheritances, and how hard it was to *find good help these days.*

"—*I* heard Doña Carmen's criada ran off her first week on the island." Sofía's ears perked up. "To join the carnavaleros, of all things. Who'd have thought such a mousy thing would have aspired to the stage?" said one of the ladies, tipping her husband's wine goblet to her lips.

"That's not the *only* rumor, of course," added the husband, smiling wickedly.

Adelina nudged the conversation along. "No?"

"Ignore him. Armando has a penchant for the macabre, he delights in speculating there is something far more nefarious happening at the Flor de Lis. More so than a proprietor in the terrible habit of poaching the help, that is."

"I hear they're offered wages too tempting to refuse," said another, a waif of a lady with buttery blond hair and a white panther mask. "It's not too bad a deal for their employers either. The couple in the suite across mine, when their criado resigned, they were gifted two weeks of room and board, compliments of the house."

That did not tell Sofía where the servants were being lodged, but it opened up an entirely new line of inquiry. Could her brother be among the carnavaleros? Was he there, even now, concealed under paint and mask? Passing her by, as he would any stranger?

She lifted her gaze to the faces of the performers, straining to peer beyond their disguises. Surely, she would have recognized him. His eyes which were the inverse of hers—the same size, same shape, but diametrically opposed in the color spectrum. Like looking at her own eyes in a tinted mirror. She would know him anywhere.

And would he? *Yes*, she felt the truth of it beyond the walls of her rationality, somewhere deep in the roots that still tangled with his. It begged the question then: If he was there, if he could see through the mask and the years that separated them . . . what, or who, was keeping him away?

THEY CROSSED A drawbridge to the next floating island. There, the dominating feature was a cavern overlaid with clumps of vegetation. Jobo trees surrounded it, standing tall with their narrow coffee-brown trunks and branches weighted with clusters of small golden fruit. Patrons picked them off the ground or shook the trees to release them into cupped palms and evening jackets held out like baskets. Sofía helped herself to a few as well, brushed the skin clean and bit in.

It tasted of summers, sweet and sour. Of mornings spent reading under a jobo tree's shade, a book on her lap and a bowl of freshly picked fruit within easy reach. She bent to pick another, and lurched back.

"What hap—" Adelina stopped in her tracks beside Sofía. *"Oh."*

The tree had eyes . . .

. . . a nose.

. . . a mouth.

The face was downturned, the features feminine: thick lashes, round cheeks, long hair draping softly over bare skin. Had Sofía been the type to indulge in fanciful notions, she would have said it looked less like a tree carved in the image of a woman, than a woman mutated into a tree. Absorbed and transformed, remade from flesh to bark, warm blood to sweet sap, her echo preserved like a piece of petrified wood. Sofía wondered, distantly, what the woman had been looking for when her bones were made wood, and her years, once bound to the Earth's orbit, could be quantified in growth rings.

What will you sacrifice . . . ? The diviner's words came to her. *What will you become?*

"Demonios," Adelina hissed, understandably perturbed. "She looks so . . . human." She swept her gaze across the copse of trees and shuddered. "There's more too. Sage above, it's as if we've stumbled into a mausoleum." One of bodies entombed within wood instead of stone.

Other patrons had also noticed the nightmarish scenery. They reeled back, laughing with surprise—genuinely in some cases, in others to save face. Those of a more curious disposition, Sofía included, leaned in to inspect the figure of the woman. It was no less impressive up close. She had watched her brother labor over his craft enough to guess the hours, talent, and effort someone must have poured into that sculpture.

A bird, somewhere up on the tree's branches, trilled a lilting tune.

Sofía's head swung up, eyes scanning the foliage until . . . there. A mockingbird, one of dozens, with tan feathers on its breast and a seashell-white throat. It nibbled at the jobo fruit, pecking the waxy skin with its small beak. She took a step closer, quietly, so as not to startle the songbird. It watched her warily with one liquid black eye.

Something stirred in the back of her mind. The faint flutter of familiarity.

A mockingbird. A jobo tree. A cave. There was a link there. A memory hidden under dust and cobwebs, set on a shelf too high for her to reach.

"Shall we go see what's inside the cave?" Adelina offered. "I strongly doubt it can be any eerier than this."

Sofía meant to say no. They were detouring off course again. This was not part of the plan. But, for reasons that were entirely beyond her, she instead found herself following Adelina through the small manmade island. Each tree sculpture was unique: set in a different pose, carved with distinct features—some male, some female, some that did not fit neatly into either category. The only similarity between them was their expression. They were caught unaware, frozen in the halfway space between realization and horror. One person was depicted with arms stretched out wide and tapering into a branch at the wrist, as if they'd fought to keep the land from swallowing them up. Another was posed mid-run, right leg bent and transmuted into a tree root.

As Sofía neared the entrance to the cave, she slowed. There was another sculpture there, this one made of rough stone the same deep gray as the cave behind it. The man's legs faded into the rock, connecting to it at knee and ankle. His arms hid his face, as if he were shielding himself from a bright burst of light.

And thus the sun turned He of the Eyes Which Do Not Blink to stone . . .

"That's it . . ." Sofía spun back, feeling foolish for not seeing it earlier. The birds, the trees, the man turned to stone. It was the legend of Cacibajagua, a story chronicled inside *A Compendium of Tales from Old Bagua*, an ethnographic work of the Taike'ri written in the first decade of the conquest. The day Don Reynaldo caught her reading it, he ripped the pages from the binding and lit them aflame with the stub of his cigar.

History is a dangerous thing to give a slave, she knew now. A story, returned to its rightful heir, could put the wrong ideas in a head.

"Your ancestors were savages, girl. Worshippers of false gods . . ."

For the longest time, she believed him. Her ancestors were childlike, he'd said. Misguided. In need of a firm hand to show them the way—to save their pagan souls from an eternity of torment. That was why, generations later, Hisperians still ruled over these stolen lands.

It took Sofía years to undo her masters' careful indoctrination.

"I know what this is," she told Adelina, words thick with emotion. "It's a Taike'ri legend, about the first humans. I read about it once, years ago when . . . Adelina?"

She had already vanished into the cave. "Mierda." Why had Sofía even agreed to this? They were wasting time.

The opening was a jagged triangle, wide as a monster's mouth, but only slightly taller than Sofía. She ducked her head and felt her way through the dark, navigating by the tips of her fingers, until she could no longer feel the ceiling above her, nor the walls at her side.

Her breath came easier then, and she felt the tightness around her rib cage loosen.

"Adelina?" *ADELINA-DELINA-ELINA.* Her voice's echo boomed, resounding for longer than seemed possible given the size of the cave. It suggested a place much larger than the exterior implied. But they were on a float, not an actual island, and despite its vast proportions, realistically, the inside of that cave could not have been bigger than her suite at the Flor de Lis. Carnaval was a stage, she reminded herself, and that prolonged echo was just another clever bit of trickery.

A blue shimmer appeared in the distance. A speck really, small as an ember.

As Sofía approached it, the pinprick expanded, flowing smooth as water down a stream. It formed luminescent lines and curves that turned into shapes along the wall. Gingerly, her fingers traced the veins of glowing rock. She studied the stone, testing for grooves or differences in texture, anything to explain the odd phenomenon.

Her hands paused their exploration, and she took a step back. The seemingly arbitrary shapes took the form of people. Four of them, side by side, with a round, basket-like object held between them. It was a simple sketch, thickly lined, like the ones Sol used to do on the packed-dirt floor of their mamá's hut, back when all they had to draw with was the sharpened end of a twig.

The air grew unseasonably cold, and in the glow of that drawing, she could see her breath misting.

A voice rose from the dark.

"The sacred sons of Old Mother Blood, Itiba Cahubaba, stole from The Great Spirit, Yaya . . ." It was female-sounding, thickly accented, with a sonorous quality that could have very well been the voice of the cave. Its echo granted words of its own. *"But before the brothers could escape with their pilfered prize, it slipped from their fingers . . ."*

A new image appeared farther down the wall, showing the brothers standing over their loot, scattered into pieces across the floor. As Sofía reached it, a stream of light poured from the broken vessel, gushing down the wall and spilling like a puddle beneath her feet.

Mother of Waters, what was happening?

"From that shattered gourd emerged all the world's oceans and seas, and all the creatures that reside within them . . ." The light continued flowing, undulating like waves and casting shifting shadows: schools of fish swimming upstream, clumps of algae rippling like a sea maiden's hair, and the occasional ominous patch of darkness.

The next scene showed the four brothers once more, gathered around a flickering flame. *"The Sacred Sons' misadventures did not stop there. They wanted more from the ancient gods; the secrets they held, the treasures they kept from the world. So it was that one day, they came by the home of the Old Spirit of Fire and took from him his flame and the secret of cazabe, bread of the gods."*

The sparks of the fire expanded, each becoming its own flame, and their warmth lured Sofía deeper into that bottomless cave. She followed the spirals of silvery blue in a trance, chasing its tail like the brothers chased the gods' secrets.

"As punishment, the Old Spirit of Fire cursed one of the brothers, causing his back to ache and swell. Little did the olden god know that from the spine of the Sacred Son, Caguama would be born. The Creator Turtle, from whom a new being is fated to emerge."

One by one, the flames winked out into curling ribbons of smoke. Sofía rushed to the wall, pressing her palms to the rock as if that would trap the fire in place, keep the heat from ever leaving her bones. Yet the cold and the dark found her anyway.

The voice, elusive as fog, echoed in the gloom. *"What the brothers took from the gods, fish and fire and bread, they gave to the humans, the children of Caguama."*

Light outlined the contours of Sofía's hands, painting around them a mountain, transforming the space between her fingers into the yawning mouth of a cave.

"*These creations were bound to the sacred cave, allowed outside only when the moon was out, and the sun was safe within its own burrow in the cosmos. Despite knowing the dangers the sun held, a day came when the humans ventured out into its path . . .*"

Sofía followed the story with her fingertips, tracing the shape of figures she thought she'd lost in the ashes of a half-read book. It unfurled across the wall, forcing her to run or miss whatever came next.

"*The first man the sun took fell asleep during his guard, and was turned to stone before the cave.*"

Her shoes skidded to a halt as the light changed direction.

"*The next humans to be caught were out fishing until dawn. On their way back, the sun transformed them into trees, and their arms grew heavy with fruit.*" Glowing branches twined like crooked fingers across the roof of the cave.

"*The third human went to search for soapberries with which to wash, and the sun transformed her into a mockingbird. If you listen closely, here, you can still hear the echo of her song . . .*" The ghost of the songbird trilled a sweet melody, and the flutter of its wings announced its flight. The glimmering shape dove between the branches, pausing only long enough to make Sofía believe she could catch up. It teased her, hopping on a nearby branch with the tune on its beak. Fleeing the moment Sofía came too close.

She stumbled mindlessly through that world of liquid light and stark shadows, reaching for something that could not be caught. Her palm hit stone, and the bird puffed into shimmering smoke beneath it. Around her, all the other lights blinked out, disappearing in the order opposite in which they came.

"Wait!" Sofía clawed at the wall. "Please! What happens next?"

"Next . . . ?" The voice deepened, becoming more resonant. Less human.

In it, Sofía heard the crash of the river, the might of the wind through the trees, the trembling of the earth. She felt it rattling through the hollows inside her, as though her body had become its cave. A house for its stories to settle.

"*They . . . leave us . . . They find their way into the sun, where we cannot protect them. They come back . . . to shelter from the storms . . . to bury their dead . . . to carve in us their histories. We sleep in the moments between, and we wake when they need us. They will not need us, not for some time. Not until the blood of their kin turns our waters red. They return, fleeing from the sun as their forebearers did. We wait until they come to fear the light, and find safety in our shadows . . .*"

A touch, soft as a sigh, whispered across the curve of Sofía's cheek.

"*We welcome them into the dark.*"

ACTO III

SHE IS OURS.

We know it the moment it happens—sense her surrender as we touch her lips . . . slide into her body . . . learn the wickedness she hides. She invites us in, splays herself open. Willingly. *Eagerly.* For there is a thirst only we can satiate, and she does not care to know the cost.

She will learn it come morning, when gold no longer crowns her head. But by then, it will be too late.

For now, she revels in us. In the silken softness of her thoughts, the way we make the world go quiet. Nothing else can soothe her yearning, that emptiness she's nursed since youth, feeding it every vice and decadence coin could buy. For years, she has subsisted on that steady diet of fleeting pleasures, each destined to stale. Fade to boredom.

Only *we* can end the wanting, the taking.

We alone are the cure.

CHAPTER 7

Saints are crowned in battle. With steel they worship, and in gold and gore they are adorned.

—Chronicler

WHEN CARNAVAL CALLS, you answer.

Teeth glinted in the firelight . . . ruby lips spread like wine spills . . . laughter knotted itself through the music, a constant pulse in the background, timed to the *tick-tick-tick* of Adelina's pocket watch, the *bom-bom* of the drums. Sweet temptations lurked in every corner—tables overflowing with fine cuisine, delights that captured the imagination, monsters eager to fill your glass with liquid courage. A king's ransom–worth of riches laid bare, an invitation for anyone with quick enough fingers.

Sofía's were quick enough. Or they had been, once.

They brushed hungrily over gilt and art and sparkling jewels, fantasizing about the years of comfort any one of those baubles could bring her, how easy it would be to pocket that spoon of fine silver, the pearls on that centerpiece, the decorative flowers cast from gold . . . She enjoyed toying with the idea. Savored the feeling of it in her mind, a lulling buzz that numbed her caution. It was like staring down a precipice, and for once not having the urge to step away. *Take it*, a voice inside her beckoned. The same voice that drove her to indulge in another sip of wine, to pile on another plate at the banquet, even when she was so full to bursting her ribs strained against the bones of her corset.

They have taken enough from you . . . It's not stealing, is it? It's justice.

It got louder, more convincing, with every glass filled, every plate laden, every breathless *yes* she muttered. She was lost in

Carnaval's magic. Endlessly preoccupied with its beautiful deceptions, the ugly truths it told in glitz and grandeur. In the monstrous masks that bared all the faces beneath concealed: the snake fangs, the wolf gaze, the devil horns. Sofia preferred the honesty of those masks to the ones the patrons wore outside of Carnaval. Pretty and powdered, all smiles and grace and genteel manners.

Here, there were no riddles to unravel, no subtext to dissect. When a spider leaned over, waxing poetic about her dress and her hair and the stormy gray of her eyes, she did not have to wonder if he was spinning her into his web. When he whispered, *"My dear, you are a vision,"* she clearly heard the words he did not say: *". . . for a mutt."*

She smiled, and he must have thought it was his flattery that did it. That she was fawning, as any lowborn girl should be, honored to have caught the attention of someone so obviously above her station, when really, she could not have cared less what he—or any of the lords and ladies who believed comparing her skin to dulce de leche was a compliment—thought of her. What she craved was certainty, not approval. And here, among the lies and illusions, people wore their darkest truths, donned the masks that showed them as they were.

It was so much simpler.

Adelina, for her part, enjoyed a different breed of what Carnaval had to offer, seeking thrills with the same hunger Sofia sought clarity. She flirted shamelessly with every man and woman she met, tempted them with fairy tales and lofty promises: romantic rendezvous that would never come to pass, personas she would shed the instant she stepped out of sight, lies crafted with the care and detail of a master artisan. She went through those lies like she went through dresses, and wore them with equal confidence, no matter how absurd they seemed to Sofia.

Time went by in a dreamy blur of excess, of riotous joy that each night left them more famished than the next, their souls like ravenous mouths that could not be sated. The more they fed it, the more it ate. Lusting for more color, more laughter, more novelty. And Carnaval, naturally, never failed to deliver. Every evening, the stage was reset, luring them from the softness of their beds with new marvels to unwrap, diversions to forget their worries in . . .

Tonight, the stage was dressed in red.

Bolts of fine crimson muslin twined into a pavilion, branching into winding paths and hidden nooks—curtained off sections furnished with plush velvet divans, perfect spots for trysts and other nightly pleasures. Shapes shifted behind the walls of the pavilion. Shadow puppets in the form of ships and knights bearing shields and swords. Sofía watched in bleary fascination as the shadow ships sailed out of view, and the knights moved to the forefront. They marched silently alongside her, matching her pace, and as she advanced down those crimson corridors, so did the story, its scenes unraveling with every step taken and corner turned.

"Who should I leave pining for me today?" Adelina asked out of earshot of their latest companions, two gentlemen from the country of Alveon. Men of commerce, come to Etérea in hopes of establishing trade partnerships for the export of rum.

Sofía did not immediately register the question, too distracted by the shadows. The intrigue. The pleasant buzz of alcohol swirling around her head. Belatedly, she offered, "Whoever makes more references to his summer estate, obviously."

"You cannot possibly expect me to keep track of that."

A laughing couple stumbled past on their way to somewhere more . . . intimate. The woman flashed Sofía a coquettish wink as she shut the curtain closed. "Then the one with distinguished facial hair." Her words came out somewhat slurred. "The scoundrel picked something off his teeth earlier, using my mask as a mirror."

Adelina covered her appalled laughter with both hands. "That's *foul*."

"He has very symmetrical teeth, I'll grant him that." A sound burst out of Sofía, somewhere between a snort and a guffaw, and it was so unfettered, so frivolous and jarringly unlike her, it took her a moment to recognize it was hers.

They ambled deeper into the crimson passages of the pavilion after their gentlemen companions, watching the shadows of aerialists dive and leap beyond the soft billow of fabric. Their legs hooked onto high beams, their bodies unfolded—dangling wrong side up—and from their fingers unspooled lengths of strings. Below them, mountains sprang from the ground, paper clouds swept into the scene, shadows flowed into the shape of a river. There were people there, splashing in the water, cooking by the fire, collecting their harvest with small children propped on hips.

There was no sound, yet Sofía heard the sizzle of meat as the fat dripped onto the flames, the stamp of small feet against the ground, and in the distance, the clink of steel, the clomp of metal boots. If she focused, she could smell it too. The smoke of barbacoa, scented with the savory char of fish and fig leaves, and underneath that, the sour must of horseflesh, the stench of tallow on iron.

How rich was her imagination now that there was so much to inspire it . . . She daydreamed beautifully, her mind dressing the wonders around her with wonders of its own.

The shadow play faded when the wind stirred, blowing the walls of the pavilion in.

Adelina, with an ecstatic shout, pulled Sofía at a run through the flutter of fabric, the way she used to on laundering days, when the bedsheets hung on the wire to dry, scenting the sun-warmed air with lemon oil and soap. They ran like they were two naughty kids playing between the clotheslines, making trouble for dear old Mamá Rosa, who'd cluck her tongue at them as if she weren't fighting back a smile.

When the fabric settled back into place, they were standing, breathless, in the shadow of the solarium. No longer a building, it had transformed into the voluminous skirts of a woman with cinnamon hair, bearing a crown that pierced the stars. Red velvet and muslin cascaded over the birdcage-shaped structure that was now her underskirt, spilling into the endless halls and alcoves of the pavilion. The regal marionette rose above the crest and crash of rippling scarlet, like a lone mountain amid a bloodred sea.

She towered above it all, lips unsmiling, face drawn into an expression of utter indifference—a gods-chosen queen among mere mortals. Her icy gaze beheld her kingdom with the look of a woman enduring someone dreadfully unimportant, and her wooden arms, draped in loose sleeves, rose and fell with stiff, mechanical motions. Golden strings looped around her fingers, their ends disappearing into the folds of the pavilion and the cage beneath the split of her skirt, as if she were a puppeteer, moving the men and women inside the solarium.

Sofia—dwarfed by a marionette the size of a palace, her neck pulled as far back as it could physically go—felt . . . *something*, a small ripple in the unyielding languor of her mind.

But no sooner did she notice the feeling than it was gone, absorbed like a pebble into the current. Adelina nudged her forward, and with a smile, she went.

Inside the solarium, they were greeted by the clink of coins exchanging pockets, the clack of spinning roulettes, and the clatter of domino pieces as they hit the playing board. The place had been turned into a gambling parlor, outfitted with tables of obsidian wood, carpets so lush you could sink into them, and cascading chandeliers twinkling with teardrop-shaped rubies, casting the room in a sultry glow.

Elegant crowds clustered around tables, trying their luck at games of chance. Dice rolled, bets were called, and game pieces fell. They cheered on a man playing three simultaneous games of chess, traded whispers around a heated game of cards, and flocked to watch a fight break out between rival players.

Sofia followed Adelina through the bustle and vice, eyes widening at the sight of reales piled into mounds, exchanging hands with the casual disregard of those who could afford to squander a fortune or two on an evening's entertainment.

Hunger reigned here. In the gazes of patrons watching the turn of a roulette wheel, in the anxious tap of gloved fingers, in the sweat collecting on temples and brows. Beneath the floral perfume and the smell of wine soaking into the carpet, the parlor reeked of desperation. With every hand played, the pressure built, and the energy edged closer to a frenzy.

"The women . . . they're playing too?" Awe laced Adelina's words.

Sofía followed her gaze to a game of cards, where a lady in a mask of mother-of-pearl played against a group of gentlemen. She was winning too, by the looks of it. There were other women hunched over chess boards and domino sets, tossing dice, and emptying reticules onto betting tables.

"Carnaval flaunting social conventions? How unexpected," Sofía said drolly. While she herself had never stepped foot inside a gambling parlor, she'd heard Adelina complain often enough to know these were gentlemen's games. A lady could do no more than observe, and only then by invitation.

"Hold on now." Sofía pulled her friend aside, noticing her expression. "Are you . . . upset?" Damp eyes, a ruddy nose, a trembling bottom lip. Yes, all the signs were there. "This *was* what you wanted, no?"

"It was. *It is.* It's just—" Adelina shook her head, pasting on a smile that did little to reassure Sofía. "Come with me . . . ? For once, I would like to try playing for myself."

They left with a promise to meet back with their companions in an hour, then commandeered a pair of seats over by the cards section. Adelina folded her hands delicately over the half-moon table. "What are we playing, gentlemen?"

The two men at the table exchanged a look.

After an uncomfortable pause, the younger of the two answered, "Brisca. You know it?" His mouth twisted like he'd tasted something sour, curving into a pronounced arch that accentuated the horseshoe shape of his ginger mustache.

Adelina did not bat an eye. "I may have heard of it."

His surly look quickly turned mocking. "Señorita, this is not the kind of game you play in your drawing room over afternoon tea. Here, we play for coin."

"Lucky then that I've some pocket change to spare. What are we betting?"

"Ten silvers to start," he said. "Bets double with each round."

She unclipped her reticule and set down a neat stack of gold and silver reales. Ginger leaned back in his seat, breezy posture suggesting this feminine threat had suddenly, and quite fortuitously, become an opportunity.

The older gentleman, however, was apparently not so easily convinced. His face was flushed a startling shade of red, and it was unclear how much of that worrying coloration was due to the weather, and how much of it was a direct result of Adelina's presence at the table.

Without a word of explanation, he abandoned his seat.

Just as soon, another took his place. The jade glint of the serpent's eye caught Sofía's gaze, but what held it was everything else about the man. Tonight, Vicente Gallardo complemented the decor perfectly, from his pepper-red cravat all the way down to his boots, buffed until they gleamed like cinnamon candies.

"Señoritas." He tipped his head in greeting toward Adelina and Sofía, reached into his coat pocket, and poured a mound of coins onto the betting table.

"Will the four of you be playing as teams?" asked the dealer, a man in a sharp suit and full-face mask of black porcelain.

Before Adelina could get any ideas, Sofía was quick to clarify, "I'm only here to watch."

"Very well." The dealer picked up the deck and started shuffling with practiced ease. "Let us begin then."

A roll of the die determined the playing order. Ginger would go first, Adelina second, followed by Vicente at the opposite end of the table.

At a nod from the players, the dealer cast three cards for each and set what remained of the deck between them. With a smooth flick of the hand, he swept a single card from the top of the stack and placed it face-side up. "Six of Cups."

Sofía was certainly no connoisseur of cards, but she had on occasion indulged the Esperanza house staff in their secret games of baraja. Enough to learn two very valuable lessons: one, kitchen pantries made poor gambling dens, no matter how much the baker boy insisted otherwise; and two, card games were entirely unsuitable to her temperament. Most required a combination of strategy and good fortune, and while she found enjoyment in the former, she lacked the strength of character to leave anything to chance. Much less for sport.

Ginger laid down the first trump card, a Four of Cups.

When it was Adelina's turn to play, instead of reaching for her own trump card, she danced her fingers along her options, tugging the corner of one card up before abruptly changing her mind. Worrying her bottom lip, she timidly set down a Six of Gold.

Sofía frowned. *Why didn't she . . . ? Ahh.*

Adelina stumbled through the game, wavering each time her turn came up, wasting good cards on bad tricks and blundering easy wins. Worse still, was that the few times she did snag a trick she beamed with novice excitement, even when the cards won were relatively worthless.

It was painful to watch. Mercifully, Sofía did not have to bear her friend's fumbles for very long. Within a quarter hour, Ginger was pocketing her coin.

"Another round?"

Adelina hesitated. "Oh. I—I couldn't possibly. Thrilling as that was, I imagine you'd much rather I make way for a more seasoned player to join. I shall get out of your hair."

"Nonsense," said Ginger with feigned benevolence. "Everyone has to start somewhere."

"Truly? You gentlemen wouldn't mind me imposing on you for another round?"

Vicente rubbed at his beard, looking deeply conflicted. "Bah." His shoulders slumped in resignation. "Not my place to tell a lady what she can and can't do with her coin, is it?"

Adelina beamed beatifically as she plucked up several reales from her stack and dropped them in the betting pot. "You two are simply *too* kind." She slid off her gloves, and tossed them onto the table. When her hands next touched the cards, that honeyed smile sharpened into a devilish half grin. Gone was the timid girl who second-guessed her moves and whose fingers dithered over the cards—when they weren't fidgeting with the stem of her glass or a loose curl of hair. Here was the enterpriser who had taken the reins of her papá's business. The schemer who could engineer any roadblock into an opportunity.

The world, ignorant to the wiles of womankind, did not yet know to fear this doe-eyed lady who carried a wrench and a pistol under silk and pearls. Who maneuvered her way into merchant circles and gentlemen's parlors. Who had learned to play their games through proxies, signing contracts in her father's pen, whispering strategies in a sweetheart's ear.

How many victories were hers, yet won in another's name?

Ginger blinked in confusion as Adelina wrested the first trick, a Knight of Clubs, with a nine of the same suit. It was not so much the win that threw him, as the confidence with which she claimed it.

Sofía pressed her fingers to her lips, trying to hide her amusement as she settled back to watch the game unfold.

The round moved quickly. Cards glided from hand to table, and table to hand, slapped down hard and swept up fast; Gold, and Clubs, and Cups, and Swords vanishing into each player's growing pile. Ginger downed his wine, face purpling as he watched his king disappear into Adelina's deck.

A crowd trickled in, congregating around the game, drawn to the thickening tension like sharks scenting blood. The stack of cards on the table shrank as the pile by Adelina grew and the ring of onlookers doubled. Soon, all three players were down to their last hand.

The crowd inched closer to watch, necks craned high as they could go. A bead of sweat trickled down Ginger's forehead, sliding beneath the rim of his mask: burnished bronze and pitted around the eyes, nose, and cheekbones like a human skull. He slammed his Jack of Swords onto the table, beside Vicente's Ten of Gold.

Adelina captured both, laying her trump card with delicate flair. She leaned back with a satisfied smile as the dealer moved to count each player's winnings. The gentlemen set their cards for him without fanfare, but Adelina—never one to pass up a spectacle—cascaded her stack onto the table, then fanned it out with an expert swipe of a hand.

"Twenty points," the dealer announced for Ginger. Followed by, "Thirty-five points," for Vicente. "Leaving . . . sixty-five points for the winner of this round."

His announcement was met with applause from the crowd, and the scrape of a chair as Ginger stormed out of the solarium. Vicente took his loss with far more grace, eyes twinkling with mischief as he bowed over Adelina's hand and pressed an extra coin into her palm. "In my field of work, we reward a good hustle with good ale. Find yourself a nice tavern back on the mainland, and buy yourself a round on me."

Adelina clicked her nail against the silver. "Señor Gallardo, you realize ale is a man's drink?"

"And this is a man's game." He shrugged. "Take the coin. Drink the ale. First one tastes a bit like camel piss, but the second just tastes like regular piss."

"I shall look forward to the third then."

He barked a laugh and left, whistling a cheerful tune.

No sooner had Vicente vacated his seat than another stepped in to claim it. It was the lady in the mother-of-pearl mask who they had seen playing earlier, raven-haired and pale-skinned. A faint smile touched her ruby lips, and she dipped her head at Adelina in greeting. Wedged in the seat between the two sat a droopy-eyed gentleman with wispy tufts of white hair, fluffed to conceal the bald spots. Sofía had noticed him a few times at breakfast. He ate the same thing each day, two eggs with a dash of pepper and a roll of sweet mallorca bread, generously buttered and powdered with sugar.

The dealer dipped his head at the newcomers and gathered up the deck.

The bets were set, the die was cast, and the cards were dealt.

The game had begun. This time, Adelina could not lean on the element of surprise to throw her opponents off balance, nor con them into complacence. She had revealed her hand—so to speak—and now had only her skill and her saints to call upon. Her gaze flicked over the cards with a knife-sharp focus, calculating risks and weighing chances. One glance was all Sofía needed to know she was in that headspace. That quiet sanctum she entered when the odds were stacked against her. When a business deal fell through. When she was told something was *"simply impossible."*

The players pulled no punches, seizing every opening, pouncing the instant she let her guard down. They yanked when she tugged and shoved when she pushed. Back and forth they went like lifelong rivals locked in a dance, wresting control in one move, losing it in the next. It was only near the end, when the stack was nearly empty, that the tables turned.

As the dealer counted each player's cards, Sofía leaned forward in her seat, silently counting with him. Twenty-five, thirty-six, thirty-nine . . .

It was a close call, but Adelina slipped into the lead with forty-six points. The air whooshed out of Sofía in a sigh of relief. To her, a game of cards might only be a diversion, but to Adelina, it was so much more. These victories were hers and hers alone, and they were long overdue. Perhaps that was why she played the way she did. Like her luck was running out, her seconds numbered, ticking toward the midnight hour when the spell cast upon her would break, leaving her on the arm of a man who would hold the cards for her. Claim her win in his name.

The games went long into the night, and the silver and gold continued flowing into Adelina's purse as she sailed from one round of baraja to the next. She gained a following of admiring suitors who scrambled to fetch her drinks and bite-sized tapas, as well as a gaggle of glamorous ladies ready to deliver on the latest gossip.

"This one pays in counterfeit coins," they said. *"That one enlists an accomplice to signal him your cards."* They floated through the

solarium like Adelina's personal circle of fashionable spies, gathering intelligence on her opponents. Sofía remained by her side, aware that the instant she left her seat, someone would snatch it up from under her.

But as the evening went on and the agreed-upon hour of cards stretched into two, then three, she grew increasingly less eager to defend her spot. After Adelina's fifth win, time became . . . slippery. The night smeared into a blur of yawns and aches, of pings and shouts and too-loud conversation. So many crowded her, pressing close, their chatter and cheer grating.

Applause rang in her ears like gunshots. The clack of a marble around the roulette wheel became the stomp of a horse's hooves, the jingle of coins, the clang of chains. When she drew in a shaky breath, she scented tallow and gunpowder. And when she shut her eyes, the darkness molded into silhouettes against a backdrop of red.

She leapt from her seat. "I need air."

Adelina looked up distractedly, eyes darting quickly back to the cards. "I'll go with you. Just need to finish up this—"

Sofía was elbowing through the herd before she could finish her sentence. The pain started at the base of her neck, working its way up the sides of her skull as she bolted out of the solarium. She knocked over a tray of wine from one of the passing servers in her rush, mumbled an apology, and kept going until she was through the doorway, gulping crisp ocean air beneath a waning moon.

Her eyes searched the night, trying to anchor themselves to something familiar. Something *real*. She found Sirik, the cluster of stars her ancestors believed were the children of the first humans, those whose spirits the gods transformed into coquíes, awaking each night to lead the islands' creatures in song as they bound down the river in the sky.

"Exhausting, no?"

Sofía turned to the voice, her gaze trailing down to the young woman sitting by the rose bushes, a sketchbook propped over bent knees, her freckled face partially concealed under a mask with branching antlers and pointed ears.

"Fátima."

The girl finally glanced up from her sketchbook, blinking at Sofía in surprise. "Oh, it's you," she said. "You were on the steamer with, um, the nice lady in blue?"

"I was, and after too . . . by the shore . . ." What had Sofía been doing there? She could picture herself and the girl, at the border where the island met the sea as the world fell into shadow, but the details of their conversation were hazy. Muffled, like words heard from the other side of a wall.

Fátima nodded, letting the silence sink back into the space between them. She appeared less eager to fill the pauses than she was when they first met. Something about her now seemed . . . subdued. A few more moments passed before either offered anything more in the way of conversation. "It's like a dream, this place." Fátima returned to her sketch, her stick of charcoal moving in sweeping strokes across the page. "From dusk to dawn, just an endless parade of extraordinary."

"That depends on what kind of dreams you have, I suppose . . ." The ache in Sofía's skull dulled to a soft pulsing, soothed by the evening breeze and the view of the open sky above her. "Mine are never quite this . . . eccentric. Even while asleep, I seem incapable of nonsense." As the words left her mouth, she realized they did not feel quite as true anymore.

"How do you—" Fátima swallowed, and when next she spoke, her voice had dropped to a near whisper. "How can you be certain you're not asleep now?"

Sofía waited, searching for the signs she'd trained herself to look for: the subtle trace of a smile, the gentle crinkling around the eyes, the playful tone assuring her the question was in jest. But she knew the mechanics of humor well enough to know there was no hint of it in Fátima's expression.

"I'm not," she admitted. "Not with a reasonable degree of scientific conviction, anyway. But, were I in pursuit of a proper answer, I'd start with a list."

"A list?"

"Yes. When seeking clarity on an unknown, I often find it helpful to begin with what I *do* know." Sofía closed the distance between herself and Fátima, "May I?" She gestured at the sketchbook.

The girl hesitated before handing it over.

A quick glance at the page revealed a drawing of the puppet queen, her proportions made all the more imposing by the forced perspective. In it, the strings she wore looped around her fingers were stretched taut, as though whatever lay at the end of them was pulling back. It was not a pretty drawing, exactly, but it was certainly poignant—all stark lines and deep shadows. And while it was nothing like the pleasant pastoral pictures one displayed above a mantel, the girl clearly had talent.

Flipping onto a blank page, Sofia plonked down on the grass beside the girl, and with the charcoal, she wrote: DREAMING OR AWAKE? in her bold, neat typography. The act energized her, brought a sharpness to her thoughts she hadn't felt in some time.

"I'd scribble the question atop a sheet of paper, divide the page in two, and on one column list everything a dream is, and on the other, everything a dream is not." She drew an even line, straight down the middle, and began filling out each column with the fervor of a person possessed. "Then I'd go through the statements, one by one, and put them to the test. Were I, for instance, to assert that a dream is nonsequential, I would catalog my whereabouts throughout the day, along with my activities and their duration, then review my findings for any logical inconsistencies. Of course, it's entirely possible that within the dream state, logic itself may fall victim to the chaotic nature of— Oh dear. I'm boring you, aren't I?"

Fátima's hazel eyes had taken on a glassy sheen.

"Please, pay no attention to my ramblings." Sofia tapped the stick of charcoal against the page, feeling unusually self-conscious. "It's been a minute since I've chatted about something other than gowns and the state of the spice trade."

The girl erupted into laughter. Not the polite laughter that greases the hinges of two strangers' conversation, nor the kind polished and practiced until it rang lovely as morning temple bells. This laugh rose from somewhere belly-deep—an abrupt and ugly sound, closer to a sob. Fátima pressed the backs of her fingers to the corner of her lashes, staunching the tears threatening to spill.

Sofía sat rigidly, stumped by the sudden display of emotion, and entirely unclear as to what the emotion even *was*. She did not know this girl. Had not spent years deciphering her contradictions, plotting them like points on a map she could navigate by. Fátima was a land uncharted, her feelings landmarks to be avoided, not explored.

"I swear I'm not laughing at you." She dried the last of her tears. "You just reminded me of someone."

Normally, this was the moment Sofía would gently redirect the girl to a more neutral topic of conversation. She had practiced the maneuver on plenty of occasions, with house staff eager to unload their worries on her, merchants who asked too many probing questions as she perused their wares, and rich folk desperate to prove themselves sympathetic to the plight of freed persons. So then, what in the devils possessed her to ask, "Who?"

Fátima rolled a small stone back and forth with the edge of her slipper. "My cousin," she said. "When we were little, she would drag me on these wild expeditions across her garden, to dig up fish bones and trinkets she'd buried the day before. She had me sketch all our discoveries in our field journal. Poor thing wanted so badly to be an archeologist. Of course, her older brothers teased her it was not for girls, but she wouldn't listen. Her mind was set on that big, beautiful dream, and she was going to prove herself worthy of it." The stone tumbled down with a soft clack. "Lucky the saints took her before the world could break her heart."

Lucky was not precisely the word Sofía would have used, but she did not comment on it. "You miss her?"

"I miss all the ones that've gone."

Sofía looked back to the sky, eyes tracking a flight of bats across the star-studded blackness, wondering if her mamá was among them, roaming free in death, the way she never was in life. Would Sol be up there with her, far from the earth he used to reap and till? Were the two of them dancing to the tune of the wind, their bellies finally full and their teeth sticky-sweet from guayaba? Sofía's chest felt heavy, and for a moment she could barely breathe.

Sol . . . His name sliced in, a blade swift and cruel, cutting deep. "Me too," she choked out, and then the pain was gone, absorbing into the depths of her, like her mind was made of quicksand. Carnaval was always there to fill the void with music, with scents that stirred in her a constant hunger, wonders that dulled the sting of memory, and sights that quieted her worries to whispers. Pain, she was learning, could not take root in a place such as this.

Consumed with thoughts of pleasant things, Sofía said, "I should get going." She went to return Fátima her sketchbook when it flipped onto an earlier page: a labyrinth, and within it, the girl herself, regarding her reflection upon a mirror. And there, on the looking glass, a man. Young and handsome, with a slight gauntness to his cheeks and an effusive smile that showed two crooked front teeth. In the mirror, he had his arm around Fátima. Outside it, she was alone.

"I've a few hours before I meet back with my husband," Fátima said, interrupting whatever strange, nameless *something* was creeping to the surface of Sofía's mind. "Would you perhaps—" a note of shyness entered her voice "—care to go exploring until then?"

"I . . ." Sofía found Adelina through the glass as she threw her head back, laughing at something someone said. It could be hours before she tired of the games, and Sofía did not want to spend the whole of her night in a gambling parlor where the wind could not reach her and the night was blotted out by the oversized effigy of a dead-eyed queen.

Besides, somewhere in that pavilion, a story was being told. And it suddenly felt important that she listen. Turning to the girl, she said, "Lead the way."

CHAPTER 8

It knows your vices, your secrets, the ugliness you do not.

—Chronicler

PALE LIGHT FILTERED in through the arched window at the end of the hall. A full moon shone through the glass, casting its silver over the walls and rust-red tiles. Sofía padded through the darkness, the floor cool against her bare feet. Had she lost her shoes again? She could not remember.

The hall was quiet save for the sound of the sea outside and the high-pitched chirp of bats as they flew overhead. She passed door after door, identical slabs of gleaming carob wood, each carved with a flower. The same flower: five pointed petals with serpentine pistils, long and sinuous as a sea anemone's tentacles.

Sofía looked over her shoulder at the hall stretching endlessly into the gloom, its rows of doors indistinguishable from one another.

That's when she saw it.

Blood. Spilling from the gaps under the bedroom doors, flowing into the spaces between the tiles like water through a ravine.

She rushed to the nearest door, shook the handle. Locked.

Her fist pounded on it until her knuckles throbbed, but it made no sound. Her vocal cords strained, yet her lips were silent. Her words vanished like a flame, stamped out of existence. Was it the ringing in her ears that muffled her shouts, the strikes of her fist?

Down the rows of rooms she went, beating on strangers' doors, rattling handles that would not budge, peering through iron keyholes that showed only darkness. How long she did that, she could not say. The hall remained the same no matter how long she walked, or how far a distance the ache in her legs told her she'd traveled.

At the end of the hall, the window blew open with a bang. Its iron casements slapped the walls, and the air whooshed in. Instead of pushing, it pulled. Held her like a feather caught in some mighty creature's intake of breath and siphoned her to the night. Onward she moved, her steps compelled by some force greater than her volition.

Blood, shining with moonlight, dripped from every room she passed, pooling into a puddle at her feet. She gathered her skirts, for all the good that would do, and her hands came up red.

Her gown was weeping, the dye trickling down the fabric in dark, sticky droplets, forming a trail behind her, long as a bridal train. It collected on the grout and mixed with the blood already gathered there in rivulets.

Sofía's movements slowed to a crawl and the hall tilted sluggishly like a ship at sea, rocking side to side. Yet the paintings on the walls did not shift an inch, the porcelain vase on that table remained firmly in place. But the blood began to stream from every closed door, gushing down like seawater in a vessel quickly sinking.

With each step, her gown bled a little more, leaving the silk a lustrous silvery white. The red draining drip by drip until—

Sofía startled awake.

Awake. In a room tinted violet-gold in the light of sunset, the air smelling of freshly laundered sheets and mild wood varnish, not the coppery tang of blood. Her gown—still a deep red—hung on the balcony to dry, its skirts fluttering in the warm salt breeze. She vaguely recalled having washed it in the tub before collapsing into bed, exhausted from another night of revelry.

A knock came at the door connecting her room to Adelina's. Sofía settled back into her pillow with a sigh, knowing very well her friend needed no invitation. The knock was more a formality than a request for entry, anyway.

Adelina sauntered in, clearly expecting to find the room's tenant up and about. Her eyes skipped past Sofía twice before finally noticing her—camouflaged from the chin down in luxuriously soft sheets.

"You're still abed."

Sofía wiggled her toes. "Quite comfortably, yes."

Adelina crossed the room to the balcony, heels clicking, and plucked Sofía's dress up from the railing. "*Tsk*. Look what you've done, it's all creased now." She laid it on the empty side of the bed and smoothed the fabric down with the flat of her hand. "Breakfast began an hour ago. I tried on five different gowns while waiting for you to wake."

Sofía poked her head out from under the sheets, rumpled hair sticking up every which way. "Am I to pretend that is unusual for you?"

"I'd certainly appreciate it if you would play along for a change." Her gaze flicked to Sofía's, then quickly away. "Speaking of . . . Celia's invited me over for another game tonight. We play a minor duke from Gallia and his infamously impetuous heir. Rumor has it they recently came upon an extravagant sum of wealth, and the poor dears have run out of luxuries to squander it on. That's where we come in, of course."

Sofía sat up in bed, rubbing sleep from her eyes. Since first meeting in the solarium-turned-gambling-den, Adelina and Celia had been playing cards obsessively. Every evening, they convened in smoking rooms and private parlors, rarely returning before sunrise. "You'll miss out on Carnaval again?"

That question wanted to be more. Sofía felt the cracks where other words should have been, each a yawning gulf of meaning. There was someplace else they were meant to be . . . or something else they were meant to be doing . . . Whatever it was, it felt unreachable.

"It'll be a quick round this time, promise. An hour, two at most. Now, look here—" Adelina held the dress out by the sleeves "—good as new." The wrinkles had been smoothed out, yet the silk itself looked dull and worn, the once vibrant dye now a muted red. Sofía would have been careful when washing it, she was sure. Had the soap been too abrasive? Or had she left it out too long in the sun? She pulled absently at a loose thread, picking at it like she did those strange little thoughts—thin and fraying, unraveling at the lightest tug. Then gone.

"Up now," Adelina beckoned, yanking at the sheets. "Before the coffee gets cold."

That was all the prompting Sofía needed.

"WATCH YOUR STEP, SEÑORITAS," said the steersman as he helped Sofía and Fátima into the canoe.

The vessel under them was shaped like a leaf, long and tapering at both ends and painted black, deep as magma hardened into stone. Its surface was lacquered to a glassy sheen, reflecting the steersman's ensemble—a white skirt-like wrap that draped down to his ankles, and a silver mask that covered all except his eyes. His torso was decorated with dots and swirls of metallic ink, and his upper arms bore platinum bands, bright against the dark umber of his skin. A foreigner from the Alkebulan Isles, probably. One of thousands brought in on Hisperian fleets a few years before Sofía was born, after a plague decimated over a quarter of the islands' native slave population. Many had arrived as children and now had children of their own, a generation with the blood of three places, three histories, their faces a vision of Etérea's future.

The canoe wobbled as Sofía settled onto the velvet-lined seat behind the steersman, skirts puddling around her like the pool of red in her dreams. Fátima stepped in next with an awkward hop, the snug hem of her dress severely limiting her range of movement. She lost an orchid in the process, pale peach with a bright pink center. Good thing she had another hundred or so pinned to the trim of her skirts, and just as many sewn through the ruffled top of her bodice.

Sofía cupped the fallen flower in her palm and offered it to Fátima. She waved it away.

"They're, um, *meant* to fall." She sighed. "It's modeled after the queen's gown from last year's Saints' Eve. I was obviously too unimportant to attend the ball, but my eldest sister, she married a courtier so *she* was there, and of course, I made her describe the whole affair. Gosh, the idea of a gown that left a trail of flowers in its wake . . . well, it sounded like the loveliest thing." Her smile grew sheepish. "I do imagine that on Her Majesty, the effect was somewhat less . . ."

"Like watching a chicken molt its feathers?" Sofía offered, with her usual sense of tact.

Fátima's mouth fell open in surprise, then she burst out laughing. "Yes, I suppose that's an accurate analogy."

Sofía placed the orchid on her lap, smoothing the petals down fondly. The girl was growing on her, despite her best efforts not to develop any more attachments. Befriending one colonist was a fluke, a pardonable exception, any more than that started to feel like complicity. Besides, her time here was finite, she would be off to her new life the moment she—

The moment she what? Where could she possibly go now that she knew paradise? What could she want out there that she couldn't find *here*?

It seemed a rather ludicrous thought to even contemplate so she swept it from her mind, turning her attention to the acrobats swinging from silver hoops overhead. Her eyes devoured the sight: the stars glittering in their hair, the silver lengths of tissue-fine chiffon they trailed like constellations, the near-liquid quality of their movements.

Below, couples spun and swayed to the sweet sounds of cuatro strings, and carnavaleros weaved between them, hands and feet gripping tall glowing rings on which they rotated, bodies whirling like the spokes on a wheel. They spun, upward and downward, between the crowds. More orbited the gathering—jugglers tossing hoops that fluoresced hot white, acrobats twisting into unnatural shapes, beast tamers with serpents coiled around their wrists.

Fátima clapped, amazed, as one performer threw a set of rings skyward, backflipping over their canoe to catch them. The steersman shouted something at the ring juggler in their shared language. The other man bowed with a flourish, touched his fingers to his silver-painted lips, and blew the steersman a kiss.

How brashly they wore their joy, flaunting it the way they did their striking costumes, their bold stagecraft, and choreography. It was still bewildering to behold, their postures proud instead of beaten down, their faces radiant. Open, instead of hardened, despairing of yet another day of thankless toil, of cruel weather and crueler masters.

Ahead, the river vanished into the rocky mountain underneath the Flor de Lis, dissolving into the dark. Sofía squeezed her eyes shut as they entered the mouth of the tunnel, relaxing only when she realized she could stretch her arms in all directions. Though the opening itself was low and narrow, inside it was blessedly spacious. Water lapped gently against the sides of the canoe, and the paddle splashed in and out of the current in a calming rhythm.

In the distant shadows, points of white light, no bigger than fireflies, winked on. They blinked beneath the surface of the river, lighting the tunnel walls like a starry night. Some species of bioluminescent plankton? Sofía knew of the microscopic creatures in the hidden bays that made the water glow bright, but this . . . this far exceeded her imagination.

The canoe flowed steadily into the shadows, and the silence, and the road paved with a universe of suns burning white. They followed that path of twinkling constellations in awed silence, the paddle dipping in and out of the stream, the waves lapping against the sides of the vessel.

Sofía leaned over, skimmed the river with her fingertips, then slipped both hands in to cup the glowing water.

As she leaned over, the surface trembled. Not from her touch, or her breath, or the glide of the paddle, but something vaster, more powerful. As though the earth beneath it were quaking. Then, a brief flicker of silver flashed across its depths, too fast for Sofía's eyes to discern, and a low rumble reverberated through the tunnel. It shook the stone like the rattle of a train approaching, but there was no train. They were coursing through subterranean waters underneath a rocky mountain, which sat underneath a hotel, which sat underneath nothing but open sky.

The rumble grew louder. *Closer.* And Sofía opened her mouth to warn the others, but it was just her, alone in the dark above the stars, and before she could wonder how that'd come to be, the river swelled and from its surface rose . . .

A river beast.

Beautiful. And terrible. Woven from night and stardust, its body long and serpentine, with spiny ridges running the length of its back and tracing the line of its throat. It pushed up on clawed hind legs, its star-stitched skin dripping gallons of water, its every motion sending tremors through the riverbed.

Sofía found herself facing a creature that did not belong to the earth, any more than she belonged in its unearthly waters. She was a tiny thing, an insect in the presence of a monstrous god, and she was frozen in terror, and *awe*, torn between the instinct to flee, and the hopeless desire to know it, this chimera with galaxies dancing in its eyes.

What are you, beast?

It lowered its great head to hers. "Beast, you name me?" it said, answering her unspoken thought in a voice that felt unsettlingly familiar. "*Mine is the womb from which the sun and the moon rise. I am mother of the rains and cloudless skies, the snake that heralds seasons and guards the earth's balance from the rivers above.*" The creature leaned forward, looming over Sofía like a ruptured storm cloud. Its torrent fell upon her, and she was not sure what she found most startling: the shock of icy volleys over her skin or the light that burned bright enough to blind her.

Still, she did not cower, for as fearsome as the creature was, she could not help but look upon it. Marvel at it the way she did an ocean. Life-giving and life-taking, a body made to nurture, made to ruin, to be both the bane and the harbor.

"And you, child?" it asked. "*Who are* you?"

"Me . . . ?" How could she even begin to explain? She had no epithets to give. Not even a family name. She was a collection of pieces molded. Borrowed. *Stolen.* She was the sculpture Doña Elena shaped and painted, the beating heart her brother lent her, the knowledge she stole from the pages of another girl's books.

"I—I am—"

"*Sofía?*"

Fátima suddenly hovered in Sofía's line of sight, one hand extended.

This new image had not eased in, it'd been violently yanked into the foreground, superimposed upon her vision like a blindfold ripped loose.

They were out of the tunnel, out of the dark where a universe lay waiting. And within it, a half snake, half lizard beast that asked Sofía the one question she'd never let herself consider. Because considering it meant turning her sight inward, looking beyond the outward neatness of herself to the mess piled underneath. And what would that accomplish in this world so determined to define her for her?

"*And you, child? Who are you?*"

She pictured her hand, gliding pen over paper, signing *Anonymous* at the bottom of yet another page.

"Feeling alright?" Fátima prompted again. "You look a little pale."

Sofía made herself reply. "Just . . . giving my eyes some time to adjust." The canoe had docked in a crypt-like space somewhere underneath the Flor de Lis. A vaulted ceiling, sculpted out of the mountain's natural basalt, soared high above them. The air there was cool and damp and the walls were slick with moisture. When Sofía finally gathered enough of her wits to disembark, her shoe slid over the wet stone.

"Easy now." Fátima placed a hand on Sofía's elbow to steady her. "Nearly slipped on my bum myself. Wouldn't that have been embarrassing, the two of us slipping and sliding like deer on ice?"

Sofía was too out of sorts to humor the girl, her mind still saturated with the haunting imagery she'd conjured from the darkness.

In strained silence, she tiptoed along the dry patches of floor, leaning on Fátima for balance, and as she wandered away from the river, the memory of it wandered away from her. Fading by degrees, like a portrait left too long in the sun, its details reduced to nothing more than a vague impression.

By the time they reached the spiral staircase at the back of the chamber, what remained was less an experience than a notion. A feeling. And when they emerged into the hotel proper, somewhere near the southern courtyard, it was easy to blame the too-quick metronome of her pulse on the climb.

Even Fátima, younger and spry, was looking a little worse for wear. "Dinner?" she huffed between breaths.

Sofía's stomach chose that precise moment to growl its hunger. "You go on first," she said reluctantly. "I should fetch Adelina."

"Playing cards again, is she?"

"Mmm-hmm. She'll keep at it until the next century too, if I don't pull her out of there."

"Well, you hurry on then." Fátima shooed her away with a grin. "I shall save you two a seat."

FAMILIAR LAUGHTER CARRIED down the echoing corridors, reaching Sofía's ears long before she turned the corner to find Adelina. She beamed widely when she noticed Sofía, untangling her arm from Celia's to rush over. The white ruffled trim on her turquoise gown rippled like sea froth as she ran.

"You would not believe the game we just had!" Laughing, Adelina took Sofía's hands in hers and swung her in a giddy circle. "It was one for the ages!"

"I've no doubt." Never mind the fact she said the same thing about every game they won, a thought Sofía graciously kept to herself. Adelina was flushed with triumph, her eyes bright with it—glowing a near-unnatural blue in fact, as though the feeling was incandescent. Her happiness was not worth risking, not for a purse full of gold and certainly not for the pleasure of a snarky comment. "You can tell me all about it over dinner. Fátima went ahead, she's saving us a table."

"Oh." Adelina glanced away guiltily. "About that . . ."

Celia approached, her face inscrutable beneath her mother-of-pearl mask. She was a statue, cold and beautiful, with alabaster skin and thick raven hair coiled into a perfect half updo, the other half falling in glossy curls over one shoulder. She did not acknowledge Sofía. Then again, that was nothing new.

"Let me hazard a guess," Sofía said, "another baron, or count, or reincarnated saint is either too smug or too foolish to think they could ever lose a fortune to the likes of you?"

Adelina flashed her a smile, showing both rows of teeth in an awkward, somewhat equine manner. "I know. It's last-minute, and I gave you my word . . ." She winced. "I understand if you'd rather I—"

"You should go."

". . . Truly? *Do you mean it?*"

"I do," Sofía said. "But you better take them for all they're worth, else I won't forgive you."

Adelina hugged her cheek to Sofía's. "I will make it up to you, I swear it."

"A thirty percent cut of your winnings will do."

"Well, that's just criminal."

Sofía spun her around and gave her shoulders a firm shove. "Quit wasting time endearing yourself to me. You have a game to get to."

With that, they parted ways, and as Sofía retraced her climb back down the stairs, preoccupied with thoughts of chicken stews and pork pasteles, freshly unwrapped from their banana leaves, there came a shout.

A commotion was brewing in the lobby—a patron, arguing with the concierge, the courteous man in the crow mask who'd welcomed them to Isla Bestia. Normally, Sofía would have gone on walking. She knew better than to embroil herself in others' affairs, having seen what happened to servants who did not keep to their own business. But as she started to turn, she caught a glimpse of the patron's mask. A silver snake with jade eyes.

Tonight, Vicente Gallardo wore a combination of colors some would politely describe as *a bold choice*. His jacket was an offensive shade of green, paired with a bright yellow vest and pumpkin-orange trousers, an ensemble which brought to mind ducklings and summer fruit baskets. It might have been amusing, was he not so obviously distressed.

"*Where?*" Vicente shouted, reaching over the counter and grabbing the concierge by the lapel. He shook the man. "Where are you hiding it?"

"I have already explained, Señor Gallardo." The concierge's response was patient. Pleasant. Even at the receiving end of a patron's ire, he was the quintessence of hospitality. "Supplies are delivered once a month by the passenger steamboat. What we can offer is to put in a special order for *La Gaceta*, to be collected in bulk and delivered with each shipment of goods throughout the duration of your stay."

La Gaceta? He was threatening a man over . . . the daily paper? Sofía edged closer, hoping to catch more of their conversation, certain she must be missing something. Not that she was a stranger to unreasonable outbursts of anger, having been the object of Doña Elena's unprovoked umbrage often enough. Vicente, however, hadn't struck her as the kind of man to act on impulse.

Then again, what exactly did she know? People were not like books. She could not pry their covers open, know them by the words on the page.

"You . . . you're *lying*," accused Vicente, pressing a hand to his forehead like it pained him. "You've done it before. You and the others . . . '*all will be well*,' you say time and again. '*We're here to serve, Señor Gallardo.*' '*Let's not do anything rash, Señor Gallardo.*' '*You're scaring the other patrons, Señor Gallardo . . .*' Well, blast it all, I'm done listenin'."

Vicente shoved the concierge and bolted. Not away from the lobby, as Sofía might have expected, but toward the reception desk. His arm reached out wildly, with the desperation of a man who had everything to lose. He nearly staggered with relief when he found what he was looking for, clutched it tight to his body like it was a raft and he a man drowning. Sofía peered closer, convinced she must be mistaken, that something as banal as a guest registry could not possibly incite such a violent reaction.

She watched in bewilderment as he thumbed through the massive leather-bound book, flipping page after page, growing visibly more frustrated the more he read. "What the devils is this, another one of them tricks?"

The concierge smoothed his rumpled suit and lifted one gloved hand, palm open to receive the registry with the distinct patience of a parent waiting out a tantrum. It was clear from the gesture he expected Vicente to return the book of his own volition. "You are unwell, señor," he said. "Please, allow us to escort you to the medic."

Us, him and the dozen masked figures that had discreetly assembled in the lobby. So silent was the vejigantes' approach that Sofía had outright missed them until they stood side by side, barricading the exits. An image flashed across her vision. Vejigantes down by the water, their shadows stretching across the sand. Waves crashing as—

Steps sounded against the tiles, even and deliberate, and from the wall of vejigantes emerged the man in the bat-winged mask. He stopped to place a hand on the concierge's shoulder, an unspoken directive to withdraw.

"Bastardos." Vicente gritted his teeth at them. "Thinkin' you can keep this up, hmm? That no one else will catch on to this charade?"

"Señor Gallardo," said the man in the bat-winged mask, his words slightly accented, his voice surprisingly soft for a man's. It was a voice Sofía had heard before, though she could not recall when. "Let's be reasonable now."

Reasonable . . . Yes. Vicente was being *un*reasonable, stirring trouble where it was not welcome. He ought to have been enjoying himself, not disrupting others' evenings—*her* evening, which had been going splendidly until she came upon that disturbance.

Yet, as much as Sofía longed to distance herself from all that unpleasantness, her body would not budge, orienting away from

Fátima's easy company, the promise of a fine meal. Here was where she was supposed to be, even if where she *wanted* to be was anywhere else.

Unlike the concierge, the man in the bat-winged mask made no attempt to retrieve the book, or even to approach Vicente at all. Considering the context, his manner might have been mistaken as deferential or even apologetic, but there was a confidence about him. A presumptuousness to his demeanor, as if all had already gone his way.

"Let us help you, Señor Gallardo."

The words, spoken with the flat, rote quality of an oft-repeated script, finally dislodged the memory: a dark figure making the same appeal of a man poised precariously upon the rocks. *"Let us help you . . ."*

It came to her in fragments. The vejigantes by the sea. The man, leaping. The figure, watching him sink into the surf.

Sofía snapped back into the present just as Vicente said, "Not this time," laughing mirthlessly. "I've had enough of your 'help.'"

With that proclamation, he pitched the registry, swinging for the nearest oil lamp. His aim hit true, shattering the glass and leaking drops of fuel onto the pages spread open below. Flames roared to life, and the air blackened and stank of burning paper, and the silence snapped with the sudden rush of movement, the crackle of fire and splutter of oil. Only the man in the bat-winged mask remained unmoving, hands folded at his back, the dark shape of him limned in red.

In the commotion, Vicente made a break for it. Heading, not away, but straight for Sofía.

She had only a fraction of a moment to brace herself as he crashed into her, his momentum narrowly knocking them both off balance.

They had just barely found their footing when he spoke. "Your friend, I saw her." The words tumbled out of him—urgent, bordering on manic. "A season ago. She was a girl then, not yet ten years of age, dancing with the other children. She wore ribbons in her hair."

Sofía shook her head, not understanding.

"The sky," he said, hands closing painfully around her shoulders, "it's wrong. I knew it when I left the river. I—I think I knew it before too."

From behind Vicente, Sofía could make out the silhouette of horned figures pressing closer. The fire he'd set was down to a few weak embers, and they were coming for him. He held her hands in both of his, squeezing, and all she could manage was to stare down at their joint fingers, at their scars connecting like mismatched pieces of the same puzzle.

What would give a child of conquerors scars like that?

"Look up," he told her, pleading. *"You have to look up."*

He was taken then, approached with soothing promises and firm hands. Forced to down a vial of something that made his eyes droop and his shouts quiet to slurred protestations. He stopped fighting. Stopped raving. Yet he did not look away from Sofía until he was gone, swallowed by the shadows of the Flor de Lis.

She stood there, watching as the glass was swept, the lantern oil mopped, all the evidence of what transpired there wiped away.

Or almost all of it.

Sofía kept her hand balled into a fist all the way to her suite. Her palm, grooved where her nails had dug in, held a wad of wrinkled paper.

A sheet torn from the registry.

Written on it was a long list of rooms and guest names, with two of the thirty-something scratched off. And the spaces beside the names? Blank. Nothing to indicate when the guest had checked in. Or out.

But that was not all Vicente had wanted her to see. No. It was the name, fifth row from the bottom, struck through with a sharp, even line of black ink. Her lip curled down as she read it.

Reynaldo de Esperanza.

CHAPTER 9

You dance between its claws and invite yourself into its teeth.

—Chronicler

WRONG. SOMETHING WAS WRONG.

Sofía scented the wrongness in the air like a stench, poorly masked by Isla Bestia's salt and coconut perfume. She knew it in her body, in the way her spine tightened like a bowstring ready to set arrows loose, and in the tremor of her hands as they laced the silk ties of her mask behind her head. But her mind . . . *Oh, her mind.* It lagged hopelessly behind, detouring toward the pleasures she once scoffed at, *oohing* and *aahing* at pretty baubles and meaningless pageantry.

It spilled. *She* spilled. Into a soft, oozing mess beyond the cracked shell of herself, like an egg yolk.

Sofía paused to watch the parade pass by, clapping on cue. She had lost the thread of her thought . . . Something about eggs . . . being . . . an egg? No. She was . . . not that. Well, almost certainly not that. She took stock of herself, inventoried her pieces and parts. Long legs and long arms and narrow hips. Hair that neither laid flat nor took a curl. Ribs she could once count in the mirror.

She was scars. On her hands and her back, lining her skin like rivers scoring paths through the earth. *Into* the earth. Into her. Vanishing into places she could not see, channels carved deep and running dry, begging her to fill them with words. Words that cooled and soothed and soaked into her brittle soul. Words strong enough to erode the old, pushing through the dirt and rock and debris to reshape her.

She searched for those words now as she drifted from dream to dream. As her awareness diffused. Scattered, blown away like dandelion seeds. There were words that could fix this, make of the elusive something tangible. Real. A thing she could hold and prod and study. If she could name it, this nebulous threat quaking through her bones, turning the rock-firm structure of her mind into molten goop, then perhaps she stood a chance against it.

Her hand stung. The pain, sharp and sudden, pulled Sofia's gaze away from the entertainment.

Look up.

The words were crudely carved into her palm, the letters jagged, as if she'd taken a shard of glass to her skin. The blood was dry, except at the bottom corner of the *L*, where she must have reopened the wound. A wound that was at least a day old.

How . . . ?

Sofia's head jerked up, compelled by the bloody command and a sudden, visceral urgency beating at the threshold of her awareness. *Look up, look up.* A waxing crescent moon hung high on a clear night sky, and she could make out the star cluster, Sirik, shining bright above it, plainly visible to the naked eye.

What am I looking for?

She knew little of the sky, aside from the remnants of lore passed down through stories and songs, and what she had gleaned from her time minding the fields. The elders, those distrustful of modern timekeeping practices, looked to the firmament to know when to plant the crops and when to harvest them. If only she had listened better, learned the skies the way she learned her books . . .

Without warning, somewhere between the closing and opening of her eyes, the night vanished, the moon and stars and shadows in between replaced by a veil of pungent smoke.

"Here again, Inriri?" said a voice within the haze. "Well, don't just stand there. Sit down or get out, you know I've got no patience for dawdlers."

". . . What?" Sofia blinked away the smoke and found herself in a familiar tent with her skirts drenched from the calves down, being berated by a woman whose expression discouraged argument. Not that Sofía could think clearly enough to even know what to argue about, or why. Mumbling an incoherent apology, she hastily backed out of the diviner's tent, feet splashing as she turned to leave.

Her palm stung.

She held it to the moonlight. And froze when she saw the uneven gashes—letters, cut into her skin. Scarred over and rewritten. Once. Twice. Three times. Sofía felt along the puckered skin and the fainter lines around it, echoes of the same two words:

Look up, look up, look up, look up—
She did.
Mother of Waters take her, she wished she hadn't.

The moon was fat and full and honey-gold, when a mere minute ago, it had been a crescent, thin as the smile Celia gave her on the odd occasion she was feeling amicable.

What in the devils is happening?

She touched her throat, reaching instinctively for the bird that always hung above her heart. The one constant when nothing in her life was the same.

Her fingers traced along the shape, slowing when they felt something warm and tacky. Blood, her blood, coated the woodpecker's beak, smeared into the patch of red along its chest. She stared blankly down at it, imagining it coming into being, spreading its wings, sculpting her flesh to re-create her, like the woodpeckers of myth.

Jarred violently into clarity, Sofía spun back into the tent.

Madame Anani dropped her divining stones and stared hard at Sofía as she took the seat across from her. Sofía returned the diviner's look with as much steel, clinging to the heat of her fear, letting it boil into anger. She understood, in that moment, what would drive a seemingly levelheaded man to shout and steal and start a fire.

Had she truly seen that? Vicente, running. Vicente, pressing something into her hands . . .

"You know what happened to my brother."

Sofía could have asked the diviner any number of questions—why she seemed to be losing time, losing focus—but it was the thought of Sol, the memory of him fading back into oblivion, that nearly choked the breath out of her. She had lost him somewhere in the opulence, the freedom, the unfettered possibility of Carnaval, forgetting his name in the music and wine. Even now, she felt the soothing touch of an invisible hand, numbing her to the rage and pain that kept her anchored. It did not, *could not*, take him from her. But it effaced him into . . . unimportance.

She felt sick to her stomach, witnessing herself sinking into apathy, drawn—again—into the unrelenting pull of its gravity. This island sang to her, poisoned her mind with the rhythm of jubilation. *Relief*, it promised with every drumbeat, horn, and strum of strings, offering her a quick remedy for heartache. Inoculation against caring.

"That a question for the stones?"

. . . A question? *Yes.* She had a question about Sol. *Sol*, who was the reason she was here, on this cursed island that gave with an open hand while it robbed you senseless with the other.

Madame Anani plucked the ceramic lid off the coin pot. "If it is, that'll be three reales. If it's not—" she waved a hand at the exit "—you know the way out by now."

Biting her tongue, Sofía tossed the payment into the pot. The coins clinked as they settled.

"The spirits thank you for your donation." With a grin that did not reach her eyes, the diviner began setting the stones face down.

Sofía hunched forward, leg bouncing under the little round table, forming ripples in the water at her feet. Her thoughts were racing, fingers itching for paper and pen to organize the bedlam inside her. To impose order upon a situation that defied all common sense.

"Will you stop that?"

She did not. Stillness was a mere step away from relaxation, and she was aware enough to understand that was a dangerous state to be in. "What do I do?"

Sighing wearily, the diviner instructed, "Choose three stones and place them along any of these nine points." She touched a finger to the circles threaded along the edges of the tablecloth, coin-sized dots of color against the deep black silk.

Dutifully, Sofía did as she was told, picking three stones and setting them down at random. When Madame Anani flipped them over, Sofía laughed. A harsh sound that toed the line of hysterical.

They were the same three stones from her first reading. "I'm going mad."

"Who could stay sane in a world like this?" muttered the diviner as she considered the stones with an avian tilt to her head.

When the woman returned that too-knowing gaze to Sofía, she felt herself dissected, the anatomy of her secrets laid bare and neatly diagramed. "Well then, diviner, have your stones revealed what's become of my brother?"

Madame Anani's expression was dark and laden with meaning when she leaned across the table, and asked, "Do you know how the sun and moon were made?"

Before Sofía could think to ask, *how exactly is this relevant?* the scholar in her leapt to an answer. "Modern cosmology posits that—"

"No, no, no." The diviner swatted at the air. "Forget all that and listen close, Inriri—" there it was, that nickname again "—for I'm going tell you a story. In this story there's an island, and on this island there's a cave, and this cave is no ordinary place. It is a womb, and from this womb the moon and sun are born, and it is where they go to die and be remade. As one falls, the other rises, for it is the balance they must keep. This world is at the mercy of contradictions, of light and dark, floods and drought, and in this opposition, this polar symmetry, there is harmony. The moon and sun, they share a cave and a sky, a birthplace and a burial ground, and they share a path, yet their journeys are not to run in parallel.

"The moon decides to change that. She knows the sun by the light he leaves behind, and so that he may know her too, she chips off pieces of herself, scatters them about their cave for him to find. And when there is nothing more the moon can give away, in the nights before she's whole and the sky belongs to neither of them . . . that is when they meet."

The diviner watched Sofía with that grave expression, as though she'd revealed something of great importance. "Really, Madame Anani?" she said, her shoulders sagging with disappointment. "A riddle in exchange for a desperate woman's coin?" To think that for a moment, she'd wanted to put her trust in this woman, to believe her an ally amid the unexplainable strangeness of this place. "I've clearly made a mistake in coming here. Know it will not happen again."

She got up to leave and was halfway through the tent's opening when the diviner spoke. "Were I you, I'd not be so quick to dismiss my words, Inriri. There's much one can learn from a story."

"Unpack it for me then, if you're so keen to help."

"Surely, a bright thing like yourself can figure it out."

Sofía laughed mirthlessly. "You overestimate my abilities, diviner. Even in full possession of my faculties, I do not think in parables."

"And *I* may not speak outside them." Madame Anani rose, hands gripping the sides of her little table with some emotion Sofía could not untangle. Whatever it was, it left her as quickly as it came, and she slumped back down onto her chair. "But perhaps . . ." She drummed her fingers over the tabletop, an idea forming. "Perhaps the right question may serve just as well as an answer."

Sofía hung her head; tension was building in the nape of her neck, and she did not think she could bear much more of the diviner's brainteasers. Her hold on her mind was slippery as it was—any more of that conversation, and she might slide straight into madness. Yet, as Madame Anani had done once that night already, she reeled Sofía back in.

"Have you tried staying up past dawn," asked the diviner, in a voice like the one she used to tell her story, "or waking before sunset?"

Had she? Sofía scanned the clouded fragments of her recent memories. What pieces she could recall ended abruptly with the rise of the sun and began like clockwork with the fall of it. "Why should that matter?" she said, knowing on some level beyond her conscious awareness that it *did* matter.

Madame Anani twirled a stone between her fingers, her expression rendering that seemingly idle gesture heavy with intent. "You've been looking for answers in the dark. Maybe what you need can only be found in daylight."

SOFÍA WALKED.

Beyond the river where the diviner had set her palm-roofed tent, through gaudy archways of crystal and gold, and beneath performers soaring like gods on gilded wings. She walked past the empty throne where earlier that evening a toad of a man had been crowned the new King of Carnaval. Then up the stairs she went, dodging glances and offers of wine, defiantly ascending the steps though what she craved was the carefree world at her back.

She slid the iron key into the lock of the Moriviví suite, stepped inside, and closed the door behind her. After only a moment's hesitation, she shoved her armoire in front of one door and dragged her nightstand in front of the other. Why she did it, she could not say. All she knew right then was that it calmed the nagging itch at the back of her mind.

Next, she went to her writing desk drawer and fished out a small jar of ink, a steel-nib pen, and her red journal, which held everything she knew about Carnaval.

Sofía flipped through the pages, skimming their contents until she reached the piece she'd written the day she stepped foot on Isla Bestia. She had penned nothing else since, or so she thought before turning to the next page.

There, an entry she did not remember writing.

> Date Unknown,
> 4th Era of the Lion Rider, Year VI
>
> More and more, I find myself losing track of time. One moment, I am watching women and men take to the skies, performing feats no human should. And then... I am waking. Here, in this room. I could blame the wine as Adelina does, if only I had not seen what I did.
> What I think I did.
> A good scholar does not rush to hasty conclusions, nor let the fear of the heart overrun the mind. That is why I write of it here. The page is where I come to make sense of my thoughts. You alone, old friend, are strong enough to bear the weight of my uncertainty...
> Could there be another explanation for what I witnessed tonight? A simpler, less convoluted one than—

The passage ended there, the last word smudging into a shadowy line of black, as if Sofía had fallen asleep while writing it, cheek pressed to the still-wet ink. The next few pages bore more questions, penned in her hand but not her manner.

There was an utter lack of order to them, which on its own was uncanny enough, but most entries also ended abruptly, switched topics midway through a sentence, or devolved into utter incoherence. Rather than the clean structure of her typical arguments, these were more like excerpts from her stream of consciousness, each shorter and more frantic than the one before. One page notably had only the words *They watch*, drawn in oversized letters and underscored until the pen nib ripped through. Tucked into the fold between two other pages was a wrinkled sheet of paper. A record of names, some of which had been crossed off, and one she was acutely—troublingly—familiar with.

Behind it, another page fluttered loose. It was roughly torn along the side, suggesting it'd been ripped off the binding, and the quality of the paper was finer than anything she could afford, so she knew it couldn't be hers even before she saw its contents. The page showed a serpentine creature, a monster, rendered in charcoal. The artist had captured it rising out of the river, water dripping down its scales, eyes gleaming like starlight . . .

Sofía rubbed a palm against her brow, trying to make meaning of all those unconnected thoughts and warnings. Who had she been when she wrote them? Who was this stranger borrowing her pen and her body? It was that mystery above all that made her tear through the journal in a feverish search for answers, reading so quickly and carelessly she almost missed it.

A question, twice circled, on the top-left margin of a page. *Cohoba?*

She frowned. Cohoba was a plant endemic to the archipelago. Its seeds bore medicinal properties and, if inhaled, could produce hallucinogenic effects. Anecdotally, she had heard her ancestors used it for ceremonial rites as a way of communing with the zemís. The few surviving diaries of conquistadores attested to the same. *But what in the world does that have to do with . . . ?*

Sofía stilled, a terrible thought occurring to her.

A *hallucinogen.* Salt and seas, was this her past self's attempt to warn her she was being drugged? It would certainly explain the gaps in her memories, the lapses of concentration and blurred sense of time. Her instincts refused the theory. A reputable hotel covertly poisoning its guests? Sofía knew how deranged that sounded. She would have put the idea to bed on sheer principle, if she were the type to let instinct dictate truth.

Facts did not care for feelings, and she could not shape them to suit her like some pillow too flat and stiff for comfort. If she wanted the truth, she needed to observe closely, test rigorously, and accept the results without imposing on them her assumptions.

This, at least, was familiar . . . A process with clearly outlined steps, built-in checks and balances, a commitment to objectivity. She could do this. *Be* this. Controlled and detached.

Grabbing her writing implements, Sofía went to the balcony and settled on a corner of the floor with the wall at her back, drawing her knees up to prop her journal against her lap. The leather spine cracked as she opened it.

Spread out below her was the Gilded Sea, vast and dark and, at first glance, seemingly knowable. Like the Flor de Lis itself, predictable on the surface, less so the farther into its depths you went. She came to a blank page and began to write, filling it line by line with questions. Questions that, until now, she'd forgotten she had.

Are other guests losing time?
Where are the servants' quarters?
Is the girl from Vicente's memories Adelina?
Why was Don Reynaldo's name crossed off?
Where is Sol?
Sol.

Sofía's pen lingered on her brother's name, dripping ink onto the page. Would he slip away again come morning? There, and yet out of reach and out of sight, like a book fallen to the bottom of a pile? She sensed she'd felt this urgency before. The evidence of it was in the pages she'd read, measurable by the uneven strokes of her letters marking the tremble of her hand. A version of herself had been just as unsettled once and forgotten all this anyhow.

She could not let that happen again.

Shutting her journal, she dipped the pen in ink, and began to write. Not on paper, but on skin. Copying onto her left arm the portents and questions another Sofía had left for her to find, filling every gap of bare skin from shoulder to wrist. The right arm, she inscribed with a list, using the crook of her elbow to divide it into two columns. On one, she wrote general symptoms of intoxication and poisoning, on the other, possible means of administration. The food? The wine? That was assuming the toxins functioned through ingestion, not touch or inhalation. She wrote instructions to herself on the backs of her hands to avoid meals and drinks. Fresh water she could collect from the river, and there were gardens and greenhouses she could pilfer food from if she was discreet.

Light began to color the sky the reddish orange of grapefruit. Sofía looked up, remembering the diviner's words. *Have you tried staying up past dawn?*

Worry pricked at her mind, foolish as a child's fear of the cuco monster under the bed. But it stuck hard and fast. She could not shake it, not until she proved her mad theory wrong.

Sofía wrapped her arms around her knees, careful not to rub the drying ink as she swayed slightly to calm the sudden jitter in her bones. The sun peeked above the horizon, painting the violet sea with streaks of fire and amber. It climbed an inch for every thump of her heart, brightening the blooms all along her balcony's iron railing to colors so vibrant they almost hurt to look at. Sofía did not take her gaze from the sky, did not even dare to blink, nervous she would miss it: the moment morning came and she was left humbled, laughing at her wild imaginings.

The moment did not come. Though she was too frazzled for sleep, the instant the day overtook the night, Sofía's vision went dark.

CHAPTER 10

*Who enters Carnaval chooses the night,
renounces all they left behind in daylight.*

—Chronicler

WARNINGS, WRITTEN ON Sofía's skin. Streaks of black running up and down her arms . . . the backs of her hands . . . a scabbed cut in her palm urging her to *Look up* in stark, crooked letters.

She studied the words, cold with shock.

Then, a calm overtook her as she inspected the scribbles, the same calm she felt piecing together bits of research, desk piled with tomes and notes and newspaper clippings. Her body had become an artifact to be examined, the archeological record of a past she could only vaguely remember.

Most importantly, it had become a thing she could separate emotion from, severing feeling from flesh like a necrotic wound.

She stood up from her spot on the balcony, stretching stiff muscles, and went to the writing desk. There, she took on the role of the unbiased observer, parsing out the mysteries inked onto her skin with a clear mind and tidy penmanship. Snippets of the previous day came back to her as she wrote—the sight of a full moon, Madame Anani's words, the sudden sleep that overcame her as the sun claimed the sky.

By the end of that writing session, Sofía had a series of tests lined up, with variables and terms operationally defined. She sat back, satisfied with her work. She had asserted a level of control over a situation that staunchly resisted it. Now all she had to do was abide by her own instructions.

A knock came at the door, followed by several grunts and huffs of exertion.

In one swift movement, Sofía pulled the throw blanket from the bed and over her shoulders, concealing the ink on her arms.

"What in the bleeding saints is this doing here?" Adelina grumbled, shoving the nightstand aside and squeezing through the opening on the door.

"A great question," Sofía whispered to herself, unsure if it was meant to keep someone out, or herself *in*. "I'm . . . feeling unwell. I think I might stay in tonight."

Settling onto the edge of the bed, Adelina only nodded, looking distracted. *Probably thinking about her games again*, Sofía thought. "Adelina . . ." She tapped a finger against the cover of her journal. "How long would you say we've been here?"

She toyed with the embroidery on her skirt, considering. "Hmm . . . three weeks, give or take a few days?"

"Right, and . . . do you remember *why* we're here?"

Adelina laughed. "It's *Carnaval*, cariño, I would think it's fairly self-explanatory." Though her words were confident, her manner was vague, her attention drawn elsewhere. Always elsewhere.

Sofía might have done it then, reminded her of the father she'd lost. Shown her his name, struck through the middle like an item on a checklist. She might have bared her arms and all the truths written there, read Adelina the secrets of a person she could not remember being.

Instead, she kept her worries to herself, needing to be absolutely sure of what was happening before embroiling her friend in the mess she'd woken to. Adelina was not exactly known for approaching matters halfheartedly. If she had even an inkling of Sofía's burgeoning theories, she would charge in headfirst with no regard for the potential danger. And there was a danger, nebulous though it might have felt just then. Someone in power, likely. That was usually how these things went.

No, Sofía was right to keep her out of this. Keep her, if not safe, then out of the direct line of fire. "Could you lend me your pocket watch?" she asked, following through on the plan she'd set for herself.

Adelina thumbed the device dangling from the chatelaine at her waist, reluctant to part with it. "What for?"

Sofía stared out into the balcony, watching the dredges of daylight disappear behind the flutter of white lace curtains. "An experiment."

THE HANDS OF the pocket watch marked 6:05.

Sofía recorded the minute in her journal, then again on the inside of her forearm, adding another tally mark to the row already inked there.

It would be daylight soon.

She looked at the line where the ocean met the sky, watching the sunlight bleed through the dark. Her toes curled and uncurled over the soft moonlit sand, and she dipped her pen into the inkpot as she prepared to record yet another minute. Behind her, Carnaval ramped up the noise and spectacle, working itself up into its nightly grand finale. The music crescendoed, growing louder, faster, the cheers becoming wilder. She felt it vibrating the air all the way from the seashore, where she sat alone waiting for the sun to rise.

The end came with a flurry of applause, punctuated by a few notably enthusiastic whistles, and then . . .

Silence.

6:09.

Diligently, Sofía logged the minute in her journal, tallied it on her skin, and—

Day 17

Waxing gibbous moon, date unknown
Experimental Condition B3, test XXII
Location: Quadrant II, Sector F
Start time: 4:25

"THIRTY-TWO... THIRTY-THREE... THIRTY-FOUR..."

Sofía counted her steps under her breath. She had tied a ribbon—stolen from Adelina's stash of fashionable accoutrements—around both ankles, so that each step measured precisely thirty centimeters in length. She marked her progress, writing the number on her journal and on the skin of her forearm before moving on.

The ribbon stretched taut across her ankles as she moved another thirty centimeters deeper into the woods surrounding the Flor de Lis. Past the river, the area was dense with vegetation, a sundry mix of spindly coconut trees, evergreens, and a few tall shrubs weighted with acerola fruit. Sofía paused to pick a few of the perfectly round, perfectly red berries and popped one into her mouth, spitting out the seeds. All she had eaten that day were a few uncooked radishes and a sweet pepper. She would have eaten more had that vejigante not shown up as she was sneaking about the greenhouse.

At least fresh water was easier to come by than untampered food. Though she did have to be mindful when crouching down to fill her wineglass, its original contents subtly emptied into the nearest bush, flower pot, or artful piece of themed decor.

Sofía wiped fruit juice from her lips and pressed on with her experiment. Thankfully, her instructions to herself, as well as her thorough record of observations, were detailed enough that she could pick up where she had left off the day prior. In her journal, she had drawn a simple map of the hotel and the areas bordering the property, then divided it into four quadrants, which in turn were divided into three sectors each. Assuming her previous observations held, she would go only another forty-six steps before . . .

Well, that was the question, wasn't it?

Her notes cut off abruptly every time. The farthest she had ever gone beyond the river line was, according to her logs, a mere thirty yards.

"There's probably a fence," Sofía mused out loud. "A tall one, with spikes." After all, in the face of competing explanations, the one requiring the fewest extraneous assumptions should be given precedence. Why let her mind run wild with speculation, when the simpler, and more plausible, reason she could go no farther was that there was a barrier? It made sense, of course. A distinguished establishment like the Flor de Lis would take measures to protect itself against pirates, freeloaders, and thieves.

Why would I not just write that then? Sofia dismissed the thought. Her memory loss and recurring fugue states she could somewhat rationalize, but the idea of a place that would not let her leave? *That*, she could not.

Distant laughter floated in on a breeze, and the leaves shivered as if they were laughing too. Fine hairs all along Sofia's arms stood on end. *Cold*, she was cold, she reasoned with herself, tightening her grip on the pen to stop her hand from shaking. She forged ahead, taking another note, another step, another shuddering breath. Twigs snapped under the heels of her toe-pinching slippers, and somewhere up in the branches, an owl hooted, the sound a low tremble, as if warning her away. Eyes the rust-red of dried blood watched her from the misty darkness.

On a whim, Sofia hooted back, whistling with a deep vibrato that shook the muscles of her throat. The creature blinked, as if puzzled by the big, featherless bird before it, but did not move from its perch. "There was a lizard back there," she said to it, hooking a thumb over her shoulder. "You might still catch it if you hurry."

It seemed to consider her suggestion, the tawny feathers of its neck fluffing as its head bobbed side to side like it was mounted on a metal spring. The creature did not call to her again, though she would have welcomed the distraction, any distraction really, for up ahead waited an uncomfortable truth: the sight of the woods uninterrupted, its verdant trees stretching on seemingly forever. She was an arm's length away from a boundary she could never seem to cross, at least not with her awareness intact, and yet . . . there was nothing there. No barrier to explain why she could never go beyond those ninety-three steps.

Perhaps this sector's different? she thought optimistically, even as sweat broke out beneath the thin porcelain of her mask. Her body had always been more honest than she was, and now was no exception.

Sofía steeled herself, and began counting the five remaining steps, her feet landing heavily, leaves crunching under the heavy wooden soles of her slippers. "Ninety-two, ninety-three, ninety—" Pausing, she hastily wrote herself a reminder of what was and wasn't there and underlined it with a sharp, decisive stroke of her pen.

Ahead, the path looked no different, *felt* no different, but her senses had betrayed her too often to be trusted. Something had derailed her every other night she dared enter these woods, evidently with enough subtlety to avoid documentation.

Her left foot hovered uncertainly, the ribbon around its ankle hanging slack. With a sharp inhale, she shoved the fear back down and set her heel firmly on—

Sofía's eyes shot open.

In a blink, the world had toppled sideways. Or had *she*? No longer did the woods wear hues of black and blue—they were now shaded in warm, golden tones.

Songbirds trilled from somewhere up above, insects chirped, and water gurgled down a nearby stream. Sofía ached in a dozen different places and her skin chafed painfully when she tried to move. Groaning, she braced her palms against the ground and pushed until the world righted itself.

Dead leaves fell in flecks from her cheek. Twigs were trapped in the knots of her hair, and her cracked lips tasted of dirt and dried blood. Her arms itched in the places where some devil-spawned mosquitoes must have made a meal of her. *Did I . . . fall asleep here last night? Why am I . . . ?*

With a jolt, Sofía came alert.

She pawed the ground for her journal, sighing with relief when she felt its reassuring bulk hidden under the pooled layers of her skirts. Her fingers shook as she flipped quickly through the pages, over to the last entry: *Day 17.* She read down to the final step logged, the last one she remembered taking before . . .

Her eyes scanned the woods again, this time with purpose, surveying the area for distinguishing markers.

There. The acerola shrubs.

Journal in hand, she picked her way through the underbrush before realizing her ankles were still tied. "Mierda," she cursed, bending to undo the ribbon. Freed, she shoved the length of silk into her pocket and hobbled over to inspect the ground near the fruit shrubs.

The seeds she'd discarded were still there, strewn among the dried, crinkled leaves. Which likely meant she'd kept most of the previous night's memories, a luxury she'd not been afforded since the start of that experiment, if not longer. Not just that, but for once she had woken somewhere other than her suite, where her evening tribulations were more easily reduced to a strange, distant dream. That is, until she saw the ink scribbled on her arms.

How she made it back each night remained a mystery. One moment, she would be tramping through the woods, and the next, her eyes would open to the now familiar sight of her bedroom ceiling, cast in the sepia shades of twilight.

Sunlight pierced through the tree canopy and Sofía closed her eyes against it, its rays a welcome change after so many balmy nights . . .

Wait. She squinted, trying to catch a glimpse of the sky through the tangle of leaves and branches.

This was not the fading light of dusk. The sun was just a little beyond its zenith, moving west. It must have been two . . . three hours past noon? She reached for her borrowed pocket watch at once. The glass had cracked in the corner—she made a note to apologize to Adelina for that later—but the hands fortunately kept on their steady rotation.

She read the time.

It was a quarter past the fifteenth hour. Sofía had not been awake during this time since . . . Well, she was not entirely sure how long. That got her moving again, nearly stumbling in her rush to see the sky in its entirety. Heels skidding down the grassy slope and hands clutching tree trunks and low-hanging branches for balance, she made it to the river's edge.

It was the hush that struck her first.

She sensed the absence of laughter and song like a giant hole punched straight through the earth. After so long without silence, the sound of her own breathing unnerved her. Dazed, she listed sideways, catching herself on a tree. She shakily gripped its rough bark as she took in the sight of the hotel grounds, unremarkable when stripped of their nighttime magic.

There were no tables stacked with shining silver and mouthwatering dishes bathed in steam. No acrobats floating on wires, or dancers painting the night with their kaleidoscopic costumes, or musicians leading them with percussion and strings. There were no contraptions to steal Adelina's attention or burden Sofía's mind with questions. No mask-bearing devils to pamper spoiled guests.

There was only the land, misty and dressed with flowerbeds that looked limp and muted, and trees that were not quite as vibrant as they had been the night before. Even the Flor de Lis's walls were more dingy gray than pure salt-white, its stucco water-stained, the vines along it growing wild rather than artfully cultivated to appear so.

This place should have been crawling with staff. No fewer than a hundred skilled hands bustling about from dawn to dusk, hastening to deliver yet another extravagant celebration in record time. Yet, not a soul was there.

Sofía touched her fingers to her temples and allowed herself three breaths, one for each certainty she could anchor herself to.

You were born in the season of storms.

You bear a name given to you by a stranger.

Your brother boarded a ship one night, and you never saw him again.

She pressed her forehead to the tree, bowing as if in prayer. "Mamá, give me strength . . ." With that, she did the only thing she could do. She kept going.

Along the river she went, until she arrived at the spot labeled Footpath on her crudely sketched map. It was a shallower section of water, marked with some sizable stones that formed a natural bridge. After greedily guzzling down several handfuls of water, she stuffed her journal down the front of her dress, pinning it to the top of her corset for safekeeping, and carefully made her way across the slick stones.

Without the trees for cover, the light of day burned too bright. She had to squint as she made her way across the endless gardens, her steps slow and heavy, as if weighed down by the mist. Was the heat to blame? Had a lifetime indoors really made her so soft that a few minutes under the sun left her knees jittering like palm fronds in the wind?

As Sofía passed a flower bed, she bent to inspect the blooms. The petals were dull reds, pinks, and oranges, their brilliance faded like gowns bleached under the light of the sun. Even the leaves drooped, their edges crisp and browning.

At the solarium, she paused again, peeking through the fogged glass. Banquet tables were shoved up against the walls with chairs resting upon them in towering stacks. Its sultry glamour vanished in the light of day. It looked smaller now, less . . . impressive. Was it just the other night that it dripped with chandeliers of ruby-red, that the crowd inside danced to the seductive rhythm of high stakes and higher chances, the jingle of pockets heavy with coins? That place had existed outside reality, yet the building before her now looked ordinary by comparison.

Turning back to the hotel proper, Sofía's pace quickened, a renewed sense of urgency propelling her across the remaining half of the courtyard, then up the steep flight of stairs.

The doors flew open, and Sofía strained her ears, trying to pick up on the friendly chatter of the cleaning staff as they went about their daily duties. Instead, she heard only the click of her own heels echoing down the too-quiet corridor. And beyond that, water streaming from the hot springs ahead, and the creak of an iron gate swinging open and shut, coaxed by a strong breeze.

Just a few more steps . . . she thought with forced conviction, even as her confidence flickered like a flame. She stoked it with the tinder of objectivity, kept it alive all the way to the main lobby.

She slid to a halt.

The concierge's desk stood empty. Only a scatter of leaves blown in from the adjacent courtyard moved to greet her.

"Where the devils is everyone . . . ?"

Sofía stepped up to the desk and tapped twice on the bell. The sound grated on her ears, too sharp against the silence. "Buenas," she called, breathless. "¿Alguien ahí?"

Again, she struck the bell. Kept at it until her hand tired and she was certain she had made enough of a ruckus to wake the gods above and the dead below. She went around the desk and threw open the curtains to each of the three rooms with their floor-to-ceiling mask displays. Pitted eyes stared back at her, eerie in the darkness.

She stepped back with a huff of frustration. "The kitchens then," she decided, pivoting on her heel and making straight for them. Surely, the ovens would be on by now, roasting meats and baking bread, the pots simmering with buttery sauces and savory stews. With hundreds of mouths to feed, the kitchen staff would have been up since sunrise, if they were ever allowed to sleep at all.

The servants' door opened with a creak onto a familiar spiral staircase, cramped and dark, without a single sconce to illuminate the way.

"Anyone down there?" It came out as a summons rather than a question. Doña Elena did always say she had too much cheek for a slave. Sofía thought it more an issue of impatience, a logical preference for efficiency over polite circumvention.

She lingered for several beats, waiting. But no response came.

"Right. In we go then . . ." As a precaution, she hefted a brick-sized garden stone over to the door, propping it open, and began her descent. Unlike last time, she did not bother concealing the sound of her passage. Her feet stomped down the steps and she pressed her palms against the walls, both to remind herself the space was not as narrow as her mind distorted it to seem, and to pretend, if only for a short while, that she could fend them off should they suddenly decide to edge closer.

The steps ended, the floor shifting from hardwood to stone. Around her, the walls opened up.

Sofía stood in the corridor she had snuck through before, allowing her eyes a moment to adjust. It was much too dark to make out anything beyond the vague silhouette of an open doorway. There were no windows to let in sunlight, not even a single lit lantern or candle anywhere in sight.

She felt her way along the gloom, navigating by memory until her fingers reached the end of the wall. The rest of her followed through the threshold of the door leading to the kitchens. The air there was noticeably devoid of heat and steam, and only slightly scented with the smells of spices, heads of garlic, and bagged coffee beans.

Sofía wandered through the space, forming a vague impression of the layout and general state of things. The stoves and ovens had long cooled, and the counters had all been wiped clean. She uncovered a set of drawers near the stoves and blindly rummaged through them until she felt a familiar shape. A quick shake of the box confirmed its contents. Matches, the long ones used for lighting stoves.

She slid out the hidden compartment, pinched one of the wooden sticks between her thumb and forefinger, and struck it against the box's grooved edge. Fire flared to life, reflecting off the rows of hanging pots and copper pans, the stacks of silver trays and fine hand-painted porcelain. She made her way around until she found a burlap sack, empty but for a few yautías, dusted with soil. She took it.

The match blackened as the fire devoured its way down. Sofía burned through nearly a quarter of the matchbox as she upturned cupboards and drawers, packing up what she could with her one free hand: food rations, a small cooking pot, a cracked dinner plate, and a knife, which she wrapped clumsily in cloth and stuffed into her pocket. Better to have it within easy reach, in case . . .

In case what? You must ward off your hosts with a six-inch dinner knife?

Right. She ought to grab a bigger one.

After a bit more rummaging, she found a meat cleaver with a wicked edge and tossed it into the sack with the rest of her contraband. Then she laughed.

Who did she think she was, sneaking about in the dark like some amateur vigilante, pilfering weapons, crockery, and produce, and plotting to swing a cleaver at some vague enemy? Her laughter had an edge to rival her new blade, though it did not last long.

The match dwindled to a stub. Cursing, Sofía scrambled to blow it out, the skin of her thumb tender where the fire burned it. "Mierda, pay attention." She struck another match and made her way back out into the corridor, her sack of stolen goods thrown over one shoulder.

Just as she remembered, the first door she opened revealed brooms and mops and feather dusters, as well as shelves stockpiled with blocks of parchment-wrapped soap, boxes of starch, and jars filled with lye, powdered and pale as refined sugar. The next door led into the linen closet, its wooden cubbies stuffed with spare bedsheets, thick cotton towels, and embroidered dinner napkins folded into perfect squares. Wooden sewing boxes were tucked into a corner. She took one and stashed it in with the rest of her bounty.

On she went, turning right at the end of the corridor instead of left toward what should have been the servants' sleeping quarters, all the while resisting the urge to pick up her pace, to run as though someone was dogging her heels. She passed the wine cellar, the laundry room filled with vats of still water, then a storage space packed with miscellaneous furniture, oil paintings, and other odds and ends strung through with cobwebs. A candelabra with a half-melted candlestick drew her eye. She lit the wick with her stubby matchstick, brushed off the dust and the cobwebs, and held the light to the room. It caught on a mirror attached to a small wooden vanity, an exact replica of the ones upstairs. As she came closer, she noticed the wood was scored through with jagged lines.

Those were no haphazard marks . . .

They were letters, a message carved into the wood. *Fools in crowns*, it read, and below that, *You are next.*

Her initial instinct was to dismiss it as some poor sod's ravings, but there was a desperation to those words that reminded her of Vicente's warning to her that night in the lobby. Of her own warnings to herself—scrawled across her journal, engraved into her palms. She laid her hand, scarred-side up, atop the vanity. Whoever etched those letters onto its surface had been like her, terrified enough to lock their fears onto something more permanent than paper. Her fingers shakily traced the lines of splintered wood, committing those words to memory.

A search of the rest of the room's cast-off treasures revealed a few valuables, including a century-old map of Isla Bestia, a pair of gentlemen's boots that fit her feet snuggly, a brass spyglass with the initials R.G.S. engraved on the side, and a pocket almanac printed in the sixth year of the Bullfighter, the same year she was born. Everything else was either too heavy to carry, or too impractical to be of use.

With her burlap sack full and weighing on her shoulder, she exited back out into the hall. Even in the dark, she didn't worry about getting lost. For all their faults, the one thing Sofía could not begrudge Hisperians was their architecture. They built in grids and blocks that could be relied upon to double back, a blessing for the navigationally challenged, or those who, like her, simply appreciated intuitive design. It was especially convenient when one was exploring shadowy passageways.

Turning the corner, she arrived at a long corridor with doors crammed close together, each barely two hand spans apart from the next. In any other property, those quarters would have housed the servants. Not here.

With surprising clarity, she recalled spying into nearly every one of those rooms her first week on the island, snooping for signs of occupancy. Each was the same—dusty, impersonal, and unused.

She walked, candelabra in hand, its shape casting a sharp shadow against the stone. It was tempting, oh so tempting, to look over her shoulder, to assure herself no masked monster followed in her wake. But there was a difference between self-preservation and overindulging one's imagination. Thoughts, she knew, were like leaks. A mild nuisance at first, but leave them unchecked and you'll have a much bigger problem when the storm sweeps through.

Sssssssssss . . .

Sofia skidded to a stop.

What was that? She spun, shining her light down both sides of the hall, scanning the dark for whatever might have made that sound. But she was alone. No sinister figure waited in the gloom, no madman stalked her steps. Had she imag—?

Ssssssssssoof . . .

Movement drew her gaze sharply down.

And there, at her feet, her shadow began to stir. At first, she thought it an effect of the wavering candle flame, then as she stared on, dumbstruck, it peeled itself off from her, like a limb removed from the rest of her body. It wore her billowing dress, her uncombed hair, yet moved with a grace she was physically incapable of.

Unblinking, Sofia's eyes traced her shadow's path along the wall, watched its form warp as it turned toward the door and reached a hand to the knob. Her likeness had no lips, no mouth, no teeth, but a crescent of pale light spread across the thing's face like a smile.

Then, it was gone. Or rather, returned to its rightful place at her feet. It moved when she moved. Held still when she held still.

Turning away might have been the prudent thing to do, but doing so would've been a kind of admission. Proof that what she saw was no mere product of her tampered mind, but a practical threat, one deserving of her caution.

No. She would *not* quake at the sight of a specter. Would not validate its presence in her reality.

In three strides, Sofía was at the door, following her shadow the way it now followed her. The knob, cool in her hand, clicked open with a twist, and the door groaned as she pulled it wide.

Candlelight spilled into the room, across the dusty floors and the too-narrow cots. That should have been all there was to see. A quick perusal of the room and then she'd be on her way, her worldview reasserted. She was so sure of it too, until the beam caught on something near the back. The porcelain gleam of a mask . . . the sharp edges of fangs . . . the curving points of a half dozen horns . . .

The vejigante sat on the bed, motionless as a doll, the chasms of its eyes open wide and watchful. Inhuman, and so very, *very* real.

Sofía slammed the door shut.

Fast as her legs would take her, she ran, making for the stairs. The candle whooshed out, plunging her into blackness. There was no time to reach for another match, so she tossed the candelabra aside and used her freed hand to find her way back.

Come on, come on, come on! Her fingers itched to grab the knife in her pocket. A few seconds was all it would take to undo the wrappings, but those seconds could cost her. Did she dare?

She did not.

Her foot hit the bottom of the stairway and she almost cried out in relief. With no time to lose, she bolted up the steps, taking two at a time, boots slipping and sliding over the wood, the burlap sack swinging against her back so hard it nearly knocked her forward.

Ssss . . . Ssssof . . .

Sssofía . . .

Sofía . . .

Finally, she burst through the door with a gasp, blinked her eyes against the jarring brightness, and ran. Ran until she was standing at the adjoining courtyard, where the hyacinths bloomed and the hummingbirds flew and the air smelled like a bowl of fresh fruit. A paradise too warm, too sunny, too *damn* beautiful for something terrible to happen.

That's what she would have thought, anyway, if she actually believed bad things only ever happened in dark, cold, ugly places. If she hadn't experienced, firsthand, the horrors that took place under the bluest skies.

Quickly, she overturned her sack of stolen goods, shaking out its contents onto a pile on the manicured grass. The cleaver's blade glinted in the sun, peeking out from behind the almanac. She snatched it up, gripped it between both hands, and waited for the door to open and the vejigante to step through. To look at her with those inhuman eyes and peel back their mask to show something just as wicked underneath.

The blade was steady between her hands, held with a surgeon's practiced calm. Not for lack of fear, of course. She was aloof, not imperturbable. But *this* was a threat she knew how to deal with, not a smiling shadow, nor the strange sleep that came with sunrise, nor the line in the woods she could not cross. No blade would save her from that, no matter how hard or fast she swung it.

But a blade might just save her from this.

This danger made tangible. Flesh that her steel could bite into, make bleed.

Her arms grew sore as the seconds turned to minutes and no one stepped through that door. She flexed her fingers, repositioned them on the handle, but kept the weapon aloft. She must have stood like that for almost a half hour, her muscles trembling with the effort, before she realized no one was coming.

Sofía sank to the grass, wiped the sweat from her brow, and gave herself permission to think nothing . . . to *be* nothing. To sit in numb silence, without the constant cycle of questions going round and round her mind like schools of fish eager to feed on her attention.

Had she imagined it all? The shadow of herself with the sickle moon on its face, the mask in the dark, and the stirring of something old and primitive within her, a fear she hadn't known she possessed.

When Sofia finally came to, the sun had lost some of its vibrance.

How long had she sat there? It was only the thought of Adelina, alone and facing unknown peril, that pulled her out of that near-insensate state. She repacked her sack, knotted it shut, and got back on her feet.

The cleaver, she kept—clasped firmly in a fist.

CHAPTER 11

*It was the first year of the Horseman when they came.
The clerics blessed the land, appointed it a patron saint.
An Empire name they gave it. In death, they consecrated it.*

—Chronicler

THE GUEST HALLS were as quiet and still as the rest of the property. Sofía peeked in on each floor, her senses alert for anything unusual. Or, *especially* unusual, rather.

As she came up to her suite, she paused and pressed her ear to the door. She heard only the sound of the ocean and the throaty cries of pelicans beyond. Still, she was careful as she slid the key into the lock and crept inside.

Her room was as it always was when she returned from a night of gallivanting. The bed was made, its silk pillows fluffed and decoratively rearranged, the bathtub drained and a fresh towel laid upon the freestanding rack beside it. Blade in hand, she made her way around the room, searching the balcony, the inside of the armoire, behind the dressing screen, and under the bed. All the places a person could feasibly hide.

They watch . . . They watch . . . They watch . . . The warning from her journal drifted back to her, hounding her as she moved from the shadowed corners of her suite to Adelina's. She opened the adjoining door and stepped through.

A narrow beam of sunlight shone through the gap in the curtains, curving over the lump on the bed. Bronze hair, twisted into little white rags, peeked out from the blankets.

Sofía released the breath she had been holding. "Wake up, Adelina." She reached under the sheets and jabbed the sole of her friend's foot. "Hurry now, we have to be out of here before nightfall. I'll explain on the way."

She tugged open the armoire and began packing Adelina's dresses into her travel trunk—not that they would be able to take it with them, if they could even leave at all. But that was a problem for later, right now she just needed to keep her hands occupied. "Are you even listening to me? Get *up*. If we don't leave now, we might not . . ." She looked back at the bed, suddenly all too aware of the silence. The stillness. "Adelina?"

Sofia unclenched her fingers from around the pile of tulle and silk, let it slip from her hands and puddle on the floor. Then, she stepped over the heap and came around the bed, peeled back the covers. Slowly, then all at once.

Was Adelina normally that still? That . . . *pale*? Sofia's hand squeezed into a fist. Breathing deep, she pressed two fingers to the pulse on her friend's neck.

At first, she sensed only her own blood rushing to her ears like water bursting from a broken pipe. Then—

Thump . . . thump.

Sofia exhaled sharply through gritted teeth and gave Adelina's shoulder a rough shake. "Quit fooling around already," she demanded. "Mother of Waters, do you even— I thought you were . . ." No. She refused to finish that thought. What good would it do her to imagine *that*, to let grief take up space in her mind prematurely, knowing well she would never get it to leave? Grief was no passerby. When it came, it settled. Bringing with it all its baggage, tearing holes into the walls she'd so meticulously built around herself. It was the worst kind of tenant—one she would not open her door to so easily this time.

Sofia marched over to the sink, filled an empty wineglass with water, then marched back and dumped its contents over Adelina's face.

"Wake up."

She did not. Not when Sofia ripped away the blankets, nor when she threatened to throw her gowns into the sea. No amount of motivational threats or creative invective worked to draw her out of bed.

This was . . . no natural sleep.

Sofía's mind whirled with questions, theories, solutions. Too many, too quickly, to make proper sense of. She pressed the heels of her palms to her eyelids and forced herself to breathe in deeply through her nose. *Calm*, she was calm. Organized. She could approach this logically.

She threw open the balcony doors, letting in a burst of sunlight before returning to Adelina's bedside. Sofía had no formal medical expertise, but there were things one picked up out of sheer necessity. How to stitch a wound, for one. How to recognize the signs of a concussion. Or sepsis. Or poisoning. Such occurrences were unfortunately common among the islands' servant class, and doctors were, of course, a privilege reserved for those who could afford them.

Given the symptoms, the first thing Sofía did was inspect Adelina's head for injuries, then her nails, lips, and skin for strange spots or discoloration. Her complexion looked wan, but that might have just been the lack of cosmetics.

Sofía forced open Adelina's eyes. The pupils were abnormally dilated, the irises a thin ring of blue, barely visible even in the bright light of day. "Some kind of toxin then . . . Probably." Bloodroot could purge it from her system were that the case, but if Sofía was wrong? In the state Adelina was in, forcing her to swallow an emetic could very well kill her.

No, there had to be another way.

She paced the room, hands clasped behind her back. Would the medic be awake? Perhaps. Could she trust him if he was? Absolutely not. It was the medic Vicente had been taken to the night he made a mess of things and, if her records were right, she had not seen him since.

Could there be a sick bay, or a storeroom stocked with herbs and medicines? She hesitated. She'd not come across one during her surveys of the property. Venturing out to find it would mean leaving Adelina alone in that vulnerable state. Could she risk it?

"Damn it." She had to.

THE MOON DID not rise that night.

And neither did Adelina. Nor anyone else.

Sofía roamed the empty halls of the hotel after the sun had set, waiting for the Flor de Lis's guests to step out through those doors. To fill the silence with their gossip, and the air with their offensive body odors and fragrant powders meant to conceal them. Yet, nothing stirred within those walls, save for the shadows under the flickering glow of her lamp.

Hours after she set out on her quest for medical supplies, she was still prowling the corridors with a hunter's unyielding focus. Returning empty-handed to sit and wait and twiddle her thumbs as Adelina lay comatose was *not* an option.

As the night went on, however, she became less and less certain her friend's condition could be remedied with a pill and a tonic. Modern medicine was not exactly equipped to handle whatever was happening on this gods-cursed island where time blurred, pleasures twisted into nightmares, and guests slumbered as though a bruja had cast a spell upon them.

So you believe in sorcery now? Sofía chided herself. The obvious explanation was what she'd predicted all along: there was something in the food or the wine, which was why, out of hundreds of guests, she alone was awake. And would remain so, provided she continue to avoid all prepared meals and drinks.

It was the kind of diagnosis Sofía liked best, one that prescribed a simple remedy to a not-so-simple problem, like those advertisements in the penny press that promised pearly teeth, clear skin, and a head full of luscious hair, all in an eight-ounce panacea.

Right, she thought to herself, *because that tends to work out so splendidly.* She swept the doubt aside like she did the kerosene fumes wafting from the lamp in her hand.

As she walked, she tried the lock on every guest room she passed. Not one of them budged, and when she held an ear to the doors, all she picked up on were the creaks and groans of an old building, and the occasional snoring. Knocking did not help, nor did shouting—she had the sore throat to prove it.

It was all feeling a little too close to that recurring dream of hers for comfort. It made her hesitant to look down, worried she'd find her gown weeping red, the gaps under the doors spilling blood thick as treacle.

On the third floor of the eastern wing, Sofía slowed as she approached Fátima's door, the glossy wood etched with a trailing bushel of sky flowers. Sofía called to her, fist beating at the door until her knuckles grew sore. She knew the girl would not answer, but hadn't she earned her right to one small act of futility? Most people made on average four or five of those a day.

"You were right, Fátima." She leaned her head against the door. She was so, *so* tired. "Carnaval is a dream, a beautiful, monstrous dream I cannot seem to wake from. Ironic, no? When it is only I who is not sleeping . . ." Laughter rattled weakly inside her chest. There was something grave about the sound, like a cough that portends illness.

At last, exhaustion dragged Sofía to the floor, and she let it, too powerless to fight it. She sat there with her back pressed against the door, waiting for tears that never came.

SOFÍA ADDED THE carrots to the pot and stirred them over a candle flame. In her free hand, she held the map of Isla Bestia, the one she'd scavenged from the storage room downstairs. It was a century old, ripped in one corner and stained yellow with age. The ink, at least, was mostly legible.

Even from a bird's-eye view, the island resembled a giant sea monster. Its tail, which the Flor de Lis sat upon, was the most thoroughly documented area on the map, while the monster's head was barely explored. Surely that was no longer the case after a hundred years. Lands rich in metals and minerals never remained uncharted for long.

Sofía traced the map eastward, toward the head. Drawn across it was a range of mountains, peaked like the spiny scales of an iguana. From it flowed the rivers that ran west. There were finer lines drawn between them. At first, Sofía thought the ink had simply faded, but as she looked closer she noticed the tiny arrows pointing east. That made no sense though—the rivers flowed downhill, toward the tail of the island.

She set down her pot, peering closer at the map.

These were not just *any* rivers, she realized, they were subterranean waterways. Of course, she had sailed one herself the night she hallucinated a beast made of stars.

Incorrectly, she'd assumed that vein emptied out into the ocean. But if the map was right . . . it actually led back east, toward the island's head. It would explain how the carnavaleros were moving all those props and set pieces in and out each day. They were obviously not being stored onsite, as there was no space large enough for all of them, and transporting such a cargo by ground when there were no roads would have been a logistical nightmare. By water, their travel time would be cut in half—more, if the westerly winds were favorable.

Her heartbeat quickened. This could be it, their way past the unseen barrier that kept them bound to Carnaval. Their ticket out of the Flor de Lis.

"Adelina." Sofía waved the map toward the bed, where her friend still slept. "I might have figured a way out of this place. Well, not *figured*, exactly . . . but it's a start. A promising one." Her soup forgotten, she went to Adelina's writing desk and cleared away the deck of cards, the jars of cosmetics, the balled-up silk stockings still clipped to their suspenders.

With the map in hand and a plan in mind, she readied her pen, cracked open her journal, and got to writing.

ACTO IV

WE WATCH HER, the one in red.

We lie beside her when she sleeps—fitful and restless—and trail her steps when she wakes. We learn the shape and measure of her breaths, the clean strokes of her pen, the stutter of her heartbeat when she feels us near. Like a cold touch along her neck, a phantom presence beckoning her into the shadows, calling for her, though we have no voice with which to speak.

We are weak. Languid under the heat of the sun, and when it sets, there is no moonlight to restore us, to return to us the words that will reach her. All there is to do is wait. For the days to pass, and the nights to settle. For the sky to wear silver and black again.

But when at last the strength reignites in our veins . . .

Something *else* awakens with it.

CHAPTER 12

Curses come in many forms. Some come wrapped in thorns and warts, steeped in poison, shaped like toads. Others are packaged under a silken bow, perfumed and handsomely adorned.

—Chronicler

SOFÍA BOLTED UPRIGHT, startled awake by the slam of a door.

Beside her, the bed lay empty. Her sleep-heavy eyes roved over the room, searching for that familiar face and finding only traces of her: gowns piled on the floor, hair rags scattered across the vanity, a fresh spritz of jasmine scenting the air.

Sofía lurched off the bed and dashed out into the hall, dressed in only her shift. Soon as she was through the door, she slammed into something. Some*one*, an older gentleman with wisps of hair fanning outward like moth wings. He dusted the front of his jacket, as if she'd sullied it, and mumbled something about "incompetent criadas."

Stunned silent, all Sofía could do was stare.

Awake. They are all awake . . .

Patrons pushed past her on their way to breakfast. Others congregated around smoky sitting rooms with doors opened wide in invitation. A few side-eyed Sofía, appearing far more scandalized by her maskless face than her state of undress.

She stared back, struck by the sight of them walking about without a care. They laughed easily, drank heartily. Did they not know what was done to them? For the last three days, they had been in a comatose state, completely unresponsive. There should have been mass panic, crowds rallying against their captors, hundreds fleeing to the coast.

Wrong. It was all wrong.

With shaky steps, Sofía backed up into the room and shoved the door closed.

Her fingers poised like claws over the wood, raking down until she'd strung her thoughts back into coherence. She could feel her mind unspooling like knotted clumps of twine, tangling to the point she could not tell where reality ended and lies began, until . . .

Until she realized how *familiar* that felt.

This was what this place did—turned your mind against you, stuffed you up with drink and dreams and doubt, so you'd blame the strangeness on your own intoxication.

She rushed to Adelina's bed, clinging to the truths before they could again dissolve like sugar in water. There, beneath the pillow cover, was a boxy lump just slightly bigger than her hand. She ripped her journal free, flipped it open to the earmarked page, and read.

SHIPS FLEW THROUGH the night.

Sofía had been searching Adelina's usual haunts in the Flor de Lis when she first spotted them beyond a window. They hovered over Carnaval on hot air balloons, navigating without seas or sails, just billowing clouds of ivory silk. Surely, Adelina would be out there, marveling up at them. She was not so lost as to choose her games over this gravity-defying spectacle. That was what Sofía kept telling herself as she scoured the grounds and skies, hoping that the next place her gaze landed on would prove her right. *Salt and sea*s, she could not bear being wrong . . .

She stared up at the ships. At the fires that lit them from within like steady bursts of lightning, and the thick cords of netting that wrapped around the balloons, securing them to the fleet. The vessels were built like the galleons from history books, the ones that brought war and disease onto Etérea's shores. Their hulls were of shining oak, decked with windows and cannons and gilt, and they floated at different altitudes. Some closer to the ground than others, and each connected via a series of rope bridges and rigging. Smaller passenger vessels were docked, collecting guests and ferrying them up to the larger aerostats above.

Sofía startled sideways as, out of nowhere, geysers of water shot upward through the luminous fog, rising with an explosive bang. The display was met with a gleeful chorus of shouts and laughter as those nearest the geysers rushed to avoid the splash. The spray caught Sofía across the cheek, a swift shock of cold to the skin.

BOOM! The night turned crimson under the flares of pyrotechnics, and just as all eyes turned skyward, a shadow burst forth from one of the cannons. It was a *person*, their body launched into a nearby airship in a blast of smoke and red luminescence. Soon, others followed like meteors in crimson leotards, shooting straight across from one floating ship to the next.

Guilt coiled in Sofía's belly. She had peeked behind the curtain of Carnaval, seen the rot under the luster, and still she could not tear her gaze away. After days of worrying and pacing, dreading Adelina would never wake, the last thing she wanted to feel was wonder. Yet feel it, she did. It was all tangled up with the horror that had taken root inside her, choking the life out of it like an invasive weed.

A vejigante in a bone-white garment and a mask as red as fresh blood offered Sofía a drink, and she froze, recalling the sight of another vejigante, lifeless as a doll upon the bed, and the sudden terror that'd consumed her when her eyes fell upon them. After, she'd been too shaken to return to the servants' quarters. *Tomorrow*, she'd promised herself, believing the fear would be vanquished by morning, the way the light unmakes all that haunts the dark—rendering ordinary all the shadows and creaks that rule the night. Then tomorrow came and the fear did not vanish with it. If anything, it dug its claws deeper, carving into her mind visions of vejigantes, their masks falling to reveal the rotting, faceless things hidden underneath.

Shame gnawed at Sofía's conscience. Odds were the vejigantes were just as trapped as she was, forced to labor for whatever madman had engineered this glamorous snare.

But . . . what if instead of cogs in a machine, they were the hands that turned it? That was the thought that always stopped her from enlisting their help. Could she risk placing her trust in the wrong person? She remembered how guarded Madame Anani had been, how reluctant she was to divulge information, as though fearing someone might overhear.

Sofía might not fully understand the what or why or how of Carnaval, but she knew that it was designed to keep them in, and no cage was ever made with good intentions. It stood to reason that whoever the architects of it were could very well be hiding in plain sight. Given all she'd seen thus far, it was no stretch of the imagination to assume informants may be listening, watching, even now. If they realized what she knew, what she'd witnessed in the three days she alone lay awake, she would never break free from this trap.

In the end, caution won out. Sofía accepted the drink with a tight smile and dumped its contents into the first flower bed she passed. Her fingers absently twirled the empty goblet by the stem as she ventured on in search of that familiar dove-winged mask. In the background, her mind was busy working out a possible means of escape, taking note of how many managed the airships, how many sets of eyes and ears she would have to bypass for a small chance at freedom.

A silver snake glinted at the corner of Sofía's eye.

She spun fast and swept her gaze through the fog. It came alight with disorienting flares of red, and in between those flashes she saw visions of masks and teeth, the flutter of silk fans, the glint of precious metals as they caught the gleam of cannon flares. Then . . .

Salt-and-pepper hair.

Snake eyes that glowed a poison green.

A smile better suited to an outlaw than a gentleman.

By the time Sofía registered the sight, her body was already moving, elbowing its way through clumps of spectators. Someone bumped into her side, spilling their drink down the length of her dress, and in the seconds it took her to recover, the figure in the snake mask vanished. She dove into the fog anyway, searching left and right for silver fangs and gemstone eyes, but amid the crush of the crowd, the flares of the cannons, the blasts of frigid water, and the looming shadows of the ships above, she did not stand a chance. It'd have been easier to find an honest man among thieves than a masked one in this ruckus.

Sofía was about to double back, retrace her footsteps, when the scent of tobacco hit her.

Not just any scent. *The* scent—the one that clung to her mother's skin and hair even after the rain came down and washed the rest of the world clean.

"Vicente."

He turned, pipe in hand, and smiled crookedly at Sofía. "By the tone of your voice, I either owe you money or I've insulted your husband."

. . . Insulted my—? "What?"

"Which one is it then?" Vicente bit the pipe between his teeth and reached inside his jacket, a hideous thing of mustardy silk, to extract a small leather purse. "How much to make whatever this is go away?"

Understanding came slowly. "Salt and seas . . . what did they do to you, Vicente?"

One eyebrow peeked above his snake mask, arched in a question.

In two strides, she closed the distance between them. "Read it." She showed him her hand, a palimpsest of the same message rewritten in overlapping tangles of scabs and scars.

His eyes, which had been tight with suspicion, softened a fraction. "Some brute do this to you?"

"*I* did this to me, but that's not the point. Read it."

"'Look up . . .'? What, this one of them tricks? I look away and you slug me in the chin?"

She curled her fingers into her palm. "These were your last words to me before I watched you be dragged away and vanished. You said the sky was wrong."

"Did I now?" Vicente snorted, clearly taking none of what she said seriously. "Must have been drunk off my wits again."

"No, just belligerent. You shoved the concierge, stole the guest registry, and started a fire in the lobby." Sofía ticked each item off on a finger, annoyed by how little the news seemed to trouble him.

"Hmm."

"'Hmm,' is that all you have to say? Mierda, Vicente. You've been missing for . . . well, I do not exactly know how long. A fortnight, at least? Probably longer."

He nodded indulgently, taking another slow puff of his pipe. "Here's the thing, lass. I don't know you, and honestly? I've no idea what the bleeding hells you're on about. Why would—"

"Look up." She cut him off. "Look at the sky just once. If nothing seems off, I promise to leave you be."

"Bah, if it'll get ya to bug off, then I'll take a gander." Vicente tilted his head back, peering through the thinning veil of fog to the expanse of stars beyond it. His gaze swept the night, cursorily at first, making it clear he was merely entertaining her silly conspiracy, then with purpose. Had she not been watching him so closely, she might have missed the subtle way his eyes tensed at the corners. "That . . . No, that can't be right."

He rummaged through his jacket and produced a small, round object encased in brass. A compass, Sofía realized. He popped the lid open and walked a wide circle around her, pausing at varying points to draw a finger across the stars like he was connecting constellations. He did this three times, growing more visibly unsettled the longer he studied the skies.

"What do you see?" Sofía asked, growing impatient.

He shoved his mask up over his head and rubbed his eyes with the pads of his fingers. Unmasked, his face was in some ways different from how she imagined it, and in other ways, exactly the same. He had a scar on one cheekbone the length of a fingernail, and a prominent nose that had been broken at least once. It was not a conventionally handsome face by any measure, but it was one that wore its hardships honestly, and for that she found it strangely beautiful.

"I—I don't know," he admitted. "This . . . this doesn't make any damn sense . . . I've been here two months at most."

Sofía knew where this was leading, had known it from the moment he planted that dangerous truth in her mind the last time they met. "The sky's telling you differently though."

"If I'm right, and by the bleeding saints let's pray I'm not, we're two months away from year's end. Which is impossible, my ship made land on the first day of spring. Surely, I've made some kind of mistake . . . I'm reading the stars wrong, I—"

"Two months from year's end?" Sofía shook her head, rejecting the possibility even as she sensed the truth of it. "That would mean . . ."

I've been here for six *months.*

Shock rippled through her, made more visceral by the ground-rattling bang that reverberated above them. Around her, the laughter and chatter and cheering dulled to mere background noise, eclipsed by the high-pitched ringing in her ears, the rapid cycling of her thoughts. *Six-months-six-months-six-months-six-months-six-months-six-months-six-months-six-months-six-months-six-months-six-months-six-months—*

Distantly, Sofía noticed Vicente sinking to the ground, sitting with his mask thrown over his head and his face in his hands. She could not save him from this, no more than a person drowning could save another. At best, they would sink together.

Before she knew it, she was walking, her feet moving with intention even as her mind scattered in every direction. She felt . . . displaced, estranged from her own body as she ran up the steps of the Flor de Lis, away from the fog, and the clamor, and the sky full of ships. As she ran, a single thought pulsed bright and clear within her.

Tonight. We leave tonight.

MUSIC DRIFTED FROM a pianoforte, the notes long and melancholy, clashing with the frenzied beats of Carnaval outside. Sofía followed the sound to a lounge tiled wall-to-wall in talavera porcelain, elegantly furnished with backless divans and chaises draped with men and women in varying states of fashionable repose. A stained glass skylight cast patterns onto a central table surrounded by a ring of rapt spectators.

On one of those seats sat a woman in a vermilion gown, the cut of it bold and its color a sharp deviation from her usual softer palettes. Somewhere deep down, Sofía had always known she'd find her there. This version of Adelina, as much as it gutted Sofía to admit it, was not the kind to look at the sky, and wonder.

Sofía marched through the charcoal haze of woodsy smoke. Her entrance caused something of a stir, her urgency a sacrilege to this temple of idle gods. She drew even more attention to herself when she neared the cards table and began shoving her way through the clutter of onlookers, inciting objections from every lady and lord she forced aside.

Adelina, oblivious to the shift in the air, did not glance up from her cards until Sofía was at the table. "Sof—"

"Get up." The brief jolt of relief she felt at seeing her friend, healthy and awake, was superseded by the harsh reality awaiting them. "We're leaving." She did not give Adelina a chance to protest—and she *would* have protested—before hauling her off the seat.

Whispers followed them through the lounge and out the set of double doors. Adelina dragged behind, her heels scraping the floor.

"S-Sofía! Stop, *stop!*" She forced her elbow free from Sofía's grip. "What are you *doing?*"

"Saving you."

"From what? A bad hand?" She waggled the cards still clutched between her fingers.

Sofía cast an uneasy glance down each end of the hall, reluctant to have this conversation so out in the open. There was no telling who might be listening in. "Let's go to our rooms first. I'll explain when we're there."

Adelina jerked her arm back before Sofía could take ahold of it. "Can this wait? I've a game to finish."

"Devils burn me. Can you quit thinking about your games for once?" In a rare surge of frustration, Sofía ripped the cards from her fingers. They fell to the floor in a flutter of black, red, and gold. "This insipid obsession of yours has gotten out of ha—" She flinched at her own words, biting down hard on her tongue before she could make an even bigger mess of things.

"No, go on." Adelina locked arms across her chest, drawing a barrier between herself and Sofía. "Tell me how you really feel for once."

"Never mind that, I . . . I meant nothing by it."

"Liar. You've never said a damn word you did not mean."

Sofía pressed both fists against her forehead, knuckles digging into her brow bone. "Can we please not do this? I've no wish to argue, not now and certainly not with you."

"Right, because gods forbid we ever argue. Let's just mince our words and talk circles around what we actually want to say." She bent to pick the fallen cards from the floor, gathering each one between clenched fingers. "At any rate, I should count this as progress. This is more honesty than you've offered me in all the years we've known each other. It'd be presumptuous of me to expect anything more."

"You want honesty?" The words tumbled out of Sofía's mouth. She tried to hold them in, pin them tight between her teeth, but they kept on coming. Kept on spilling. "Then shall I confess I've scarcely seen you since you fell into your games? That you play like a woman bewitched? I am sick with worry, watching you reach for your cards night after night. How is this any different from the way your mamá reaches for her sleeping tonics?"

Hurt flashed across Adelina's eyes.

"No, Adelina. I—" Regret seared through Sofía. "I didn't—"

"Yes, you did." She retreated a step, putting distance between them. "But that's my fault, I reckon. I asked for your candor, I just . . . didn't imagine it cutting quite this deep."

In a last desperate attempt to stop her from leaving, Sofía grabbed for her wrist.

"Come with me, please. This place, it's . . . it's messing with our heads. You feel it too, don't you? If we stay here any longer, we will not leave the same as we came in." Eyes squeezing tight, she appended, "If we ever leave at all."

Adelina's eyes widened. "Is *that* what this is?" The news seemed to temporarily detract from the wound Sofía inflicted. "You mean to leave?"

"I have to," she said. "*We* have to."

"When?"

"Tonight."

Adelina's gaze strayed longingly toward the room where the cards, the coins, and the victories lay waiting. "But we only just got here . . ."

"If only that were true." A sound too haggard and worn to be described as laughter escaped Sofía's lips. "Do you even remember why we're here?" She could not recall the last time Adelina spoke of her father. Truthfully, she seemed to have forgotten she even had one. "Or do you actually believe we came all this way just to—"

Steps echoed down the hall, and two servers in crimson masks came into view.

Doomed scenarios flitted through Sofía's thoughts. The vejigantes dragging her away as they had Vicente, pushing a vial to her lips, forcing her to drink until her legs grew heavy and her mind pliant. And when they had raked her memory clean, they would empty her suite of the secrets she pressed between pages, the trail of breadcrumbs she left for herself to find.

Sofía held her breath as the vejigantes approached and did not release it until they vanished into the lounge. Then instinct took over—instincts she assumed had atrophied before stepping foot on this island, if she were ever in possession of them at all—and she sprang into action, her body poised toward survival like a rifle aimed to fire.

We'll go to our rooms first, Sofía thought as she made off with Adelina in tow. *Pack the journal, a practical change of clothes, and whatever essentials we can carry. A satchel would be too obvious, but if I'm quick, I could sew some pockets into our petticoats. Yes, that could—*

Mired in the details of her escape plan, she grew insensate to her surroundings. Only when Adelina tore her hand away did she finally come to, and by that point, they were almost at the stairs.

Sofía pivoted to face her.

"I am not going anywhere," Adelina said, massaging the fingers Sofía had gripped between her own. "And I would appreciate it if you stopped pulling me about like a hound on a leash."

Mother of Waters, give me the strength not to throttle her . . . "You realize what you're asking of me? To go, and leave you behind?"

"You've done it once already. Why should this time be any different?"

And there it was, the wound festering between them. There since the night Sofía packed her belongings and left but a note. She could have tended to it that night at the pier, when the wound was still fresh, but to do so required the courage to face the damage she'd done and the skills to fix it. She had neither.

With a smile and a quip, they'd haphazardly bandaged the hurt over, like every other nick and cut they had ever inflicted upon one another. Staunching the bleeding, but not the infection setting in. That was the way of things for them, skirting around any and all unpleasantness the way others might sidestep a bit of horse muck on the road. How else did a friendship like theirs stay afloat, when a wobbly piece of driftwood was all that held it above water? Any sudden movement could upset that precarious balance, so they'd learned to ride the waves. To endure the slap of cold, the stinging salt, the dangerous surge of the high tide, because when the surf was low and the sun bright, that rickety slab of solid ground was the only safe place they knew.

But no longer.

With those words, Adelina tipped the fragile thing they balanced on.

"You *selfish* girl." Tears burned in Sofía's eyes. "Do you know why I left?"

Adelina balled her hands into fists, her own eyes shining.

"Do you think it was easy? Two years it took me. Two. Years. Enduring your mother's slights, my brother's absence, the constant reminders of who I'd always be. I left so I could *live*, Adelina. I stayed . . . because you are my heart." Her sister despite all the reasons she shouldn't be. "But go on, stand there and shame me for leaving. Tell me that the six hundred days I chose you over my own blood meant nothing. Tell me I was wrong to want a life away from the girl who once *owned* me."

Adelina lurched back. "Saints damn me if I ever once thought of you as my . . . my property. Gods, I feel queasy even saying it."

"Was I not, Adelina? Your mamá, did she not give me to you?"

"N-no. I mean, *yes*, she did. But, it wasn't—" She clutched an arm to her stomach, folding a little into herself. "We played together, you and I. We read books, and snuck sweet rolls from the kitchens, and put on puppet shows in the gardens. Mamá . . . Papá, they might have seen you as *that*, but to me . . . to me you were always just . . . Sofía."

"And yet when you slept, I remained awake to do my day's work. The work I left unfinished because you'd wanted to play and read and stir up trouble. Because *you* were a cherished daughter, free of burdens and care, and did not understand that the dresses you wore, someone had to iron. The hem you tore climbing up the tree? Someone had to mend. My duties did not go away by virtue of our friendship, nor did Doña Elena once pardon my mishaps because of your attachment to me.

"By the time you woke, refreshed and ready for another morning of leisure, I had already washed and dressed, fetched the water for your bath and boiled it to the perfect temperature. And when I brought your breakfast tray, I prayed to gods that weren't mine that you would not care much for the food that morning, because your scraps were the only meal I'd have for hours." Sofía stopped, wiping roughly at the tears on her cheeks.

"You caught on some years after, when you saw me scarfing down your leftovers out in the hallway. I must have looked desperate, for ever since you left exactly half your meal untouched. I waited for you to ask, but the questions . . . they never came. Not about why I was so hungry . . . or why I so often came back from your mamá's apartments with a limp, or a bloody gash on my hands. Did you actually think me so clumsy that I'd cut myself on broken crockery every other week?"

Tears tracked kohl down Adelina's cheeks and she looked down, ashamed. "I never meant to hurt you, Sofía. I was just . . . I was just a child."

"I know." Of course she knew. "But so was I."

Uncorked, the resentment and pain Sofía had pressurized into a bottle surged out into the open. Her body was a stranger to this, untrained to bear so much emotion. From the tremor of her bones and the weakness of her knees, she knew that a minute more of this would undo her. Break her limb by limb.

Adelina appeared to fare no better. She staggered, catching herself on the wall with a shaking hand. "I told myself, over and over, that I was better than *them*. But . . . I am no different, am I?" Her voice broke with the admission. "You were right to leave me, Sofía. I see that now . . . If I could, I'd leave me too."

Sofía was too deeply buried in her own pain to spare Adelina hers. So when Adelina left, she did not call after her, did not try to stop her. When the click of her heels vanished down the hall, Sofía did not follow.

Tonight, the storms roaring through Sofía drowned out the voice that begged, *Go after her!* Tomorrow, she might finally hear it, once the winds had settled and the rains had passed.

Tomorrow, she might even remember she loved her.

CHAPTER 13

*In blood and sand their lives were written.
Alas, there came the wave.*

—Chronicler

ON THE THIRD KNOCK, the door swung open.

"I need your help," Sofía said.

Fátima stood at the doorway, wearing a rumpled nightgown and a headful of knotted rags—a few unraveling into springy curls. Her face was blotchy and bare, and without her usual layers of cosmetics, she looked even younger. *Damn it all, she's a child . . .* Sofía had naively presumed her to be about sixteen, but she could not have been more than a year or two into womanhood. Yet they'd made her a bride.

The girl wiped at the corners of her eyes, as though she'd been crying. "What do you need?"

"A pair of your husband's trousers, a vest, and an evening coat, to start. Something not too eye-catching," Sofía said. "He's about as tall as I am, I would imagine?" Most Hisperian men were, on average. "Give or take an inch or two?"

"Uh . . ." She blinked. "Yeees?"

"Good. That should do nicely then."

Looking utterly mystified, Fátima stepped aside to let Sofía in.

"*Oh.* Before I forget." She spun to face the girl. "How do you feel about heights?"

SOFÍA'S HANDS GRIPPED the ropes, the bridge swaying beneath her. From that high up, the solarium looked like a bell jar, the patrons roaming the misty gardens far below like bright feathered insects. If she shut an eye, she could hold them in the pinch of her thumb and forefinger.

Her gloved palms slid farther up the handholds, the rope chafing slightly against the words broken into the skin. As she climbed the wooden slats to the next ship, a nearby vessel blew a flare from one of its prop cannons. The flash, a crimson starburst, bloomed against the backdrop of night, leaving ghostly embers in her vision and a sudden gust of sweltering air. She lowered the brim of her borrowed top hat over her forehead, careful to keep her locks tucked away under its bulk.

The bridge creaked as she pulled herself onto the next deck over, boots squeaking against the polished wood. Though not as mighty in size as the steamer that had carried her across the sea, its hulk was impressive. Presumptuous, even. *See?* It seemed to say. *As I conquered your oceans, I conquer your skies.*

It had no equal either. Of all the ships to swim the stars above Isla Bestia, it was the largest. Holding it aloft were three balloons twice its height and just as wide. Flames lit their moon-pale silk like paper lanterns, and Sofía shivered with pleasure as the heat absorbed into her tailcoat, thawing the ice in her bones.

While her decision to change into menswear had nothing to do with the crisp, high-altitude weather, she was relieved to be wrapped in cottons and wools. As perfect as her scarlet dress was for the tropical heat, it would've offered little more protection against the chill than her underthings. Indeed, the women she spied roaming the flying ship were quivering in their summer fabrics.

A sudden shout, like a war cry, rose above the howl of the wind. Sofía looked up, just as rows of performers in baggy trousers and belted tunics climbed over the railing. They perched there only long enough to call attention to themselves, and once all eyes were on them, they plunged over the edge.

The deck lurched with the motion, and everyone on it rushed to peer over the sides.

To Sofía's great relief, the carnavaleros had not plummeted to their doom. They swung in and out of view, suspended upon ropes tied like nooses around wrists and ankles, their bodies gliding out from under the hull in coordinated synchrony. On the ship across, figures in elegant naval garbs, complete with long vermillion coats and rows of shiny gold buttons, climbed the rigging. They too leapt in unison, gripping the ropes with one hand and their swords with another.

A mock battle erupted in midair, both parties brandishing weapons, their sword points nearly touching as they arched across the divide like pendulums. Back and forth they went, their combat a dance, their shouts a song scored by a symphony of cannon blasts, incoherent exclamations, and the furious strum of guitars.

An arm hooked around the crook of Sofía's elbow.

"Find anything?" she asked Fátima, her eyes fixed on the daring performance before her. So far above everything, and without a safety net to break the fall, if anyone were to slip the rope or slightly miscalculate a swing, the cost of that error would be certain death—a morbid possibility that kept every observer enthralled.

"There are rooms belowdecks. Plenty of spots to hide in too, barrels and treasure chests and shadowed alcoves," said Fátima. "Problem is, they only let a few patrons in at a time—to keep the weight even, is what they said. A doorkeeper's posted at the entrance to track everyone going in and out."

"That . . . that might actually work in my favor. Any carnavaleros inside? Servers, performers?"

Fátima opened her mouth to respond, then hesitated. "I . . . no. At least, I think not." Her head angled in concentration. "You'd reckon I would remember, seeing as I was only just— *Oh!*" She clapped her hands together. "Did you see that flip? Saints, my heart nearly stopped."

No, Sofía was no longer watching the performers tempt the gods with their tricks, she was watching Fátima's awareness melt off like rouge on a hot day. *No, not you too . . .* The girl's memories were eroding before her very eyes, the sharpness of them being smoothed and rounded like river stones by Carnaval's corrosive touch.

"Your sketchbook, Fátima. Do you have it with you?"

"Always," she said, and tugged it out of her reticule.

Sofía opened it to a blank page and set it back on the girl's hands, along with a freshly sharpened stick of charcoal. "Here. Draw what you saw."

The fog did not lift from Fátima's eyes, nor did her attention once stray from the performance, but her hands moved independently of her, capturing all that eluded her awareness in swift, bold strokes, as though her fingers held the memories her mind could not. On the first page, she drew men and women dancing, smiling wide. On the next, a long, dark passage rendered at a sharp, sideways angle. The page after that was a solid canvas of black, with no other feature Sofía could discern.

It was the last sketch that most intrigued her. She watched the shapes coalesce into the image of a room. An ornate desk. A chest, filled to the brim with jewels and gold.

"This—" Sofía tapped a finger against the page "—I can work with this."

Fátima finally glanced down at the sketch, and frowned. Her finger ran along the lines of it with that same hazy recognition Sofía had felt upon discovering the writing on her skin, at once familiar and so acutely foreign. It was the worst kind of betrayal, the one done onto the self. How hostile and unsafe her own body had felt to her then.

The girl smiled to cover her unease, yet it did not escape Sofía the way her hands trembled as they stowed the sketchbook away. She felt a sudden, fierce protectiveness of the child. If she'd been certain of what awaited her beyond this dark splendor, she would have taken the girl with her. But safety was a hope, not a promise. Here, the threat was insidious, yes, but not fatal. At least, it did not appear to be . . .

Out there in the wilderness, however, the threats were of a more practical nature. Predators. Dehydration. Dengue fever. Fátima was strong in ways Sofía had just begun to uncover, but the reality was she had lived a sheltered life. One of regularly scheduled meals, consummate idleness, and modern conveniences.

Leaving her here was risky, but bringing her along could be a death sentence.

Worried she might blurt it all out, Sofía said the first thing that came to mind. "I knew a pirate . . . once."

"Oh?" Fátima sounded reasonably perplexed by the new direction of their conversation. "Were they—" she motioned toward the performers "—this acrobatic?"

Sofía laughed—a rare, true laugh—that strained some seldom-used muscle in her chest. "Skies and stars above, no. He was many things alright, but no one would ever have accused him of being nimble." He came to the hacienda the summer of Sofía's eleventh year, rolled in on the same rusted, stinking cage that had brought her and Sol years earlier. He had a raggedy beard, shoulders wide as an eagle's wingspan, and a voice that life at sea had honed into a permanent bellow. It was only when he sang shanties to the oxen that drew the carts, or told tales of adventure and heroism to the children, that it ever softened.

It was at the age of eight, during a raid of the Alkebulan Isles, that he was captured and placed on a slave ship bound for the Gilded Sea. Along their journey, pirates had commandeered the vessel, taken its loot, and freed the captives. Some found passage back to their homes. Others, like him, joined the motley crew of *El Cofresí*. Life amid the waves was not an easy one, he said, but it was better than a life spent bowing and scraping at a master's feet.

As a child, Sofía had envied that freedom, longing for the idealistic existence he told of in his stories, the justice and order the crew imparted through their codes and systems: the fair division of spoils, the plundering from the rich to give to the poor, the liberation of ships that carried men, women, and children as their cargo.

She had never been one for dreaming, yet for a little while she dreamt.

When he escaped from the hacienda, he took more than a dozen slaves with him. Half returned a week later, shoulders slumped and heads bent. Eyes haunted.

Sofía soon stopped dreaming.

As Fátima appeared to be waiting for her to elaborate, Sofía said, "He was a good storyteller. Ghastly singer."

It was in that precise moment that the ticking in her coat pocket became a metallic buzz. She pulled the watch into the open—about an hour to sunrise.

"It's time." Sofía drew Fátima by the arm. "For this next part, you will need to lose your wedding band."

The girl listened and nodded shakily, subtly slipping off her ring and tucking it into the small pouch on her bodice. "And you're certain this will work?"

"About as certain as I am that this ship will not crash under our weight. Which is to say, not very. What I *am* certain of is that your saints, dear girl, have blessed you with a face that eschews all suspicion. You could plunge a knife straight through the chest of a man and he'd die wondering who did it."

Another might have thought the analogy tactless, but Fátima's cheeks puffed like she was holding in laughter.

"Point is, you've nothing to worry about." Sofía paused under the fire-warmed cavity of the central balloon, behind a group of women seeking shelter from the cold. She angled herself slightly toward the ship's stern, scouting the door leading belowdecks.

"At least tell me what all this is about then." Fátima gestured vaguely at the ship, the door, the disguise Sofía donned, plucked from her own husband's armoire.

"My brother," she said, owing the girl at least that truth. "Five years ago, he left for Carnaval and never came back. I'm . . . trying to find out what happened to him."

Though Sofía stared at a point in the distance as she spoke, sparing herself the pitying look that typically followed such a confession, she heard Fátima's voice soften with compassion. "And you believe this will get you closer to an answer?"

"Assuming it all goes well."

"If it doesn't, what then?"

"Then I need you to find Adelina and give her this." Sofía pulled out a cream envelope from her inner jacket pocket. Folded inside it were copies of her last journal entries and a letter explaining where she had gone and why. An identical envelope lay inside Adelina's trinket box. Another beneath her vanity tray. This one was just insurance.

Fátima blanched with worry. "Sofía . . ." She clutched the envelope to her chest. "What are you getting yourself into?"

"Trouble." The real question was whether she could get herself out. "Come on, we've got an opening."

They made their way separately to the back of the ship. Fátima first, Sofía second, strolling some distance behind. Patrons queued up by the door, eager to explore the entertainment underdeck, as though floating above the earth while sailors and pirates fought for their claim of the skies was not sufficiently diverting.

As planned, Fátima cut through the line, dashing straight for the doorkeeper. Sofía, for her part, watched the scene unfold while pretending to inspect a scuff on her boot.

"Ayuda, señora." Fátima huffed and puffed, feigning breathlessness. The delivery needed considerable work, but all in all, it accomplished what it was meant to. "My wedding band, it's slid between the floorboards over there. Please, *oh please*, come help."

The doorkeeper, with an indifference that belied her words, said, "Has it now? That's unfortunate."

To Sofía's surprise, it was a voice she recognized. When last she'd heard it though, it had belonged to a man in a bat-winged mask.

It couldn't be.

. . . Could it?

The woman wore a sun-gold coat, bone mask, and a plumed tricorne hat. Her dark hair was not tied at the neck, as the man's had been, but hung long and loose past her waist. At her side rested a dagger, and at her hips, a woven belt of crushed shells and precious stones. "Let us hope then that your husband buys you another," she said, her tone decisively final.

Fátima staggered back, startled by the treatment.

Sofía had not accounted for the doorkeeper's dismissal. Luring the woman away from her post should have been the easy part.

This was Carnaval after all, a place of *Sí, señorita*, and *Whatever pleases you, señorita*. A mode of hospitality that, while only for show, was reliably consistent. She could not have predicted such an abrupt departure from the pattern.

Fátima's eyes found Sofía's in the crowd, an urgent plea.

Sofía mimed a *try again* gesture and she made her approach, slinking slowly along the sides, willing herself into wood and wind, a part of the scenery so dreadfully average it would invite no gaze to linger. Her disguise did most of the work, concealing the features that had elsewhere rendered her invisible, yet here made her conspicuous. Too tall, too dark, too female, a combination of qualities that made those around her look. And remember.

Yet, as a man, no one cared to peer too closely at her. In this world, a man was assumed, and so in a way, unremarkable. Add to that a mask that concealed her face from forehead to chin, and she became near impervious to attention.

Still, being who she was, she could not settle for an approximate. She needed full assurance that once she slipped belowdecks, no one would come find her. Devils only knew what might happen if they did.

She paused in her approach, waiting for Fátima to stomp her foot, set her jaw to iron, brandish her wealth and title as a knight wields shield and sword. But the girl had frozen under the doorkeeper's uncompromising stare.

Worse, tears were starting to well in her eyes.

"Mierda." Sofía cursed as she backtracked, her mind already spinning alternate strategies, coiling those loose threads of possibility like a weaver at her loom. She should have known better than to entangle the girl in this madness, but in a rare burst of optimism had convinced herself that the plan would play out as designed, as it always did when it was the tough-as-nails Adelina de Esperanza taking center stage. Fátima was loyal and eager, but she did not devour attention as witchweed devours crops. She angled to it, shy as a bud that'd grown in shade and now sought sunlight.

The threads of *maybes* and *almosts* began unraveling in Sofía's hands, and as she scoured the remaining warps and wefts for the ones that could become a tapestry—a plan—she heard: "Not all things are so *easily* replaceable."

Fátima spoke with a quiver, yet her voice was loud enough for all to hear. She was, to Sofía's utter astoundment, sobbing in earnest now. There was no telling if it was due to the nerves, the doorkeeper's abrasive manner, or if she was simply that immersed in her role. "You may think it no more than a trinket, but to me . . . it's . . . it's everything." Her breathing thinned to a shallow wheeze, growing more rapid with every exhalation.

An act, surely.

It had to be.

Sofía had no time to ponder that as, all of a sudden, the girl was falling. Like a tree before the ax, sans the practiced daintiness of ladies who've mastered the art of politely wriggling out of unwelcome situations. She toppled straight into the doorkeeper, whose arms tensed, jutting out like oars at her side, braced to row her away from that predicament. As Fátima began to slip—for the woman made no attempt to catch her—those in line rushed forward to help.

It was certainly not the distraction Sofía had envisioned, but she grabbed at the chance all the same.

The whole ordeal took just long enough for her to slink through the door and into the dark, damp, creaking deck below.

SOFÍA'S BOOT FELT along the gloom.

She braved a step into the dark, then two, then—

Music found her, the long, scratchy notes of a guitar coiling along the shadows. Light came next, a small flame jarred inside a hanging copper lantern, suffusing the hall with the fatty stink of oil. Another door waited at the end, and with one hand, she pushed it open.

Buttery light flooded the hall, and the music surged clear and bold. The mess deck gleamed with gilt and candlelight, with treasures displayed upon rows of shelves and framed paintings coated in glassy varnish. On one side of the room, a long table was laid out with pans of saffron rice, lobster stews, and seasoned crab meat. A few patrons occupied the seats, scarfing down the fare with such gusto they hardly came up for air. The rest of the deck's occupants were busy dancing to a slow bolero, feet stepping to the sultry beat of guitars and castanets.

Where the music was coming from, however, she could not say. It played loud in her ears as though it'd crawled inside her, its volume unvarying no matter which direction her head angled.

Uneasy, Sofía stepped through the chamber. She resisted the temptation of a meal, the pleasure of a warm room, and as she went, she probed her mind for weaknesses—unexplained gaps in time, wrinkles in the otherwise smooth fabric of her thoughts. It was becoming routine to question her own mind's reliability. Impersonal even, like diagnosing a faulty sewing machine, her troubles tantamount to a loose bobbin and a jammed needle.

Across the deck, dance partners glided in harmony, heads bowing intimately toward one another. Joy tugged their mouths open wide, peeled their lips back from their teeth. They smiled, exuberant.

Eyes flicked to Sofía as she skirted around and between dancers, heading for the door on the opposite side of the mess. She felt their attention hot on the back of her neck and worried they could see the woman under the gentleman's tailcoat, the mestiza behind the mask. What they thought of her was inconsequential, but she'd rather they not think of her at all. Her plan only worked if she was forgotten.

Quickening her pace, she reached the door, pushed her palm to the wood, and—

"*Ayúdanos!*"

Sofía whipped around, searching for whoever had uttered that plea.

Not one face among the dancers and diners wore an expression to match the urgency in that voice. No one even spoke, their mouths were too busy grinning, slurping, and chewing to waste breath on words.

A sudden, sharp awareness cleaved her with a violence. This time, when she looked at the dancers, she noticed the tight stretch of their grins, the unnatural synchronization of their movements. When she came closer, stepping between this foot and that, their eyes followed, straining toward her as they dipped and twirled, clinging fiercely to the sight of her, even as their heads bent in the opposite direction.

She waved a hand between a pair of dancers. Yet their steps did not falter, and neither did their smiles.

The next dancers to brush past her, she hauled apart. Tore the lady from the gentleman's arms and dragged her even as her body jerked toward him—slippers sliding left and right into a box-step, tears gleaming in the cobalt of her eyes. She continued her bolero between the tight tether of Sofía's arms, not missing a beat. The gentleman too went on, his fingers laced around a ghost's, reclining the suggestion of a woman into a low dip.

Sofía released her hold, and the woman went, fit herself to her partner's arms as though they'd never come apart. But their eyes . . . *Mother of Waters*, their eyes held hers, begging.

She backed away, step by step, until her hips struck the edge of the dining table. A glass toppled. Crashed, its contents running over the shining wood, dripping onto the lap of a man who cracked into a lobster tail, splitting the carapace with his nails, biting hungrily into the meat. The butter and juices dripped down his chin, soaked into his scraggly beard.

His free hand stretched across the table, reaching past the dinner napkin to grip a steaming pan of shelled shrimp. He drew the dish toward him, snatched the ladle up with oil-slick fingers, and piled on another heap of food despite his plate already being filled to bursting, his mouth stuffed to its teeth with lobster meat.

Sofía forced her gaze over the rest of the table's occupants, noticing for the first time the desperate wanting on their faces, the restlessness of their grubby fingers as they scooped up another generous serving. They ate like urchins who'd not tasted a proper meal in a fortnight. But these weren't scrawny orphans abandoned to the streets, these were the folk who tossed at them their spare coins. The crop of society that had a fork, spoon, and knife for every dish, a glass for every wine. Who ate delicately, wastefully, because hunger was not suffered among their class, it was *endured*. Borne like the sting of a night cream that burns away unsightly freckles.

Nausea swelled inside Sofia, leaving a trail of heat from her belly all the way to the back of her throat. And still, the spices and herbs tickled her nose. Garlic, rosemary, paprika . . . Warm butter and salted meats . . . Sauces and stews . . . Rice fluffed and seasoned to a perfect shade of sunflower yellow. She took one step back, and another forward, aching toward the salt and fat and warmth, even as her stomach churned, the taste of bile thick on her tongue.

Her arm lashed across the table.

She grabbed a boiled crab—still in its sand-pale shell—from the nearest pan and brought it to her mouth. And froze, her lips an inch from the creature's claw, her teeth poised to bite straight through, carapace and all. She released it, flinging it onto the table like it'd stung her, and in the same movement, pivoted into a run.

The deck tilted, hurling her toward the dancers.

She fought through the tangle of arms and swishing skirts, the stab of heels and swing of hips, and burst through the door at the opposite end. It opened wide for her and no one else, and as it slammed to a close, she saw them. Their eyes still straining toward her.

The door locked into place, swallowing the music, the dappled fire-gold glow, the rich aromas that hollowed out in her a monstrous hunger. Her hands trembled where they pressed to the door, her fingers still sticky with the buttery glaze. Sofia hurried to wipe them on her coat, and the smells clung to the fabric. To *her*. She popped the buttons loose and shook it off, fast as if it were crawling with spiders, letting it fall to the floor and staggering away, down a narrow passage that smelled of damp and sea salt.

The deck swayed beneath her in that distinct rocking motion of a ship upon the waves, rolling over the ocean's swells and drops. She braced herself against the walls, tipping this way, then that, her feet clumsily dancing themselves back to balance. She heard the stretch and groan of wood, the grate of a rusted hinge, the thump of a thick rope hanging from a hook on the wall. And then, she heard the sea. Not the gentle susurration of waves one might hear from a distance, but the drag and slap of water, the thunderous rumble that warned a storm was upon her.

The floor pitched Sofia forward, slamming her into a wooden barrel, hard enough to bruise. She latched on, dug in her nails and rode out the worst of it. In her mind, she saw the flying ship, the white silk of the balloons scored through, flapping in the wind as the vessel plummeted.

Only when the ship seemed beyond saving did the storm finally temper. Mellowing suddenly, like a colicky babe snuggly swaddled. Then, beyond the crash of what was either wind or water, came the creak of iron, the faint notes of a shanty sung by distant voices.

Addled by the violent to-and-fro, Sofia followed the song into a darkened space off to the right. The voices strengthened the deeper she went, unmelded into distinct sounds. Words in another tongue, the cadence of which she recognized. It was the language of Carnaval, passed like a secret between those who dwelt in its shadows and its limelight.

Their singing was no shy canticle for weeping saints, meant for temples of marble and gold, where even whispers echoed like bellows—amplified for the ears of gods afar. *This* song was harsh and haunting. Grief, melted down and reforged into retribution. Its rhythm was unforgiving, the notes striking hard as the pound of fists against the floor, building gradually to something that required time. Patience.

Instead of drums and strings, it was the rattle of chains, the growl of thunder and the seething sea that carried the voices, shoring them up in a way no instrument could.

In the dark, a lightning flash showed the glint of iron swinging like a maiden's braid from the ceiling. The next bolt of light showed an image—an impression, really—of phantom wrists crossed and shackled, their silhouette upon the gloom glowing like moonlight over water.

Darkness fell again then, as a curtain closes over a stage.

Sofía should've been frightened, alone with the ghosts and the shadows and their violent elegy. Yet she felt the singers' rage hot in her blood, their pain setting her own aboil, transmuting it to something that would burn the world with her still in it.

With that came an unexpected sense of clarity. She understood what she had once in the depths of a cave that echoed stories. In a river full of stars, faced with a monster and a question. Those stories . . . those stars . . . this song, were *hers*. An inheritance denied, a history buried, dangling before her now like a piece of fruit for the taking.

Could she take it?

As Sofía moved through the rattling dark, she hummed. She was no singer, and she did not know the phantoms' words, but her voice stuttered along the song's pulsing rhythm, gaining confidence as it went, finding the peaks and dips, losing herself in a language she ached to learn the shape of.

A square of faint light appeared before her, and her hand reached forward, fingertips brushing something solid. A door.

It opened with the turn of the knob.

Sofía let herself linger a moment at the threshold as she whispered her goodbye to the ghosts and the dark, and the song she almost knew.

She stepped through.

Her eyes squinted at the light from the next room, blinking its features into gradual focus. It was the captain's cabin, laid out exactly as Fátima had sketched it, and shaded in warm reds and browns that shone amber under the flickering glow of candles. A sturdy desk strewn with maps and scrolls and stacks of leather-bound books sat at the center, framed by tall, mullioned windows and thick curtains of scarlet velvet. Every shelf, chair, nook and cranny teemed with treasures: wooden chests overflowing with coins and jewels, tables bearing golden busts and fine vases, bolts of rich cloth spilling like streams, statues and framed artwork propped against whatever would hold them.

There was a clatter, then the sound of beads spilling across the room. A shining pearl rolled into sight, bounced against Sofía's boot and wedged itself into a narrow gap between the floorboards. She traced the spill to a corner of a room, where a man hunched over a treasure chest.

"No, no, *no*." He fretted as he bent to pluck the fallen pearls, the string they'd presumably been attached to lying limp on his hand. The man was on his knees then, crawling around like a rat scavenging up the crumbs of someone's supper. He jingled as he moved, his pockets heavy with his loot.

When he pinched the pearl near her shoe, Sofía expected him to notice her, but if he did, he was too preoccupied to look her way. He was flat on the floor now, arm elbow deep beneath a bookshelf.

"Get up, you fool." She kicked at his boot. "Your pockets cannot bear another coin. Take your reward for making it this far and run."

He wriggled his arm deeper and his lips moved, muttering some nonsense to himself that sounded vaguely like *one more, just one more*. Sofía exhausted her charity. There was only so much sympathy she could conjure for a man who had everything, yet wanted more.

She went around the room, throwing open cabinets and crates, looking for the one that would best suit her needs. Over there, near the corner window, a large wooden chest containing a crown, a jeweled goblet, and her weight in gold. She dragged it from the wall with some effort and tipped it forward, letting its wealth spill out. Was any of it real? she wondered as she shoveled out the remaining dregs.

"This should do."

From her waistcoat, she removed her pilfered kitchen knife and used the tip to puncture a hole in a discrete section of the empty chest. The wood splintered around the wound. It looked more organic that way, she thought, like it'd gotten chipped while being carried in.

Now all that was left was for her to climb inside.

Sofía looked sharply away. Toward the windows, at the expanse of black beyond them, then at the man who'd likely never bent his knee to another but now contorted his entire body for a few pearls. Her eyes found Adelina's pocket watch last, gazed through the crack on the glass at the hands warning the arrival of dawn. She made a disgruntled noise as she slid her top hat and mask off, loosened the knot of her bow tie, and began emptying her pockets.

Her hands fell still over the waistcoat.

"Maldición." Her journal was in the jacket she'd shed two rooms back, along with the map of Isla Bestia, the spyglass, and every other damn thing she'd thought to pack. She had the pocket watch, at least, and the knife. It would have to be enough.

The first step was the hardest, that's what she told herself anyway as she climbed into the empty belly of the chest, only to be immediately proven wrong. She lay down on her side and drew her knees toward her chin, fitting herself to that cramped space like a child playing hide-and-seek. Her breathing grew shallow as she looped the watch chain through the hook on the lid where a lock would have been, and pulled.

The lid creaked as it lowered, its hinges stiff with rust.

Sofía drank the sight of freedom above her, gulped the wax and dust in the air as if she was about to plunge herself below waters. Then, as the weight of the lid tipped forward, it slammed shut. Clamping over her like teeth.

Inside, the darkness was broken by a mere thread of brightness where the watch chain kept the lid propped a hair's width open. It was also what would keep it closed, should a light-fingered scavenger come near. With any luck, if a carnavalero happened to tug at it, they would think it jammed. All she had to do was hold on tight, stay still, and keep quiet. Long enough to make it out of there. When the sun rose, she would be sailing down the river and below the earth. And when she emerged, she would be elsewhere. Free from the fog, and the night, and the arbitrary line she could not cross with her consciousness intact.

Sofía pressed herself to the vent on the side, held her lips as close as she dared to the splinters and breathed, timing each inhale and exhale to the tick of the watch. Six in, eight out. Her mind, she kept busy generating a list of words ending in *ción*. It was the kind of task Adelina's old tutors used to assign them, and she found comfort in the simple rules and structure of it. *Porción, canción, localización, segmentación, satisfacción . . .*

Outside, the man continued to forage, and Sofía found she could trace his path along the cabin by the clink of his pockets. He must not have found all his pearls yet, based on how he kept doubling back, huffing in frustration.

Motivación, celebración, murmuración . . .

Was the air getting thinner? The walls of the chest tighter?

Nación, bifurcación, aclamaci—

Her eyes squeezed shut, her lungs rasped in another inhale as her body jerked, arms opening, legs folding in, caught between the competing urge to be smaller, and so large that her bones would break through the cage.

Not a cage, she reminded herself. A treasureless chest, one she placed herself in. One boot after the other, one limb after the next, arranging elbows and knees and ankles and feet like toy blocks, packed neatly into their box. *You're safe*, she insisted, but her lungs would not listen to reason, the ache along her skull would not surrender to her arguments.

Sofía's fingers scraped the sides of the chest, feeling the smooth curve of iron bars instead of the flat, rough wood. They were cold and slick with rain—*rain?*—her cheek pressing into them as another's pressed into her back. The weight of shackled bodies crushed her head to the metal and mud, her ribs to the unbending bars below her.

Sweet gods above, she could not breathe.

She could not breathe.

She could not—

CHAPTER 14

Unmade, they were. Remolded—in the heat of the branding iron, in the foreign names sealed for them in ink.

—Chronicler

TERRIBLE THINGS DID not happen on beautiful days.

At least, that was what Sofía believed once, before she learned the world liked its irony. That its cruelties would not wait for shadows and storms, some ambience properly befitting the shade and texture of its punishments.

On a blue spring morning, a man could buy a life for the price of grain. A family could be ripped apart as mockingbirds sang. Beauty and horror were not mutually exclusive.

It was a lesson that would be drilled into Sofía at every juncture of her life, but it'd started on this day, barefoot at the edges of a field that had not yielded its season's crop. Disease had rampaged through, turning the crop mottled and brown, leaving the soil a mushy tangle of shriveled roots and stinking rot.

A yellow moth hovered near Sofía's toes, its soft wings tickling her skin. Some other time, she would have bent to inspect the critter's stripes and patterns, counted its legs, and maybe even brushed a gentle finger along the fuzz on its back. This time, however, her eyes were on her mamá. On the quick rise and fall of her chest, the tremble of her jaw, the fullness of her lips pressed flat and sealed tight as a dam. As though opening her mouth would unleash a flood, or something equally destructive.

Looking back on it, she might have just been holding in a scream. But back then, more than a mother, more than a woman, more than bones and curves and a beating heart, she had been a force of nature.

Which was why Sofía stared, and waited. For Mamá's lips to open wide and let out fire, for her wild tresses to turn to wilder snakes, for her sun-god eyes to transform the men who'd taken her son into stone.

Instead, she stepped forward with Sofía's hand crushed in hers. Her body folded, her knees pressed to the dirt, and her silken mane, unbound and uncombed, sagged over her cheeks as she bent into a low bow. When her mouth did open, there were no fires, no floods. Just a hacking cough and a mother's desperate plea.

"Take her too," she begged the man who owned the ground she knelt upon, and every soul that worked it. Including her. "Please, they have only each other."

Their master smoothed the cuffs of his white frock, unmoved. "The gentlemen here are looking for laborers," he said, his voice different from how Sofía imagined it—quieter, as though he expected others to strain forward to listen. She had seen him on a handful of occasions, but only from afar. The closest he had ever come to the field was his manor's second-floor balcony. "In a year or two, she'll fetch a better price as a domestic. Keep her away from the sun until then."

"It'll be too late!" A sound, something between a growl and a sob, tore out of her mamá's throat. She wrenched Sofía in front of her, swept the unruly mop of hair off her cheeks, and forced her to face the man. "*Look* at her. Look at her eyes."

His own eyes were the misty gray of rain. A color that would mean nothing to Sofía until two years later, when she finally met herself upon a mirror.

"Mamá . . ." Her scalp stung from the tug on her hair, and the muscles of her neck pulled taut as her head craned backward.

"She did not come into this world alone. That boy you bartered and bound came with her, and I swear to the earth and sea I will burn your house with both us in it before I let you tear them apart." Her words cut through, sharp as daggers, but all Sofía could hear was the rasp of her voice, the rattle of sickness inside her chest.

The master's oiled mustache twitched, amused. "I always did like your spirit, girl." He took a deep drag of his cigar. "She could be some noble lady's maidservant. She'd be comfortable, well fed. Might even earn her favor. You'd rather she spend her years planting sugarcane?"

"I'd rather she be free." The wish was an ember on a dying hearth, a thing Mamá guarded but did not dare stoke. "But we both know you will not grant her that."

Thick tobacco smoke blew from his nostrils as he studied both mother and daughter. Without looking away, he summoned the men who'd come with coins and cages, and directed their gazes to Sofía: a scrawny young thing with sunburnt skin and deadened eyes. "You can have her for the same price as the boy."

The heavyset one crouched, appraising her like he might a horse. "How old's she?"

"Five summers this year," her mother answered.

"Tall for her age, ain't she? Oye, Ramón," he called back to the other man. "What say you?"

"She's got all her fingers and toes, don't she? That's all Don Reynaldo cares about. Now, quit wasting time and load her in with the rest."

Hands reached for Sofía, pulled her kicking from her mamá's arms. Her mind went blank, her mouth forgot the words it so eagerly gobbled up. All she could do was touch her fingers to her mother's tear-damp cheeks, feel the heat of fever on them, and quietly beg her not to let the bad men take her.

"Te amo, mi cielo. Mi Hurakán." She pressed a teary kiss to Sofía's palm. "Take care of each other, you hear me? Let no one or anything come between you, and—" Her step faltered, her body too weak to keep up with the man's long gait. "Keep chasing your frogs and hummingbirds, sweet girl. Keep asking your questions." The space between them widened. Her voice grew faint. "Skies know someone has to . . ."

The rain did not come until after.

After two days on the road.

After Sofía's body had learned the chafe of iron, the weight of her brother's fingers across the bars.

There were six others crammed into her cage, all broader and taller, better at keeping their feet steady as the wheels bumped along the cobblestone streets and wooded back roads. The terrain was rough and muddy, the landscape a haze of wet gray.

Sofía's eyes were heavy, just beginning to close, when shouts from the traders' carriage jolted her upright. She heard a ground-shaking thud, like a felled tree slamming down, then the anxious whinny of horses, the stamp of hooves.

Everything toppled sideways: the beasts, the carriage, the cages bound to it. And everyone in them. Bodies crushed Sofía to the bars, pressing her face to it at a wrong angle, twisting her limbs and trapping them beneath her. Muffled by the pitter-patter of the rain were cries and groans. Men shouting. A scream that sounded like her name.

She knew that voice like she knew her own, but could not call back to it. Could not move. Speak. *Breathe.*

She could not breathe.

She could not breathe.

She could not—

SOFÍA WOKE UP GASPING.

The wheezing rush of air raked her lungs, her throat. Leaving her insides raw and . . .

Where was she?

An azure sky was painted bright above her. The smell of musty old wood and the soreness of cramped muscles told her she was still inside the chest she'd stowed away in, but the lid had been flung open, and beyond those close confines she heard the trill of songbirds, the burble of water. On the balmy air, she scented fresh green and ripened fruit.

With a groan, Sofía sat up, arms stiff and shaking with the effort.

She was not alone.

Across from her was a figure cloaked in morning mist and honeyed sunlight, sitting against a backdrop of dense, dew-covered leaves and a frothy lake of turquoise water. The stranger wore dark trousers and a white button-down shirt, sleeves rolled up to the elbows. Their face, obscured from view, was bent low over a book, their fingers skipping through the pages, browsing the contents with cursory interest.

"Such meticulous recordkeeping . . ." The voice was female, husky, and lightly accented. Familiar in a way Sofía's muddled mind could not yet define. "I would admire your obsession for detail, if you had not gone and ruined it all with your mediocre speculation."

The woman waved the book at her in a manner Sofía thought approximated a crude gesture, before tossing it to the ground between them.

Her journal.

"Do you know what I find most disappointing?" She did not pause long enough to invite a response. "That your arrogance should be so much stronger than your intellect. You take of the world whatever fits into the box you've made for it, getting so distracted by what you *think* you are looking for that truth is displaced by expectation."

The woman leaned beyond the veil of light that kept her features hidden. Her eyes were dark as volcanic stones, her skin the brown of clay, and her hair smooth and shining black, sharply fringed over a solemn brow. Around her waist she wore a woven cotton belt, beaded with a thousand fragments of colored shells and bits of precious stones, and over the skin of her heart, a bird was tattooed in obsidian ink.

"It's you, isn't it?" Sofía thought aloud, and because she could manage only one emotion at a time, she neglected to feel properly offended at the woman's comment. "The one in the bat-winged-mask . . . On the galleon too . . . you were minding the door." Where else had she been? What other guises had she donned without Sofía knowing?

"And *you* were sneaking past me as your horrid little friend made a scene."

"How did . . . ?"

"Please." The doorkeeper held out a hand to stop her. "You are subtle as a hundred-pound dog barking for a bone."

Sofía locked her jaw, clamping her mouth against the flurry of questions eager to break out of her. She needed to think, dissect the woman's words and their intention. Was she a savior, or a foe? Clearly, she had known she had a stowaway. If she wished Sofía ill, she would have stopped her. Instead, she'd brought her here—wherever *here* was.

Sofía considered her surroundings, building in her mind a picture. The area was dense with vegetation, walled by hulking mountains blanketed in lush greenery, their peaks rising so high they disappeared beyond the cloud cover. Sparkling waterfalls rushed down their side, into the vast pool on her left. The land around it was unpruned, uncultivated, its verdure tall and full and imperfect. Colors clashed, vines knotted into clumps, mushrooms grew fat and wild around the bed of trees.

It was paradise.

In her mind, Sofía saw the crinkled, age-stained map of Isla Bestia. The spine of hills and mountains bisecting the island in half, running from the top of the tail to the base of the creature's neck. A second mountain range lying like a crown along the head.

From the position of the sun rising above the peaks, she suspected that was where she was: the easternmost side of the island, opposite the Flor de Lis. At least a day's journey by foot, maybe three . . . four hours by riverway?

"You knew I was aboard the ship when you brought me here . . ." The doorkeeper had just short of admitted to it, but Sofía needed to work through those words aloud, strip away the obliqueness to extract the facts.

"Nothing happens in Carnaval without me knowing," confirmed the woman. "I am everywhere, child." It was the way she said it that triggered a memory. Or rather, *memories*. The voice of a cave that told the tale of four brothers. The serpentine monster of the river deeps, its body made of night and starlight. The singing ghosts in the dark of a ship.

Sofía swept the memories to the back of her mind with a note to revisit later. Right now, she had more pressing matters to contend with. "Why not stop me then?"

"I was . . . curious."

The word was incompatible with the context. An offer of aid, she would have understood, even a warning would have been expected, albeit unfortunate. But *curiosity*?

The woman met her eyes, her gaze humorless. "You arrive arm in arm with some moneyed heiress to a sugar empire. You share her table at breakfast, toast her glass at sundown. When Carnaval beckons, you accept its invitation. It is a game, a new one each night, and you learn to play it well . . . *Most* of the time anyway. Other times, you're restless. Asking too many questions. Sticking your nose in places you have no business being in." She laid each word down like a stone in a match of hooks and rooks. "So yes, child, I was curious. Curious to know why a loyalist would go to such lengths to ruin the fun for herself."

The implication sank slowly, burning on the way down. *Loyalist*.

"We get others like you now and again, those with just enough Hisperian in their bones they can almost pass for the part. They act it too. You see them flaunting the latest fashions, showing off how fine and proper they are for their mothers' masters. Scoffing at the lives they might have led had they been just a shade or two darker. They prefer to blend in usually, not stir the waters too much lest it attract the wrong kind of attention."

"The kind *I've* attracted, I presume."

The woman stared intently at Sofía's hand over the ledge of the chest. The one missing a glove, revealing knuckles webbed with the lessons of her youth. "I believed you to be one of them." She worked her jaw, the admission seeming to stick to her teeth like taffy. "Now . . . I am less sure."

Sofía pored over the woman's words in her head, drawing mental lines and circles, linking together threads of meaning.

"So, if I'm to understand correctly, I stow away on your flying ship and rather than be rid of me, you abduct me, bring me to some undisclosed location in the middle of devils know where, read my private journal, and start accosting me with questions before I've even had my morning coffee. Also, let's not forget—" she counted the armed figures hidden among the trees "—the six . . . no, *seven* archers pointing arrows at me. Am I to actually believe you've gone to such extraordinary lengths just to ascertain my allegiances?" Shaking her head, she said, "Respectfully, I call horseshit. You'd not have brought me here unless I was stirring up the kind of trouble you could not make go away."

Her dark eyes settled on Sofía. "As I said. Arrogant."

"My previous employer would have agreed with you." Her muscles protested as she climbed to her feet and out of the chest, stretching cramped limbs. "Who are you anyway, doorkeeper? Why are you doing this? Is someone . . . is someone forcing you?" Some sadistic hotelier with too much coin and time to spare? It was what she'd expected to find and could not yet reconcile this apparent reality with the story she'd built up in her mind.

Archers smoothly peeled off the trees and boulders, a silent warning to Sofía. The other half remained poised on the branches, weapons trained on her. "Or perhaps it's you who's at the helm of this. In which case, mind ordering your archers to stand down? Surely a lone, unarmed woman poses no threat to you. Or them." Sofía turned out the pockets on her waistcoat and trousers, showing they were empty. Of course, the doorkeeper already knew that. "You've relieved me of my knife. Though even with a weapon in hand, what chance have I against your trained bow bearers?"

The woman remained seated, scratching lines into the dirt with the butt of her spear, the shaft of it etched with a symbol reminiscent of a sunburst. "They are to dissuade you from leaving, should you resort to such action."

"After the lengths I've gone to get here I'd be mad to leave without answers."

The archers settled into a loose circle around them, holding the strings of their hunting bows taut and ready. Sofía took quick stock of their appearances: the artful sigils and geometric patterns painted along their skin, their bodies boldly decorated with septum rings in guanín and gold, thick armbands of polished stone, and necklaces of carved bone dyed in brilliant colors. They wore light, comfortable garments—loose trousers or slitted skirts, articles that left the stomach and arms exposed, intricately woven and braided through with precious beads.

Sofía knelt to pick up her journal, carefully brushing the dirt and leaves off the leather binding, flipping through the pages to check all was still there. When her gaze lifted, she found the point of a spear aimed straight at her, the blade hovering a finger's width from her nose.

"Do not mistake me, child of arijua," the doorkeeper said, her hand holding the weapon steady. Unflinchingly. "You are in no position to expect answers. It is not mine, but the island's will that you be given fair trial, a chance to convince us you are to be trusted. Were it my judgment alone to make, you would not be here at all." A fact, one delivered with appropriate sharpness. "I have watched you make of invaders, murderers, and slavers your friends. You are a traitor to your own, that is plain to see. What remains to be known is whether you are also a danger."

Slave . . . Mestiza . . . Freedwoman . . . Loyalist . . . And now, *a danger.* Yet another label to add to her collection. Another identity imposed, clamped on like a collar around her neck. Squeezing more with every move she made to shake it. "I . . . I understand." And she did. The weapons aimed at her were not for theater and the woman's callous threat was no empty promise.

Relief should not have been her response to the woman's brutal honesty, but after months of lies, any kernel of forthrightness was welcome, even one underscored by the point of a blade.

It was in that precise moment that a shout rang from the mountains.

Birds startled off their branches, and every head and arrow swiveled to the source of that sound. From the corner of her vision, Sofía registered a blur of movement. A flash of brown arms and legs skidding down the ragged base of the mountain, throwing up rocks and earth. A cloud of sand-fine soil trailing behind it.

In a matter of heartbeats, the figure was before her—no longer a blur, and no longer shouting. Speaking softly, yet firmly, in that language born out of a drumbeat. His back was to her, his feet planted solidly between her and the doorkeeper, his arms spread wide as though any moment now he would burst into flight.

Sofía knew him instantly though he was only a shadow, his outline cast in sunlight like a saint ascending, silhouetting the new strength of muscles, the width of once bony shoulders, the now unbending length of a spine that, for as long as she could remember, had been perpetually hunched, bent into a question mark.

"Please, Kaona . . ." he said, switching to Hisperian. It was deeper now, his voice. Confident.

"You would vouch for her, Kachi?"

"I would. I trust her with my life."

The woman, Kaona, took a step toward him, her shape vanishing, eclipsed behind his much larger frame. "And with ours?"

There was a pause, a hollow between her challenge and his answer that he filled with the heave of his labored breathing, long enough that an aching worry lodged beneath Sofía's rib cage. "Yes," he said finally, his tone steady as the feet below him. "I do."

"Then she is hereby your responsibility." Kaona stepped back, visible once more. "If she is to stay with us, she will learn our words and our ways. She will earn her keep and travel with a chaperone until I permit otherwise. If I sense her bringing danger to our home, it will be I who personally escorts her off these shores. Am I understood, boy?"

"Yes, Cacika." He bowed his head in respect.

Kaona shot a last warning look at Sofía and turned sharply on her heel toward the water. At the edge of the pool, she kicked off her boots, undressed down to the bare skin, and dove beneath the water's surface. No one batted an eye at her nakedness, nor her abrupt departure.

The archers, taking her leave as their cue, lowered the bows and retreated into the surrounding forest, blending into the bramble and bark.

Sofía was still on her knees, her journal cradled in her lap, when the shadow turned halfway around to face her.

Her heart swelled painfully inside her chest.

Until that moment, she had not truly let herself believe it was him. That she had found him after five long years of hoping and waiting, of pushing down the stomach-twisting fear that he was already dead and she had crossed an ocean chasing after a ghost. He was different, the sweet lankiness of him remolded, the softness of his boyhood face whittled into hard angles. He was all sharp lines and lean muscle. And hair, *so* much hair. On the planes of his cheekbones, the arch of his brows, grown long and sleek and tied into a knot atop his head.

This man before her was at once familiar and not, a house Sofía once knew, now changed. The wallpaper replaced, the rooms refurnished. The bumps and dents covered over with a fresh coat of paint. His scars, which she had once memorized, line by tragic line, were redrawn in ink, transformed into a piece of artwork along his back, the length of his arms, and around the small scar on his left temple. The one he got when they were six, after taking a strike to the face meant for Sofía. It was now a coin-sized sunburst, the tallest ray curving along the corner of his eye.

It was really him, for who besides her brother could make beauty out of nightmares?

"Sol." His name came out strangled, the reality of him a shock to her system, like the first drink of water after too long without. *"Sol,"* she cried out again. Because she could. Because he was there, whole and beautiful and *alive*. Alive. Her brother, her only blood, standing close enough for her to see the flecks of gold in his copper irises.

She took his hand, and he was solid. Real. Her fingers squeezed, needing the reassurance. The tangibility of weight and pressure that bordered on pain. Her brother squeezed back, and his head fell to his chest as though in prayer. For a moment, as his hand gripped hers, she glimpsed a telltale sheen in his eyes. But then . . . he was letting go of her, opening the space she'd closed, and whatever emotion she thought she saw was gone. Stamped out so completely, it seemed impossible that it'd been there at all.

"Can you walk?" Sol's gaze moved beyond her, landing on some vague point in the ground. "We should get you inside before Kaona changes her mind."

"Right. Y-yes," she stuttered out a reply, his sudden distance stumping her into near speechlessness. "Sol . . . have I done someth—"

"Kachi!" A voice came from the lake, and Sofía looked to find a woman wending through the water in a small canoe. She was drenched, her dark hair plastered to her skin, her face paint running in charcoal rivers down her cheeks. Despite all that, Sofía recognized her immediately.

Madame Anani?

"You reached her in time," said the diviner, sounding relieved.

"Almost didn't." Sol drew the edge of the canoe with one bare foot, helping her dock along the bank. "Thanks for knocking me off my hammock," he said, "must've been quite the run."

"Did it piss off Kaona?"

Sol ran a hand along his beard. "I'd wager so."

"All in a good day's work then." She grinned sharklike, all teeth and predatory glee. Sofía thought back to their first meeting, the dangerous gleam in her eye as she read her future in fire, turning the tiny tent into a flaming inferno.

"Ey! Inriri!" she called to Sofía. "About time you found your way."

Sofía furrowed her brow, stumped as to what to say. What to think, even. All her mind could conjure was *how . . . what . . . why*? In the span of minutes, she'd been threatened, reunited with the brother she'd thought lost, and greeted as if she were late for an appointment, by the most enigmatic individual she'd ever encountered, no less.

"*In, in.*" The diviner waved her paddle at them. "Hop on already, I've got places to be."

Sol paused before Sofía, tilting half to her, half away. "Need help climbing in?"

"I think I can manage." Her voice came out small, almost timid. *Timid*, before this boy with whom she had shared a womb, a cage, and a pair of worn-down sandals. Until they'd outgrown them, at least. Now he seemed to have outgrown her.

He climbed into the canoe first, taking the seat behind Madame Anani. Sofía went in last, testing her balance with a foot before coming all the way in. The canoe wobbled under her weight as she settled in. Had she been in her right mind, she'd have wondered why they were sailing through a lake that led nowhere. Her mind, however, had become a fragile, brittle thing, a brain-shaped sculpture of molded sand that alternatingly crumbled and reformed. Elation and heartache taking turns building her up and breaking her down.

Paddles dipped into the water, turning them away from the bank. There were fish in the lake, swimming circles around the canoe, their rainbow scales iridescent in the sunlight. The water was so clear Sofía could see all the way to the rocks and sandy soil underneath. The sights and sounds and fresh, clean smells were almost enough to distract her, pull her eyes away from the ink on her twin's back, make the fist around her chest ease its grip. But then, there were the old words, tumbling from his mouth; his answering nods to that name that was not his; the gaze that refused to meet hers, no matter how desperately she sought his.

It seemed another cruel trick of Carnaval's, like the image of his boyhood self in the mirror maze, evading her as this version of him now did.

Look at me, Sol.

And then he was—looking at her, that is. Or well, in her general direction, his focus hovering somewhere between her left shin and knee.

"Don't be scared. This . . ." He swallowed. "Just trust me."

For a hopeful, childish instant, she thought he was referring to the strangeness between them. Then, she woke to the world beyond the shape of him and saw the massive wall of water coming toward them. Her mouth formed a warning, *Stop!* But Madame Anani was cackling, her arms thrown out wide, and Sol was paddling determinedly *toward* the danger. And even if Sofia urged them away from it now, they would not hear her over the crash and roar of the waterfall, could not paddle hard nor fast enough to escape it.

Too late. It was too late.

She squeezed her eyes shut and braced for the impact.

CHAPTER 15

They serve their gods in conquest.
They honor them in war and glory.

—Chronicler

WATER THUNDERED AROUND SOFÍA, deafeningly loud. Enveloping. She had been swept up into a storm, thrown into the eye of it. Yet, it did not pummel her bones or toss her into the deeps. It whispered along her skin. A mist.

One eye cracked open.

All around her was froth and gray. The canoe traveled through it smoothly, the water parting for it like a bride's veil. For a moment, she felt . . . something. A weight in the air, as though eyes watched her from the mist. Then the water cleared, and the odd sensation vanished with it.

They had gone beyond the waterfall, into a long, dark, and cavernous passage. The walls stretched high, carved by the river flow into flat, square columns, pressed tight and overlapping like the folds of an accordion. The cave was formed from a white shimmering stone, opaque in places and translucent in others, with finger-thin stalactites of quartz dripping from the ceiling like an upside-down forest of ice.

"What . . . what is this place?" Sofía's question echoed along the channel, pleating back into itself until it grew distorted. Unrecognizable.

"Home," said her brother. The word sat strange on his lips, stranger even than the words he traded with the diviner. Home. That concept had always been beyond their reach, meant for those who had the coin and king-given rights to such privileges. Sure, they'd had a roof over their heads, a place to lay their heads each night, but never a *home*.

Sofía tried the word out, rolled it around her tongue just to see how it felt. Overly sweet. A thing she could not quite bite into, slipping between her teeth like a slice of overripe mango. She fell silent, listening to the gentle lap of water as the paddle dipped back into the stream, the ripples it made glowing faintly silver—too evenly for some bioluminescent organism to be causing it. She leaned over the canoe and combed her fingers over the dark surface, as if she were running them over the strings of a harp. The river answered, radiating pale light along the path she drew.

Perhaps the glow was coming from the rock around them, or the stalactites above?

The passage widened, and they came to a forking path: three identical openings, side by side. Sol propelled them to the right, and they entered another blocky tunnel with ruffled stone walls. The crystals grew thick on them, dusting the rocks like oversized sugar grains, sometimes jutting out at precarious angles, their points long and sharp as swords. They had to duck low in the canoe to avoid an especially massive one, its girth wider than the circle of Sofía's arms.

When they came back up, she caught the sound of chatter. Voices so tightly woven into a tapestry of noise, the individual threads became indistinguishable. The light came after, a bright spectrum of violet, blue, and sunset pink washing over the faint, pearlescent glow of the tunnel. Sofía had to shield her eyes against the sudden harshness of it.

When she opened them again, she was . . . *elsewhere*.

"Welcome to Coaybay."

The diviner puffed with pride, as if she herself had built the secret city spread out before her. It floated on an underground lake, vast as the mountain around it. The cavern domed over the water, its marbled stone hanging with braids of flowering vines, tangles of leaves and moss-covered stalactites. Swirls of multi-hued agate and quartz ribboned along the walls like the cloudy, star-dusted spirals of the galaxy, smooth in places and thick with coarse crystals in others.

Enormous towers of deep purple amethyst surged above the water, rising to hold the ceiling aloft. Vast islands of rock made a ring around the lake, each at a different height above the water level and connected by stone bridges. Everything seemed to glow, the stone and the water, the plant life suspended high above it.

Sofía soaked that world in, slack-jawed.

The canoe glided beneath arching bridges and along the edges of solid land. They had neared what appeared to be a plaza, where dozens labored in and around huts draped in bright fabrics. Men and women worked metals, wood, and clay, weaved baskets of palm leaf and clothes of dyed cotton, bartered for jewelry and statuettes carved of precious stone.

A tawny-skinned woman carrying an infant in a sling and a basket over her head stopped as they passed. "Anani!" She greeted the diviner, exchanging several words in their language while keeping pace with their vessel. Midsentence, her eyes shifted to Sofía, and her entire face lit up with a smile. "Mabrika, ituno. Welcome, sister." She traced the curve of her brow, left to right, with two fingers. "Moon be with you."

Sofía nodded, unsure what else to do.

Others soon came and went, wearing airy fabrics, and donning jewels around their necks, arms, and ankles or hooked around ears and noses. Their attire—or occasional lack thereof—would have stirred up a scandal among Hisperian circles, but here it was Sofía's layered garb that was out of place.

She didn't think that was why so many of them were staring at her though. Most greeted her warmly, calling out *Mabrika! Mabrika, ituno!* as she passed, but a few among them wore stoic expressions, their eyes trailing her with the cold look of suspicion.

Eventually, the canoe would sail past those individuals, and some new face or oddity would distract her again. Passengers paddled alongside them, humming in harmony. Vendors waved from canoes stacked with baskets of fresh fruits and peppers, roasted nuts and cocoa beans, leafy vegetables and hardy roots. Under the lake's surface, luminescent water sprite fluttered their leaves, and above it, a blanket of round leaf waterlilies bobbed to the gentle current. Wild green orchids grew over the rocks, their thin petals curving like spider legs, and flowering moriviví shied inward at Sofía's touch.

The current object of her fascination was a system of lines and pulleys high overhead, crisscrossing the cavern from left to right and vice versa. Cargo zipped in and out on the ropes, safely stowed within large lidded baskets.

Not just cargo, she realized. People too rode the lines. They flew in from shadowed passageways onto nearby platforms of rock that spiraled down into staircases. Some vanished into other hidden tunnels, traversing from one to the next within the span of three breaths.

"Incredible . . ." She sighed. Every inch and sight ignited another spark of earnest, tongue-tied awe—a sense she'd figured was lost to her after so many nights in the grip of Carnaval's magic. But whereas the dazzle and glamor of Carnaval was a show, all smoke and dreams, *this* was real. Its magic solid and lived in. She swallowed around that nameless lump of emotion wedged in her throat. If there was a word for what she was feeling, she had not learned it yet.

Past another amethyst tower, a dock came into view, the length of it lined with canoes. They slowed as they approached, then wedged their vessel into an empty spot between two others, tied the rope to the post, and hopped off.

Madame Anani assumed the lead, weaving a path out of the dock and through the back end of the plaza. There were over two hundred people scattered throughout, and all appeared to know the diviner. They waved, called her name, and made way for her as she passed. Twice, someone pulled her aside to speak in hushed, worried tones, and she listened and nodded, patting shoulders and backs, impressing upon everyone a sense that all would be well.

Who was she, Sofía wondered, this bruja who brewed up chaos as easily as she instilled calm? The mask of kohl she wore at Carnaval might have devolved into a mere smudge across her face, her hair and vestment may have been a sopping mess, yet she commanded attention more now than she ever did confined inside that tent. Was more a mystery, in fact, without the shroud of fire and curls of sagey smoke.

She walked between the stalls and tents with confidence, touching cheeks in greeting, looking completely at ease among these people. This place. "Tí-ni-ma!" she singsonged as she climbed up a set of stone steps, ducking into a curtained passage—a person-sized hole, really, set into the farmost wall. If the cavern were a compass rose, this spot would be the point on the star's northern spike.

Past the jingle of beaded fabric was a room shaped like an obelisk. A relic, it seemed, some temple built centuries before and returned to the earth's hold. Nature rose, as nature did, overtaking its walls with thick vines and dense greenery that draped and curled and dangled. An enchantress tree grew, half embedded within the stone like a moth trapped in amber, its branches pressing against the ceiling, reaching for the wispy beams of light shining through the cracks. The flowers on it were waxy and red, their delicate perfume a drink of bittersweet nostalgia.

Over the bark grew chunks of raw amethyst like wild mushrooms, spreading over the walls, the ceiling, between the rosy buds of maiden's blood and the bursts of fire-star orchids, around the endless shelves stacked with vials of liquids and powders and clay jars, and across the edges of a long counter where someone stood, crushing herbs into a paste.

"Taiguey, Tínima!" Madame Anani called again. "Not ignoring me, are you?" She switched to Hisperian, presumably for Sofia's benefit.

"Ignoring you, rahe? Wu'a. No more than the scorch of midday sun can be ignored."

She smiled, pleased by this response. "I've come for a favor."

"Of course you have," said Tínima, back still to them, hands still busy crushing herbs between mortar and pestle. "What's it this time, another burn? Let me see."

"Please, I already know where you keep the salve for that, old friend." The diviner leapt onto a tall wooden stool by the counter and pushed the seat into a whimsical spin. "Third shelf from your left." She pointed. "The red one."

The comment confirmed what Sofía had already gathered from the rows of woven mats on the floor, the pungent scent of healing herbs: hints of mint and ginger to clear the lungs, iron grass for stomach pains, chamomile to settle the nerves. This was a place for the injured and ailing.

"Humph." Tínima eyed the paste on the mortar, made a sound of displeasure, and began rifling through the clinking vials, bottles, and urns on the shelves. "Something for our new sister, then?"

"A restorative." The diviner sniffed the ingredients on the counter and let out a sneeze. Tínima smacked her hand away.

"She drank the wine, did she? For how long?"

Anani glanced at Sol, then quickly away. "Six moons?" Her nails tapped the countertop. "Maybe seven?"

Sol stiffened where he rested cross-armed against the wall. He tried to meet the diviner's gaze, but she was studiously looking everywhere but at him.

Tínima immediately stopped and spun to face the diviner. "*Seven* moons, rahe? And we are just now getting the poor thing out of there?"

She lifted her hands defensively. "Take it up with Kaona. I am only her eyes and ears. What the Cacika does with what I see and hear is up to her."

Tínima spat what sounded like a curse and moved to Sofía. "Let me take a look at you. Sit, sit." Madame Anani was shooed off the stool, and Sofía ushered onto it. "Your name, sister?"

She looked to Sol, feeling herself a child again. Lost in a world that did not make sense to her.

"It's alright," her brother assured her with the polite gentleness of a stranger. "You can trust them. Tínima is a Behíke."

Sofía noted her brother's phrasing, and the title. It was an old word, that. Healer of spirit and flesh, wisdom-keeper, and arbiter of all matters between humans and the divine. Before, a Behíke would have occupied a powerful and respected role in a Taike'ri tribe, second only to the Cacike or Cacika.

Tínima, stooped and stalk-thin with sagging bags under eyes deeply wrinkled with age, did not fit the grand image Sofía had built in her mind—this enlightened figure that chased off illnesses and petitioned gods. The robe sitting on the Behíke's shoulders, fine as it was, seemed to highlight the spindly arms and scrawny legs drowning under all that fabric. By Hisperian standards, the overall vestment would have been considered women's wear, but Sofía strongly suspected those conventions did not apply here. Indeed, nothing about Tínima's appearance abided tradition. Not the thick obsidian collar encircling their neck, nor the coin-sized disks stretching the lobe of each ear. The look was utterly un-Hisperian, and it made Sofía dizzy with something like relief, knowing there was this entirely different way to be.

"Sofía," she answered at last, drawing her name out of herself like a confession.

"Well, Sofía, this will not hurt a bit." The Behíke examined her, pressing fingers to the sides of her neck, the insides of her wrists, asking her to open wide as a wooden spatula pressed her tongue against the floor of her mouth. "Pupils are dilated," they said, pouring sudsy water from a vase onto a clay basin and dipping both hands in, "but her pulse is stable and she's otherwise healthy. How long has it been since you drank the wine, Sofía?"

She counted in her head. "Twenty-two days, at least." If her writings were accurate. What she did not say was, *What the godscursed seas was in that wine?*

"Good, good . . . that ought to make this part easier." Tínima procured several items from the shelves and brought them to her.

The first was a ceramic vial the length and width of a thumb. "Take this one on an empty stomach as soon as you're settled. Keep a bucket nearby, you will need it." Next she was handed a hollowed gourd, round and stoppered with a wooden cap. "This one's for when you wake up—drink it to the last drop. It tastes the way a wet goat smells, not going to lie, but if you can stomach it, you'll be on your feet before you know it." Last was a small clay pot. The scent of witch hazel wafted up from it even through the lid. "For the bruising."

"Bruis . . . ? Oh." It was then that Sofía noticed the soreness along her cheekbone—naively dismissed as the beginnings of a headache. At the first brush of her attention, pain sprouted like leaf-buds following an overdue bout of rain. Her entire body ached, and not just with the lingering effects of her cramped sleeping quarters. She must have been bumped and jostled a dozen different ways on the ride out from Carnaval. "Thank you."

Tínima's answering nod was less an acknowledgment than a dismissal. "Off with you all then. I got work to do."

Anani kissed Tínima's cheek, Sol dipped his head goodbye, and Sofía bit down on her impatience. They all ducked back out through the curtain.

THIS WAS A MISTAKE.

Sofía gazed over the side of the footpath, a narrow arch of stone set so high above the lake her eyes had entirely missed it. It was one of five bridges, linked by a central point and radiating outward like the arms of a sea star, each connected to a different tunnel.

"You alright there, Inriri?" Madame Anani stared at Sofía over her shoulder. She stood poised over the rock with a sort of . . . effortlessness, as if her feet had worn this path smooth, learning to walk its heights as others learned the ground. It did not seem to concern her that the path was only wide enough for one, or that it had no handholds, or that people and cargo whooshed past on ropeways so fast her hair tangled in the winds of their flight.

"Is there not . . . some other way across?"

"Sure." The diviner nudged her head toward the ropeways. "The way of the air spirits, if you care to brave it."

"Right." Sofía threaded her fingers in front of her, affecting a calm demeanor.

Sol's voice came from behind her. "It's not so terrible once you get used to it," he said. "Take a deep breath in and list out your favorite trees in alphabetical order. I'll be with you the whole way."

It was his promise that propelled her onto that first horrid step. *Salt and seas* . . . Her stomach plummeted and her vision shadowed at the edges, but she could weather it. All of this—*anything*—with her brother at her back. She walked, hands held out to her sides for balance, safely bastioned between a ghost and a fortuneteller. Below, the plaza was alive with color and movement, and if she ignored how dangerous this all was, she could almost find pleasure in the view.

From up here, there was a symmetry. A clear intentionality to the design of this strange and secret world where each island of rock was arranged like a petal around the center of a flower. Or . . . *Wait, I've seen this.* It was the symbol on that stone, one of the three Madame Anani had plucked from the fire the night of their first encounter, and again, on that desperate night of her second reading.

"What does it mean?" She traced the pattern's outline in the air, for a moment forgetting to feel afraid.

"The sun god," said Sol. "We . . . follow the old faith here."

The faith handed to her in fragments, snuck into hymns of bloodied saints and prayers to three-headed gods, wrapped in the cloak of legend and myth. Her mind buzzed at all she might recover here. Words her lips had only tasted, a whole history unabridged.

Sofía followed in contemplative silence down the rest of the footpath and through a tunnel that rippled and curved like sand dunes, stretching tall and wide, then narrowing so they had to squeeze through its gaps. Swirls of red, orange, and yellow bled through the clear quartz as though the walls, the floor, the ceiling had all absorbed a giant flame, pulled it from the air and fossilized it.

She trailed a hand along it, anchoring herself in the solid strength of the stone beneath her palm.

"Here's where I make my exit," the diviner announced. "All this heroism's wrung me dry. It's exhausting, really, no wonder I so rarely try my hand at it." She continued down the passage, fluttering her fingers goodbye. "See you both in the Guatiao."

". . . Guatiao?" Sofía asked.

"It's, eh, how do I put it . . . A naming ceremony, I guess you could call it? Here—" Sol paused in front of a square opening in the wall, one of many along the passage, and parted the curtain to reveal a small, dim chamber. "You go in first. I just need to have a quick chat with . . . ey, Anani, ukajá! Be back soon," he told her, and trotted after the diviner as Sofía slipped inside.

She remained by the doorway, ears straining to catch snippets of their conversation. They were careful to keep their voices low, but there was only so much privacy one could expect from an echoing passage. Their whispers carried with enough clarity that, if Sofía concentrated, she could make out most of their exchange.

Understanding it was a different matter, however.

". . . *Did I not deserve to know?*" her brother was saying, switching easily between Hisperian and the old tongue. ". . . *I could have . . . doesn't belong . . .*"

Next, came Anani's voice. ". . . *a risk . . . you never said . . .*"

"*No point . . . already gone . . .*"

". . . *did what I could . . .*"

The bits of conversation Sofía could work out did not click together in her mind no matter how she twisted and rearranged the fragments to fit. But she moved beyond the words to read the pauses, the inflections, the fall and rise of pitch. The tone that conceded what language hid. Her brother's: wounded and imploring. Anani's: composed and resolute, though . . . not unsympathetic.

Whatever it was they were arguing about, Sofía guessed it had to do with her.

Outside, the hall went silent.

Sofía moved quickly back from the curtain as footsteps approached. Sol swept in a moment later, and the light from the passage chased the shadows from the room.

On one side, tucked into a nook, she could now make out the shape of a maroon hammock suspended from the rock on a pair of hooks. A low stone table took up the center of the chamber, stacked with wood scraps and a scattering of carving tools. Cushions of sun-bleached palm formed a ring around it.

"Kaona should assign you your own room soon," Sol said. "For now, you can share mine." He pulled a thick knitted blanket from one cabinet, a clay vase from another. "You'll have a rough few nights once you take that restorative. Most people are back on their feet within a day, but that's . . . only after a few doses of the, um, wine. It might take your body more time to purge it. Chills are common. Fevers, nausea, hallucinations too, so I hear . . . I'd taken only a few glasses myself before I came here and was spared the worst of it."

He continued moving around the room with a nervous kind of energy, lighting candles that floated in bowls and basins, rummaging through drawers for a change of clothes, pouring water for her from a ceramic jug. "This should get you through the night." Sliding his tools into a pile, he laid the blanket, the clothes, and the cup of water on the low table beside them. "I'll be in the room next door if you need anything."

Sofía tracked his restless movements. "Sol . . ."

"My friend works the day shifts," he went on. "He won't mind if I take a rest over at his, I'm sure. Don't worry, I'll come check in on you every other hour, and—"

"*Sol.*" Sofía stopped him, clutching his face between her hands, one palm over each scruff-roughened cheek. *"Look at me."*

He did, finally.

And his eyes gave her nothing.

She could read them no more than she could the walls of this place. It was not just his face that had changed, his boyhood softness whittled into edges. There was a hardness to his gaze she did not recognize.

"What happened to you?" Sofía was not exactly sure what she was asking. *What happened to make you disappear*, or . . . *what happened to make you look at me like I'm a stranger?* She felt his jaw tense as he withdrew from her touch. Putting distance between them. With his face shuttered, he turned to the shadows of his room. Unable, it seemed, to bear the sight of her.

It struck Sofía that in finding her brother, she had lost him as well.

And yet . . .

And *yet*, even in the grip of that realization, the tears that sprang to her eyes were of overwhelming relief. He had a place of his own. Friends. A home. There was no price she would not pay, no piece of herself she would not give for this life he so obviously deserved.

Slowly, she bent, picked the blanket from the table, and pressed its warmth close to her chest. "I kept all your things. The others, they . . . they told me to bury them. To bury you. I didn't. I . . . couldn't."

Sol touched the back of his neck, looking everywhere except her. "Rest up now . . . You've had a long night."

"Will you be gone when I wake?" Banished by the light of morning, faded into another dream? Would the clock spin her back, back, back, unwinding her from this island, tugging her from one shore to another. To her bed at the hacienda, where she would wake to another day of house duties and slow, quiet mourning.

He said nothing, simply stepped up to the doorway, gripping the length of ombre cloth that covered it. After a moment's hesitation, he was gone.

CHAPTER 16

*Savage gods, those that let the land grow wild . . .
Nature, like lesser men, must be tamed.*

—Chronicler

IT WAS NOT love that brought Sofía and her brother into this world. But it was love that greeted them.

Love had strong hands, a fierce smile, a songbird's voice.

Sofía came first, on the tail end of a hurricane. She burst into this world a wailing, wriggling, blood-slick bundle of indignation. Mamá spun the tale of their birth for them often: How it was the worst storm of her lifetime, how it'd blown clean through the walls of her hut, razed the wood and thatch to the ground. That night, she had gone into labor on the floor of her master's kitchens, where forty men, women, and children huddled together against the wet and cold.

"Your wails beat out the rain and wind, like you were Guabancex, the goddess of storms reborn." Her mother laughed. She'd had a great laugh, full and unapologetic. "You were a menace. Unsoothable till your brother arrived, quiet as the breeze that came behind him."

He was born eleven minutes after, bringing with him the first gleam of good weather. Warmth had always followed her brother, bright child of the sun.

That was how they had earned their childhood names. The ones their mother called them, Sol and Hurakán. Not the ones a stranger put to paper, inventorying them as they did sacks of corn, coffee, and cattle.

Sofía would not answer to Sofía until her fifth summer, and would not become her until her seventh. When she entered a world where little girls who were wise survived, and the ones with storms in their veins had the wildness bled out of them.

Huracán had died long ago with her mamá, yet Sofía felt the pulse of both the name and namer as she twisted and turned. As chills racked her bones one minute, and fevers boiled the sweat from her body the next. She rolled out of the hammock in a daze, half crawled to a nearby basin, and emptied her stomach.

Her legs hung tangled in the knot of blankets and hammock behind her. She only managed to wriggle one foot free before sleep dragged her back under.

Between the flashes of those bleary waking moments, when her body went too cold or too hot, or she groped the ground unseeingly for another desperate gulp of water, she found . . . clarity. A sense of, *ah, I see now*, even among all that mess. In the way a room must be overturned, the clutter dug back out of boxes and dark, dusty corners before order can be imposed upon it.

She found herself there, recovered those days and nights she thought she'd lost. All the evenings spent pacing, writing warnings to herself she would soon forget. The meetings with the diviner that always ended with three stones, one lie, and a million questions. How many times did she barge into that tent, demanding the same answers? Ten? Twenty?

There were nights Carnaval burrowed beneath her skin, moved her like a doll from one pretty thing to the next. She followed it obediently, as did all the others. Ambling listlessly to their beds when summoned, rising only when the moon demanded. She never questioned it, that sweet, sudden yearning for sleep, the orderly way all patrons, en masse, would ascend the stairs to their rooms just as the sun itself ascended.

Then there were the nights she felt Carnaval's teeth.

Those were the nights she ran. Barricaded herself. Wrote until the paper could no longer hold her truths.

She saw it, the first of many times a scared man's words cut into her palm. She felt the shard of a wineglass, smooth and cool against her shaking fingers, then sharp and jagged where it pressed into the skin.

Its shape transformed in her grip, its texture taking on a sandy roughness.

"Kán-Kán?" Her brother's face faded in and out of her watery vision, drawn with concern. In a blink, he morphed into his boyhood self. Another blink, and his features rippled like a pond at the throw of a stone. He became almost unrecognizable again.

"Kán-Kán. Get up . . ." Her childhood nickname rang like an echo from somewhere far away. She could have wept at the sound of it.

Gentle hands lifted her from a puddle of sick on the floor. Removed the shard of a drinking cup from her grip and bandaged the wound, then replaced her tunic, soaked and soiled with her own sweat and vomit. He tucked her back into the cradle of the hammock, brought water to her parched lips, then covered her with a blanket that smelled faintly of star fruit. As the shadow of her brother turned to leave, she seized his wrist. "I am so, *so* sorry . . ." She thought she might have said, "for not finding you sooner . . ."

She slept again after that. Dreamt of bodies interred within bark and a man made of stone. Of a half lizard, half snake that mothered rains and clear skies. Of a hummingbird searching the flowers for a love lost, a ship haunted by singing ghosts, and a maze built from the locks of lady earth, her skin green grass, her hair a burst of flowers and cascading leaves.

In her eyes, the rivers ran.

When the giantess turned to look at her, Sofía jolted awake.

"FINALLY."

The diviner stood at the doorway, arms crossed, and hip propped against the wall. Instead of a mask of kohl, she wore stripes of white paint across her cheeks and two dots on her chin. A beaded band circled her forehead, adorned with a single nighthawk feather, nearly as dark as her hair and spotted white.

She sniffed. "You smell like death. Come, let's get you to the baths, Inriri."

Still groggy from two days of sickness and sleep, Sofía let herself get dragged out of Sol's room and down the tunnels.

"Madame Anani—"

"Just Anani here."

"Right. Anani . . . Did you . . . How many times did I . . . ?" She rubbed the bridge of her nose, trying to make sense of what she saw when she slept. "Before all this, I would have said we'd only met twice, but now . . . I think I may be slightly . . . misestimating that number."

"Bit of an understatement, that." The diviner yanked her aside as two men strolled by, fingers laced together. She greeted them each with a pat on the shoulder as they passed. "Fifteen times I turned you away," she went on, "before you stopped taking no for an answer. Kept finding me too, no matter where I plopped my tent for the night. You just kept pecking and pecking and pecking, like the little inriri at your neck. It was maddening. Thought I'd wronged some spirit and was being punished for it. Here, this way now."

The path led down to where the fire-gold striations along the rock expanded, overtaking the pearlescent white.

"So that's why you helped me?" Sofía asked, thinking of the last night they met at Carnaval. *Have you tried staying up past sunrise?* "To get me off your back?"

Anani's mouth softened into something like a smile. "At the beginning, perhaps, back when I was still naive enough to think I could. But once I knew better, I wanted you off that place and across the river, where your insufferable tenacity could be put to good use."

What Sofía had interpreted as anger when last they met, had it actually been frustration? They'd been having the same conversation for months, and she was nowhere closer to freeing herself from Carnaval.

"Our fearless Kaona might not think it, but you belong here. With us."

Sofía stopped, forcing the diviner to face her. "And who exactly is *us*?"

Anani smiled in earnest then, flashing a canine that was slightly crooked. "The guardians of these lands, of course. We, sister, are the Taike'ri."

The Taike'ri.

The islands' first people had not called themselves that in . . . well, centuries. Not since the bloodlines mixed and the culture was carved open, the warm life of it let out like an infection. Now they were Taike'ri descendants, mestizos and mestizas with the blood of both conquerors and conquered. A people of two worlds able to claim neither.

"The Taike'ri are dead," said Sofía.

"I can assure you we are very much alive. Pinch me, go on." Anani offered up her arm. "See for yourself."

At Sofía's stoic expression, she sighed. "Not much fun, are you? Look . . . some three hundred years ago, when the Hisperians arrived, a group of Taike'ri escaped what you now call mainland Etérea. They came here, to these mountains, where they began to rebuild. Some of us are their direct descendants, others, like your brother, like me, escaped slaves and servants offered a home. Not all are Taike'ri by blood, but we are *all* Taike'ri: The Brave Ones of this Good Land." She held up a finger, anticipating another question. "No, no more of this. Wash first. Talk later."

She shoved Sofía through an opening and into a wide cavern. Inside, the air was fragrant and pleasantly warm, the rock around them damp with steam. Voices echoed beneath the gentle lap and burble of water.

"Mixed baths are through there." Anani pointed at a path leading to a central pool where Sofía could vaguely make out men and women through the steam, sitting naked on the rocks or soaking in the softly glowing water. "I assume you'd prefer the women's baths?"

Sofía shrugged a shoulder. "I don't much care either way." She'd never understood why people made such a fuss about the unclothed body. It was not as though there was anything inherently scandalous about a leg or a breast, it was all just flesh in the end. Tissue and fat and varying quantities of body hair.

The diviner, apparently unconvinced, led her down the steps to the right, between two towers of rough uncut rock and along a winding path. A wide pool ringed by a few pond-sized springs came into view. Fresh water poured down the rock from an opening in the ceiling, mixing with the steaming baths below.

Anani handed her the basket strapped to her back, unhooking the lid to reveal a change of clothing and a thick bar of herbal soap embedded with orange petals. Sofía brought it to her nose. It had a mild citrus scent.

"You can leave the basket atop that rocky ledge right there. Use one of those pitchers to rinse before you go in for a soak. I'll be just outside when you're finished." She turned to go.

"Wait." Sofía clutched the basket to herself. "Will I . . . see my brother after?"

A flash of something crossed the diviner's features. Sofía couldn't be sure, but she thought it looked a little like pity. "Soon," she said. "I promise. Now, go on already, you reek."

"COME ALONG," Anani commanded the moment Sofía emerged from the baths, not once looking back to see if she had heeded her instruction.

Sofía trailed dutifully behind, the soft hem of her white wrap brushing her ankles. She went barefoot, as was apparently the norm here. Better for walking these uneven paths, she supposed. Without shoes, the soles could bend to the dips and ridges of the stone, the toes could curl at a steep incline for a better grip.

Just up ahead, a woman slowed as she came across them. Her skin was oak brown, wrinkled as a sun-dried fruit, and her shining long hair silver with age. Like Anani, her green eyes were framed with chalk-pale paint. Sofía stared. She had never seen a mestiza that far in her years. Most were lucky if they lived to thirty.

"Mabrika, ituno," said the elder mestiza. With the tips of four fingers, she traced the shape of Sofía's brow. "Moon be with you."

After parting ways, they turned into a passage where a crowd was gathering, all dressed in different styles and variations of purest alabaster. Everyone was shuffling toward the other end, where the path tapered down into a staircase.

"What's happening?" Sofía was jostled onto the line, wedged between Anani and a bare-chested man carrying an overexcited child on his shoulders. The little one squeed, her tiny fists gripping the man's hair like horse reins. Sofía half walked, half stumbled down the enclosed steps, pushed along by the press of dozens filing in behind her, her breath hitching despite having just spent a night inside a much more tightly cramped space.

"It's the Guatiao," Anani said over the chatter and noise. "Once a year, at the end of each harvest season, we celebrate our new kin. Tonight, they take on a Taike'ri name and bond themselves to the island's zemí."

Sofía froze at the base of the staircase. They stood by the bank of an underground river vein, where rows of canoes waited to be boarded.

"Anani—" she felt her temper splinter "—I am not a daughter of your faith. Moreover, I have endeavored for near a month to free myself from a devils' fete and am not in the mood to make merry. Now, I've been patient. I have drunk your cure that fell on me like poison, and followed you with my teeth on my tongue. If one could die for want of answers, I would have perished three times over. So go on then, enjoy your ceremony. If you will not yield me an explanation, then I will find myself someone who will."

The line parted around them like a stream around a stone, gravitating toward the canoes.

"Are you done?" the diviner asked, expression flat. "If you are, quit your whining and hop in. You'll find your answers at the river's end."

"Will I, though?" When last she rode the river, she came out with more questions. "How do I know I can trust you? How can I know if what awaits me is yet another version of Carnaval?"

Anani swiveled her toward the stairs. "Trust *him*."

Just then, her brother emerged into the open, laughing widely at something someone said. The joy in him reshaped his face into something she almost knew.

Sol noticed her, and his smile fell, weighed by that ineffable thing that toughened his heart to iron. Sofía took a small, unconscious step toward him, and his mouth opened around a word—

An arm came around his shoulders, yanking him to the side. A circle of laughter and warmth enfolded him, the way the earth wraps its green and bark around all that's left too long neglected. It was a scene from a different life: Sol among friends, bantering in that distinctly teasing manner that was recognizable in any language. They wrestled playfully, fighting for the chance to board first. A child's game, played by men who—like Sol—must have grown too fast, too soon.

In her mind, she heard the word *home*. It wrote itself into the dark behind her eyelids in looping letters, and she traced this moment into its lines and loops, like the word was a scrapbook she could fill with her brother's new life.

"Well?" Anani braced a hand against her hip. "What will it be?"

Sofía stared after Sol until he was one shadow among many. "I doubt you need your stones to intuit this one, diviner."

Anani grinned. "To the river's end it is then."

THE SONG RAN UPSTREAM, echoing through the tunnel. It traveled from voice to voice, injecting into every listener its tempo. The music leapt with confidence and dove without warning, switching course abruptly, almost cheekily, as another mouth caught it and breathed a new rhythm into it. It was alive. Feline in its mood swings, its sounds a gentle purr one minute and the next, a roar.

Every voice on that river sang. From the young to the old, the musically gifted to the offensively shrill. The tunnel rang with words and ululations, the clap of hands, the drum of palms against thighs, knees, the sturdy wood of the vessels. The oars dipped in and out of the water in gentle swishes and violent splashes, whatever the music demanded at that given moment.

Sofía watched bodies swaying to the beat, dancing their arms to the fluctuating rhythm. Mostly, she watched the river itself, how its glow seemed to brighten and dim with the highs and lows of the notes.

Is no one else seeing this?

Neither Anani nor the two passengers behind Sofía reacted.

She trailed her fingertips along the water experimentally; it did not feel any different, at least. She cupped it in both hands, and even there, between her palms, it pulsed in shades of silver when the music climbed. Darkened in the silent seconds between.

"Anani." She nudged the diviner with her elbow. "What is—"

The question died on her lips.

There were parts of this world Sofía had long resigned herself to never fully understanding. How energy conversion actually works, for one. The exact evolutionary purpose of socially responsive yawning. The mechanics of sitting while wearing a bustle. Yet, in the face of seeming impossibilities of science and machine—and of course, those of the carnivalesque variety—there had never once been a moment she had stopped believing that all in the world, impossible as it seemed, could be explained.

In her language, *inexplicable* was hyperbole. A word existing to define a concept that itself did not. Like brujería and miracles and magic, placeholders for questions pending answers. Because there always *was* an answer. Perhaps not in that precise moment, but surely someday someone more clever, better resourced, or more experienced could make sense of the seemingly senseless.

Yet the word hung there on her tongue, stripped of its semantic guises, no longer a metaphor for some mystery waiting to be solved.

It was acid in her mouth, burning through the truths she had once spoken with such certainty.

Gasps of awe and elation went up around Sofía, yet all she could feel was horror. At the knowledge that no matter how hard she looked, or how long she studied, there would be no tricks or gimmicks here for her to unravel. And if *this* was not the lie, then . . . everything else was.

She was relieved to be sitting, otherwise this moment would have driven her to her knees. For here was these people's god. A zemí in the shape of a sacred ceiba tree, nearly as tall as the cavern itself. It sat on a lone island of moss and rock, immersed in water lit like liquid moonshine. Its roots spilled outward, like an ocean wave petrified to wood. Thorns lined its bark, thick and sharp as arrowheads, and on its many twisting branches bloomed silken flowers, white as snow. How she'd *imagined* snow, anyhow.

Each flower glowed bright enough to light a room. They blossomed before Sofía's eyes, bundles of perfectly round buds poking out from the branches and bursting into petals. They dangled there for only a breath before fluttering down to the waters below, making way for new life to bloom. A process that should have taken days, if not weeks, over in seconds.

Anani and the others continued to row closer to the impossible tree, but Sofía's own paddle lay forgotten on her lap, her mind too tangled up in once-truths to signal her muscles to move.

The cavern arched high overhead, vast and round, a giant geode of smoky crystal. A gentle stream from somewhere higher up the mountain poured through a break in the ceiling, creating a misty, ethereal backdrop for an already otherworldly tree. Blooms continued to grow on it, and the sight was even more remarkable up close: soft petals soaked in moonglow, pollen dusting the air like glimmering motes of light.

Of its own volition, Sofía's hand rose to catch a fallen flower drifting over their canoe.

With painstaking gentleness, she held it in the cradle of her palms as if it were a wounded bird.

Anani turned to Sofía then, gathered the flower from her hands and tucked its fragile stem into her hair, still damp from the baths. Her fingers tipped Sofía's chin upward, forcing her eyes to hers. "You're looking for fire in the middle of an ocean, Inriri"

Sofía frowned, and Anani made a small huff of frustration at having to explain herself. "What you seek, you won't find it here. Reason can no more kindle in this place than a flame can ignite among the water." In a slightly more sympathetic tone, she added, "This is hard for you, I know. It was for me too. I was a bit like you once, believe it or not. One of those . . . 'grounded sorts.'" An echo of her words from their first meeting, once spoken with the snide tone another might say *divorce*. Was it truly half a year ago that Sofía first sat across from the diviner, debating faith and logic?

"Life had not given me much reason to believe there was any force in this world greater than the blight of man. If it had existed, it'd have seen us for the sickness we were and put us back into the dirt." That kind of statement was not one often said with so little emotion. And yet, Anani's manner was matter-of-fact. If rage had ever taken up space inside her, it had been hollowed out.

She nudged her head toward the tree, where a familiar figure in a black feather headdress stood, waiting. "Kaona found me then. Made me believe in *us*, so I could believe in *this*."

This. An island-god that drank moonbeams. A civilization thought dead, secreted away within the mountains of an island in the form of a beast.

Kaona noticed Anani as she steered into the outermost band of the hundred or so vessels ringing the ceiba tree. Her mouth was a stern, unyielding line, taut as the ropes the carnavaleros walked, yet there was warmth in the way she looked at Anani. Sofía knew this expression. In her memory, her mamá had often worn that soft-edged anger, weary of her and Sol's antics.

With a tired shake of the head, the Cacika continued her sweep of the crowd. The canoes were still pouring in and the music was still going strong, bending to the hands and lips that molded it. Laughter wove in and out of the beat, and howls and trills of joy rose above it.

Sofía followed the thread of the voice she knew, catching a flash of him six rows over. Her brother had his head tilted back, one hand cupped around his mouth as he sent his voice into the night. How long had it been since she'd seen him that carefree?

Once, he had been a wildling, dancing under a different sky, a different ceiba tree. Once, his candlelight warmth had been a blaze.

Though her world was breaking, a smile brushed across Sofía's lips.

It was in that moment that Sol's eyes caught hers. She stilled, waiting for him to look away, to dodge her gaze as though one glance her way could strike him dead. Instead, he held her eyes, tentatively mirroring her fragile smile.

The singing quieted, replaced by the low, long-drawn beat of the paddle-blades against the hulls. Kaona's voice rose above the music, commanding and sure. "On a night like this, we welcomed the first new member of our tribe," Anani translated for the Cacika. "Stole her back from the invaders, who dared take a girl of one and ten for a bride . . ." At these words, the Cacika's gaze flicked to the diviner's, a look passing between them. Brief yet laden with meaning. "All of us gathered here share a similar tale, of our wills shackled, our spirits smothered, our voices silenced."

The drumming continued, interjected by cries of woe and fury, and grumbles of assent.

"But by the Mother's mercy, our story is also one of transcendence. Great and gracious Atabey awoke from her sleep so that *we* would wake with her, pulling us back into the world of the living, bringing us together under one home. One people. The Taike'ri, reborn. Tonight, our new kin break the last link on their chains and claim themselves with a new name."

The crowd erupted in noise and cheer, banging paddles and splashing water. In all her nights in Carnaval, Sofía had never seen the like. This riotous glee, honed to a knife point. Half battle cry, half jubilee.

"Come, those who are ready. You have learned your ancestors' words, embraced their ways, and served Atabey, Great Mother of Mothers, ruler of waters, wellspring of the moon and earth. Drink from the sap of her bark so that you may know her as we do."

One by one, figures dove from their canoes into the water, becoming vague, shapeless shadows under its bright surface. They climbed, sopping, onto the stone steps, paint dripping down their skin in white streaks. Then up, between the ripples of massive roots, toward Kaona. In her hands, the Cacika held a ceramic jug, heart-shaped at the base with a tall rounded spout. She lifted it skyward, as though it were a gift meant for a king, until the applause had died into anticipatory silence.

The first man to drink from the vessel let out a cry. His spine curled, trembling, and he crumpled to the stone on all fours. A sob burst out of his throat, something primal and wounded, helpless as the sounds of a newborn freshly torn from the womb.

"The Mother welcomes you, brother," intoned Kaona, laying a gentle palm on his head. "Tell us your name, so we too may welcome you."

His fists beat the ground, and the paddle-blades drummed the water to match their slow, erratic tempo. Like a puppet yanked upward, his head flung back, and the name tore out of him as the music crescendoed. "EYDUAN!" It came out a growl, a warning to any fool that would dare take it. *Let them try*, it said. They would have to rip it from his tongue, slice through the marrow of its letters and bleed the sound out of him.

Sofía's bones sang in answer. Shivering as if it was her atop those steps, claiming herself back from those who should've never had a claim on her in the first place.

"Welcome, Brother Eyduan," said Kaona, a half smile softening her face.

"Mabrika, Atiao Eyduan!" the other Taike'ri echoed.

On the Cacika went, down the line of initiates, handing each the jug to drink. Standing by them as they wailed, broke down at her feet, or were overcome by tearful laughter. The kind that leaves a body all atremble and wheezing for breath.

The song did not rest. It changed, degree by degree, as the sky gives way from light to dark. As the night now deepened to a blacker black. The music bowed to each's rhythm, fitting itself to every new name like it could pour itself into them, filling the negative spaces between each line and loop, each fragile letter.

Not for the first time, Sofía felt the hollows of her own name gaping open like wounds. In her mind's eye, she saw it written in blood and ink and sugar dust, and she wondered what it would feel like to have it washed clean by these waters, to write herself a new one in tree sap and moonbeams. To have it sung by those who understood the weight and ache of a name. The subtle power given and taken in the simple act of naming.

Her hands reached into the white-glowing water and cupped it as though she held in her palms the last drops in the desert. Her head bent to it. Her lips parted.

She drank.

SOL SPUN INTO the arc of a young man's arm. He was a full head shorter, with a nose too large to be considered handsome, but he grinned with a devilish charm that made her brother blush. It took her a moment to reconcile the smiling face with that of the man who'd wept and raged over the ceiba's roots mere hours before. Eyduan, that was the name he'd given himself.

Sofía was watching them dance and flirt without a care when, for the third time that night, Sol's eyes met hers. Not that it was hard to notice her; she was the one figure standing still among the rabble, nursing a cup of something tart and warming while watching the celebration unfold with the scholarly interest of an anthropologist.

The festivities had migrated over to the plaza, a place the Taike'ri called the Batey. The revelers were spread across water and land, dancing atop the bridges, splashing down in the lake, sharing meals around one of the many low round tables.

Sofía made her way along them, moving toward her brother as he moved toward her, the man who'd made him blush now forgotten. The whites of Sol's eyes were tinged red from drink, but his sight was focused, his step steady. He gave her his hand, palm up. And just like that, they were children again, moving clumsily to the beat. Or rather, it was Sofía that was clumsy, her feet dragging and muscles stiff, limbs jerking in a manner that was not so much a dance as a series of elaborate spasms. Fortunately, Sol could feel the rhythm for the both of them. He was not exactly a gifted dancer, meant to grace the stage of Carnaval, but he was so wholly himself, so blissfully devoid of self-consciousness that those nearby could not help but watch him.

"Loosen up, Kán-Kán," he beckoned. "You don't have to do it right, you just have to have fun doing it."

There it was again, that name. She was never Sofía to him, as she was to the world, nor Hurakán, as she had been to their mother. When her brother was a boy, the *R*s had lain heavy and round on his tongue, swelling into the gentle curve of *L*s. With enough time and practice, the letter roughened, rolled like gravel off his lips. But the nickname, Kán-Kán, had stuck.

"What precisely is fun about—" she swiveled left "—coordinating one's movements to—" Sol swept her right "—arbitrary patterns of air vibrations?" She attempted it nonetheless, allowing him to guide her, to spin her round, to twine her hands in his and sway their linked arms side to side like a swinging hammock. It was silly, and joyous, and it made her chest swell with a kind of effervescence, a champagne fizzle that might have been laughter, or tears, or both.

"Synchrony," Sol answered as he tugged her sharply forward, then back in time with the music. "Connection." His head tilted to the side, eyes shining as they watched the crowd dancing. "I see the music, a glowing web that ties us. Moves us—moves *through* us. I feel them, everyone here . . . we are bound by song."

Once, Sofía might have rolled her eyes at his unprompted poetry. Tonight however, she could almost see that diaphanous web woven through the gathering. It was like she could borrow her twin brother's sight, peer beyond the worldly realm to the extraordinary—the color, radiance, and wonder that always came so easily to him.

"There is art here," she said with a quiver in her voice. Was it longing, perhaps? Regret that she was not sooner a part of this? "I can see why you would choose to stay." *To leave me*, she thought, but did not say.

His head dipped low, his lashes fluttered closed. It was not an expression she had ever seen on him, and so she had no name for it. He rocked, gently at first, slowly building up to faster motions. Back to the foot stomps, the dizzying twirls, the rhythmic wave of arms.

There were no more words after that. As though they had clogged up inside them after five years without an outlet. Or maybe, for her, they had become irrelevant. The brother she had gathered those words for was one in need of rescue—if not *beyond* rescue. A captive, a fugitive, or a man long dead . . . She had not prepared for a scenario in which he'd chosen a life without her.

She could not fault him for it. He belonged here, more than he had ever belonged with her.

Just this once, Sofía let her questions rest. Made a sturdy box for them, shut the lid, and locked them inside. There were things better left unsaid and unanswered, truths that could not be buried back down, no matter the damage they wrought once unearthed. And was this not worth it? Having her brother back at her side, laughing with him as though no time had passed?

There had never been a price she would not pay for knowledge, unless—it seemed—that knowledge cost her him.

All the *whys* left unspoken rattled inside their box, but she could hardly hear them over the drums and shakers, the chatter and song, the clink of ceramic bowls and clay cups, the swirl of water below and the echoes above. Another night, one less vibrant, less rowdy than this one, she might inch the box open, let a *why* or two slip. Wonder, perhaps, at the beauty and horror being wrought at the other end of this island, and the part of her she left behind.

But not this night.

This night was for dancing, imbibing, and believing in gods. A night in which her ancestors lived, a tree bloomed moonlight, and her brother was here. With her.

It was a night for miracles.

ACTO V

VELVET ARE HER thoughts when the wine coats her tongue. It is its sweet heat that she craves upon waking, the hush it brings to the howling, aching thing trapped inside her head. It pours into her wounds like resin over bark, sealing the cracks, and with them, all the life and warmth bleeding through. Until all she feels is the smooth glide of cards along her palms, the cool touch of the coins she's laid claim to.

She laughs. Laughs until her throat is raw and the bones of her jaw are aching.

Only when rest comes to her at dawn will she weep, shedding the tears her eyes deny her beyond sleep.

On a nearby shore, another will be waking . . .

Her mind is no kinder, no less loud. It throbs with each strike of memory. Bang! *You selfish girl.* Bang! *Did she not give me to you?*

After so long trapped in unrelenting bliss, every fall of that hammer feels seismic. Not that she's ever known a steady ground. What she *does* know are the places amid that volatile world where one can take shelter, the nooks and hideaways where the rattle outside becomes a soft rumbling. It was there she stowed away the orphaned girl named Hurakán. And there, the slave who made of a master a friend. Here, the sister who grieved her brother for five long years.

Now she finds somewhere new to settle, burrows in like a mollusk to a shell, the fragile softness of its body hidden from all that might harm it. She promises herself that this time, *this time*, she'll not brave the shaking of the earth for the dream of something surer elsewhere. If such a place even exists, it will demand a toll. A dangerous gambit, for what else can she forfeit when she's already traded half her heart for another? To greed for more, she might just risk losing both.

This, she tells herself, will have to be enough.

This place that is almost quiet. Almost still. Almost safe.

Almost enough to make her want to stay.

CHAPTER 17

Alive she is, within the stone and in the water.
In the root and in the leaf. By moonlight, she is born.

—Chronicler

WALKING WAS NOT the most efficient mode of travel through the caverns of Coaybay, but it was the least hazardous of options. A canoe could capsize, a ropeway could snap as one swung across it, but Sofía's two feet were as dependable as the rest of her. They did not slide, hedge, or bumble a single step as she climbed up, up, and up the tall, narrow arch of the bridge.

Practical reasons aside, the route allowed for observation as she went about her daily duties. She had acquired a new journal from a man who made paper from coconut fibers. It was darker than parchment, and the ink did not go on it as smoothly, but it was sturdy, and she didn't have to worry about her words bleeding through to the other side.

She wrote on it her detailed records of the cavern system's flora and fauna, the customs and culture of the Taike'ri, their stories and beliefs. She documented the zemís she saw vesseled in stone, and the petroglyphs that told of gods and spirits and men, and the words that sang to her, strong and rhythmic. Words without Hisperian equivalent. Words that captured the scent of morning dew, the pleasure of rest after a long day's work, the sensation of a once familiar place rendered suddenly foreign. It was a language of bold strokes and vivid colors, so unlike the soft curves and pastels of her own tongue.

Sofía's latest journal entry described a colony of bats, consisting entirely of females and their flightless offspring. They were feeding on the nectar of the flowering vines overhead as she crested the footpath, and the flutter of their wings stirred the tangles of greenery, the vines so long their tails kissed her cheeks. She observed the female bats and pups for another few minutes, making notes about their size, wingspan, and other aspects of their external morphology, until someone coughed pointedly behind her, urging her to get on with it. She did, reluctantly, and then only because she had a shift to get to.

"Taiguey." Sofia bid a quick good morning to the other transcriber at the palm-roofed hut, a woman close to her own age with owl feathers in her braids and a long burn mark across her left eye, pink and puckered.

She waved a hand in acknowledgment as her quill moved across a sheet of coconut paper, but her eyes remained on task. Sofia settled onto the low table beside hers, straightened the stack of blank sheets and envelopes, replenished the inkwells, and lit a candle for the wax.

By the time she was done organizing her materials, there were several in line waiting for their missives to be written and read. They came in one by one, sat cross-legged on the cushion by her table as she inked their words onto paper, sprinkled a powder mixture of sand and cuttlefish bone on them to dry, and folded them neatly into tan envelopes. Once the wax had cooled, she addressed the letter to whatever friend, family, or loved one the sender had left behind on the mainland, or some other island amid the Gilded Sea. On occasion, the missives were to travel even farther—to the Continent, or the Northern Colonies, or the Alkebulan Isles where they last saw their mothers and fathers, their spouses, siblings, sons, and daughters.

Not sure if these words will ever reach you, was how many of those letters began, each a hope made tangible, pressed into a form that was as vulnerable as what it carried. Absurd, that the most precious things should so often be entrusted onto paper, to sail oceans and weather storms that could render their fibers to pulp, their ink mere blots of color. Flames could gnaw the words to cinders, and Renata would never learn that her father, torn from her at the age of three, still scoured lands far and wide for her. A gust might steal the letter from Joaquin's lover, or Mariana's son, or Coa's nieces and nephews, and then who but the sky would know their story?

Is that what happened to Sol's letters? Did they dissolve in the waves and in the fire, wander off on a breeze? Sofia pictured him there and wondered if he was like them, those who sat across her table every morning with their bodies hunched and faces weary, carrying the same message, the same words recited by rote.

It took an extraordinary effort not to say, *Don't give up yet*, to promise them that *the wait will be well worth it*. Having found her way back to the person she herself had lost was making an idealist of Sofia. Fortunately, she had just enough good sense to remember that her story was the exception, not the rule.

Her assurances, no matter how well-meaning, had no bearing on whether their letters made it safely to their destinations, or whether they even reached the hands they were meant for. These, after all, were people fated to impermanence. To be vanished, sold, or worked to an early grave was not so much a probability as a statistical certainty. Further complicating matters, since the Emancipation two years before, many had also left for other haciendas and households, if not other islands entirely, leaving behind no record of where they'd gone.

When missives *were* answered, Sofia unfolded the letters with the tender care of someone unearthing a rare, archeological artifact, feeling at once humbled and daunted by the immense responsibility of reading them. Someone had waited weeks, months, even years to hear these words. Was it everything they needed? Was her tone too flat, too forcefully chipper? Was she inflecting in the right places, in the right way?

Transcribing was much better suited to her strengths, requiring diligence, patience, a keen attention to detail. She found pleasure and pride in her duties, and the letters she wrote, unlike her essays, did not need her to mark them, to claim them as Anonymous or otherwise. She was merely the instrument, making herself invisible so that another could be seen. It made her realize there was honor in obscurity, when freely chosen.

All in all, there was so much to see and learn and do, that it was easy to get swept up in it. To forget the state she'd been in a mere few weeks ago when she arrived in Coaybay.

It was impossible to reconcile the harsh realities of Carnaval with these people, this place. The dissonance was too stark for her to even begin digesting, so she'd thrown herself headfirst into her new life. Leaving no time for her mind to idle. Or wonder. Or worry.

She'd made the choice to stay, and that meant looking resolutely forward. The past, and all she'd left there—*who* she'd left there—could not coexist with this life she was building for herself. It was selfish, yes, but *gods*, with all the world had taken from her, was she not due a bit of selfishness?

It was almost midmorning when a transcriber arrived to relieve Sofía from her post.

Having some time to spare before her next shift, she left to explore the Batey's trading market. She roamed the colorful aisles, collecting payment for services rendered. From the soapmaker she earned three lumps of papaya soap, one for each letter written. Another vendor gave her a comb of dappled shell and a corked potiza for carrying water, vaguely shaped after the creation turtle, Caguama. In exchange for five readings and some light mending work, one small cheerful-looking fellow with an incongruously baritone voice offered her two inkpots and a wooden box to store her quills in.

The Taike'ri did not deal in coins. Theirs was a bartering system whereby goods and services were exchanged, to be traded promptly or at a future time per the agreed upon terms. There were no contracts drawn or receipts issued. The system relied wholly on the other person remembering what it was they'd offered and choosing to honor it. Sofía, being the meticulous recordkeeper she was, obviously kept a running ledger.

Within a half hour, her satchel was round and heavy with her week's earnings: essentials mostly, as she was still settling into life at Coaybay. She had been given her own room, but there was little in it that was not a gift or a loan. If next week turned out to be as profitable as this one however, she would no longer be reliant upon Sol's kindness or Anani's charity . . .

It struck her then, that she was envisioning a life here—planning for it, as though it were a given. Her future a right, rather than a rare and extraordinary privilege.

The thought was too big, too messy, to contemplate so early in the day, so she took out a small notepad from a pouch in her satchel and wound her way along the trading market. By the light of the cavern, glowing in hues of deep blue and violet, she crossed off names and logged payments issued.

At the margins of her awareness, she registered little details she'd missed when she first arrived at Coaybay. For one, the unnatural symmetry of the lake and the islands of rock around it, each a perfect circle. How the petals of the waterlilies were always dancing, even though there was no breeze, and how, despite the Taike'ri's world being consigned to these caves, there was a never-ending bounty of root crops, greens, and grains that should not have thrived without sunlight.

Then there were the secrets Coaybay revealed as the days went on. Flowers perpetually in bloom, neither fading nor wilting. Passages that appeared where before there'd been a wall. Mushrooms the size of coconuts, sprouting on the ceiling of her room overnight. Specifically, the Marasmius purpureostriatus, known for its purple pinwheel stripes and usually dainty size.

It had been several days since that particular development, and if she lost any more sleep pondering fungi, she might just have to find herself new accommodations.

Sofia finished updating her accounts just as she arrived at her next destination.

The hammock weavers glanced up as she entered the hut. They stood at their looms, structures consisting of two vertical poles over which the dyed agave leaf fibers were threaded through with a large wooden needle. She started sliding off her satchel when the most senior weaver popped his head up from the worktable where he was extracting fibers from a long leaf of maguey.

"You're being called to the tailors'," he said, dumping the ropy fiber into a large basin of water.

"Now?" Sofía dropped the strap of her satchel back over her shoulder. "My shift's not until midday."

"The Carnaval folks are in a pinch, they say. Anyone with a lick of talent for sewing's been pulled to help with costuming—something about a fire that got outta hand, or was that last week's debacle? Hard to keep track of that lot's messes."

Sofía stared after the looms with longing. She had been assisting in the preparation of the fibers for over a week now—the sorting of the agave leafs, the extraction and cleaning—and had been looking forward to learning the weave. Tomorrow then, she thought. Surely, she could endure a few blank journal pages for another day.

After a quick goodbye, she ducked back out of the connecting huts, past the work and storage areas, over to the storefront where the finished hammocks were showcased and bartered for. They hung from ceiling hooks like banners, proudly displaying the vibrance of their dye, the quality of their weave. The fabric rippled as she moved between them toward the tailors' hut at the other side of the bridge.

"Oh, thank the Mother, you made it on time," said the head tailor, Inoa, as Sofía walked in, thrusting an unwieldly large wooden sewing box into her arms, along with several bolts of fabric, fine and gauzy as dragonfly wings. Without another word, Inoa hefted their own stack of supplies and led their small army of tailors to the edge of the bank, where nearly a dozen canoes waited to be boarded.

They managed the entire process with a general's tactical efficiency, darting about on their prosthetic leg. It was unlike the discrete, organic-looking devices Sofía had seen before, designed to blend neatly into the skin. This one stood out boldly against the head tailor's peachy complexion, carved from jagüey wood into the shape of a tree on which nested owls, woodpeckers, and hummingbirds. It was as much an art piece as it was an instrument, and Inoa wore it the way other Taike'ri wore their paints and ink—deliberately showing off its mastery through the slits on their wraps and skirts, or the rolled-up hems of their trousers.

Sofía set her load onto one of the canoes, beside the rest of the tailors' cargo, then left to search for an empty seat. She found one near the end of the row, behind a boy half her age whose skill with a needle was already more impressive than hers would ever be. Pablo, she thought his name was. A newcomer, like her, brought to Isla Bestia as a dressmaker to a wealthy merchant family, alongside a bevy of other servants now living in Coaybay.

From somewhere up ahead, Inoa hollered a command, and they were off, rowing along the southern channel toward a part of the cave systems Sofía had not yet explored. The Batey, with all its noise and color, faded behind them, and in front of them, the lake tapered into a riverway that was only slightly wider than the canoes themselves.

Overhead, the rock split open a crack, revealing glimpses of the living quarters high above them. Sofía could just make out the shape of feet moving about, hear the garbled echoes of conversation. Then the trench knitted shut, and the passage went dark. Or at least, it seemed to in the seconds it took her eyes to adjust to the water's gentle light.

The strands of conversation lapped over and under one another, flowing into a knotted spool of words impossible to separate. Sofía lost herself in the cadence of it, even if she only understood a small fraction of what they said. The Taike'ri language did not abide by the rules of Hisperian. *This* language belonged to the salt and earth of these islands. You could feel them in it, the grit of the islands' sands, the sting of brackish waters, and the sweetness of their fruits. The words were not forged like foreigner's iron, between hammer and heat and anvil. They were woven. Like leaf, and palm, and cotton. Shaped like clay by deft fingers to bear the mark of those who made them. It was a language that had survived storms and siege and bloodshed to climb its way out of near extinction.

Sofía hungered for it the way she'd once hungered for the words in books, for the power to imbue her thoughts onto paper. Hungered for it to the point of obsession. It kept her awake, turning the pages of her journal long into the night, branding each sound onto her tongue, learning to bear the weight and sting of it, its salt, grit, and copper tang of blood.

"Hold tight now!" Came Inoa's raspy voice from further down the passage. "Coming into the curve!"

The tailors eased up on their rowing as the river slanted sharply left. Sofía had zeroed in on the task at hand, and nearly missed the mouth of the tunnel opening out into a wide chamber, with its roof fissured to let in ocean air and shafts of golden light. It had been some days since Sofía had felt the sun on her skin.

The river bent, making a circle around the chamber. Along its bank grew shrubs and small trees, their leaves dewy and green, their twisted trunks and roots swaddled in mosses and veiny filaments of brightly colored fungi.

Sofía was stretching an arm to pluck a leaf from a low-hanging branch when her ears perked to the not-so-distant echo of laughter, hard labor, and hearty conversation.

She looked down.

The river did not stop at the chamber. It *spiraled*. A hundred feet downward, around a deep shaft built like an upside-down tower. Sofía tried blinking away the sight. It seemed . . . impossible, a view of the world from the wrong way up. Yet, there it was. Impossible and not.

How fitting that Carnaval would be born somewhere as unfathomable as it.

The canoe slowed as it rounded the bend, and down the river went, tracing circles around the wide, bottomless tunnel. At that angle, the current should have dragged at them. The canoes should have been rocking and bumping along choppy waters, the paddles slick and slipping from cramped hands.

Yet the river was as tame as a creature well-fed. Bound by its own gravity, or perhaps, Sofía mused, some force greater . . .

She had not forgotten that this island was these people's zemí—Atabey, Mother of Waters and goddess supreme. Come to this earth by way of the ceiba tree, the mountains' heart which was her heart, and the cave the womb from which all is born. *Her* womb, from which she too is born. Legend said Atabey gave birth unto herself, that from her divinity rose the beginnings of the world, and with her aid, her sons filled the heavens with stars and sky beasts, the earth with its seas and its green.

It was no wonder that this island, with its strange happenings, would be thought divine. Religion was a natural result of the mind's need for order, rationalized Sofía. Deprived of explanation, the brain imposed its own flawed logic upon whatever eluded it.

Sofía herself nearly fell prey to this instinct at the Guatiao over a fortnight ago, and in moments such as this she could still feel herself grasping for that simple wellspring of sense and certitude. How much easier it would be to let faith patch the cracks in her knowledge, to accept that there were parts of this world not only beyond *her* understanding, but beyond *all* human understanding. Perhaps that was comforting to some, the cosmic absurdism of a universe that is inherently chaotic, defying comprehension, but how could she survive a place so unpredictable, so outside of her control?

As they wound their way along the inverted tower, she curbed her awe and observed instead with a scholar's gaze, taking every detail in. Each level they passed was bustling with fabricators, potters, and painters, alive with the sound of conversation, the hot crackle of flames forging gold and guanín, the strike of hammers on wood, the grate of chisels against stone. The river glowed bright, casting the artisans' creations in silver light. Among the half-finished works, Sofía spied flowers of ebony glass, a woman's body sculpted of clay, and several hound-like creatures carved from smooth dark wood.

Watching Carnaval come into being transported her back to her nights on the other side of the island, when the wine sweetened all mortal things with legend and myth. She thought of all she saw and experienced in the months she was there . . . just how much of it was a figment of her drink-addled mind? With Coaybay distorting Sofía's understanding of what was even possible, she could not confidently say what of Carnaval was real and what was fantasy.

Sofía snapped out of her reverie when she noticed her brother standing among the artisans, dwarfed by a tall monolith of matte stone, black as the volcanic sands of Playa Negra. He was shaping it with a pointed chisel and hammer, patiently cutting out a vague humanoid form.

It was striking to see the scale of his work now. Before becoming Don Reynaldo's valet, he used to carve amulets and figurines from rocks and bits of bark no larger than his fists. After his so-called promotion, he was given blocks of fine teak and precious marble to turn to busts, miscellaneous home decor, and whatever else the master coveted for his collection. Now Sol worked a stone so massive its top could only be reached by ladder.

Sofía knew better than to try for his attention. The earth could shake under that boy and his focus would not falter from his work. Although opposite in so many ways, he was her twin in that at least—a servant to his craft, losing himself in his passion just as she lost herself in hers.

The canoes continued their journey until the scent of metal, wet clay, and wood dust faded above them, and the heat of the furnaces melted to a gentle warmth. The next level down was crammed with racks and shelves bursting with every weave and shade of fabric imaginable. Cotton and velvet, suede and silk, lace and damask. Each arranged by type, color, and hue. Tables lay buried under piles of ribbon and trim, spools of fine thread, strings of pearl, and feathers dyed a rainbow of colors. The costumers darted through the chaos with pin cushions strapped to their wrists and needles gripped between their lips, tape measures draped around shoulders like scarves.

Up ahead, a wooden gate swung shut over the river, and one by one the canoes drew to a stop. Just as soon, they were each tied to a post and unloaded.

Sofía still had one foot inside her canoe when a harried-looking fellow with soot marks on both cheeks approached. "You three. With me."

He spoke in Taike'ri, and while Sofía understood the words, she failed to recognize their urgency. She lagged behind the other two tailors, who dove straight into the action with the haste of physicians tending to a medical emergency. They sidestepped a bundle of red chiffon, scorched black at the edges, and ducked as another tailor scurried past them, bearing an enormous roll of metal sequins upon one shoulder. Tulle flew and orders rang. Someone nearby cursed at the prick of a finger, another shouted for a *Saints-fucking bobbin!*

Sofía had known hurricane preparations to be less frantic than this.

When she finally made it over to her assigned workstation, their guide was gesturing at a pile of fabrics in sunset shades. The tailors she had ridden with were nodding at his instructions, but she only caught every other word.

At her blank expression, he paused.

"Buk'guároko ke' irája?"

Sofía interpreted this as, *Do you know the earth's song?* Which she presumed, from context, meant *Do you speak Taike'ri?* She shook her head.

He slid a hand down his face, tracking soot all the way to his pointed chin. "Half the eve's costumes have gone the way of the flames," he continued in Hisperian. "The half that did not succumb to ash needs fixing." He held up a gown, its hem seared into uneven tatters, the bodice spotted brown and black. "You have five hours to make this mess look 'artfully scorched.' All performers are to be in costume and en route to Carnaval soon as the sun slips west. Questions? No? Fantástico. I'll be just around the corner, sewing till my fingers bleed."

With that, he left them to patch and mend, to tack on layers of scarlet chiffon or—on occasion—strip them away, curating the burn marks to look intentional. Designed.

Carnaval always seemed so effortlessly grand. Too perfect to have been sculpted by flawed, clumsy, pin-pricked human hands. Even after everything, a part of her dared long for the nights she believed in the illusion. When the drink was strong and the mysteries endless, and Carnaval was not made, but *willed* into existence.

Sofía busied herself with the snip-snip of scissors, the rise and fall of her golden needle, the chafe of fabric against her fingertips. All the while, a question was forming in the back of her mind. Just a small thing at first, but she could sense it stretching beyond the space she'd made for it, taking up more room in her mind than any question had a right to.

She felt it as she glided her scissors through a length of tulle.
Why?
As she stitched the fraying along the hem of the gown.
Why?
As the point of the seam ripper bit through the fabric.
Why? Why? Why? Why go through all this effort to entertain those they despised? Why shower conquerors with feasts and dance and spectacle? Why make them stay, when they could make them *leave*? They had a drink that could make a mind pliant and forgetful, why not use it to take more than just these mountains? This whole island could be theirs.

Sofía worried she'd been too quick to abandon her initial theories. Recent evidence might indicate the Taike'ri were the ones running the show, but she could not discard the very likely possibility that there was another hand behind this. One that *actually* made sense.

"Ay!" The woman Sofía was fitting a gown to recoiled at the jab of her needle. If the glare she sent Sofía was any indication, it was not the first injury she had endured at her hands.

"Hold please. Just a few more stitches," she said by way of apology.

Performers crowded her. Some were being stitched into their costumes, others were milling about in their smallclothes, waiting for their turn. At the other side of the rotunda, carnavaleros were being brushed with red, gold, and yellow paint. Carbon black lined their eyes, and flames spread up their cheekbones and beyond the arch of their brows, ending at the edges of their hairline. Sofía watched as one performer was outfitted with giant wings of steel wire, braided in red cord and set aflame. Another donned a similar contraption above their head, the fires flickering bright.

All of this . . . for what?

Sofía worked furiously, trying to chase the suspicions from her mind, her thoughts swirling with that same sense of wrongness that drove her out of Carnaval, to this place where others like her came to be . . . *safe*. She was content here. Free to learn any trade. Free to be whoever she wanted. Here, she lacked for nothing. The food was plentiful, her living quarters generous, and the knowledge waiting to be discovered endless.

So what if it did not make sense? Would she pick at this loose thread and risk unraveling her new, fragile life just to sate her damn curiosity?

"Mierda . . ." She could dismiss it all she wanted, but for every reason she had not to raise questions, she thought of another dozen why she should. Even if she did need only one.

The reason had a face, and it flashed in Sofía's mind. Not the version that she knew, the radiant smile that could endear a devil to her, but the one from the night it all went wrong, the one so foreign to her now it could not hold its shape. Within Sofía's memory, the face she knew morphed, iterating on itself the more she conjured it. Transforming into something almost monstrous.

Sofía bowed her head, and when she lifted it again, her brother was there. The piece of her she'd gained at the cost of leaving behind another.

One corner of his mouth twitched, and then, he was laughing, his voice echoing in the sudden silence of the tower. That was when she realized the clink of tools and grunts of labor, the swell of voices all rushing to talk over one another, had faded. A handful of stragglers still loitered about, sweeping floors and putting away materials, but the rest had gone.

Sol bent to where Sofía sat against the leg of a sewing table and picked a few scraps of fabric off her hair. She sputtered a protest as he scrubbed a strip of silk roughly against the bridge of her nose. It came away dusted black with soot.

"Where is everyone?" she asked blearily, voice thick with exhaustion. She vaguely recalled sliding to the floor after what must have been hours of costume repairs and fittings. A thimble sat forgotten on her thumb. She clicked a nail against it absently.

"The night shift's gone off to Carnaval. The rest are scarfing down their evening meals, I'd assume." He untangled yet another bit of fabric from her hair, and she let him, taking every shred of kindness he'd extend to her.

These days, their connection was a delicate thing—built on nostalgia and heartbreak and jokes only the other would ever understand. But a relationship, even that of twins, could not be sustained on memory alone. And yet, memory was all he was willing to give her. The rest, those five long years they spent apart, he guarded closely—almost jealously—shutting her out the instant she dared pry.

"And you?" he asked. "You eaten anything today?"

"Not since this morn—" No. She had gotten distracted on her way to breakfast, first by a small stone zemí near the women's baths, and later by the bats. "Last night . . . ?"

Sol pulled her to her feet, angling his head for her to follow. "Let's go fix that."

A RUMBLE MADE Sofía's hand still halfway to her mouth, a crisp piece of cassava flatbread pinched between her fingers. The floor of the Batey shook, rattling the bowls and cups on the dining tables, yet no one reacted. Not in the way Sofía expected, at least. There was applause and cheers, a smattering of good-natured heckling, and then, she saw it.

The platform rising above the water, its edges lined with hulking slabs of dark amethyst. Carved into each slab was a petroglyph. On one, the double spiral she now recognized as the cosmic energy that knows no beginning and no end. On another, the face of the sun. The moon, like a smiling half mask. The god twins, Marohú of the Clear Skies and Boinayel, Herald of Rains, bound together by a cord around their waists. She recognized a few others, the simple image of a heron. A snail. A coquí. They could be found throughout Coaybay, etched into the walls and the floor, on necklaces of stone and amulets of shell and fishbone. Some were woven into hammocks and rugs, others tattooed onto skin, and Sofía had been obsessively collecting them all, gathering their meanings like artifacts to be placed in a museum.

Though the platform had just barely broken through the water, over a dozen Taike'ri had already launched themselves onto its slick surface, splashing noisily as they assembled at opposite ends.

"What are they doing?" Sofía asked.

Sol glanced over his shoulder, appearing to only just notice the commotion behind him. He shrugged, returning to his bowl of spiced sweet potato, corn, and boiled yautía. He scooped up a generous spoonful and folded it into his cassava flatbread.

"Batú," he said, and took a bite. "Sometimes a ceremonial ball game, others . . . eh, how would you put it? An elaborate means of conflict resolution? They'll fight it out for a few hours and be good and civil by morning." Noticing Sofía's expression, he clarified. "Not *fight* fight. Blows and swords are not the way here. If you've a problem, you talk it out or deal with it in the ball court."

"Oh." How . . . novel. "And they *all* have a problem?" There were well over twenty gathered on the floating platform.

"Nah." Sol waved his spoon. "These lot will just grab at any excuse to muck around."

All across the Batey, people were turning in their seats, drawing closer to the edges of the bank or climbing the stone bridges for a better view. Those who had been rowing past in their canoes dropped their paddles over their laps and lingered to watch the match unfold. A few whistled, or clapped, or called out words that sounded distinctly like a taunt.

The players had scattered into mixed-sex teams, a dozen to each side, a sight that would have surely caused an uproar anywhere else in Etérea. Men and women mingled in ballrooms and tea rooms, where the blending of the genders was deemed proper, but never in sport and play.

Then again, that would not have been deemed the most shocking of the players' offenses, not when the very concept of gender itself was as fluid as it was among the Taike'ri, and when a quarter of the players evidently regarded clothing as optional.

The only item every one of them wore was a stone belt around their waists, green for some, blue for others. The players bounced the ball against the curious accessories, relying on those belts as much as they did their knees, ankles, shoulders, and elbows.

Observers jeered and clapped when the ball was dropped, or a pass was made, or a player accidentally touched their hand to it. A lively chant that sounded like a name went up from those gathered at the bridge, growing to a cacophony when one of the players from the blue team scored a point.

Sol joined the celebration, not that he very much cared who won. He cheered on both teams with equal fervor, his twinkling eyes straying to the crowd more often than the game. It was the people, not the sport, that tugged his mouth into a wide boyish grin, crinkling the sunburst inked from brow to cheekbone. She watched him as he watched them, wondering how he could love this world so fiercely when it had shown so little love for him.

When he caught her staring, he rubbed a hand across his beard, as though he worried there was a bit of food stuck in it. "What is it?"

"Nothing, I just . . ." Her words felt brittle, too soft against the noise. "This life . . . it breaks things, and when I first saw you again . . . I . . . I was afraid it'd broken you. All good must either bend or fracture, and I knew which way I'd gone, and thought I knew which *you'd* go." She met his gaze, storm-gray on gold-flecked ochre. "But if you can still laugh like that, then I was wrong, and I've never been so glad for it."

At her words, Sol's expression changed. Shuttered, the same way it had that morning outside Coaybay. A moment later, he was pushing away from the table, gathering his cup and bowl and rising to his feet. When he smiled this time, it looked strained. "I should get back to work now."

"What? At this hour?"

In reply, he bent to brush a quick kiss against the top of her head. It felt like an apology. "See you tomorrow, Kán-Kán."

With that, he was gone.

CHAPTER 18

The zemí is the spirit in the islands above, as it is the wood and rock below, the carved bone and forged guanín that houses it.

—Chronicler

SOFÍA WAS IN red again.

Not in her usual silk gown. In a costume, like the ones she had bruised and pricked her fingers over to mend, an extravagant thing of chiffon and beaded tulle, winged in fire. She felt the heat of it against her back, her shoulders, her neck; felt its searing brightness against the corners of her vision, though it did not burn her.

Down below, the river too was in flames. A million candles floated on it, washing all of Carnaval in deep shadows and tangerine light. Sofía watched the show unfold from atop the solarium, unsure how she'd gotten there—or how she would get down, for that matter.

From up there, she could clearly see the embers over the stone paths, traipsed by barefoot carnavaleros in burning crowns, trailing behind them long, glowing trains. Elsewhere, fire breathers performed for a crowd of patrons, lighting the night sky with their conflagrations. The flames glinted off the performers' large bronze masks, shaped in the image of Bayamanaco, the wrathful Old Spirit of the Fire. The eyes were pitted, the mouth wide and lined with gritted teeth.

Arching arbors, trellised with flames instead of vines, made a luminescent path for whoever dared cross them. Totems of the old fire god rose tall over the landscape, and atop them performers spun rings of flamelight. Even the sky burned red. With a whoosh and a bang, flares surged from the roof of the Flor de

Lis, exploding against the dark in a shower of sparks, rattling the air that hung thick with clouds of smoke. They came one after the other, bursts of heat and sound and light, barely winking out before another series of explosions rose and . . .

Stopped.

Or rather, *slowed*.

Powder and debris ignited, the tiny specks winking in place like starlight. The music slowed with it, the notes stretching taut, growing rhythmless and discordant. Fire hung in the air in a sinuous ripple, hands froze midapplause, and the din of celebration became a strange, muffled hum.

In the light of the moon, Sofia saw her dress was dripping. The red dye so thick it looked like blood.

The sleeves melted to drips of red down her arms and around her fingers. The skirt bled from the hem, streaking across the glass of the solarium, soaking into the earth below. Then . . . it was not just her dress. The river too was turning crimson, seeping into the soil and the green, flooding the land with violent color.

Sofia scrambled back, felt the glass beneath her crack and shatter.

She fell. Straight through the solarium, landing as the bloody river rushed in like a tidal wave, breaking her fall. It filled her mouth with the taste of copper, thick and warm as though freshly spilled.

Her head broke through the surface, and her eyes burst open to the sight of the moon, swollen and full above her. As Sofia sank, its silver light engulfed more and more of the dark, swallowing the stars and the cloud and the smoke, until there was nothing left of the night.

The moon ate the world whole.

THE REAL MOON was a waxing crescent, its light too weak to even navigate by. Not that Sofia needed it. The water fluoresced a gentle white even beyond the caves.

It had been morning the last and only time she was in the valley outside Coaybay. Now that there were no arrows pointed at her head, she could appreciate it properly. The place was a paradise safely nestled into the nook between mountains, vibrant with color and fragrant with passionflowers. It played a different symphony in the dark. The song of the coquís had replaced the morning chirp of mockingbirds, punctuated by the somber hoot of owls, the splash of fish beneath the canoe.

Where the waterfalls met the lake, a gentle mist rose, diffusing into an even blanket across the water and rolling over the edges of the bank. That was why Sofía did not notice the figure at the base of the guayaba tree until she was out of the canoe and the two were only a span apart.

Kaona's eyes opened, their shape rimmed with coal dust and painted flames. There was no surprise in them, merely resignation. She must have seen Sofía long before Sofía saw her.

"Running away, daughter of arijua?"

Sofía did not rise to the Cacika's taunt. It was not especially creative, and her self-esteem was not so fragile it could not withstand being called a foreigner's daughter. Besides, the insult lacked the venom of their first encounter. If anything, Kaona sounded more exhausted than malicious.

"Couldn't sleep, Cacika?" Sofía resisted the urge to step back, unwilling to let herself be cowed.

"I do not sleep," she said, offering no further explanation.

In a typical conversation, it would be Kaona's turn to ask, *and what of you?* But the Cacika was not the kind to bother with pleasantries and Sofía was not the kind to demand them, so instead, she said, "I dreamt the moon grew so big it gobbled up the world."

At her words, Kaona glanced at the slice of silver floating in the dark above them. "Would that be such a terrible thing?"

"Sometimes, I wonder." Sofía wrapped her arms around herself, warding off the evening's chill. "There are days I've wished the next storm that blew through would leave nothing behind. That it would wash this earth clean of all the blood and sin, and maybe whatever life grew on it next would be . . . *better*."

Kaona regarded her intently, letting the pause linger before saying, "And other days?"

Sofía gave a small shrug. "I'm plagued by a strange . . . sentimentalism." Her lips twitched into a wry smile. "I start believing that we might *grow* into something better, instead of simply making way for it. Or I'll catch myself mulling over the morality of things. Is it right to erase all for the wrongs of a few? That kind of thought."

"It is not always about whether it is right or wrong though, is it? But whether it is inevitable. You can cut away the rot, or leave it until the rest of the flesh festers." Kaona brought a bottle to her lips, hovered it there as she said, "Not all healing restores. Some requires destruction." She drew a long, deep gulp before extending the drink to Sofía. A peace offering?

The uikú, fermented from the juice of cassava, sent a gentle warmth through her. It was an acquired taste, a bit like ale. Sofía made a face before tipping the bottle back for another swig. "Can I ask a question?"

"No."

She asked it anyhow, emboldened by the Cacika's rare gesture of . . . not friendship exactly, but something that might lead to it. A promising start.

"Why do all of this . . . ?" She waved at Kaona's costume, so tattered and blackened the tailors had thrown it in a pile to discard. She had chosen it herself, ignoring the pristine piece already set aside for her and sliding the burnt thing on before anyone could try to change her mind. "The likes who attend Carnaval are, by your own admission, your enemies. Why put on a spectacle for them?" *Who is forcing your hand?* is what she wanted to ask, but doubted the Cacika would take well to the insinuation that anyone could force her to do anything.

"Not every weapon draws blood."

"What's that supposed to mean?"

"You were there," she replied. "You drank the wine, clawed at your cage while others reveled in it. So desperate were you to escape that 'spectacle,' you stowed away in a box. You have the pieces—" she flicked her wrist dismissively "—put them together yourself."

With that, Kaona got to her feet and stalked away through the mist.

She was waist deep in the lake before Sofía could react.

Sofía's hands balled into fists, and her nails dug into the soft, scarred flesh of her palms. Something frayed. In *her*, some broken thing she kept on stitching. Rebinding with fresh sutures soon as the old ones snapped apart. It had been there, a constant ache deep beneath her rib cage, tearing a little at a time.

Once, under a blue sky, when her mamá gave her over to the bars and chains while whispering she loved her.

Again, when Adelina saw the bloodied bandages on her hands yet looked the other way.

When the brother she thought dead came dashing to save her, but could not bring himself to meet her gaze.

Sofía was *so* exhausted of trying to make this life—these people in it, so rife with contradictions—make sense. Before she knew it, she was moving, splashing into the lake after the Cacika.

"Then allow me to speak plainly." Her voice, normally so even, struck the silence like a cord of thunder. "I witnessed yours taking a man away, and the next time I saw him he'd forgotten my name. For three nights and three days, I kept vigil over my friend's unconscious body. On the fourth night, she rose like one of her saints, returned from the brink of death. And what did she do? Left to play cards and down a few glasses of wine as though nothing had happened."

Anger simmered in Sofía, warming her despite the cool bite of the water. "I am no fool, Cacika. I know there is a darkness beneath all the glitter and gold of that place. But I have met your gods and dined among your people, read them tear-soaked letters and written their hopes and hearts in ink. My brother has found a home here, and I—" *refuse to believe he is a part of this* "—am trying to give you the benefit of the doubt, Cacika. I want to trust that whatever horrors are being wrought upon this island are not your doing. Please do not mistake my wishfulness for ignorance."

Kaona's teeth glinted in the pale light. "'Ignorance'? No, that is too passive of a word for what this is. You say you've met our gods? You've merely studied them. They are a myth to you. These waters a thing to be explained by your science." She nearly spat the word. "You think you know us because you watch us, make notes of us. Like *they* did when they came, worming their way into our homes with the promise of peace and friendship. It was not our gold or our women that they first stole. It was our *words*. Our stories. They took them, butchered them like they did our bodies. Gave them to their kings and queens as curiosities. Our ways, shared in good faith, in their hands became the first weapon to be used against us. So forgive me if I am not eager to expose our lives and choices to an outsider's judgment."

"Would I be any less an outsider if I made your stories and your gods my own?" Sofía asked, feeling the cold seep back in. "Or would you still hate me for loving one of them?" That was what it came down to, after all. Sofía had made a sister of her slaver, and the Cacika could not forgive her the transgression.

No answer came—not in words anyway.

"*Please* . . ." Sofía's eyes squeezed shut. "I . . . I just want to know she's . . ." *Safe?* No, Sofía had no illusions of safety. She knew very well what she'd abandoned Adelina to. "Unharmed."

"Go back to her then," said Kaona, "if you're so worried." With that, she turned and waded deeper into the water, until she was only a ripple on the surface, a shadow against the pale light.

Sofía let her go.

"STOMACH PAINS, IS IT?" The Behíke lifted an eyebrow.

Sofía clutched her arms around her abdomen harder, bidding her facial muscles to look appropriately aggrieved. She had practiced that morning in front of a mirror, pulling the corners of her eyes and lips down until it looked as though her face was melting.

"That's right," she said, tugging her brow deeper. "Perhaps . . . the tincture from last time might help?"

"Perhaps it would." Tínima's tone was one she would have described as amused, had their concern not seemed so sincere. "Any pain when I apply pressure here?"

"Yes," she blurted, perhaps a little too eagerly. "There, and . . . there too. All over, truly."

The Behíke clicked their tongue in sympathy and stepped away to rummage through shelves stocked full of stoppered vials, dried herbs, and colorful powders. "Let's see what we've here then. No, not that. Not that either . . . Maybe . . . hmm . . . something with anamú? Or . . ." They trailed off. "I have the perfect thing here somewhere, I'm sure."

"Why not this one?" Sofía grabbed from the shelf a stoppered gourd, similar in size and shape to the one the Behíke gave her when she first arrived at Coaybay. "It did a fine job before."

"*That* is a wart treatment." One bony hand reached over to pluck it from her grip. "*This*—" They held up the correct bottle, as she'd been hoping they would do. It was slightly thicker at the bottom, and the carving on the wooden stopper was different, more angular. "—settles a stomach ailed by a toxin. It will do nothing for your . . . particular affliction. For that, we'll need a different remedy."

Sofía was only half listening as she watched Tínima place the little bottle back, committing its location to memory: fifth row from the left, second shelf from the bottom. Now, if she could only get them to tell her where the other one—

"Drink," said Tínima, and she did automatically, downing the medicine offered in a single gulp. It was cool and quenching. Tasteless.

She looked at her empty cup, and frowned. "What was that?"

"A treatment befitting the affliction."

Nervous, Sofía rolled her tongue along her teeth, trying to pick up on any warning notes she might have missed—a bitter aftertaste, a tingling sensation, a slight burning along her gums. Nothing.

What had she just taken?

"There, it's only water. See?" said Tínima, pulling a second stool from under the counter and motioning for her to take her own seat again. She did, after a brief pause of hesitation. "I gather it at each rainfall and infuse it with hibiscus petals. Lovely, isn't it? Adds a mild sweetness, I think."

"And . . ." she said slowly, unsure where this was leading, "does hibiscus treat afflictions of the stomach?"

"Not at all." The Behíke chuckled gaily. "I'm just fond of the taste."

"Fond of . . ." Sofía shook her head to clear it. "Forgive me. I appear to have misunderstood. I thought you were giving me something for the pain."

The Behíke reached for the water pitcher atop the counter and poured themself a cup. "The treatments I prescribe are proportionate in strength to the ailments themselves. As yours is not one of the body, it cannot be treated as such."

"That's not—"

Tínima held up a hand. "I may be old, but I've still got my wits about me, ituno. Enough to know when I'm being played for a fool. That being said—" their eyes lifted to hers "—you are ailed by something. Everyone who comes here is, be it something that troubles the body, the spirit, or the mind."

Sofía's mouth gaped, racking her brain for an answer that did not come. The Behíke used the moment to refill her cup—a pink petal falling with the pour and bobbing to the surface.

"Now, how about we start over again? Without the lies this time. Tell me, what brings you here today?"

Sofía's shoulders fell on an exhalation.

There had always been the possibility she would walk out of there empty-handed, her mission thwarted, though not entirely lost. She'd come in with a contingency plan already in mind. At dawn, when the day shift slept and the night shift was some twenty kilometers west, busy entertaining their unwitting captives, she would slip back into this shop. With no locks or bars or even doors to block her entry, breaking in wouldn't be a challenge. All she had to do was get Tínima to show her where the restorative was beforehand, and she'd be on a canoe traveling west before anyone noticed her absence.

Could she figure it out on her own? Maybe, but there was a risk she'd abscond with a skin rash ointment—or something equally useless—instead of the thing that could bring her friend back to her senses.

"I . . ." Sofia's reflection looked back at her from the drinking cup, distorted by the slight tremble of her hand, the puffs of her breath. "I left someone behind." She had tried so hard to put Adelina out of her mind. Thinking about her would lead to worrying, and if she worried, she'd have to act. To uproot this new life she was building for herself, risk losing all she'd just found: the brother she loved, work she found meaningful, a place that did not continuously demand she prove her right to *be*. And she was so weary of this trade, this constant bargaining with the world, exchanging one good thing for another as though one good thing was all it would allow.

Tínima did not ask who she'd left or where she'd left them. They must have known by now why Sofia had remained at Carnaval for as long as she did. Had she not come in as a guest, Kaona would have smuggled her away from the Flor de Lis as she had every other servant that sailed in on that same steamer. "The Hisperian girl," they said without reproach.

"Carnaval has got a grip on her. I've tried breaking her away from it before, but . . . I need the restorative, the one you gave me, if I'm to stand a chance this time."

Tínima nodded, dark eyes narrowed in contemplation. "So you give her the restorative, then what? You bring her here?"

"I take her home."

"Oh, child." A weary sound escaped the Behíke. "No one comes or goes from this island's shores without the Cacika knowing. The few who ever make it out of Carnaval do so only by her will."

Sofia frowned. "You all speak of her as if she's a god."

"She is the voice of one. The vessel through which the rivers speak. What this earth knows, *she* knows."

It was not the first time she had heard someone proclaim Kaona the voice of Atabey, Mother of Gods and Waters, but it sounded no less absurd coming from the Behíke, despite their venerable position as healer, wisdom keeper, and spiritual mediator. Everyone whispered of the Cacika as if she were a deity herself, a woman chosen by a great divinity to lead.

"Then let her gods tell her what I've done. I will take my chances."

"I can see you will."

She leaned forward, solemn. "Would you help me?"

Tínima barked out a laugh, and Sofía flinched backward.

"Forgive me," they said, placing a hand over their heart, just beneath the curve of their obsidian collar. "I am not laughing at you, child. I swear it. You are just . . . so much like her. How had I not seen it before?"

"So much like . . . who?"

"Her. The woman you've dismissed for a fraud. She sat there too, once. Asking me to make what *you* now ask me to unmake, as though I could have ever said no." The sound of their laughter grew wistful. "I was just a child then . . . eager to please the Mother and her chosen vessel."

Sofía struggled to unpack those words. Tínima looked to be twice Kaona's age. Surely, they must be misremembering, or maybe she'd misheard . . .

"I can see your confusion," said Tínima. "No one has told you yet. Or maybe they have, and you've not wanted to listen."

"Told me what exactly?"

The Behíke let out a deep sound of exhaustion, as though regretting what came next. "May I see your hand?" They motioned at the one with the words *Look up* branded into the palm.

Sofía hesitated. The wounds had healed into faint lines in places and thick scar tissue in others. They no longer smarted, not even when she dipped the hand into the heat of the baths or scrubbed at the broken skin with rough soap. It was therefore not the potential of pain that gave her pause, but the earnest, almost apologetic expression the Behíke wore.

Slowly, she uncurled her fingers, extending her hand out with the same uneasy curiosity she once approached an ox, knowing nothing of its nature.

The Behíke accepted the hand, holding the palm to the light with a gentle grip. "The waters here," they began, "can heal in ways my elixirs and unctions alone could never hope to accomplish. The right words and herbal mixtures can rid a body of illness, mend broken flesh, and soothe the pain of childbirth. These waters bear the Mother's power. Raw and ready to be molded by our will and hers. You may have heard others tell of it, how they petition the zemí for soil that grows rich, crops that withstand plague, wood that will not wear or rot."

While Tínima spoke, they applied a poultice to her palm, a thick cooling paste that smelled of cloves and something earthy. Finished, they placed the clay jar back on the countertop, then wrapped the poultice with a length of pressed moss, bright green against the sand-brown of Sofía's skin. They coiled it around her hand like it was a bandage.

"Those the Mother favors may be given stronger bones or lasting youth. For some . . . the waters do more." Tínima carefully undid the dressing, and folding it, used it to scrub off the paste. Each swipe exposed another glimpse of skin, the scar-roughened layer peeling away like caked-in dirt, leaving behind a smooth, unblemished palm. "Some, like our Cacika, the Mother keeps long after they should have gone."

Sofía stared.

She could sense herself nodding, a compulsive motion rather than a conscious one. Her body quickly coming to acceptance, so that her mind could follow suit.

Tínima sat quietly as Sofía flexed the healed hand experimentally, ran a finger over the unscarred skin, brought the palm to the light and set about inspecting it from every possible angle. All the while, her chin bobbed up and down mechanically. *Yes, I see*, the gesture seemed to convey. *Yes, this makes perfect sense.*

"Do you understand now?"

"Of course." The words came out quick and breathless. "The curative powers of these waters are truly remarkable. Even the medical advances from the Northern Colonies cannot hold a candle to this."

Tínima took the hand from her again, gently pressing it between both of theirs comfortingly. It was only then she realized she was shaking.

"You know there is more to this." It was not a question. "You wouldn't be eyeing the exit if you didn't. This scares you, ituno. Down to your bones, it scares you. You are not the first of our children to feel this way. They often return to us with the wrong gods, praying to warring saints and fearing all that's different is devilry. Some, it takes years to believe in anything else."

"That's not—" Sofía shook her head. "I am godless," she said, almost in defiance. "Scholarship is the only altar I bend a knee at."

"A devotee of truth." Tínima leaned back, arms crossed over the opening of their overrobe. "Tell me then. What truth do you see here?"

She rubbed circles into her palm. Hard. As though she could wipe off the unbroken skin, scrub the strange perfection away like she would face powder. "One I have no explanation for." The admission pained her, unsettling the plinths she had built her world upon, in neat blocks and with clear delineations. This truth was all angles and pointed edges, a shape she could not make fit no matter where she put it. The kind of truth to undo all truths.

She knew it before, floating beneath a moon-soaked ceiba tree. And she knew it now, sitting here across from this living relic of a people thought dead.

"It doesn't make it any less real though, does it?" said Tínima.

Sofía inclined her head, less in agreement than surrender. The Behíke gave her shoulder a pat as they slid off the stool, walking heavily to one of the floor-to-ceiling shelves cut into the stone. They stretched to their full, lanky length and plucked up a stoppered bottle. "Here," they said, offering it to her along with the tincture.

With eyes wide, Sofía cradled both remedies in the cups of her hands.

"Wait until the next full moon," they told her. "There . . . may be others leaving the island that night. That might be your best chance to slip by unnoticed."

"Why? What's happening that night?"

The Behíke's expression grew grim, their spindly frame and weary face weighed by something heavier than fatigue. "An . . . anniversary of sorts."

"And the island, the Cacika, she will not sense us leaving?" The implication was absurd, a farfetched thing of daydreams and storybooks. An island alive, a woman the conduit through which it spoke.

"If all goes to plan, she'll have other things to deal with."

Sofía did not know how much of this she was ready to accept, but if what Tínima said was even remotely true, she could not risk a premature rescue—if that was even the right word for it? Who or what she ought to fear, she no longer knew. Besides, she had been in Coaybay near a month already, she could wait a few more nights if it meant getting Adelina home safely.

And then what . . . ?

The bottles clanked softly as Sofía set them carefully into her satchel. "Kaona would not want you helping me, would she?"

They stroked a hand along their chin. "Probably not."

"Then why do it? You were in awe of her once . . . are you no more?"

"Sweet child, she saved our people from extinction. Her hands built the vessels that carried my ancestors off Taike's shores, and her spear drew the blood of those who would have defiled the Mother's sacred waters, drained them dry to fill their coffers. I will *always* be in awe of her." Respect and admiration rang clear in Tínima's voice. "But . . . the Cacika . . . she is not who she was in her youth, before the ships came and with it the men who took and took and *took*. She is old, and she is weary, and the fire with which she once lit our way now consumes her."

"Before the ships . . . ? Tínima. That would make Kaona . . . what? Over three-hundred years old?"

"Three-hundred and twenty-four by her count."

"But that's . . ."

"More years than a spirit can bear, yes," said Tínima, sorrow dragging at their shoulders.

"I was going to say *impossible*." Sofía was on her feet then, pacing the short length of the cave. "These waters have kept her alive all this time?"

"They have preserved her body, but those closest to her can tell you she has not been of the living for some while. She is, in some manner, an opi'a. One bound to her physical form," they said. "On the very eve of her death, the Mother brought her back from Maketaori's land and rebound her spirit to her flesh. Since then, she has not aged or slept or sickened. Nor will she for as long as she is bound to this island."

"An opi'a . . ." A spirit, like the ones from the stories Sofía's elders told. Again, she found herself nodding vigorously through her denial. Bodily shoving past the voice that dismissed all this as nonsense, in hopes of arriving at a more comfortable place of begrudging acceptance. "That is, um . . ."

"Enough for one day. I agree." Tínima placed a gentle palm on Sofía's cheek, the stone rings around their fingers cool against her skin. "I gave you the truth not so that you would believe me, but because it is yours as much as it is mine. This place, this history, it belongs to all the children of those we left behind. To you, kin of my kin, blood of my blood, our fire is yours and you may warm yourself by it."

Sofía's throat tightened, and she felt a pricking sensation at the backs of her eyes. Not tears, no, she would not call them that, for that would imply there was a hollow in her that the Behíke's words could fill. Without cracks, the offer of home and belonging would slide like rain off her skin, finding no firm purchase, no dents to hook into and settle.

So she did not call them tears. Not when her vision blurred. Not when she tasted salt on her lips. Not when, later that same day, she slid into a room that smelled of paper and ink and felt it *hers*. Hers. This rug and that hammock. The quills on the table. The basket of unlaundered clothes by the door.

Hers, but for how much longer?

CHAPTER 19

*Beasts are born,
and so too are they made.*

—Chronicler

COAYBAY WAS A creature holding its breath. Within its walls, there was a pressure building, the feeling of too much air gathering too quickly, taking up space, pushing against stone already stretched rubber thin. It built in sighs and whispers, in weighted silences, too-long pauses and meaningful looks—each a fragment of another language for Sofía to decipher, one which ceded to her more than their words did. The ones they chose with care. The ones they left unsaid, fading into an ellipsis.

Whatever was happening on the next full moon was not to be spoken of out loud. At least, not overtly.

"This is the year . . ." was a sentence Sofía heard more than once. At times whispered with dread, at others, with anticipation, and always intended for another's ears. She grasped onto it anyway, every piece of information she could pocket, all of which amounted to little more than crumbs. Some she found slipped into the reprieves between errands and work, in the steam of the baths where tongues loosened as muscles thawed, and in the letters that warned *Not yet*, and, *Wait until the next moon*, and *Stay, I'll come to you* . . .

More often, the truth lived in the passages, filtered through thick curtains and thicker stone. Sofía might not go so far as to linger by strangers' doors, but she did relax her step as she made her way to and from her daily duties, enough to reel in gossip as she passed.

It might not be ready . . . We might still have time.

We can't tell the children yet. Not until we're sure.
Would you take this to my father if . . . ?
If you stay, I stay.

There was more that reached Sofía's ears that she could not understand. Words not yet in her vocabulary, or exchanged too fast for her to tell where one syllable ended and another began.

Was she wrong to worry? Doubt crept in from time to time, and with it, the urge to brush off her anxieties as paranoia, some leftover malaise from her days trapped in Carnaval. Until she remembered she had merely crossed the curtain, she hadn't left the show. And sure, she might have been fonder of life backstage, but its shadows held just as many secrets, if not more.

If only her brother would stick around long enough to have a conversation, she wouldn't have to go skulking about Coaybay, pulling scraps of knowledge from the dark. Yet dawn to dusk, his room lay empty. The only sign of him, the growing pile of unwashed clothing by the door. Most days, she was lucky to catch a glimpse of him on his way out of the Batey, a half-eaten guayaba between his teeth and a goodbye in his hand. *Work*, he'd mouth, already shifting away from her.

He was not the only one keeping busy.

On the rare occasion she saw Anani, the woman stalked after the Cacika like a storm cloud, her mood foul and steps thunderous.

Usually, Sofía's eyes followed them only until they vanished from view. But today, her feet moved to follow too.

The two were arguing. Or rather, *Anani* was arguing, lobbing harsh whispers at Kaona's back, and though Sofía kept a generous distance, sound traveled far along these tunnels.

As they passed, heads swiveled. Conversations stalled. Bodies leaned in to listen. Noticing, Kaona snatched up Anani's wrist and dragged her deeper into the passage, down the nearest outlet to the river. Sofía waited for their shapes to disappear through the stone staircase and for the remaining bystanders to move on before shadowing them.

She paused, foot hovering halfway to a step when she heard voices. A few snatches of their conversation carried up through the stairway, muffled slightly by the rush of water.

"You ask too much of me," said Anani with a note of defeat.

"This is what the Mother wants," Kaona replied, her own voice giving away nothing. "She does not ask for more than you are capable of giving."

"And what if I'm not willing to give it?"

"You knelt at her roots, rahe. Fifty years ago you offered your life to her. To us."

"*My life!* Not . . ." The next words were a tangle, too complex or too garbled in Anani's anger for Sofía to pick apart. "I can't lead them. Not under the same laws that made me an orphan, slave, and child bride. The goddess can have my life. *Here*, among her dirt and bramble I'll forfeit my years, this unending youth I never asked for. I'll give my bones and my blood for this justice, but I won't die in a land that took my name, my voice, and my body. I will serve her here, or not at all."

"They need you." The Cacika's voice softened a fraction. "*I need you.*"

"Don't—"

Footsteps, at the base of the stairs.

Sofía scrambled up the steps, back toward the passage as quickly and as quietly as she could.

As she turned, Kaona's last words drifted to her. "Not all of us get to choose, rahe . . . Leadership is thrust upon some of us, whether we welcome it or not."

ON THE NINETEENTH day of the eleventh moon, Sofía woke in her brother's room.

"Demonios," Sol cursed, tripping over her leg in the dark. "What are you doing here?"

She rubbed her palm over her eyes, and when she spoke, her voice came out hoarse and groggy. "Waiting for you." How long had she been asleep? It was somewhere around midnight last time she checked. "You've been impossible to get ahold of."

"Have I?" He heaved a breath, sounding tired and . . . guilty? "I've been busy, I suppose."

"I figured, with the way you've been racing off soon as you see me."

He ignored the accusation and offered her a hand. She took it, letting him tug her to her feet.

"Go on then," he said. "What's this about?"

She did not waste a moment. "I need your help. Tonight there's a chance I c—"

The sound of a horn blasted through the tunnels.

Around them, a silvery light pulsed along the clear striations of the stone, making the swirls of white and red quartz glow like flames. Sofía took a step toward her brother, reaching for his hand in the face of this unknown danger. The way she always had, and always would. "Sol. What's happening?"

In the fluttering light, she saw her brother's eyes fall shut, his mouth press into a bloodless line. "Come on." He brought an arm around her, guiding her gently out the door. "We have a ceremony to attend."

SHE SENSED THE thrum of the crowd before she saw it.

Over a hundred vessels floated around the lone island of mossy rock in concentric circles, like petals around a flower's center. Their passengers gazed up at the luminous ceiba tree expectantly, looking restless and eager for the ceremony to begin.

Sol maneuvered them into an open spot in the water, and the canoe groaned and bobbed as it settled.

Sofía squinted up at the dawn light streaking through the gash in the cavern's ceiling, its pinks and violets muted against the tree's radiant white. Not for much longer though; the sun would be blazing bright within the hour, showering gold over the cavern's jagged crystals, lighting the whole place up like a kaleidoscope. If the ceremony went on long enough, they might even watch it happen. Sofía did not know if she'd get another chance, not if tonight went according to plan. Would she return a traitor? Would she be allowed to return at all?

The idea of never again walking the caverns of Coaybay, never knowing who she might become were she to stay, left her with a soul-deep aching for all her lost tomorrows.

Not everyone would resent her choice; her brother, Tínima, perhaps even Anani would understand. Sofía could hope that counted for something in the Cacika's eyes.

As though she could sense her thoughts, Kaona's gaze seized Sofía's across the distance.

The Cacika sat upon her ceremonial stool, her shape half hidden among the thick tangle of tree roots. Her head was framed by a headdress of night heron feathers, and on her shoulders rested a matching mantle, open at the collar to expose the bird tattoo over her heart. To her right stood Tínima, pale hair flowing loose and crowned in owl feathers, white paint streaking both cheeks, and to her left was Anani, looking stubborn and grave. She wore no adornments, save for a guanín septum ring and the usual belt of shells around her waist, a near-identical match to Kaona's.

The three held themselves in silence, though around them a chorus of questions and anxious murmurs rippled through the gathering. Sofía could feel the charge of tension in the air, could breathe it in, the suspense, the desperate anticipation.

All at once, the hum of conversation ceased.

The Cacika had risen to her feet, and her gaze fell like a weight upon the crowd. "The moon rises full and heavy on this fated night." Her voice sang clear in the hush. Not as a cry or a clamor, but steady and strong. Powerful, without resorting to loud. "When it crests the sky, She will be ready."

The reaction was immediate.

A roar of exultations swept through the chamber, fierce and frantic as the shouts before a battle charge. This was not the sweet and simple sound of contentment. This was older. Grittier. *Messier.* The sound of bittersweet triumph, bled and fought for. Of vindication.

But not all rejoiced at the Cacika's words. Some, like her brother, appeared resigned. Many more sat in stunned silence, muffled sobs against their hands, or locked fingers across the water. Children were soothed, hugged close. Faces vanished into shoulders. Tears were stifled against whatever would absorb them. There was pain hanging heavy as a miasma. You could breathe it, pass it from body to body like lungs exchanging oxygen. Even Sofia, ignorant to the source of that pain, sensed it settle inside her chest.

Kaona went on, "On this day three hundred years ago, on the nineteenth night of the eleventh moon, three ships blew into our shores . . . and loosened onto our lands an infestation." Her words rose above the din, mighty as the easterly winds. "We shared our fire with these strangers. Offered them salves for their sun-seared skin, fresh fish and good drink, a seat of honor, from where they could watch our dances and hear our songs. We led them to our rivers when they asked after our gold, showed them our cotton trees when they praised our weave, gave them shelter after many nights knowing only the harsh, cold spray of the sea . . ." A pause, leaden with grief. "Within six moons, more ships came. And by the next year's harvest, they had a fleet parked at every coast."

Kaona's head fell back, face tilting to the light. Tears glimmered there, in streaks along her brown cheeks, at the edges of her lips, pulled back into a vicious snarl. "We'd shown them friendship, and they showed us the barrel of their guns."

Shouts and cries rose to meet her words, *her* pain calling to *their* pain.

"They fought us with steel and greed and disease. Set their hounds on our children, forced our women to their beds, sent our men to work their fields and mine their gold. Our zemís they tossed into crates and carried to foreign gods' lands. Lands that remade them into savage men's idols, treasures for their galleries and showrooms, to be bartered for with the gold they wrung our people and our rivers dry for."

The Cacika spoke to the sound of fists pounding against chests, striking wood and splashing water, a ruthless beat that grew with her telling of their cruel history.

Rage, that's what this was.

It took Sofía a moment to recognize it. Her own rage had always been a simmer, a quiet thing, constant yet contained. But here, she could bring it to a boil. Here, there was room for it to steam and spill, and enough fire to keep its dangerous heat rising steadily. Here, she would not rage alone.

"Those few of us who survived their chains and their gunpowder fled south, sailed through a storm, evading enemy ships to shelter here, in these sacred caves. We rebuilt . . . sowed our crops . . . crafted our tools . . . carved into this new home our gods. For a time, we knew peace."

A shining bloom fell from the ceiba tree, and the Cacika's hands drifted up to cup it in her palms.

Bringing it to her lips, she opened her mouth wide. Devouring the flower whole.

Others were following her lead, picking fallen blooms as they fluttered in the air or floated along the water. They folded the petals and slid them between their teeth, mouths glowing white as they bit down. Some let out soft sighs of relief then, as though finding rest after a long day's journey. Others cried and grasped their canoes with white-knuckled grips, or laughed until fat tears poured down their cheeks. Everyone took part in the strange ritual, from the very young to the very old.

Sofía observed, but did not rush to join them. Likely wouldn't have joined them at all, had her twin not turned to her then, holding in each palm a star-shaped flower.

She started shaking her head. "Sol, I can't—"

"Do you trust me, Kán-Kán?"

"With my life."

"Then trust me when I say this won't hurt you," he told her. "Take it. You should see this. You should know what all this is for."

Sol waited, patient as ever, until her hand closed firmly around the flower.

He bit down without hesitation. Sofía watched closely as his eyes crinkled, emotion welling in them. "Your turn," he said, his cheeks rounding in a smile even as he blinked away tears.

Sofía nodded once, determinedly, and the petals slid between her teeth. She chewed without tasting. If the flower was bitter or sweet, she couldn't tell. All she could focus on was the butter-rum warmth coating her tongue and spilling down her throat.

A flash of searing white washed across her vision.

She was in red then, watching her dress melt over the terracotta floor. Her feet moving endlessly down the same hall, past doors carved with the same star-shaped flower. Toward a window.

The moon hung full beyond it. And *above* her too, as the glass of the solarium shattered and the river turned to blood. As she drowned in it.

Sofía gasped out of the visions, the afterimages clinging to her eyes like cobwebs, and the sickening smell of death overwhelming her senses. She felt a hand on her shoulder give a reassuring squeeze.

"Easy now, *shh*, you're alright. This is the Mother's doing," said Sol, looking toward the side, at something or someone beyond their canoe. "I see them too, we all do. These are her memories."

"Her memor—? No . . ." Sofía pressed the heel of her hand to her forehead, reeling from the violent images. "Those were dreams. *Nightmares*, not—"

Movement drew her gaze a little to the right. To where a figure rose out of the water.

Or rather, where the water rose in the form of a figure. A woman, naked to the waist, moving her arms back and forth like she was paddling. A breath later, the paddle materialized from the mist, beading into droplets and binding itself into a translucent shape. The canoe came next, building itself up drop by drop, as had the paddle.

The water woman traveled through the world of the living without disturbing it, passing through people and objects as though they were the spirits instead of her.

Sofía did not dare look away.

"Tell me you see this too, Sol. Tell me I haven't gone mad."

Her brother offered a sympathetic smile, the black sun around his right eye creasing.

The watery spirit had disembarked, and now knelt by the ceiba with a basket of cassava bread wrapped in cloth. She offered the bread to the tree and lay it at its roots.

Her image evaporated then, replaced by the ghosts of people dancing. One of which had satin hair and a crown of feathers, and the small tattoo of a bird above her breastbone.

Kaona.

The Cacika regarded the memory of herself, dancing where she now stood. That version did not look much younger, yet she smiled as though her burdens were not quite so heavy. "This peace we'd found would not last," she said. "We knew there was no land that could hide us. No weapon we could build that would protect us. Our spears and our arrows, no matter how finely crafted, could not win against their blades and their bullets. We had not evaded our fate, merely delayed it."

The dancers vanished, returned to the mist. Then, from the river that flowed into the cavern, another memory took shape.

Armored gunmen stood at the prow of a rowboat, weapons ready.

"Legends of these waters had reached the ears of greedy tradesmen and thieves, hungry to make their fortunes selling miracles. Discovering our tribe of runaways . . . Well, that was a pleasant happenstance . . .

"We had no warning. The Mother slumbered then, rising occasionally to meet our petitions for good health and good harvest, but she hadn't yet a vessel through which to speak, and no words to warn with. When the occupiers arrived, those who resisted met their end. Those who didn't met the worser fate."

More figures materialized from the mist—thirteen Taike'ri, bearing bows and spears. They stood on the crystalline rocks that rose over the water and around the tree in a protective circle. "Those of us still alive and free of their iron took up our weapons. Determined to save this sacred site, even if we could not save ourselves."

The first ghostly bullet struck, taking down a male Taike'ri whose arrows had pierced one man's eye and another's arm. He fell backward into the water, gaze unseeing.

Somewhere in the cavern, someone screamed. Not a spirit. One of the living, a girl with pink sprigs of jagüey woven through her curls.

Another soundless round of shots, and three more Taike'ri went down. Sofía wasn't sure when she'd started gripping her brother's hand, but her fingers already lay numb between his.

"We fought, a dozen and one to their twenty. And we lost."

The armored men spilled from the rowboat and charged at the five warriors still remaining, Kaona among them. The present Cacika walked along the memory of herself, watching the battle play out as she must have done a thousand times inside her head.

Arrows flew. Weapons clashed. The enemies fired.

Soon, young Kaona was the last one standing, her spear point striking steel, weaving expertly around the swing of her attacker's sword. She parried every blow with a flurry of her own, teeth bared and mouth open in a vicious scream. Though the memories carried no sound, Sofía could almost hear it.

Suddenly, the ghostly Cacika jerked backward, her spear arm stilling midstrike. For several heartbeats, neither she nor her opponent moved.

Her eyes traveled slowly down the length of her torso, finally landing on her stomach, where a dark stain bloomed from the tear in her flesh. She touched a finger to the blood in confusion. She'd not seen him, the one holding a still-smoking rifle. Had not noticed him lining up his shot as she fought the swordsman.

Trembling, her hand pressed firmly to the wound, and the present-day Cacika did the same, mirroring the motion as if she could feel the ache of it still. Then her spirit-self fell, down the stone steps, over the edge of the rock, and into the water. A splash, and she disappeared beneath its surface.

No one made a sound, not when the seconds stretched into a minute. Then two. Not until the water rippled.

A hand broke through, slamming hard over the base of the stone steps.

The memory of Kaona rose from the depths, dripping and angry and *whole*—without even a scar where her body had just ripped open. And with her came the others, returned from death.

The invaders panicked at the sight, stumbling in their effort to take up their weapons once more. Not that fire and steel could save them. Beneath their boots, the ground trembled as the woman they'd murdered ascended the steps, slow and purposeful. The tree roots slithered, the branches cracked like old bones, and the water rose behind her in a massive wave.

"The Mother awoke in her fury. Mended our bodies and stole our spirits back from the sands of Coaybay, where the great Maketaori watches over the dead. To our flesh she returned us—to right a wrong, to exact justice on these parasites who taint her waters, who take from her earth what has not been given, who dare spill the blood of her children at her roots."

Kaona's hand pressed reverently to the spiny trunk of the ceiba as the grim memory came undone, dispersing into floating beads of water and fading back to mist. "From that night, her strength grew, her awareness spreading beyond this chamber, beyond these caves. Finding new paths for her rivers to take. She awoke into the soil, and the grasses, and the leaves. Into the mountains beyond this valley, to the farthest edges of herself, where her island meets the sea.

"A half century ago, it was *she* that warned us when the ships landed on her western shores, waving flags of scarlet and gold. We watched, outnumbered, as upon her earth they built their palace. The Mother filled their gardens with rot and drained the water from their wells, but it was not enough . . . Their walls came up, and our island was overrun by pleasure-seekers, our home once again taken over by those who already had too much. And among them were our people, the children of those we left behind. Made to dance to their masters' godless tunes, to sing their canticles. To serve, as *they* rejoiced."

"So we took it back!" someone yelled.

"We did more than that," Kaona answered, locking eyes meaningfully with Tínima beside her. "We slipped among them, concealed under the very masks they wore to hide their sins. And as they would wield their swords, we wielded our songs. Our dances. Our stories. Drawing strength from areyto, the way we had in days gone by. Before they made us believe that power was the edge of a blade, the point of an arrow. For centuries, we fought in the battlefield they'd designed for us, meeting weapons with weapons, blood with blood. But that night, we found what our wars had buried: *our* way of fighting."

A smile unraveled across the Cacika's lips. "Never had I felt the Mother so alive or known her with such clarity. Areyto did that, made her stronger to make *us* stronger. Bonded us to our zemís, the way it always had our people before we lost our songs to grief. It is a radical act, to lift our voices when they would have us silenced, to move our bodies when for so long they've kept us bound. To tell all they tried to make us forget—just as now we make *them* forget, every wanderer who drinks the Mother's sap, her raw power steeped in prayers and poisons. She grows seeds inside their minds, tangles herself in all they are. Their thoughts. Their memories. They are undone, erased from the lives they led before they came to us, estranged from even themselves. All they are left with is what drove them here, the knowledge that they *wanted* this."

Kaona descended the steps until her feet sat submerged in glowing water. "A life without rules, without consequences. A life of distraction and riches and endless entertainment. We gave them that, a place where the pleasures do not stop, not for weary bones, nor sickness, nor pain. In Carnaval, they feast long after the food has lost its taste, dance when their bodies are weak, and laugh when their hearts ache. And tonight, on this day of remembrance . . ." A smile tugged at her lips, and behind her, the tree shivered. "Tonight, they will cheer as justice comes for them."

SOL DRAGGED SOFÍA down the tunnels, one hand clamped around her upper arm in a vise, keeping her from getting trampled by the crowd. She'd still be floating along in the canoe if he had not hauled her out himself.

She had meant to move, her body just . . . hadn't listened.

Elbows dug into her ribs, hands shuffled her out of the way, and someone stomped hard on her foot. Children cried. People shouted for their loved ones. Voices fought to rise above the clamor. It echoed inside the caves, all that noise, amplified to disorienting levels.

And *her head*. Salt and seas, how it pounded with visions, the fabric of her mind distending past the limits of herself. It was the ceiba flower; she could feel its moonlight in her veins, coursing through the rivers of her body. Past her body, into *theirs*—the Taike'ri, each of them an island connected by the Mother's waters.

Almost there, Sol mouthed to her over his shoulder.

They passed room after room, and through the curtains, Sofía caught movement. Glimpses of hasty packing in between quiet, more intimate moments.

Unbidden, she poured into them, became the lovers gripping each other close, the parent soothing the infant at their chest, the family deciding what they could bear to leave behind.

In that confluence of minds, Sofía recognized the tailor, Inoa, begging their wife to *stay, stay with me*. The soap maker, standing motionless amid the shove and drag of the crowd. The transcriber with whom she'd shared so many shifts, smiling weepily as she banged on the ceremonial drums.

Sorrow sat right alongside laughter there. Music played as kith and kin said their goodbyes. And an ending was mourned, and a beginning celebrated. Sofía felt it all. The dissonance of heartbreak and jubilation, triumph and despair, the whole spectrum flowing into her with a devastating force.

Then Sol was pulling her through a doorway and sliding the curtain closed, dampening the noise, but not the sights, feelings, and thoughts that threatened to displace her own. Within moments, he had a bag in one hand, and was hurriedly stuffing his belongings inside it—an ornate box of marbled stone, a gold ring gleaming with a fat ruby, a pouch that jingled with the telltale clink of coins. "The canoes will be set to sail by eventide." The words spilled out of him in a rush. "And be gone before the sun's down."

"Sol." Exhausted, Sofía pressed her back to the wall, letting it bear all her weight. "I'm not leaving."

He stopped and set the bag down. Hard. "There'll be nothing of this island come morning. Of course you're leaving."

"I *can't*." Her words came out as a shout, and she reeled back in shame. Never had she raised her voice at her brother, but then, her mind was buckling under the weight of so many others'. Breathing deeply, she gentled her tone. "Not without Adelina . . ."

At that, he grew very, very still. "What do you mean?"

"It was why I came here last night. I meant to tell you I was getting her out of Carnaval—please, do not try to talk me out of it. My mind was made even before I learned what would become of this place." The words left Sofía in a flurry, tumbling out before the psychic tide could come and pull them back under. "Now, I'm not naive. I know Adelina can be flippant and brash—I offer no excuses for her. But, Sol, when all is said and done, the fact is that my life at the hacienda was kinder with her in it. And sure, you could argue there's a degree of dysfunction to that, but what about the way we're made to exist *isn't* dysfunctional?

"This world is all turned around, and I've run myself ragged trying to make heads or tails of it. All I know is that amid all this wretched madness her friendship made sense, even when it shouldn't. So, no matter where tomorrow may take us, today I . . . I just need her to be well."

The longer she spoke the more Sol seemed to shrink, his shoulders caving, expression going bleak. "Adi's on the island . . ." he muttered, as if he needed to say the words aloud to believe them.

Though his emotions were as plain to read as the swirls of ink on his skin, much like those tattoos, Sofía could discern only the shapes, not their underlying meaning. His face flashed hopelessness. Confusion. Shame. Mere data points, devoid of context. If only she stopped resisting, let her goddess-touched mind steal into his and wrest away his truths.

No, that was not how she wished to know her brother.

Looking resigned, he slowly dragged his fingers through his hair. "Of course Adi would be here. That girl would follow you to the ends of the earth. How could I've thought otherwise?"

"You . . . you're saying you had no inkling of this? That, what, it never occurred to you to wonder why the Cacika is so distrustful of me? Or here's a radical idea, *ask me outright?*"

"You'd arrived as a guest," he started to explain, but Sofía wasn't done.

"Never mind that I was trapped in Carnaval for half a year. My mistake for assuming you'd care enough to wonder *anything* about me—heavens forbid you actually talk to me."

The accusation sent a shock through Sofía, and it was only in hearing it from her own lips that she realized that was no throwaway remark. It rose from somewhere deep and dark and painfully true, where it had been quietly fermenting. "How little I must mean to you . . ."

Sol's eyes widened, and there was something almost fragile about the way he looked at her, but it was gone before she could be sure. He ducked his head and returned to silently dragging items out of drawers.

"What is this exactly?" She placed herself back into his line of sight and gestured at the nebulous strain between them.

"Packing. You ought to do the same."

"Enough with the misdirections, Sol. We're done treading lightly. If we cannot be honest at a time like this, then when can we? Tell me truthfully, are you . . . angry that I did not find you sooner? Is that why you can barely look at me, why you run off every time I attempt a real conversation?"

"That's not—"

"Or is it that you never wished for me to come and insert myself into your new life and—"

"*I was trying to protect you!*" Emotion twisted his sculptor's hands into trembling fists at his sides, transformed his face into a sight that was wholly unfamiliar.

"Protect me from *what*?"

"From *me*." Sol slammed a stack of papers atop the cabinet, swiping his forearm roughly over his eyes. "It's all there," he said, catching the tears before they fell. "Everything I became, everything I never meant for you to see."

Tentatively, Sofía came forward and picked up the bundle of crinkled pages. There were at least a hundred letters, each written by a different hand, but all addressed to her. "You . . . wrote to me." Many times over many years, if the fading of the ink was any indication. She parsed through that stack, moving her gaze over the words but comprehending nothing, for the story they told was not of a brother who'd resented her, forgotten her, evolved beyond her, but one who thought of her as often as she'd thought of him. "Why not send them?"

"I . . . I was . . ." His hands opened in a helpless gesture, and he tried again, "I was unrecognizable, and it wasn't until you'd lost me that I finally found myself. By then, you'd grieved me once already, how could I put you through that again?"

Again . . . ?

His meaning landed like a dagger through her stomach, and Sofía had to grip the cabinet to keep from falling. "Tell me, please, tell me you don't intend to stay, Sol. Tell me I'm mad to even think it, that this is not why you've kept me at arm's length all this time."

He said none of that, choosing instead to remain silent.

A bark of manic laughter tore out of her throat. It all made a sick sort of sense now: his reaction upon first seeing her; the walls he retreated behind; why the nearer they drew to this day of reckoning, the more he pulled away. With grim clarity, Sofía now saw the letters in her hands for what they were. Her brother's parting words. His final will and testament.

In one quick motion, she reached for the bag he'd left on the chest and spilled its contents. Jewelry. Precious stones. A small fortune in gold. "So what's it going to be, brother? You send me off with my inheritance and I leave you here to die?" Hefting a handful of coins, she flung them at his feet, wanting him to seethe, shout, tell her she was out of line, to counter with *anything* but this calm surrender.

Yet his face remained carefully blank as he lowered himself to his knees and began picking up the fallen coins. "What else is there for me? There's no home for me beyond this island."

"There's no home for you here either. Not after tonight!" She knelt by her brother, gripping his hands between hers, desperate for him to see reason.

"At least here," he said, "I die a free man."

"The laws have changed, brother."

He fixed her with a look, resolute and grave. "And have the people? I might get paid my due wages, but would I be any less a slave?"

Sofia's head dropped. What could she say to that? *Give it time? Have hope that things will get better? Endure until one day those who hold your chains deem you sufficiently a person?* "Sol . . . please . . ."

"I've had every choice taken from me, Sofia." He unlaced his fingers from hers and bent to scoop up the last of the silver and gold. "This one, at least, will be mine to make."

ACTO VI

"ARE YOU READY, MOTHER?" The question is a murmur, quiet as a leaf on the wind, but she has never needed to speak for us to hear her. Her voice is ours, her mind the one place we always return to. In every other, we are a passerby, a guest, sometimes welcome, sometimes not. But *she* is where we come to rest.

How easy it is, how familiar, this woman untouched by time.

Her spirit makes way for us, and we settle into the shape of her. Into her hands, clenched at her sides. And her feet, perched high above the world. Her muscles are taut, poised for action, but at our arrival they loosen. Her shoulders fall in relief. *We are almost there*, she thinks, *it is almost over.*

Tonight, her part in this tricentennial war will be done. And she will sleep at last, knowing she did right by those she lost. Others forgot. Forgave. Moved on. Yet, she molded her life into a shrine for them, honoring them in death the way she failed to do in life.

She is stronger now, wiser. No longer that girl who sang to our trees and made wonders from their wood. She is, as her mother before her, the leader of her tribe, and this time, she will make the choices—the hard, gut-wrenching choices—her younger self could not. It is her burden to bear, her duty to fulfill.

She will bring her people liberation.

CHAPTER 20

Ojo por ojo, diente por diente.

—Chronicler

THE ISLAND CAME alive that night.

Its waters rose beneath them, its branches bowed as they passed, and its night creatures steered their way with song—hoots and chirps and the rhythmic *co-kee, co-kee* of small frogs. Cucullos, glowing a vivid green, fluttered among the leaves and over the enchantress flowers on Sofía's dress. Instead of red, their petals were a deep glossy black, clinging to the sheer fabric of her bodice, trailing down her bare arms like vines and falling in billowing layers past her ankles.

Already, she was regretting her choice of attire. It chafed against her skin, and her hands had nowhere to settle comfortably. But they were Mamá's flowers, and on a night such as this, she could allow herself some degree of sentimentality. Besides, tonight she was among the carnavaleros, whose standard attire consisted of four-foot stilts, head-to-toe body paint, and flaming crowns. Her chosen ensemble was almost sensible by comparison.

Sofía weaved her way toward the front of the barge, hesitating only a moment before joining her brother at the bow. Sol too wore black: a mask of obsidian bark, covering all but his eyes and mouth, and on his shoulders, plates of reedy branches protruding outward and upward, like the skeletal arms of a tree.

Sofía forced herself to remain silent, for every time she let herself speak, the two would fall into another argument, an infinite back and forth which boiled down to wanting to keep the other safe, even at their own personal peril.

Neither was particularly good at it, what with having so little practice. Growing up, they'd had their share of disagreements, sure, but nothing that wouldn't go away eventually if left alone. They had been too busy fighting this hostile world of theirs to fight each other, so now they fought the only way they knew how: Sol with heart, Sofía with logic. And, of course, neither could get through to the other.

"You should have gone with the others," he said, his first words to her since she, in direct defiance of his wishes, boarded the barge heading for Carnaval, and not the canoes evacuating to mainland Etérea.

Sofía's reply was a firm, "I go where you go. I haven't gone through all this trouble just to lose you now."

"Then you will fall with this island."

"Or we'll leave it together."

"My decision stands."

"But I'm a great deal more persistent." She emphasized this with a staunch set to her shoulders. The end result was another broodingly silent stalemate.

Before them, the earth was growing shadowed with dusk. They had been on the river for several hours, and still, the Flor de Lis was nowhere in sight. If possible, the trees grew even denser up ahead, their foliage blotting out the sky.

She looked closer. The trees . . . they were moving. Not sideways, in the way of things waving on a breeze, but *upward*. It took Sofía several moments to realize what she was staring at. A wall of bark and bramble was rising high over Carnaval. The branches reached up like fingers toward the darkening sky, twining themselves into a cage.

A *cage*, that was the word her mind went to. She could have called it something else—a pavilion, a dome—but that would not have felt as honest.

"Aren't we stopping?" Sofía shot an uneasy look at Sol. They were drawing dangerously near to the structure, which grew taller by the second. If they kept on this way, they would crash right through the thick weave of sentient earth.

Her pulse had started racing, her eyes darting rapidly for some escape, when the branches quivered. Wood cracked and leaves rustled, and the path yawned open. Just long enough for them to pass. When they were through, all aboard the float rushed to join Sofía and her brother at the barge's prow, pressing in around them, their elaborate woodland costumes jabbing at her sides and scratching at her skin.

This was it, the culmination of an event begun half a century before, on these very grounds.

Carnaval's grand finale.

The island had engulfed the Flor de Lis. Dark roots slithered over the hotel, tangling themselves along the staircase banisters, crawling over its salt-white walls and wrapping like greedy arms around its roof. Moss carpeted the steps and clay tiles, and the flowers that once grew in a riot of colors along the balconies and archways were now a pure, oily black. Even the fires burning in the lanterns were an unnatural shade, fading from silver to deepest gray at the edges, as though it was the Mother's sap that fueled them.

And where there had once been two rivers, there was now only one. The waters had overflown from their beds, like in her dream, rising and splashing, overtaking the earth. Upon that small ocean perched the gods, giants come to them in wood, and glass, and stone. In earthenware, unglazed and unpainted, and in guanín, gleaming a reddish gold. They had each a barge crafted in their tribute, a seat of honor from which to watch the island fall.

On one side was Guabancex, the Lady of the Winds, whose fury destroys all. She was carved from a smoke-colored crystal, her face fierce and her body half transformed into a storm. On the float next to her was Itiba Cahubaba, Old Mother Blood, depicted in moss and stone, her belly swollen with the four zemís who would go on to create the ocean and the humans who would one day sail it. Then there was Bayamanaco, Old Spirit of the Fire, shown with a silvery flame burning between his gritted teeth. And the twins, Boinayel, Bringer of Rain, and his brother Marohú, Bringer of Clear Skies. The two were crafted from a glassy stone, one opaque, the other translucent. A rope of shining silver bound them together at the waist.

Sofía herself had arrived in the company of a god—Yucahú, son of Atabey and the lord of good harvest. His face was etched into a mountain that was not, in fact, a mountain, although its size was similarly impressive. Its peak crested over a miniature rainforest, bountiful with seemingly real greenery, dewy grasses, untamed shrubbery, and several species of fruit trees.

Despite everything Sofía had already seen, she still half expected the vessel to sink under all that weight. These things were massive, almost as tall as the Flor de Lis itself and wide as ten men stacked atop another. Each was adorned with the motifs of their respective gods. Fire and storm. Earth and sea. Yet, shadows were the evening's reigning theme, painting all of Carnaval a shade darker.

She saw it now for what it was: a place of power, grown and nurtured like a lichen, flourishing where power should've never been allowed to breed. An altar, on which her people lay their offerings, paying tribute to the foremost creator through their own creations, strengthening Atabey as she strengthened them.

They could have done it quietly, covertly. Instead, they built their insurgence out in the open and invited their conquerors to watch.

"This is how we show them," said Sol, seeming to intuit Sofía's thoughts. His words bore the mark of a well-worn mantra, a rallying cry he'd recited many times before tonight. "This is how we show them that though they took our lands, they could not take our stories. With our dances, we reclaim our bodies, with our songs, we take back our voice . . . Our joy is a radical act of rebellion."

A revolution, come in the form of a celebration, for to celebrate was a bold declaration of their humanity, an honoring of the self through laughter. Community. Remembrance.

Sofía closed her eyes, overcome by some emotion she had no name for. Sweet and tragic, a feeling of finally *arriving*.

She mourned for all the days she would not wake in Coaybay, the people she would never meet, the pages of her journal that would remain unwritten, a blank slate in place of who she might have been.

Sofía's gaze roamed over the zemís she'd only just begun to know, lingering on Marohú and Boinayel, twins born from the Great Serpent. Two forces opposite in nature, achieving equilibrium through their coexistence, defining themselves in one another.

"Your art," she told her brother, recognizing his craft in that vague, intuitive way one can recognize another by the fall of their footsteps or the measure of their breath, "it is extraordinary . . ."

He shook his head. "It's the canvas that's extraordinary. My work is only as good as the bounty the Mother grants me. These hands of mine may have cut into the stone, but the true artistry is hers."

As much as she would have liked to object, Sofía did not get the chance, for in that moment, a familiar voice rang out above them. The words drew all their gazes upward, to the roof of the Flor de Lis where the Cacika stood, her features obscured and her figure brightly outlined in the remaining threads of daylight. She was a dark shape, masked and bearing wings like those of a bat.

"On this night," she said, "we bring the world of the dead to the living, and our zemís from the islands above to this one of the earth, to bear witness to this justice, to reap the rage the Great Mother has sown for them since her awakening. Atabey, let your sons and daughters hear our refrains, and the ground of their bohíos shake to the rhythm of our feet, and wake, *wake* into all their bodies, here and beyond these seas . . ." Kaona's arms rose to the heavens. "Come into your eyes, zemís, and see how they entomb you—display your corpses on their palaces, built from the gold they stole from your Mother's rivers. Feel how they bleed us, how they plough our spirits just as they break and tame these lands. Listen to how we, children of

Caguama, still lift our voices to you, how we stir the embers of your memory until you are reborn again, ready to *fight* again."

Applause met Kaona's proclamation, reminding Sofía that those gathered here had volunteered. To tithe to the island their power: the sway and music of their bodies, the stories they carried on their tongues.

They would fall, so that Atabey could rise.

If she focused, Sofía could still feel the thrum of their minds in hers, a ripple of hurt and hopelessness that made her see red. Whereas in Coaybay she'd felt the full spectrum of the loss to come, it was battle lust that reigned here. It filled her head with beautiful, terrible visons of a world in flames, singed like a blighted crop to flourish in the next harvest, all strong and new and prosperous.

She could almost see the smoke, smell the sickly scorch of loam and root rot.

She could almost believe she wanted it.

"Tonight, by the full moon's light, this island takes back what it is owed," proclaimed the Cacika. "And tomorrow, the world will know our gods."

With that promise, the last filaments of daylight faded to black. Stars dusted the dark above, twinkling silver between the web of briar and bramble encircling Carnaval, their reflection wavering in the dark of the water below. Then, the river's surface rippled, and the mirrored light of the stars scattered, and the floor of the barge Sofía stood upon tremored.

Around the Cacika, the roots were stirring, consolidating into a distinct shape: a giant skeletal figure with hollowed eyes and a wide grin. Bat wings stretched across the figure's back, extending beyond the edges of the hotel's roof, while its arms lengthened and its fingers curled around the iron rungs of balconies.

Sofía recognized the idol. It was made in the image of Maketaori, Lord of Coaybay. Not the Coaybay she had slept in for the past six weeks, but the one of myth, where the dead roam until nightfall before escaping to the living world for dancing and feasting.

Caught in the zemí's terrible embrace, the hotel seemed no bigger than a toy. The Cacika, small as its smallest finger, should have looked just as frail, just as . . . inconsequential. Instead, she seemed fearless facing he who watched over the dead. Wistful even, as her hand alighted on the god's wrist, as though she had been waiting a long time to meet him.

She is an opi'a, Tínima had said. A ghost returned to her flesh on the eve of her death, left to wander this earth for centuries after everyone she ever loved had gone. It was no wonder she stared up at the zemí with such longing.

Again, the river shuddered. Sofía's reflection on its surface swelled and stretched into something unrecognizable. And then, from the solarium came a crack, the sound of scratching glass, the roil of water as the river bubbled within its walls. Suddenly, there was a bright burst of white light and the solarium exploded with leaves and thorns and flowers black as the night. Vines twisted. Moss grew in clusters. The water filled with brushwood and fern. When it all finally coalesced, Atabey was before them, a bust sculpted from the earth with the river as her plinth. A goddess, trapped within the solarium's walls like a figurine inside a water globe.

Her floating hair was a wild mass of green, her nails giant thorns, her eyes twin moons glowing white as the one above them. It was a different version of the zemí than the one from the mirror labyrinth, with her serene features and welcoming hands. This Mother did not cajole her children forward, she *demanded*. She did not quell tears or soothe scuffed knees, she *punished*. Swiftly and thoroughly, with the same callous efficiency that nature bears its whip.

From outside the solarium, vines thick as tree trunks emerged. They broke out of the water with a splash, wrapping like tentacles around the glass and scuttling across the river's surface in spiraling paths, toward land. There, gathered all along the grand staircases, were carnavaleros in sweeping cloaks and long trains, obsidian masks and black silk wings. As each stepped over the boulder-sized vines atop the river, ropes of root and ivy dropped from the domed ceiling into their waiting hands. Then they were airborne, gliding high over the Flor de Lis as though suspended on wires. They swung and twirled, and turned themselves wrong side down, their costumes swooshing and bat wings fluttering in the wind.

From the float nearby, came a rallying cry. Others responded to the call with a cry of their own, until the bellows turned to chants, and the shakers rattled, and the drums banged.

On the roof of the Flor de Lis, the Cacika lifted a guamo shell to her lips, and blew the horn. That was when the doors burst open, and the patrons flooded into that new world of ghosts and gods.

"YOU HAVE MY WORD," Sofia told Sol as their barge made its round through the water, approaching the Flor de Lis. "The second I get Adelina off this island, I'm coming back for you."

He reached for her hand, eyes darting between her and the staircase they were fast approaching, his expression torn. "Kán-Kán . . ."

"There's not a thing you could say that would stop me. Persistent, remember?" Squeezing his hand as if it were a vow, she said, "I'll be with you before long." Then, as the steps came within range, she relinquished her hold and vaulted from the float, landing smack-dab in the middle of a crowd who initially startled, then clapped as though her sudden leap was all a part of the show.

From behind her came a dull thud, and she turned to find her brother, unfurling from a crouch.

"Sol. Why . . ."

"You and me," he rasped, and contained in those three words was their whole history. *You and me*, through the storm, and the rattle of her lungs, and the iron walls, the shivering nights, the sweltering days, the sugarcane. *You and me* through the years and leagues and secrets. Through every beginning and every end.

All Sofía could muster was a nod.

Her brother led the way through the tight knot of spectators gathered all along the staircase and she followed, muttering a continuous string of *permiso, perdón, permiso*, and limping slightly. Her heel had caught in the gap between two tiles, forcing her left ankle to bend at a wrong angle. She pushed through the discomfort, gathered her skirts, and kept up the steps—fast as her swelling ankle and the crowds allowed. Up she went, nudging patrons aside with the quick jab of an elbow here, the slam of a heel there.

Then Sol was extending a hand to help her across the last few steps. He pulled, and she went, and together they waded through the noise and the rabble gathered all along the terrace. It was easier with him at her side, and not exclusively in a figurative sense. Patrons made way for him, intimidated by his size. He had only to stand there for a direct path to clear for them.

His hand stiffened in hers as they neared the doors, his pace slowed. Sofía, moving ahead, tried drawing him in behind her, but his arm yanked back.

Beneath his mask, his eyes were shut tight. She grasped his fingers between hers and felt them shaking.

"I can't," he said. "I thought I could, but I—I can't."

Sofía's chest constricted painfully. "You've had a change of heart?"

"No! That's not . . ." A storm of emotions hailed him, the same she had picked up on back in his room. Anger. Revulsion. Shame. "I *can't* go back. I can't return to those halls, those *rooms*. I'm sorry. I'm sorry I'm not strong enough. I'm sorry, I—"

"*Shhhh*, it's alright. You're alright." Sofía hugged her brother to her, gently patting his back as he curled—trembling—into her shoulder. Not even as a child had he leaned on her, not in his darkest days had he let her share his burdens. "Wait for me out here. I won't be gone long," she said to him, stamping down on all those questions desperate to break loose. *What happened, Sol? What have they done to you?*

On the surface, she portrayed calm, but underneath there was a violence brewing. She could not tell if it came from the island, whose nectar pulsed through her bloodstream, or from somewhere that was hers alone, that dark little voice that whispered, *See? These people deserve what's coming to them.*

Reluctantly, she took a step back, releasing her brother. "Keep an eye out in case Adelina wanders over? She'll be wearing a dove mask, white and winged at the edges." And with that, Sofia slipped inside.

She hobbled down corridors draped in snarls of weeds and roots and climbing snowberries, their fruit and trumpet-shaped flowers dark as ink. Nature had swallowed up the Flor de Lis, inside and out, forcing its way out through the tiled floors, crawling up the walls and over the ceiling. The courtyards, which had always been so flawlessly manicured, with their trees evenly spaced and their shrubs pruned to the exact same height, now grew wild and tangled. Their reds and pinks and blues were bled out of them, repainted the black of Coaybay. The black of the flowers on Sofia's dress. She tried to ignore the dark satisfaction that thrummed through her at seeing this place be devoured, the ugliness of it buried beneath new life.

Around Sofia, patrons walked daintily along the grasses and the moss, fretting over their shining shoes and expensive silks. Some slowed to a halt when they spotted her, expecting her to lavish them with dance and song and looking disappointed when she brushed past them, offering neither.

As quickly as her injured ankle allowed, she prowled the halls, searching Adelina's usual haunts—the salons and leisure rooms and garden terraces—hoping she would not have to scour the guest suites for her tonight of all nights. Navigating the Flor de Lis was challenge enough, with its once even floors transformed into harsh terrains and its corridors nearly unrecognizable beneath that cloak of wilderness.

Sofia limped through its rough new topography, her skirts snagging on bramble, her skin catching on thorns, and not by accident either. The island was . . . reaching for her. Twining tendrils of green around her wrists, coiling around her ankles, knotting its fingers in her hair. Sofía growled, clawing at the ropes that held her, ripping through her bindings with nails and teeth and sheer force of will.

Despite her best efforts, her progress stalled. She would get no further than three paces before another vine coiled around her, tugging back. Yet the more the island fought her, the closer she drew to the sound of unruly laughter and clinking glasses. Its resistance was a compass, pointing to Adelina.

A little farther down the hall now. If she could just—

Sofía tore through a tangle of weeds as she launched herself forward. She clung hard to the door frame of the leisure room, fingers curling into talons and teeth clenching into a snarl. Already, she was panting and dripping with sweat, and her arms trembled as they strained against their ropes.

Through the haze of tobacco, she spied floor-to-ceiling shelves filled with leather-bound volumes, several pool tables of filigreed wood and burgundy velvet, ornate chess sets and round tables for games of baraja.

Adelina was not among the card players this time. She was near the back of the chamber, leaning against a bookshelf with a lace fan fluttering in hand. From across the room, Sofía could hear her laughing in that saccharine way she did when the joke was not all that funny. Her real laugh was explosive, more akin to the wheezy bark of a seagull than any sound a human could generate.

Without looking away from her, Sofía tore free from the island's grip—finally—and marched across the room. The noise and conversation tapered to a hush when she entered, until the only sound was the clop of her heels against the porcelain tiles. There were dozens of eyes on her, sparkling with curiosity, if not outright anticipation. Dressed as she was, they must have been expecting a show.

She stopped, now just an arm's length away from Adelina.

The memory of their last conversation came at her like a fist, knocking the words right out of her. She had been rehearsing what to tell Adelina all the way from Coaybay, outlining her arguments and building her case, approaching their feud like a treatise to research, compose, and defend.

Instead, when Adelina turned to face her, Sofía found herself stepping forward—wrenching her friend into her arms in a fierce embrace.

"What's gotten into you, cariño?" Adelina laughed, pulling away to study her. "And what *on earth* are you wearing?" She probed at the dark flowers, plucking a petal to inspect it in the lantern light. "How very fashion-forward, do color me impressed."

At Adelina's blithe tone, Sofía felt the weight of their reality crash over her. She had been arming herself for friction, assuming the tension—if not the memory—from their fight would have lingered, or that in the time since, Adelina would have grown reproachful at being left behind. But of course, the island-god had dug its roots into her friend's mind, dulling all that was real. All that mattered. She remembered the feeling well, that heavy fog where only the brightest pleasures shined. Where her hunger grew bottomless and her passions corrupted. Everything else, her misgivings, her loneliness, her pain, became muted. Fuzzy.

"Answer a question for me, Adelina. How long has it been since you last saw me?" At her look of befuddled amusement, Sofía added, "Please." It was a quiet plea. "Indulge me."

"You'll tell me what all this—" she gestured broadly, as though to encompass both Sofía's ensemble and her unusual behavior "—is about if I do?"

"I swear to it."

With a roll of her eyes, Adelina relented. "Very well, shroud yourself in mystery you little sphinx, I'll play along. What was the question again? Ah, yes, last I saw you was . . . um, well, it was just . . ." Her fingers toyed with the edges of her mantilla, twisting and untwisting the lace as she sifted through her mind for the answer, uncertainty creeping into her expression. "Last night," she declared with forced confidence. "We dined together."

"Where?"

"Pardon?"

"Where were we? What did I eat? What did we talk about? Was anyone else with us?"

A response faltered on Adelina's lips. "I—I'm not—" she stammered. "What exactly are you getting at here, Sofía?"

"The truth," she admitted, "which is that it's been weeks since you last saw me." The confession was a whisper, quiet as secrets and sins. "I've been gone for *weeks*."

Adelina's face wavered between a grimace and a smile, fixing somewhere in between. "We're a little old for pranks now, aren't we?"

"Is that what you think this is? That I've belatedly developed a penchant for tomfoolery?"

"Always figured you for a late bloomer."

"Adelina." Sofía met her gaze, serious. "I was *gone*, and deep down you know that."

"Stop. Why are you saying that?"

"Why are *you* crying if you don't believe me?"

"I am not—" Adelina opened her mouth to protest just as the tear clinging to her lashes fell. It dragged through the heavy powder under her eyes, exposing a thin line of bruise-colored skin. "Oh . . . oh . . ." She caught another tear before it slipped beneath her mask and stared at it in puzzlement.

Sofía took both her shoulders between her hands, gripping firmly. "Do you remember climbing the magnolia tree when we were little? How, when you reached the top and realized how far you were from the ground, you panicked?"

"You climbed up after me." Her breath hiccupped inside her chest, and the tears fell harder.

"What else was I to do? You refused to open your eyes, you fiend. I had to guide you down every step and handhold, it was that or leave you for the crows to peck at." Something like laughter raked against Sofía's throat. "That day . . . you trusted me to keep you safe. I need you to do the same now, Adelina, even if it feels like you cannot see where you're going. *Especially* then. Tonight, before the moon hits its zenith, we need to leave Isla Bestia." Expecting her to object, Sofía scrambled to add, "I'm aware this won't make sense to you. You'll want to fight me . . . tell me the wine's gone to my head. I ask only tha—"

"Sofía." Adelina took her hand, holding it like a promise. "Lead the way."

CHAPTER 21

The Earth was silenced, her lips sewn shut.
When at last her mouth opened, she let out a scream.

—Chronicler

THEY RACED THROUGH the corridors, shoes dangling from their fingers and skirts crumpled between their fists. The island chased them. Its arms snaking tight around their waists, its bark snapping like broken bones as it shattered through the floor to wrap around their feet. It spread thick as a cast over Sofia's legs, transforming her lower body into a tree.

She dug her nails in, ripping off chunks of bark as fast as it could grow.

Adelina rushed over to help. "What is *happening*?" Gripping her heel like a weapon, she hammered the fine point into the bark. Over and over, grunting with each swing.

Together, they clawed and struck until Sofia was free. Her palms were scratched raw and bitten through with splinters. Adelina looked no better, standing there with a ruined heel, her breath heaving, and her flawless updo now a nest of sweat-damp curls. It lent her usually refined appearance a wild edge.

"Devils take me, that was *brilliant*," Sofia blurted as she accepted Adelina's outstretched hand.

They took off at a run, dodging the island's onslaughts. It forced them down a winding, roundabout path that took twice as long to traverse. There were times they could elude its dangers by escaping down another hall, another door. Other times, the only way forward was through.

"What now?" shouted Adelina when they turned to find themselves blocked on either side. The path ahead was overgrown with thorns sharp as swords. Behind them too, the hall was mutating into a skewering death trap. Sofía's mind whirred as her eyes swept the hall, looking for . . .

There.

She saw their escape route mere moments before Adelina cried out, "You're mad."

Sofía moved to peer beyond the stained glass window. It faced east, and through it, she could make out a few distorted glimpses of Carnaval. The terrace where Sol stood waiting was a hop and a step away. If they climbed through it, then . . .

"Do you have your pistol on you still?"

"My pist— Sage above, you want me to *shoot* at it?"

She considered this. "No, you're right. Terrible idea." If they were not careful, someone could get hurt. "Something heavy then, like . . ."

A wrench was out of Adelina's reticule in seconds. "Here."

"This will do."

Sofía was turning back to the window when she heard a *riiiiiiiiiiiiiiip!* The hem of Adelina's teal gown, roughly shorn, now hung from her teeth. "Bind your hand with this," she commanded, wrapping the fabric thickly around Sofía's hand.

"Good thinking." She flexed her fingers around the wrench, adjusted her grip, and positioned herself to strike. "Get back."

The glass shattered from the first blow, raining shards over Sofía's bound hand. It took several more whacks to remove the jagged fragments stuck to the frame, but the entire ordeal was over and done with in under a minute.

Wind blew into the hall, ruffling her hair and cooling the sweat on her cheeks. "There's a ledge, thank the seas," she noted optimistically, leaning her head through the opening.

"And you realized that only *after* smashing a wrench through the window?"

"I made an educated guess. Now, go," Sofía urged. The thorns were pressing in on them, encroaching into their already meager stretch of safety. Bending, she netted her fingers and boosted Adelina up to the window. She went, muttering prayers and profanities in the same breath.

As Sofía rose to follow, she caught a flash of movement in her periphery.

Thorns, long and thin as rapiers, shot toward her.

In the two heartbeats it took for them to reach her, she could have made a launch for the window. Instead, she felt her posture righten, her pulse even with an uncanny calm. *You won't hurt me* . . . That certainty hit her like a lightning strike, sparking and buzzing along her skin as though she'd swallowed it whole. It settled into her belly with the weight of fact, real and incontrovertible. And so, rather than dive out of the way—as she ought to have done—she set her feet and faced the island head-on.

Thorns froze midair, their wicked points hovering so close to flesh it was dangerous to even breathe too deeply.

"You *won't* hurt me," she repeated aloud, the words tearing out of her throat. Not as a command, but an inevitability.

The island appeared to regard her for a moment—curious, considering—before, at last, conceding. Its thorns drew back inch by inch, clearing just enough space for her to hoist herself over the window and onto the narrow ledge outside. Sofía looked over her shoulder, watching the island's final retreat. Had it had eyes, she would have sworn it watched her back.

Adelina sighed with obvious relief at the sight of her, a bit of color returning to her deathly pale face.

"Can you make it?" Sofía shouted over the noise and wind. It was a short distance to the terrace, but the drop below them was steep. A fall from that height would end in more than just a few broken bones.

Adelina gave one shaky nod, hugged her palms to the wall, and began the slow, sideways walk to safety. Sofía followed closely, clutching the black roots that wrapped over the building for leverage. Keeping a lookout in case the island changed its mind about letting them go.

At last, the terrace appeared below them and she nearly cried out in relief. Adelina jumped first, and Sofía followed an instant after, knees bending to absorb the impact. "Come on," she said, catching her breath. "We have to find—"

When Sofía looked up, Adelina was gone.

SOFÍA SCANNED THE crammed terrace from left to right, shouting her friend's name. *Where the devils did you go?* Her pulse leapt against her neck, and her hands tensed against her skirts, crushing the flowers beneath them. Masked faces blurred across her vision, a tableau of oversaturated colors and striking imagery. There was no place her eyes could land that offered relief to her senses, already overwhelmed by the noise, the crowds, the high-pitched hum of fear building inside her.

She saw it then, not far from where she was. The torn hem of a teal dress.

"Adelina!" Bracing herself, Sofía pushed through a swarm of patrons packed tight against the balustrade. They gawked at the evening's spectacle, waving arms and silk handkerchiefs as the floats passed by. With one arm, she reached to catch a fistful of Adelina's mantilla.

"We don't have time for this!" she shouted, at the same moment Adelina cried, "Cariño, there you are! Where've you been all night?"

Dread iced in Sofía's veins, rendering her body numb, her thoughts sluggish. *No . . . this isn't happening.* Not again. Not so soon after she'd finally gotten her friend back. The walls of her mind closed in, trapping her, and she pressed her eyes shut against the first whispers of a headache.

Overhead, an acrobat swooped past, bat wings outstretched. Adelina clapped, as mesmerized as the rest of the crowd. If she remembered their frantic escape, the memory was too deeply buried for Sofía to draw it out now. Not that she was in any state to try. The only coherent thought her mind could form was, *Out, out. We need to get out.*

She surrendered to the impulse.

"Ow— *Stop*. What are you doing?"

"Saving you from yourself." Sofía's grip on Adelina's wrist did not loosen, no matter how much her friend protested. "If I can just get you far enough from here, I know you'll remember why we're running."

"Running where? What in the bleeding saints has gotten into you, Sofía?" Beneath her mask, her pupils were unnaturally dilated, swallowing nearly all the blue of her irises as they strained to catch another glimpse of the floating altars for sleeping gods, the artists worshiping at their feet with dance and song, the art, the magic, and the horrors underneath. It was as though she was under a spell, cursed to look upon Carnaval or else be turned to stone, like the cave dwellers who first abandoned the dark to gaze upon daylight.

"Mierda," Sofía cursed as Adelina wrenched herself out of her hold, slamming backward into a tall, broad figure donning twisting branches and a scaled armor of coal-black bark, like he was a warrior of the forest, born from the heartwood of an ancient tree.

As Adelina spun, ready to break away again, Sol called out, "Adi!" and tore off his mask. "It's me, Adi . . . It's me," he said, arms extended wide in a placating gesture.

"Sol . . . ?" She took a step toward him.

He took a step back.

"Saints. It really is you, isn't it?" The bewitchment was clearing from Adelina's gaze as she searched his face, finding vestiges of the boy she once knew.

His own eyes would not meet hers, a reaction Sofía recognized from when they first reunited outside Coaybay. At the time, it had been a rejection, but from this new vantage point—knowing all she did now—she saw it clearly for what it was: an act of self-preservation.

Distance was a shield, his way of protecting himself. But from what?

"You . . . you're all grown up," Adelina went on. "And you're here. How are you here, Sol? We searched for you . . . You were just . . . gone."

He opened his mouth to reply, but Sofía cut in before he could. "There'll be time for that later," she said. "Right now we have t—"

The ground moved. Not with a warning tremble, but a brutal shake.

Sofía's eyes snapped to the moon at once. She traced its trajectory across the sky, calculating the time until it reached its zenith. They had, at most, a few hours before the island was no more.

Another rumble shook the earth, reverberating up the building's foundation, rattling the floors beneath their feet. The tiles clacked, the walls splintered, and all around them, people screamed. Patrons clung to the banisters, folded onto their knees, or fell limp where they stood. A howling cry rent out of Adelina, and before Sofía could reach her, she was on the floor.

Whatever was happening to her was also happening to the hundreds around them. The only ones seemingly unaffected were Sofía and Sol.

No, not the only ones. The Taike'ri stood steady through the island's violent quakes, looking on at the crowds with unreadable expressions.

"The island . . ." Sofía rode the quakes, arms spread out for balance. "What is it doing to them?"

"Returning what it took," her brother answered, "forcing them to remember all it sealed away. The Mother, she wants them to know all they've lost, all they stand to lose when . . ." He didn't finish the thought. He didn't need to.

Among the patrons, Sofía noticed Fátima, curled on her side against the rungs of the staircase, her frizzy auburn ringlets spilling over her cheeks. Some ten steps down lay a man with a silver snake mask, a tailcoat in jade and gold. Could she save them, too? Whisk them away before all this came crashing down?

And what of those who'd made this island their home? Those sailing to lands that, come morning, might know the wrath of waking gods. How many, she wondered, felt as her brother did? Trapped, knowing the world beyond these shores was not one they could return to? Heartsick, to be forsaking the life they'd built in Coaybay. And how many, like her, heard the island's dangerous song? Did it thrum through them, crooning blood and vengeance? Had it sung in their ears for so long that its tune became theirs?

She heard it now, tempting her to bask in this victory, to add her voice to that hymn of blood and war, to transmute her grief into devastation.

No, that was not all there was . . .

Beneath it, playing so quietly she almost missed it, was a lamentation.

Unaware she'd even made the decision, Sofía began to move. She was at the wall, her hands clutching the thick roots twined over its facade, climbing as Sol desperately shouted her name behind her, as her own inner voice warned *this is a terrible idea*. At least, she was relatively certain it was hers. Hard to gauge when her brain was porous and leaking, and loud, getting louder as she ascended higher above the ground. The ground that was splitting apart as she herself split apart.

While the world trembled, she heaved herself from one root to the other, climbing mindlessly. Determinedly. Every distraction, be it falling debris, the twinge of pain in her ankle, or her own turbulent thoughts, fading out of focus.

Then one wrong step, and Sofía's foot skidded. Her fingers lost their purchase. She felt the telltale drop in her stomach, the awful weightlessness as her body slid backward into empty air. Her arms flew up, reaching for something to save her, and grasping nothing.

This was it then. After a life of overzealous planning, her final act would culminate on a snap decision. Here, of all places, on this island that was a god. Or perhaps, this god that was an island. Either way, what it was did not matter much. She was falling, and soon, she would be dead, and all that mattered now would stop mattering then.

Suddenly, there was a crushing pressure against her rib cage. Something coiled tight around her, circling her waist and squeezing until it'd wrung the air out from her lungs. The muscles in her neck pulled painfully as the thing pressing on her midsection yanked. The sudden, violent break in momentum wrenched Sofía's head toward her spine, even as the rest of her jerked skyward.

For a brief, utterly surreal moment, she dangled in the island's grasp—dark hair flapping in the wind, petals flowing from her gown—far enough from the ground to know with complete and utter certainty that she would not have survived such a fall. There were snaps and rasps as the roots holding her aloft coiled back into the wall, settling her on a solid perch a short way down from where she'd fallen.

The island . . . it had *saved* her. It had chased her down halls, trapped her in its clutches, and now she was alive because of it. It made no sense.

Shakily, Sofía gripped the next handhold. Pulled and pushed, until her aching fingers were gripping sun-warmed clay and she was dragging her weight over the edge of the roof. She crawled on hands and knees up the incline, muscles throbbing, breaths flowing in and out through gritted teeth.

Under the great and terrible shadow of Maketaori stood Kaona, winged and clad in the death god's black. From the way she watched Sofía, it was clear she had been expecting her.

"Cacika!" Sofía shouted over the roar of the wind and the breaking of the earth. "This night doesn't have to end in tragedy. Intercede with the goddess, I beg you. Save your people. Save their home."

Kaona turned her gaze back to the unraveling of the world. "This is the Mother's will and mine," she intoned without emotion. "Take your mistress, girl, and leave while you still have the chance."

Sofía's jaw clenched. Her blistered fingers drew into fists at her sides. "You're meant to protect them, not sacrifice them for your revenge!"

Kaona spun on Sofía, her composure fracturing. "Call it what you will, but this night is *ours*." She beat at her chest. "*Our* justice. *Our* sacrifice. *Our* lives to give for the lives we are to take. It is the way of our people to reap as we sow, not that I would expect you, daughter of arijua, to understand."

I am no daughter of theirs, Sofía wanted to argue. *I am daughter of she who gave her body to the earth and her heart to your gods, sowed her life into this world that gave her nothing but pain in return.* But she had not scaled a wall to prove that in her veins ran the salt of these seas. That she'd been forged from Taike's blood-soaked sands, the scorch of its sun, the bittersweetness of its storms. So instead, she said, "This place could be so much more. *You* could be so much more, Cacika. You are . . . a miracle to your people. To us. A connection to a past we have been denied from birth. There is nothing you could do for us as a martyr that you could not do for us alive."

"What would you have me do, then? Set the vermin free to build their palaces over our lands and their kingdoms on our backs?"

"I would have you live." Sofía dared another step closer. "*Live*, and find another way to fight."

"Do you think I haven't tried? That I haven't spent every day since those ships made land *enduring*? Waiting and waiting for that *other* way?" Kaona's gaze snapped to Sofía's with palpable hurt and fury. "Did I not beg when they put their sword through my mother's throat? Or lay jewels at their feet when they stole my wife to bed? When our son, barely six summers old, vanished into enemy arms? I have pleaded mercy, offered peace, and granted bribes. And for what? The only language they have ever understood is violence." Tears sprang to the Cacika's eyes. Time was said to heal, and yet the passing of centuries had not lessened Kaona's grief nor cooled her anger. It had cemented it, calcified around it like bone.

"When their gore paints our spears," she spat, "that is when they stop taking."

And who knew that better than she? Having lived through every raid, every battle, every butchery. In the shadow of the Cacika's history, the brutality she had endured, Sofía's arguments felt terribly naive. There would never be peace for the islands' people, not without bloodshed.

Our conquerors will yield these lands by force, or not at all . . . The thought reverberated loudly within Sofía, again and again, with the strength of certainty, nearly drowning out the part of her that cried, *and what will it cost us?*

"This will be the catalyst," Kaona said with a sweeping gesture. "Our zemís, they have slumbered since their bodies were stolen, our areytos silenced. But the Mother will wake *them* in her death as our deaths woke *her*, rouse them into their fury—into the flame that does not warm, but burns; the skies that know no temperate weather, only droughts and torrents; the earth that bears no sweet harvest, only wild growth and dangerous poisons. Across the seas, our people will know the gods are with us, they will see them and know they do not fight alone. There will be rioting and insurrection. A revolution."

Freedom, paid for in fresh blood. Justice, won through suffering.

With tears spilling down her cheeks, Kaona smiled wide. "These lands will be ours again, do you not see? The wrongs done unto our people will at long last be righted."

Her promise tore open a desperate wanting inside Sofía, sudden and visceral. She had dreamt of this, *lusted* for it. Alone, in the dark, when the world went quiet, and it was just her and the walls and the wounds still tender on her skin. Yes, she'd dreamt of it. And she might even dream of it again, if she made it past this night.

"In righting those wrongs, what is to become of us? Where do we shelter while our gods unleash their devastation—or are we to soldier on as they wither our crops and flood our rivers, ravage our islands with storm after storm? The people of these seas . . . how long before they finally know comfort? How many of them will live and die with a blade in hand, bleeding for the home they might have found *here*?"

"A home they are bound to, and beyond it, a world that will never again belong to them." Kaona's hands tightened into fists. "But you'd have us show our enemies mercy instead. Allow them to go unpunished."

"This is not about *them*. It's about *us*," Sofía shouted over the wind. "We have a choice for once. We can make this place a battleground . . . or we can make it a sanctuary." A place where peace was won over ball games instead of war, a home for every child who'd never known one, a place where existing meant more than just surviving. "Blood is *their* way, Cacika, not ours. Was it not you who told us that this very morning? We wield another kind of weapon, you said. Yet is it really any different if it cuts just the same?"

For the briefest instant, Kaona's resolve seemed to waver, sputtering like the dying steam of a kettle gone cold. Sofía felt it, the Cacika's tender hope that the sun would rise over this island come tomorrow, that on this soil might grow a place where joy was not proportional to one's sacrifice.

"You see it too," Sofía choked out. "What this land could be . . . who *we* might become on it."

Kaona's eyes fell closed, her ire yielding to a gentle yearning, as if picturing that other future, losing herself in the possibility of it. Yet, in the way of all reveries, it vanished the moment her eyes reopened, and the next words she spoke were decidedly, painfully, final. "This cannot be undone."

Screams rent the night as the rumbles heightened to an earth-tilting, ground-splitting shake, the force of it strong enough to knock Sofía and Kaona both off their feet.

Sofía grabbed fast onto the roof, digging her nails between the tiles to stop her fall.

She dared to look down. Below, the river was churning violently, tossing the barges and their occupants who rocked and spun to its rhythm, adjusted to its tempo their refrains, singing the songs their ancestors did to call upon their gods.

Cracks appeared along the walls of the solarium, its cast-iron framework rattling and creaking.

Then, the structure exploded. Blasting outward in a shower of glass and torrential waves as the water within it drained, spilling over the sculpture of Atabey, down her skin of leaf and moss, her hair of tangled earth. The zemí's eyes were open, full moons shining a brilliant white, dousing the world in its pearlescence. Patrons and Taike'ri alike had to shield their gazes from its blinding brilliance. And in that burst of harsh light, Sofía saw it. Docked on the coast, a familiar vessel flying the red and gold of Hisperia . . .

Before her racing thoughts could coalesce into a plan, she was climbing back over the edge of the roof and down the wall, scrambling along roots fast as her hands and feet allowed.

"Sol!" She landed unsteadily, stance wide and arms held out to ride the shockwaves. "Sol!"

Her brother maneuvered between the prone bodies of now waking patrons to get to her. "Have you gone mad? What were you thinking, going up there? You have to get off this island *now*!"

Sofía steadied herself against his shoulder, only half listening to his protests as she threaded together pieces of seemingly disparate memories. The bloody nightmares that felt like omens. The three days she spent awake, roaming the empty halls of the Flor de Lis while every other soul inside it slept. The times when she spoke to the island, and the island spoke back.

And then tonight. Mere moments ago, it had come to her rescue.

Why? Why spare her now, only to have her die later? Why hunt her for near an hour, to then free her from its trap? It was as if the land was at war with itself, a raging god one moment, a merciful one the next.

Sofía straightened.

She had been thinking about it all wrong, imposing her human ways on an entity that was anything but. Assuming it to be a cohesive existence, the total sum of its parts. She was wrong. The island was not a body, with one heart, one brain. It was an ecosystem, connected, yes, but not of a singular mind. How could it be when its tendrils wrapped around every soul upon it?

"Sol." She turned to her brother. "I have a theory . . . a supposition, really. I could use your help rendering it less hypothetical."

A large block of masonry fell from the roof, crashing not three paces from them. Sol studied her like she'd lost her mind. "Is this the best time for an experiment, you think?"

Another crash, a planter from one of the balconies above. Dirt and broken clay sprayed across the tiles.

"You have petitioned the Mother before. For your carving work?" Sofía's gaze wandered to the sculptures of the twin zemís, Boinayel and Marohú, formed by her brother's own hands.

"What is this about, Sofía?" His eyes roved across the destruction, growing increasingly more worried.

"We'll return to Coaybay," she said. "There, you will petition the Mother to save the island. To save itself."

Her plan was met with incredulous laughter. "I appeal to her for stone to grow. To change color. I'm not so dear to the goddess that I might sway her will, let alone undo it."

"And if there's a part of her that wishes it undone?"

"What . . . what are you saying?"

Sofía touched her fingers to her head. "The weeping, Sol. You hear too, don't you?" The lamentation was a constant underscore to the battle anthem. "It is ours, but is it not also the island's?"

He stared helplessly at her. "Does it matter when our rage is so much louder?"

"Rage is always louder. If in spite of that, this island-god can be moved to mercy, should we not at least try? For *us*. For the others right there on those barges who feel as we do? For those at sea, sailing away from the only place that has ever felt theirs. That has ever felt *safe*."

She thought of all the letters she'd transcribed in her time at Coaybay, the stories of family and friendship, found and grown within those walls. She thought of mealtimes at the Batey, of the market with its brightly colored stalls and bohíos, of the tunnels and their sleepy nighttime sounds blanketing her as she dreamt. And she thought of Sol.

Sol, who smiled, and danced and lived so intrepidly within its walls, but would rather make the sea his grave than endure what lay beyond it.

He let out a humorless laugh. "Subverting a revolt . . . gambling your life on the off chance a god has a change of heart . . . You really have gone mad."

"Then let us lose our wits together." Sofía met his gaze squarely. "If you could stop this, Sol, would you try?"

He swallowed, made a motion with his head that was somewhere between a shake and a nod. "We're hours away from Coaybay. There's no way we'd get there in time."

"That was not the question."

"Kán-Kán . . ."

"Would you?"

The answer tore out of him in a growl of frustration. "Yes, *yes*. I would! I'd rather live for this place than die for it. I want to make art in it, find love in it, grow old in it. To call this home until my skin wrinkles, and my hair grays, and the years have softened the sting of all these wretched memories." With urgency, his palms rose to frame her cheeks. "Damn it all, I want to try. Desperately, so will you please tell me you've got a plan to get us there?"

Eyes misting, Sofía grinned up at him. "I may have something in mind."

THE STEAMER ROCKED wildly where it was tied to the dock, straining against its ropes as the waves pulled, ramming its hull against the rocks as it pushed. The seas were restless, the waters rising against the seismic shocks from the land.

"If the island doesn't kill us," Sol said, pausing on the step beside Sofía, "the sea surely will."

With their roles apparently reversed, Sofía was left with no choice but to affect optimism. "We'll make it." She imbued those words with confidence she did not feel. "We have to."

Jostled by the island's tremors, they staggered down the long set of stairs to the dock, taking turns helping a semiconscious Adelina. A wave came in as they crossed the boardwalk, drenching them up to their ankles, rendering the already treacherous path even more precarious. Behind Sofía, Sol braced his side against the gangway's railing, fighting the waters that tried to drag both him and Adelina down.

Sofía reached, and heaved them up to the deck.

The steamer was empty. Pitch dark, save for a single lantern swinging at its bow. The last passengers must have disembarked just hours ago, and the crew had gone with them. If Sofía had to guess, she'd wager they were in on the plan, likely Taike'ri themselves.

The deck listed, and all three of them went careening. Sofía slammed backward into the salon, hitting the glass wall with a heavy thump. Sol and Adelina landed in a heap beside her.

"Saints' balls," he grunted. "That hurt like—"

His invective was cut short by a groan. Adelina was stirring, her long-lashed eyes blinking back into awareness. Up until that moment, she'd been like a sleepwalker, able to move when nudged but otherwise unresponsive.

"Welcome back, you fiend." Sofía let out a tremulous laugh despite the pain shooting up her shoulder blades, her neck, the small of her back. Her emotions were all muddled up inside her, bloated and cumbersome. "Can you captain this ship?"

"Ship . . . ?" With Sol's help, Adelina groggily pushed herself to a seat. She took a moment to collect her bearings, taking in the waterlogged deck, the Flor de Lis looming over the rocky hill, the turbulent seas. Then her attention settled on her companions. First on Sol, whose hands hovered just above her shoulders, ready to catch her should the need arise. Then, on Sofía.

Adelina's expression crumpled, a sharp *knowing* replacing her previous look of confusion. The crease between her brows softened into an apology. There was so much between them still unresolved, so many words unsaid, but that all would have to wait.

"We have only a few hours until this island drowns," Sofía told her bluntly. Were this a different time, a different person, she might have tried smoothing the edges of her voice, dampening the severity of their predicament. "However, if we can make it to the eastern end of the island, there might be a way to save it."

It was a testament to her friend's unwavering trust in her that she did not ask why or how. She only closed her eyes. Took one breath in, and another out. "Sol can captain," she uttered decisively. "You and I will work the engine room. It's usually a job for a half dozen men, but I dare say the two of us can handle it just fine."

Sofía could not hold back her smile.

"This may come as a shock to the both of you," Sol said, "but I've never piloted a ship."

"You've good eyes, careful hands. I've seen enough of your carvings to know that if you can manage that, steering a helm left and right should be no problem." Adelina pushed herself to her feet and laced an arm around Sofía's. "Upstairs with you then," she told Sol. "Look for a voice pipe when you get to the bridge—it's a long tube, open on one end. Keep an ear to it, we'll send word to you once we're belowdecks."

From the confident way she carried herself, one would think she had spent her life at sea, ordering sailors about. "Sofía, with me." They parted ways in silence, Adelina directing her to the steamboat's stern with unwavering focus.

A door creaked open into a dark narrow flight of metal stairs that rattled at their footsteps. The engine room was cramped and muggy with the lingering heat of steam and machinery. The stale air hung with the scent of salt and paraffin, and an industrial grease that smelled mildly of rotten fish. On the wall to the right hung a lantern. Sofía switched the knob to light the wick. Its glow bounced off a complicated latticework of copper tubing along the wall and ceiling, enormous iron rods connecting to pistons, panels of gold-ringed dials, and assorted wheels and gears.

"Can you light those too?" Adelina nudged her head toward the rest of the lamps. "I'll go warm up the boilers."

Sofía made quick work of her task, and joined Adelina just as she was shoveling a heap of coal into a firebox.

"What else do you need?" Sofía grabbed a spare shovel and began digging coal.

Adelina brushed a curl off her forehead, smearing soot across her mask. She tore it off in one quick motion, as though she'd only just remembered she was wearing it. "Can you take over?"

Sofía nodded firmly as her friend went to inspect the gauges above the flames. "Temperature looks good . . . Pressure's building nicely." She sighed in relief. "It must have docked just a while ago. The water's still hot, see? We'd be waiting here for hours otherwise."

That possibility had not occurred to Sofía, and she chided herself for the oversight. She ought to have known better, given how often Adelina gushed over every gizmo and gadget on land, sky, and sea. But as it was, she had been too busy unraveling the mysteries of the living world to pay attention to one of the metal beasts.

A high-pitched noise, like the whistle of a tea kettle, piped out of the boilers. "Is that a good sign?" Sofía asked, wary.

"Excellent, actually." She darted past, cheeks flushed with excitement. "Come on!"

Sofía whirled around to follow.

Adelina fluttered about the engine room, mumbling beneath her breath as she poked and prodded at this and that, seeming to forget, in her bliss, what waited for them beyond the deck. "Let's see . . . if I turn this just so then . . . No, that can't be it. What about . . . ? Oh . . . *Ohhhh*. Yes, that might . . ." She clapped her hands emphatically. "Ha!"

The engine room filled with the groan of machinery rousing awake. Pistons shuffled ploddingly, noisily, in place, clattering like a train in its tracks. Steam whistled, and the air grew instantly warmer by several degrees.

Adelina rushed over to the voice pipe on the wall to her right. "Sol? Are you there?" She spoke into the golden tube, bracing herself as the floor tilted sharply beneath them. "Listen, somewhere nearby should be the engine telegraph—looks a bit like a clock, with letters instead of numbers. See it? Good. Now, grab that lever and yank it to the side."

A shrill bell rang from a similar device behind Sofía, the pointer on the face of the device veering toward the word *Slow*.

"Sofía, cariño, if you would be so kind, please tug the crank to match the dial."

Sofía did as instructed.

"It's working!" Adelina's cheeks flushed with triumph.

"When you hear the bell, Sol, you'll know we've received your order. I'll start us off slow, once we're off the coastline, ring the order in and I'll bring us up to full speed." A shaky smile. "Now, grab on to that helm, Captain."

OF ALL THE reckless things Sofía had done since stepping foot on Isla Bestia, this one ranked among the highest. Her feet scrambled unsteadily across the deck, knees wobbling and ankle smarting as the ship jerked her from side to side. She clung to whatever she could as she stumblingly carried out Adelina's orders. *Shovel more coal. Check the water pressure. Ring the bridge.*

Adelina, meanwhile, marched barefoot across the engine room checking machinery, monitoring various gauges, and exchanging hurried words with Sol through the voice pipe. Sweat plastered her curls to her temples, her neck, and she'd slashed all along the side of her fitted skirt for ease of movement. Coal-stained and disheveled, she seemed more herself than she had in all their time in Carnaval.

Outside, a wave smashed against the hull, sending them both skidding portside.

Sofía caught herself on the rail bordering the rods and pistons, and wrenched Adelina up beside her. Gravity tugged them sharply left, then jostled them side to side as the vessel righted itself.

"You deserved better—everything, Sofía, you deserve *everything*," Adelina blurted, knuckles white where they gripped the rail for balance. "I should have protected you from Mamá. From Papá. From *me*."

It was not the most opportune time to be having this conversation. Then again, time was not a resource they had in abundance. "I should have been honest," Sofía shouted back over the racket. "I should have opened up years ago, trusted you to do the right thing. Instead, I let this fester."

"Oh, shut it." Adelina rolled her eyes, exasperated. "That isn't your fault to bear. I *knew*. I'd always known, but I was . . . ashamed. I'd held my tongue for so long, turned the other way so often . . ." She scrunched her eyes shut. "It made me sick knowing I'd hurt you. That nothing I did would ever redeem me. Not to you, not to myself."

Another wave hit, and Sofía lost her hold. Her feet skated across the damp wood, sliding further.

Adelina caught her by the back of her dress. "But I want to do better by you," she shouted, "if you'll let me." With a low growl, she gripped a fistful of fabric and hauled Sofía to her side. "Not to be forgiven, Sage knows I am beyond that, but because you're my family. The very best of it. I may not be able to right all the ways I've wronged you, but I owe you that much and more."

The door to the engine room burst open, and the sea rushed in, splashing down the metal stairs.

"Mother of—"

The surge knocked them off their feet, and in an instant, the deck was six inches below seawater. There was more coming in, flowing down from the upper deck.

"Can you manage here alone?" Sofía shouted over the rush. "Go!"

At Adelina's urging, Sofía splashed up the stairs, fighting the downward drag of the torrent.

The sea pummeled into her the moment she was through the door. Her vision became a blur of black and her nostrils stung with salt. She could taste it on her lips, in the back of her throat, could feel its grit against her skin, rubbing raw the wounds on her palms as she pushed herself back onto her feet.

The main deck was flooded, the water coming nearly to her knees. On it floated broken drinking glasses. Wine bottles. A broom. Grabbing a wooden bucket from the slosh, Sofía began the tedious job of draining the deck, one gallon at a time. It did not help that her drenched skirts weighed heavy on her, or that for every twenty bucketfuls of water she emptied, another wave swept in.

She tackled the task with focused desperation, scooping and tossing, over and over and over, until a familiar hand closed around her wrist.

Her brother stood there, wan with worry.

"Sol! What are you *doing*? You should be—"

"We're here."

She turned, dazedly, bucket still in hand. He was right. They had driven the steamer onto the sandy shore—crashed it, by the looks of it—and just beyond the beach was the forest buttressing the mountains of Coaybay.

Sofía's legs buckled beneath her in equal parts exhaustion and relief.

Adelina emerged from the door behind Sol, looking as tired as she suddenly felt.

"There are canoes along this shore," Sofía told her, wringing water off her skirts. "Take one, and row as far away from here as you can."

Adelina's brow creased. "And leave you?"

They didn't have time to argue. "Adelina—" Sofía rubbed the bridge of her nose "—this island will be destroyed, any moment now could be its last. You have to leave while you still can."

"But is that not why we're here? You've a way to save it."

"A way? No, a mere idea, and a bad one at that. Look, it's too big a risk, you have to—"

"If you stay, *I* stay." The fierce set of her expression brooked no objection. "Let's not waste any more time debating. You and I both know my mind is made." She brushed coal dust off her glove, as if the thing were not already beyond repair. "Now, be a dear and lead the way."

CHAPTER 22

They worship her with story and rhythm and craft. With the dough they bake over the fire, and the babes they grow inside their wombs. To her, they tithe creation.

—Chronicler

"WE'LL HAVE TO SWIM," said Sol, expression grim as he stared up at the mountains of Coaybay. Heavy rockfall blocked the passage up the valley. More stone crumbled even as they watched, and the earth sloughed off the mountains in sheets.

The riverways were only marginally more viable a path, the waters rough and flowing dangerously fast toward the caves. At that rate, there should have been nothing left but a dried-up lakebed, yet every drop lost was rapidly replenished by the great waterfalls rushing groundward, dragging with them driftwood and debris.

"Grab on to that." Adelina pointed to a fallen tree trunk floating along the lake.

Sofia bit back her objections. It was too late now to slide back into her role of doomsayer. After all, it was her half-baked supposition that had brought them here. Clenching her jaw, she dove into the water. Her skirts billowed to the surface and her toes curled at the fresh bite of cold, despite already being sopping wet from the sea.

Two more splashes sounded behind Sofia just as her fingers gripped a nub on the log. She folded her arms over it, legs paddling against the vicious current as Adelina caught up to her. "Hold on!"

Adelina clung to the other end of the trunk, blinking away water. Behind them, Sol had found another piece of driftwood to use as a makeshift flotation device.

With that, they let the waters wrench them onward, through the tunnels of crystalline stalactites, glowing and thin as icepicks. The river was aroar, its rush and roil echoing off the glowing stone, drowning the sounds of their panic. Sofía and Adelina took turns finding handholds on the walls to temper their speed, paddling hard and fast when the river took them too far to one side or the other.

A cauldron of shrieking bats flew over them, moving as a cloud of writhing black, rushing to escape the impending destruction. At the same time, pebbles loosened from the stone overhead. A stalactite fell, its bladed edge cutting through the water, missing Adelina by an inch.

Above the sounds of the river, they heard a rumbling.

"Sol! I think the tunnel is—"

Sofía was midway through her warning when the ceiling collapsed. Rocks rained down. Her body twisted aimlessly within the water's hold. A jagged pebble grazed her cheekbone, another sliced across her forehead, dripping blood into her left eye.

"Sofía!"

She tried calling back to her brother, but every time she opened her mouth to speak, water poured in. Her arms flailed wildly, hands searching blindly through the fog of pale light and rock dust.

Finally, she felt stone, firm and solid under her hand. Her fingers clawed at the wall, digging until they found purchase. There, she clung with all her strength.

"Are you alright?" Adelina clutched the opposite wall some distance away. Something had sliced open her chin and there was a nasty bruise forming over her right temple.

Sofía coughed and wheezed in dusty air, trying and failing to find her voice again. "Wh . . . Where . . ." Her eyes refocused, straying slightly to the left. Toward the mound of fallen rock blocking the tunnel. "No . . ." She swept her gaze across the water. "Sol?" Her breath pressed painfully against her chest, stretching the bones of it thin. She moved along the wall, pushing up against the current.

"Sol! . . . *Sol!*"

His voice at last came through a small gap in the rockfall. "Here! I'm here."

Relief washed over Sofía. She felt dizzy with it. "Are you hurt?"

"No, but . . . there's no way through."

"There has to be, water's still flowing in from your side."

"The openings are too small. I can barely get a hand across. I could try digging through, but . . . we don't have time." He went silent, considering his next words. "You two have to keep going without me. I'll find my way back somehow."

"No."

It was not a refusal, as in *no, you cannot*, nor a command—*no, you must not*. It was a correction, a *no, you are mistaken*, as though he'd uttered a fallacy and she was dutifully rectifying his error. "It . . . it's supposed to be you. I—I can't." How could she petition a being that up until that morning she had not believed in? "It *has* to be you."

"Is that a fact?"

"What?"

"Have you clear, incontrovertible evidence to suggest it *must* be me?"

"I—" The question stymied her, as her brother very well realized it would. That was the problem with twins, they knew exactly how to outmaneuver you. "Sol . . ." She let her forehead fall against the wall.

"If it mustn't be me," he posed, "why can't it be you?"

Excuses rose to Sofía's lips, but never made it past them. *It must be you because . . . because you are easier to love.*

Because your hands create, whereas mine only synthesize.

Because I read the world in patterns, not poetry.

Because if one of us can inspire a god to mercy . . . it isn't me.

THEY DRAGGED THEMSELVES out of the water.

Sofía and Adelina managed only a half crawl, half slither up the stone steps, pulling loose clumps of moss as they heaved their aching bodies upward.

They'd made it.

The ceiba was only steps away, its once gentle glow now so bright it was like staring straight at the midday sun.

Sofía pressed her cheek to the rock, shut her eyes, and listened to the earth tremble beneath her, alive and angry. She wanted so desperately to remain that way, not moving, not seeing, letting sleep claim her.

The soft touch of a hand brought her back to the present.

Adelina lay beside her, wet hair dripping onto the stone, smiling feebly through a bleeding lip. She squeezed Sofía's fingers gently.

Sofía squeezed back. "Ready?"

"Cariño, I've never been less ready for anything in my life." Despite her wounds—both visible and not—and the threat of impending death, Adelina laughed. And Sofía loved her a little more for it. "Don't suppose you'll clue me in on what exactly we're doing here?"

"We're here . . ." Sofía began, "to confer with a goddess." They rose on shaky legs, arms thrown over the other's shoulders, leaning close as they lumbered up the steps. "They say she is this island, and this tree is her mind," she continued, knowing how preposterous it all sounded. "Her consciousness awakened here, and so here is where she is strongest. Most . . . aware."

Soft moss pillowed Sofía's knees as she knelt over the ceiba's roots, her fingers feeling along the bark, the thick spines on its trunk, before settling over the roots again. She spoke to the tree, hoping it could hear her. "If I may be so bold, Mother, I come to ask of you a favor." Palms facing down, she bent until her forehead touched the ground. "I realize I may not be the dearest of your children, if you would consider me a child of yours at all. My brother, he'd have known just the right words to say, the right way to . . . *be*. It should never have been me, yet here I am, and I pray that is enough. That *I* am yours enough."

Beneath Sofía's left hand was a fallen flower. She picked it up, ran a thumb along its smooth petals, and placed it on her tongue. It went down warm and sweet as coconut rum, reviving the link that had begun to fade. "I come to ask that you not leave us, Mother, that you not take our home from us."

A familiar presence grazed Sofía's mind.

It had been there many times before, muddling her thoughts, stoking her wants to the point of obsession. This time, the island did not tamper, it watched, studying her as she studied *it*, the connection going both ways. It inundated Sofía with a torrent of disparate emotions or, at least, what she interpreted as emotions. Many were unrecognizable, so foreign to her body she could not wrangle their meaning into words. What she *could* decrypt bore only a vague likeness to her own experience, as much as a child's chalk drawing can resemble its subject.

There was rage . . . sorrow . . . a fierce, all-consuming desire to protect. But what Sofía recognized most clearly was the island's distrust, its confusion as it tried and failed to make sense of her thoughts, her intention. In that at least, she and the island were more alike than they had any right to be.

"You've protected me." She kept her head low, anchored to that single point of contact on the ground. "Whatever else you may feel about me, Mother, I believe there's a part of you that thinks me worthy of your goodwill, worthy of saving even, if your actions from this night are any indication. I appeal to that side of you now."

The earth rumbled its response.

Sofía pressed closer to the trunk of the tree, curling her fingers around the thick spines, bridging the physical distance as though that could bridge the mental one as well. "If what they say is true . . ." She swallowed through the thick knot in her throat. "If you are Atabey, then you are first and foremost a zemí of creation. You made the lands and the waters that nourish them. You shaped the gods that would give shape to us. Why destroy all this you've made?"

The question went unanswered.

It felt so foolish suddenly, to have hoped for more. She could glean nothing concrete from the island. A scatter of hazy impressions—images and sensations—was the most it would give her.

"Won't you speak to me, Mother, as you speak to the Cacika?" Fear settled into the pit of Sofía's stomach. Up until that point, her newly discovered optimism had quelled her anxieties, but now, so far from shore and with the moon cresting the sky, she felt the full weight of the island crashing down on her.

Adelina's hand slid over her shoulder and Sofía sagged under it, reminded, with sinking horror, that she'd doomed her friend as well as herself. And worse, had abandoned her brother to the dark and the cold. He'd come to this world with her, yet he would depart from it alone.

"Sofía . . . maybe we should . . ."

"No. This is *not* over." Sofía pressed more flowers into her mouth, gnashing the silken petals between her teeth, tasting warmth and nectar. She ate and ate and *ate*, until the warmth turned to stinging heat and she'd made herself sick.

Adelina knelt down, stroking soothing circles over Sofía's back as she emptied her stomach over the web of roots. "There, there," she assured, cooing kind, comforting nonsenses. *"Sana, sana, colita de rana . . ."*

Sofía's mouth tasted of bile and there was a burning in her chest, as if the ceiba's nectar had come aflame inside her.

"Is this your answer, Mother? Has my petition been denied?" she shouted up at the tree, delirious with sickness and grief. What the devils had possessed her to think she could do this, presume to know the mind and motives of a divine being when she could barely make sense of other people, her own self even?

Sheer arrogance, it was.

Hope, countered another voice inside her.

From somewhere in that fog of fear, remorse, and self-reproach, a dangerous thought took shape. "Adelina," she began, rolling the jagged contours of the idea around her head. "Do you still have your pistol on you?"

Adelina glanced down at her reticule, still clipped to her skirts despite their evening's tribulations. She opened it, revealing a small silver weapon against the silk lining of the purse. "What will you do with it?"

There was no delicate way to phrase what she was about to request, and thus, Sofía wasted no time sweetening her words. "I need you to shoot me," she said. "In the heart, preferably. A quick death would be best—we are working against the clock here, after all."

Laughter, loud and with a ragged edge of exhaustion, filled the silence. But only for an instant. When Adelina realized Sofía was serious, her amusement quickly faded to horror. It was not a smooth transition. The emotions collided on her face, each usurping a different feature, splitting her like a land among warring factions. Her eyes were unblinking and wide, but her lips still bore the lingering trace of a smile when she said, "You aren't genuinely asking me to put a bullet through you."

"I am."

Adelina's mouth fell open, anger flaring red on her cheeks. "You'll *die*."

I might, she thought, but did not admit out loud. Instead, she said, "For a while, yes, if all goes to plan. Look . . ." Sofía reached for her friend's hands and held them firmly. "Either I die now for a chance to live, or I die later. All of us do. I know how this all sounds, but this island . . . Well, just *look* at it." She did her best to hide the cracks in her conviction. "Look at this place and tell me you wouldn't call it a miracle."

Tears spilled freely down Adelina's eyes, and Sofía's own vision began to blur.

"Think of what you're asking me to do." Her chin wobbled, adding a tremor to her voice. "If you make me do this, I . . . I will not survive it."

"You have to," said Sofía, her words stern but not unkind. "We both do. So please, pick up the gun."

"Do it yourself, you miserable wretch." Adelina shoved the pistol across the ground, toward Sofía. "Go on, pull the trigger if you're so eager."

"It . . ." She faltered. "I think it has to be you." She'd seen what had happened here. The enemy fire that'd flown within these walls, the violence that'd awoken the island. If they could replicate the events of that night nearly three centuries ago, approximate them at least, then perhaps . . .

Adelina hung her head, rested her face against the cradle of her palms.

Sofía picked up the pistol from the ground, and folded her friend's hands over the cold silver of the barrel before pushing to her feet. Determined to stand tall in this moment, even though she felt like crumpling.

"You'll come back," Adelina said. Not a question, but a decree, upheld by something stronger than the law of men. And gods even, if she thought Sofía had any say in what happened next. "Promise me you'll come back."

"I promise I will try." It was all she could do.

The pistol shook between their joint fingers as Adelina lifted it. Sofía met her eyes, nodded once and stepped back. "If I don't come back—"

"You will."

"But if I don't . . ." A small, sad smile tugged up the corners of her mouth. "I hope there really is an After, and that someday we may read again under the jobo trees. If this is to be the end, sister in heart, then may our next beginning be kinder."

Tears poured down Adelina's cheeks as her pointer finger hugged the trigger. Her lips formed words, words too quiet for Sofía to hear. And then, just as her eyes squeezed closed, the gunshot rang.

CHAPTER 23

Nature knows no morality. Unless . . . you give it words.

—Chronicler

SOFÍA OPENED HER eyes to moonlight.

She floated in an ocean of it, a bright, endless white that curled over her skin like smoke. Above her, or perhaps in front of her, appeared a flutter of ghostly leaves, diaphanous and drifting in swirling patterns. They coalesced into a pulsing form, vaguely female in shape.

"Atabeira . . . ?" The name came out soft and reverent as a prayer.

The translucent leaves shuddered, dispersed like moth wings before transforming into a howling gale of petals. They flew circles around Sofía, building into a cyclone. The bands of wind glittered like iridescent threads and brought with them the scent of brine and morning dew.

Sofía fell to her knees, as much as one could fall in a place without beginning or end. "Is it you, Mother? Are you . . . Atabey?"

"Are we?" The voice that spoke was an echo of her own, yet silkier and richer, with a quality that could only be described as otherworldly.

"Her names we have been called so long now," the zemí said. *"They are as ours as the springs and creeks above our surface."*

In those words, Sofía heard the babble of a brook, the rustle of dried leaves, the groan and crack of swaying branches. Not as an undertone, but as a focal feature, there in the way an accent might curl the edges of another's speech. "But . . . you are not her?"

At that, the island made a contemplative sound, an inhuman vocalization akin to the pull of the tide, the sigh of air through the trees. *"We do not know if we are her . . ."* it said. *"But she is us."*

The storm of glassy petals became a twisting river flowing ever higher, its towering shape undulating amid the blank canvas of that infinite space. It came crashing fast as it'd surged, raining shimmering drops over Sofía, reforming into the wide expanse of a lake with her at its center. It rose around her ankles. Her knees. Her chin.

She was drowning in it, fighting for air when she finally remembered . . .

I am already dead.

And with that realization, her body settled, the imagined pressure of the water against her throat and rib cage fell away. It was all little more than an illusion conjured from moonglow and mist. Even if the threat *were* real, what difference would it make? Death no longer held power over her.

The thought emboldened Sofía. It was a new kind of freedom, a sudden rush of invulnerability that left her buzzing and heady, ready to confront the island-god. "Mother." Rather than gawp at its immensity, she fixed her attention on a nearby point in the water. "How was it that you came into being?" If she stood any chance of convincing the island not to destroy itself and everyone in it, first she needed to understand it. To know what, if anything, would sway it from this fatal course.

As she waited for an answer, Sofía felt the weight of the ancient being's observation, the uncanny presence of a gaze that could follow where human eyes could not. It was a gaze unmoored, unavoidable, and all-pervasive, as though the air itself watched her. "Will you not grant me this truth? After all, who would I tell your secrets to now that I am no more?"

The island's form destabilized, fracturing as though it were in conflict. At last, it spoke. *"We have existed since the darkness and the silence. Since our rock was molten and buried beneath the sea. We came into being long before our surface greened and grew, and life became upon us . . ."* Mountains and forests rose as the lake around Sofía transformed into a sea, its gossamer waves rolling over the sandy shores of a small, beast-shaped island. *"We came into being long before we knew we were."*

The island evolved rapidly before her, shedding the weaknesses of its infancy, strengthening itself against the droughts and the storms. *"Then . . ."* It paused, remembering. *"Then came the children born of earth."*

Humanoid shapes of light rose from the ground to walk beside Sofía.

"They carved their gods into our walls. Filled our halls with song. Brought to us their ailing and their injured, their newly born and newlywed, to mend and bless. At times, they lived within us, but all soon yearned for the sky and sun, the heat our stone kept away. We woke when they came . . . slept when they left. Before their blood soaked our waters, we were but a seedling of awareness. It was through our bond with our children that we came to be . . . more."

Sofía roamed a translucent facsimile of Coaybay, depicted, she assumed, as it was before the Taike'ri made it home. Though its beauty was not yet preternatural, it was still formidable. "In saving them that night," she said, knowing what came next, "you bound your mind to theirs."

"And since, we've not once fallen to slumber."

"That is a very long time to go without rest." Sofía turned down an unfamiliar tunnel, knowing she faced no real risk of getting lost. "Do you even remember what it was like having your mind be your own?" She came to a stop at the end of the path. "All that rage . . . How much of it is even yours, Mother?"

The stone responded with a growth of crystals sharp as thorns. A warning.

Sofía did not back down. "How much of your rage is actually *ours*? How much of it is *theirs*, the ones who drink your poisoned waters, whose heads invite you in? What do you see when you're in there—twisting up their memories, molding what they want and need and crave into an affliction?"

More crystals emerged from the walls, the floor, the ceiling of the tunnel. Growing into a mouthful of razor-fine teeth. Sofía skimmed a finger over the sharpened points, her hand passing right through the illusion. "You resent my scrutiny, yet is that not why I am here? Lured by your dreams of blood and moonlight. Was it not you who roused me from sleep on those nights no other lay awake, revealed to me a truth I was too obstinate to see?"

The island's answering rumble was reminiscent of a grunt, a vague approximation to a human sound of . . . confusion? Frustration?

"Were I feeling brave, Mother, I might even go as far as to say there's a part of you that wants me to question you. To question *this*."

The tunnel dissolved into particles of floating dust, glinting as they settled against a canvas of white, like stars into a constellation. Without moving, Sofía again found herself beneath the ceiba tree. Her eyes went to the roots, half expecting to see her own body laid across them.

"Of all our children . . . why choose you to carry our portents? To challenge our resolve?"

"*Choose?* Stars above, no, I do not claim to be your divinely chosen champion—if anything, a 'last resort' is a more apt descriptor. My guess is that no one else heeded your warning. Would you not agree that is the likelier scenario? After all, who would be so arrogant as to presume the Mother's true will?" Sofía allowed herself a small smile. "Only a godless woman would have such conceit."

The island fell quiet.

"I could go on speculating, Mother, but surely you could ascertain your own intention far better than I ever could."

"Assertion . . . intention . . . How effortless it must all seem. To you, this is a matter of yes or no, of simply . . . knowing." The island sounded almost wistful. *"Your kind . . . Your minds are ponds. They ripple, they dry, they overflow, but always they remain a pond, contained to their one existence. Whereas our mind, it . . . diverges. At times, we are the leaf, others, we are the branch that holds it, or the soil that nourishes it. We are often all, and rarely one."*

"Could you not fathom then, how some part of you might want to put an end to this?"

"*And how would we know whether that will is ours, or another's? You said it so, we are tangled in our rage. Could the same not be said about our lenience? Is it really ours, this unwillingness to do what must be done?*"

Images flashed against the moonlit landscape. A mosaic of ghostly faces blinking in and out of being, their spectral voices whispering their secrets into Sofía's ears. Wanting respite, wanting war, a way to stop the hurting. She glimpsed their lives in vignettes, their stories colliding in a jarring symphony.

Over there, Anani—play-chasing a gaggle of rowdy children. And there, in genuflection. Her lips no longer smiling but bending to the shore she will never return to. Beyond her, Tínima—relishing their winning round of guamajico. And there, singing through tears as all around them the earth keeps breaking.

Then . . . there's Kaona.

Kaona, a babe on her lap and a woman beside her, her heart inked with a matching bird tattoo.

Kaona, when the first shots ring and her tribe dwindles.

When she finds refuge beyond the waves.

When death calls, but she calls to the waters.

When she frees a girl she would raise as a daughter.

Grieve as a daughter when she sends her away.

"How can you bear it?" Sofía gasped out. "Feeling this, *all of us*, all the time . . ." It was brutal, the constant pendulum of emotions tugging toward justice, toward life, as if the two were mutually exclusive. "Perhaps if you were to make your mind your own again, then—"

"*No.*" The specters vanished and the image of the ceiba tree shivered, its lines loosening into individual points, as though it had been sculpted from shining grains of sand. "*That we cannot do.*"

"Why?"

"*We need the words you give us . . . We need to understand.*"

Sofía stepped forward to trace a hand along the tree's suspended fragments, reaching for the island-god. "Understand what?"

"Everything."

Everything . . . everything . . . everything . . . The confession reverberated through Sofía as if her body was a cave, holding that word in its bones. She felt it deep in her marrow, that same drive to know, to understand, the instinct vital as food and shelter and water. For most, knowing was a want. For her, it was survival.

"*You feel it too*," the island said, discerning her thoughts before she spoke them. "*It gnaws at you, how much of this world you are yet to make sense of.*"

Sofía rasped out a laugh, but there was no joy in it. "I endure hunger better than I do unanswered questions."

"*Then you, better than most, know why we cannot abandon these ties.*"

"But our minds . . . what could you find in them that you could not in your own? We're mere fish in the vastness of your ocean. Is it even worth knowing the world as we do?"

Within the starburst fragments of the ceiba, the figure of a woman flickered, breaking apart before once again consolidating into a discernible form. "*In your minds . . . we become. Are named. Defined. We do more than exist,*" it said. "*In your minds we are, and thus know the world is.*"

"That's . . . no. You *became* when you protected those who came to you for shelter. When you took the pain and sickness from those who bathed in your waters." Sofía stepped toward the flickering figure, her skin a galaxy of diamond-shaped droplets, her long mane a river curling at the ends. "It seems to me you were making your own choices long before you bound your mind to ours."

The woman lifted a hand, rested her shining fingertips softly over the slope of Sofía's cheek. Her touch was light and cool at first, like that initial dive into water, before it faded to a pleasant warmth. "*How fierce you are in your resolve, rahe, yet why deny your people their vengeance when you clamor for it too? We hear it. We hear you, child of the summer storm. Orphan. Captive. Powerless. Girl of two names, and yet, Anonymous. Made to bow, to forget, to erase yourself. This is your chance to make them pay, why not take it?"*

"Because . . ." Sofía let herself sag. "Because I'm exhausted. This world has worn me down to the bone and I can't keep giving pieces of myself to fight it. Because within these walls, I learned that the sweeter vengeance is just . . . existing. Because so many found in you a home, and I—I think I could have too." Strange, that she could feel a thing of brittle glass cracking inside her chest, as though she had left her flesh but brought her heart with her.

"I don't know if this is the right choice—" *was there right a right choice?* "—but neither is going to war today to be at peace tomorrow. There has to be a better answer, and until we can find it . . ." Tears fell, hot against her cheeks. "Until then, I just want us to *live*."

That yearning blazed bright at her core, igniting her like she was coal, metal, and machine. But even her stubborn desire to live could not keep her from fading—all it did was make it harder to let go.

Against the pearlescent white of that in-between place, Sofía's arms were becoming translucent, evanescing as rain does under the heat of the sun. She clung to her own body, sank nails deep into the skin as if that could keep her from disappearing. It mattered not that she was already gone, her true body lying elsewhere, she felt so *real*. So solid and whole and unprepared for what came next.

"Mother." Her breath hitched. "I wish I could've known you . . ."

The figure angled its face of pale stars as around it the world shook, and the ceiba dispersed even farther apart, scattering into a shapeless shimmer.

Sofía grew fainter, losing her grip on life even as her taste for it grew sharper. She was not done with life, even if it was done with her. There was too much left to see, to learn, to write about. How could it end here?

She held on until there was nothing left of herself to hold.

No hands to grip, no feet to stand their ground. Amid the fear, the tremors, and the fall of moon-bright dust coming down like snow, Sofía faded.

The last she saw was the Mother's inhuman face, shining bright against the rising dark.

CHAPTER 24

*Guardian, she is, of a mother in birth.
Nourishment she brings to the green of her earth. Yet, as she calms the tides, so does she bring the storm. Destruction and life are but two sides of the same coin . . .*

—**Chronicler**

A VOICE CRIED out Sofía's name.

She was cold. The only warmth was the pressure of a hand against her cheek, the spill of blood above her heart. Her vision was a dizzying blur, revealing flashes of searing white between gentler glimpses of cerulean blue.

She knew that color, and the face that framed them—blotchy and tear-stained as it was.

"You came back," Adelina stuttered between racking sobs. *"You came back."*

"I . . ." Sofía forced the words out hoarsely, every sound an enormous undertaking. "I promised . . . I'd . . . try . . ."

A kiss was brushed against her hairline, more peppered across her brow. Then a weight settled on the curve of her shoulder and tears soaked into her tangled tresses, mixing with the salt and damp already on her skin. Sofía reached a trembling hand, gently cradling Adelina's head as she wept.

Above, branches rocked to a gentle wind, cottony flowers opened to a full bloom, and a round moon looked upon her from its zenith, bathing the obsidian sky in a halo of soft light.

The night was silent.

The earth, at last, stood still.

THE WINDS CARRIED the musky scent of crushed earth, traced with notes of something sulfurous. Over the ruins of Carnaval hung a film of dust, veiling the night in muted shades of sallow gray. At least the sky no longer hid behind blackened bark and bramble. The cage over Carnaval had caved inward, and what little remained upright was brittle and saw-edged as a cracked eggshell. Its remnants lay scattered amid the debris, a few pieces floating along arteries of murky water—all that was left of the once sprawling river.

Nothing had survived the night intact, not even the Flor de Lis upon its firm bed of stone. On one side, the roof had collapsed right down to its foundation, revealing the shattered skeleton of the building underneath.

Sofía climbed over what was left of the arcade that once bordered the hotel, stepping from soft sand onto sodden earth—patched with limp grasses, clumped roots, and shining bits of glass. The surface had ruptured in places, leaving gaping fractures across the ground. "Mind your step," she cautioned as they moved between trees half buried in the soil, branches and roots protruding into their path.

Adelina lagged some paces behind, leading Sol carefully along the space Sofía had cleared for them. Her brother's limp was more pronounced here where the ground was cratered and uneven, and where his improvised splint, assembled from a broomstick and some rope they'd found aboard the steamer, kept snagging on the wreckage.

He was hurt during the cave-in, though he kept it to himself until they reunited outside Coaybay. Sofía was furious at him, never mind the fact he had done it for her, hidden his injury knowing what leaving him behind already cost her.

Self-sacrificing fool, she thought, not entirely unaware of the hypocrisy.

Wordlessly, she drew his arm over her shoulders and slung her own around his midsection. Adelina let her take some of the burden, but not all. She was adamant about helping, despite sporting more than her fair share of aches and pains.

Of the three, only Sofia had escaped the night seemingly unscathed. The island-god had healed more than the broken muscle tissue and ruptured blood vessels of her heart. In returning her to life, it had soothed every inch of torn flesh, every aching bone across her body. Only her old scars it left untouched, and for that she was strangely grateful.

What this second life meant, she was not yet sure, but that would reveal itself in time. However much of it she had.

Just beyond the copse of fallen trees, near a thousand patrons huddled outside, pale-faced, bloodied, and motionless with shock. Most had removed their masks, revealing faces smudged with sweat and tears. They sat bent over the steps, or slouched against the balustrades, staring listlessly into the distance—if they stared at anything at all.

Others lay prone and ominously still, the pall of death hanging over them. Even from a distance, Sofia could tell that theirs had been no natural end. There was an eerie similarity to the way they'd fallen prostrate, bent earthward and humbled. The Mother's doing, then.

Having seen into each of their minds, she would've had her reasons.

A man, golden-haired and grimy with rock dust, took down the stairs at a rush. He seized patrons by the shoulders, forcing their blank gazes to his. To each, he asked the same question, "Have you seen my son?" One or two answered with a shake of the head, but most appeared to hardly notice him. Some fear had spawned within those who had survived the night, seeded by something greater than their brush with death.

What final terror had Isla Bestia sowed in them as it left their minds? Sofia might never know for certain. The island no longer spoke to her, nor did she suspect it ever would again. Should she hazard a guess, she'd say the island-god had not spared them without some measure of . . . assurance. Too much Taike'ri blood had already spilled for it to be so reckless.

Whispers drew Sofía's gaze forward.

There was some commotion ahead, where the Taike'ri crowded along their grounded barges. The crowd stirred and shifted to let someone pass.

It was Kaona, her eyes veined red and blazing with condemnation. Stripped of her headdress and mask, and without the bat-winged god at her back, she was just a woman, one suspended in vengeance and grief, as if the same magic that preserved her body also kept her mind trapped in some bygone time.

Sofía made to withdraw from her brother's side, to face the Cacika alone, but he clung to her with a determined expression.

"Sol, you don't—"

"You and me," he said, an echo of his words from earlier that night, and from his tone it was clear he would brook no objection. Not that she could summon the energy to argue.

Thankfully, though Adelina appeared just as reluctant to leave Sofía's side, having taken quick stock of the situation, she prudently remained behind.

Together, Sofía and her brother approached the Cacika.

"Years we spent building toward this night," said Kaona, her voice a strangled rasp. "A perfect storm to wash away what did not belong, to return to those lost to us their ways. Their rightful lands. We were to remake them a people servant to no one but this earth and its gods. Yet you would have us remain nameless. Conquered and bowed to a tyrant's might."

Sofía bore the sting of that accusation. She had known, and had accepted, that their intervention would not be universally well received. What they'd done lived somewhere at the intersection between selfishness and selflessness—an act that altered the fate of a people would never be morally clean.

"And *you*, Kachi." The Cacika turned to Sol with a wounded look. "How could you?"

"I—" He hung his head. "I never meant to turn my back on this. This night was to be my last, that had always been the plan, but then I stood there watching it all end, and it . . . it didn't feel like winning."

A few of the onlookers nodded wearily.

"And this—" She shot a hand toward what was left of their revolution. "*This* does?"

Before anyone could respond, a tall, stooped figure broke away from the crowd.

Tínima.

"My dears . . . this has been a long and grueling night. We're all tired and our tempers are being tested, but we mustn't forget that this is not our way. We do not war amongst ourselves." At that, their eyes locked meaningfully with Kaona's. "Dividing us is the arijuas' job. Let's not make it easier for them."

The Behíke turned to Sol and Sofía then with something like encouragement . . . perhaps even relief? "Go on then, say your piece." It was just as she'd glimpsed through that window in the Mother's mind. Tínima too had been dreading the island's end, praying they would not have to break the world to make it better.

Nodding her gratitude, Sofía addressed the Cacika in her stilted Taike'ri. "It was my idea to petition the Mother," she admitted. "If one of us is to bear the blame, it should be me."

"What are you doin—"

"That is a given," Kaona responded before Sol could properly interject. "Your loyalty was compromised from the start. What I failed to foresee was the extent of your betrayal. Had I known you would corrupt the Mother, undoing everything we had been working for, I would've never let you in."

Sofía felt that cut deep into the softest parts of her. "Would you believe me if I said the Mother made a choice?"

"Brought on by your manipulations."

"You think far too highly of me. I am flesh to her earth, what power could I possibly hold over the divine? My talent for rhetoric, while above par, is certainly no match for the likes of a zemí. Not enough to sway her lest she already willed it—some small sliver of her, at least."

Kaona ground her teeth. "And what would you know of her will, when it is I who have shared her mind for thousands of moons?"

"Did therein not lie the problem?"

It was only when the Cacika recoiled as though struck that Sofía realized that had been the wrong thing to say.

Sol, far wiser about these things, leapt to intervene. "She means no disrespect. Her words, they just don't always come out how she intends them." But the damage was already done and there was no deescalating it. All Sofía could do was steel herself for the inevitable vitriol. *Maybe you deserve it*, whispered something small and hurt inside her.

That was when the vines sprang out of the loam. The knotted threads circled the ground at Kaona's feet. Grew tall, twining up and around her ankles—restraining her, Sofía mistakenly assumed, yet the island's hold was gentle. Cocooning.

It seemed to stir something within Kaona, some too-big emotion that left her wavering on her feet. She fell to her knees and the blanket of green settled around her like a warm cloak.

"Atabeira . . . *why*?" Her dark eyes stared at the earth that held her, uncomprehendingly. "Why have you abandoned me, Mother? Why does your voice no longer sing inside my head? It's quiet here now, I . . . I can't remember it ever being this quiet . . ."

The Cacika's gaze found Sofía's, and in that rare, brief moment of vulnerability, she did not seem ancient and unbreakable. She was lost, and lonely, and maybe even a little afraid. "Is she with you now?"

Sofía shook her head, unsure if that made it better, or worse.

"She's forsaken us then . . ."

"Is this the act of a god that's forsaken you, Cacika?" asked Sofía. "Salt and seas, she's swaddling you like a child."

"Then why do I not feel her?" Tears dragged through the black paint on Kaona's cheeks.

There was a rustle, and something brushed against Sofía's feet. A vine, weaving up her ankle, along her calf. Coaxing her forward. "Sol . . . can you manage?" she said to her brother, and when he was safely balanced on his uninjured leg, she allowed the island to guide her. Draw her closer to the chieftain of the Taike'ri.

Weighing her options, Sofía decided she was tired, and her feet were sore, and it seemed rude to loom, so with a sigh, she picked up her ruined skirts and joined the Cacika on the ground. It was strange, bizarrely funny even: the two of them sitting amidst the remnants of a revolution, face-to-face as though about to clap hands in a game of Aserrín, Aserrán, meanwhile the island fussed and fretted over them, its touch soothing as a mother's fingers through the hair.

It was a long while before either of them made a sound.

"When I spoke to the zemí," Sofía began, treading with care, "it was like calling into a cave. Everything I poured into it came back an echo, amplified and distorted. Toward the end, it all started to blur, what was mine and what was hers. I think . . . I think the Mother left so she could remember." *And you could too*, she thought but did not say.

"Then that . . . that would mean . . ." Her voice trembled. "We shared a vision of what this world could be once we'd remade it, but if *this* is what she would choose, then was that vision only ever mine? Did I . . . did I do this to her?"

This time, it was the island that answered.

Delicate, moon-pale flowers budded from the blanket of green around the Cacika. She blinked large, wet eyes and let out a racking sob. "Have I been holding on too hard, Mother? All these years, is that why you stayed? Would you have left had I not been so afraid of living in myself without you?"

In its language of velvet blooms and twisting green, the island seemed to say, *I needed you too*, and held the Cacika as she wailed and raged and pounded her fist against her heart like she might beat the pain out of it. Dislodge from her body the history she'd been carrying inside it; a whole museum contained within one deceptively small woman.

There was no comfort Sofía could offer, but she could listen, bear witness to Kaona's centuries of grief. And so that's what she did, remaining long after the sobs had quieted to whimpers, and the strikes weakened to thumps, and the cloud of dust cleared enough to show the stars.

FROM BEHIND THE MONSTER, a man emerged.

A flash of silvery lantern light rippled against the vejigante's enameled mask, catching like moonlight over dark water. Slate hair peeked out from behind the horns. Next came the brows, thick and meant for scowling. Then, a crooked nose, broken one too many times during his years in battle, followed by a thin-lipped mouth. A square jaw. Wrinkles set deep as ravines.

The man was as still and gray as a photograph. Only his eyes stood out against those ashen hues, their irises a familiar shade of cerulean blue.

"*Papá.*" Adelina held a hand to her mouth, stifling a sob. She had known the state she'd find him in. Awake, but unresponsive, his expression vague and lifeless. Over a dozen others she had unmasked before him. They sagged like rag dolls across the ruined courtyard, drool dripping down their chins, empty-eyed and staring at nothing. But even the sight of those men and women lying listless and languid, as though sedated, could not have prepared her for this.

Adelina's father was nearly unrecognizable.

When last they saw him, he'd been a man capable of silencing a room with his presence. His every word resounded; his marching steps boomed across all levels of his manor. Some passed through life fading into shadowed corners, but even when standing idle, Don Reynaldo de Esperanza never went unnoticed.

Now the only striking thing about him was the gauntness of his cheeks, his soldier's brawn reduced to little more than bones. He was aged far past his years, his skin chapped and sickly pale, the area under his eyes puffy and bruised.

Adelina reached for her father, tracing the sharp jut of his cheekbones, the hollows underneath. If he sensed his daughter's touch, he showed no sign of it. He sat there like a stringless marionette, his weight drooping against the fountain at his back.

Sofía felt no pity for her old master, but her heart ached for her friend. He might have been a beast of a man, but to his daughter at least, he was a kind father. One who smiled when she came to supper stained in engine grease, who taught her industry and trade, and doted on her endlessly.

Beside Sofía, Sol stood rigid. When she twined her fingers along his, he gripped them hard, like he might fall straight through the earth without her. It had not been easy for him, stepping back into this place. Even in ruins, the Flor de Lis was a painful memory.

He did not look at Sofía when he spoke, as though he were recounting the story to himself instead of her. "Each full moon, a king was chosen," he said, voice strained. "The most rotten among the rot. We'd give them a crown, a special drink . . . and by the night's end, the goddess would slide into their skin, make a host of their bodies. Their wills would give way first, and with time, their minds."

The island-god made slaves of the slavers, robbed them of name and voice and memory, and bade them to her command. Sofía thought of the vejigantes serving her meals, pouring her coffee, dressing her bed with fresh linens each night. They were empty husks in devil masks, puppeteered by a power born of rock and root and moon and water. The truth should have horrified Sofía, but after the night she'd had, her capacity for such emotion was spent.

"Most hosts she burned through in a year or two. Few lasted as long as him." Sol did not bother concealing the bitterness in his tone. "Is it cruel of me to feel no sympathy, when he sits here frail and broken, neither living nor dead?"

Sofía wrapped her free hand over Sol's knuckles. "Don Reynaldo owned our bodies, our sweat, our labor—he is not owed our kindness." She watched her brother fight for control. He did not want to fall apart before this man, not even this version of him. "He hurt you, didn't he?"

"No," Sol said, not taking his gaze away from his former master. "Pain was not what brought him pleasure. It was others' eyes, their hands . . . their *envy*. I was a piece of his collection, put on for display. *See the boy? What beauty he sculpts . . .* He entertained at night, belting out old sailors' tunes as I set my chisel to stone. His guests only watched at first, but people like that aren't ever satisfied with just watching. And he, of course, was the kind to base the value of what he owned on how much another wanted it."

Sofía clung to Sol, needing him to stave her hands from the sudden violence roaring through her. Mother of Waters save her from striking a man already half-dead.

"Like a good businessman, he waited for the right bid to be made. The one to pay it was some Northern industrialist with a fondness for younger boys, so the rumors said. I was to remain in my suite until my guest arrived." Sol's mouth twisted into a grim smile. "The Taike'ri got to me before the old bastard could."

"If . . ." Sofía bit the inside of her cheek until she tasted blood. "If he recovers, Sol—"

"He won't," he said quickly. "We've . . . retired hosts before, when they get too frail or sickly. They might learn to sit up on their own, or eat when prodded, but they never go back to who they were. Thank the Mother for that mercy."

Sofía looked at the other unmasked vejigantes, scattered about what remained of the courtyard. "The rest of them . . . Did they deserve it?"

Her brother followed her gaze, pausing on each face as though he could read the sins that led them there. When he spoke, his voice was grave and firm, bearing no trace of uncertainty.

"They did."

THE SUN SPILLED over the rubble of Carnaval, yet for the first time, its warmth did not compel the island's guests to bed, drawn to sleep as the goddess in their heads demanded. They remained as they were, watching the night turn rose-colored and gold.

Sofía shielded her eyes against the glow of morning and moved to join the figure on the balcony. Sunlight silhouetted the girl, rendering her another featureless shape among many. It was the way she stood, hands clasped in front of her, feet angled like a skittish rabbit's—poised to leap—that made her instantly recognizable.

As Sofía stepped beside Fátima, she took in the girl's tattered gown, drooping curls, and scuffed elbows and chin. Blood had seeped through the cream silk of her gloves and dried on her palms.

"Let's take these off, shall we?"

Fátima did not protest when Sofía began sliding the gloves off her hands. The girl seemed unaware of the world around her, remaining pliant and uncharacteristically quiet even when Sofía shook a few drops of bromine onto the ragged skin of her palms. The rust-colored liquid seeped into the open wounds, and still the girl did not flinch. An hour ago, Adelina had cursed all nine saints when Sofía administered the same treatment.

She dropped the vial into one pocket. From the other one, she retrieved a roll of leftover bandages. There was just enough to bind both hands, but not enough to do it properly. "This'll have to suffice for now." Sofía moved with gentle precision, wrapping each hand in a thin layer of cotton. She was fastening the ends of the bandage, when at last, Fátima spoke.

"He's gone," she said. They were fragile things, those words, cursed to crumble if she dared utter them too loudly.

With a final twist, Sofía tied the bandage over the back of Fátima's hand. She brushed her thumb over the knot, choosing to hold instead of letting go. "Was he ever here?"

Fátima turned her face toward the rising sun, and her eyes closed against its warmth. "You knew, then."

"I . . . suspected. You seemed far too besotted for a wife so neglected. At first, I blamed the foolishness of young love. And then—" Sofía's gaze wandered "—I saw your face the night I donned his clothes. I've lost people before. I know what that pain looks like."

"The gods took him two nights before we were to journey here." The measured cadence of Fátima's voice could have been easily misinterpreted as calm, but Sofía knew enough to recognize the deep weariness in it. "We'd known when we married that our days together were numbered. He'd had a weak body ever since he was a boy. A doctor was at his bedside seemingly every other evening, mixing draughts and sticking him with leeches. Their official prognosis was that he'd not live past his tenth year. But Felipe . . . he was determined. My father told him he could have me for his wife when he was sixteen, and not a minute sooner. And so, he pushed his heart to beat until the day we could be wed." The memory thawed through the pain of his absence, and Fátima's lips softened into a small smile.

"The morning after his birthday, we were on a ship, setting sail across the sea. In secret, mind you. His dear mamá would have barred the doors had she known what we were planning. Sweet saints, I might have done it myself, had I not known just how badly he wanted a life beyond his bedroom walls. Felipe . . . he had dreamt of adventure since before he understood he'd have none."

Sofía joined her at the balustrade, leaning her elbows against the flower-wreathed railing. "And did he find it?"

Fátima smiled in earnest then. "Enough to make up for all the years he did not. I think that was why I came here, even though I'd only just lost him. He'd have wanted me to keep adventuring, to soak in all the life he couldn't. That same night I boarded the steamer, he was laid to rest in the meadow by our inn, near a patch of blue widow's tears—seemed only fitting. Then I packed my things and his, and set off. There was so much to do here, so much to see, it was easy to pretend he was somewhere near, lost among Carnaval's wonders.

"I can't say when it was that I started to believe it. It was such a relief, imagining he was out there dancing and drinking, eating all the chocolate flan he wanted . . . Until in forgetting my grief, I forgot him too. All the reasons he deserved my mourning. It hurt more, somehow, to lose him and go on as though I'd never had him."

A gust of balmy wind blew through the salt-sprayed tangles of Sofía's hair. She tilted her face toward it. "Carnaval took something from me too," she said, as she traced the spiny edges of a leaf on the railing. "My twin brother. I had come here to find him, and yet there were days I could hardly remember his name. But you . . . you were strong enough to grieve your grief, to cry when this place demanded laughter. If all of us could love another even half as deeply as you did, this world would be far better for it."

Fátima bent, leaning her forehead over Sofía's shoulder. She could feel the girl trembling against her.

"If I close my eyes, will I still remember?" Her voice broke with her next admission. "I am terrified I'll forget."

SOFÍA FOLLOWED THE sounds of music to the shore. Tens of Taike'ri had taken to the water with their rattles and their drums, and the tempo they set was bittersweet. Neither fast nor slow, but as constant as the waves they splashed within.

Sofía was unsure if they would welcome her, but some residual boldness compelled her to shed all her salt-stiffened layers as the others had, and let herself in. The sand was soft under her feet and the water refreshingly cool against her bare skin. She ran her fingers along its sun-dappled surface as a low, quiet hum played at the back of her throat.

A half smile brushed her lips when she spotted Tínima, swaying with their arms outstretched, a rattle shaking rhythmically in each hand.

She stepped alongside the Behíke, who smiled broadly enough to show two crooked front teeth.

"This island is my birthplace . . . did you know?" They told her without preamble. "I'm the ninth of my line to be cave-born. My daughter too—may Maketaori watch over her spirit—and my grandchild, that gangly one over there."

"The one belting off-key?"

"Their talents lie elsewhere." Tínima's lips twitched into a wry grin. "This island is all we've ever known, all we've ever needed."

Sofía tried picturing what it must have been like to grow up with a zemí in the earth and water all around you, promising that the soil would thrive and the walls would hold. A vision flashed inside her mind's eye of Sol and herself as children, dashing like wildlings through the Batey, playing among the rainbow of hammocks on display and knowing all the best places to hide in. They would come home to their mother—whom they'd call bibi, not mamá—and she would sing to them in the language of their blood until they slept.

A tear slipped across Sofía's cheek as the vision ended. "It must've been beautiful."

Tínima nodded. "It still is."

They spoke of simple things after that. Sofía told them of the journal she kept, the bats, and plants, and mushrooms she was cataloging, and Tínima gave away the secret to a perfectly crisp cazabe, revealing in the process a deep fondness for culinary experimentation. They were enthusing over the versatility of malanga when, around them, the music gradually faded to silence.

Tínima trailed off and turned their sight toward the horizon. Sofía followed their gaze, her heart thudding when she saw the shapes in the distance. "Are those . . . ?"

"Yes."

Canoes, outlined in the morning sun.

The Taike'ri were coming home.

A HORN BLARED.

From the smokestacks, steam and engine exhaust blew in a jet of soot, just as a man leaned out the side of the pilot's house, shouting, "Get in already, you gibbering muck! If you ain't up here by the next whistle, you're swimmin' back mainland!"

The captain prowled along the cabin as people rushed aboard, stomping his heavy leather boots, gold-buckled and tanned the burnt yellow of saffron rice. He wore a matching vest and eggplant-colored trousers embroidered with some kind of long-necked bird. Swans, perhaps—or geese? It was hard to tell from a distance.

As the man went about his rounds, he spotted Sofía.

She waved up at him.

"*Oye!* You really did quite a number on this old girl." Vicente rapped his knuckles against the wood. "Water rot on every floorboard. Scratches all along her keel. Windows cracked to bits. You even broke my damn broom."

"And how gracious you've been not to remind me at every turn, Señor Gallardo." Sofía flashed him a half grin. "It must be the fleet of passenger ships at your disposal that makes you so forgiving. How many do you own again . . . twenty-seven?"

"*Owned,*" he corrected, biting down on his cigar. "Ten years, it's been. Who knows what's happened to the business."

It was a decade ago that Vicente had come to the Flor de Lis, intent on negotiating exclusive docking privileges for his line of steamers. Needless to say, his trip had not gone according to plan. He faintly recalled signing off on contracts and correspondence over the years, blearily approving crew rosters and ship repairs, unknowingly foregoing more and more control to the Taike'ri.

"You don't seem terribly upset."

"Bah." He flicked his wrist dismissively. "Good riddance to it, I say. Never did acquire a taste for all the bluster and preening that comes with this line of work—bunch of peacocks, us enterprisers." At that, he winked. "Now that I've gotten grayer and more ornery, not to mention more likely to strike up a brawl than a deal, perhaps it's time I go back to swabbing decks. Remind myself of that raggedy lad that once dreamt of the open sea."

"And perhaps after, you might try your hand at a new venture," said Adelina as she came to stand beside Sofía on the boardwalk.

"Got something in mind?"

"Oh, just a few fledgling ideas . . ." By which she meant several long and rigorously researched business plans with multi-year projections, market analyses, and detailed footnotes. "Let's discuss over coffee if you're ever in Etérea."

"Assuming we make it there, seems my engine officer's wandered off the ship."

"Oh, hush, you," Adelina scolded good-naturedly. "You cannot expect me to leave without a proper farewell. Besides, Ramona's keeping things running for me."

For over a week, they had been traveling to and from the mainland, conveying patrons away from Isla Bestia—which now belonged solely to the Taike'ri—and back to a very loose version of the lives they'd left behind. Lives altered by absence and time, and whatever the Mother had sowed inside their minds right before she left them.

The steamer could only safely fit about a hundred passengers, and each round trip took roughly half a day, counting the hours it took to restock and refuel. This trip was to be their last.

Once the steamer left its berth, it would not turn back.

The fact seemed to sink in for Adelina when Vicente vanished into the pilot's house, gearing up to set sail one final time. As she spun to face Sofía, her smile slipped a fraction. "I . . . This is . . . I mean, we . . . *Oh, fiery hells*." Adelina threw her arms around her. "How am I supposed to do this? You and I, we were to take on the world together, *fix it* together. How are we to do that with an ocean between us?"

Sofía tucked her friend under her chin, holding her there. "Don't sound so dramatic now, it's barely a dozen leagues."

Not that it mattered—distance was the least of their concerns. It had started four nights ago. A heavy fog had formed like a bolt from the blue to wrap around Isla Bestia. The steamer had wandered the sea aimlessly for hours, until a few of the more competent Taike'ri rowers offered to guide it to shore.

The moment they touched the water, the veil lifted.

Every night since had been the same. A mist descended right as the ship neared land and parted for the Taike'ri alone, a warning to those who might seek the island's shores uninvited.

The Mother's message could not have been any more obvious. *So much for needing words . . .*

"I wish I could stay." Adelina pressed the confession into Sofia's shoulder, as if by muffling it she might also dampen its effect. "But that's not what you need, is it?"

The answer stuck in Sofia's throat. The best she could muster was to hug her friend tighter.

"No, I don't suppose it is . . ." Adelina answered for her. "Gods, my every instinct is screaming at me to fight for you even though I know—*I know*—the best thing I can do is let you go. I'm horrid, aren't I? I ought to be gracious and supportive, yet here I am, acting like some mewling moppet because I can't stand losing my best friend. Saints, what is *wrong* with me?" Adelina's face had quickly devolved into a blotchy mess of snot and tears. "I should confer with my physician, surely there's some sort of overactive gland or imbalanced humor. There must be a remedy he can prescribe me. A pill or a tonic, maybe a lobotomy."

"Adelina." Sofia seized her firmly by the shoulders. "When the steamer leaves, will you be on it?"

"Wh— Do you mean to say that was not implied?" She made a spasming sound that was either a hiccup or a laugh. "Sofia, dearest heart, I gave you my word that night in the engine room. I vowed that I'd do better, and I *will*, even if . . . even if that means I don't get to be by your side."

Sofia swallowed back a sob, pushed it down and locked it tight inside her chest. Her voice, she was pleased to note, wavered only slightly when she spoke. "In that case . . . it's my professional opinion that all your glands and humors must be perfectly balanced."

"Why then is this *so* hard?"

"Endings always are."

Adelina's hands reached for Sofía's. These were not the pristine hands of the girl who had clung to her over half a year ago, afraid to be alone. These were blistered and scandalously ungloved, one finger bound in gauze and the nails caked with coal dust.

"I'm going to go now, cariño." She said this as though summoning the courage to leave. "Any longer, and I might be tempted to say goodbye."

They let go the same way that once upon a time they came together. Slowly, by degrees. An unraveling of fingers as their fates themselves unwound, a yielding after a lifetime of latching on too fiercely. They had been children when the universe, troublemaker that it was, thrust them onto parallel paths, making sisters of two girls who, at best, should have been strangers. How guileless they were then, to believe that someday love would be enough.

Sofía's memories flashed against her mind's eye like a zoetrope. *Your brother, he said you like frogs?* Adelina had parted her hands in the way of someone unfolding a present, and she had caught a flash of a wriggling body, golden and small as a thumb, before it leapt—absconding into the braided depths of Adelina's hair. The first of many sweet, many terrible memories Sofía would spend years trying and failing to compartmentalize.

"If by some chance," said Adelina, already turning toward the steamer, "you ever find yourself wanting to write to me, I will be at the pier on the first morning of each month. Your courier may find me by the statue of the lion."

"It could take years, Adelina. I might never actually be ready . . ."

"I know." A small smile touched her lips. "If you ever are though, that's where I'll be." With that, Adelina was climbing the gangplank to the steamer and stepping onto the deck.

Gradually, the knot in Sofía's chest loosened into something approaching bearable, the pressure of it like a thumb against the inside of her rib cage, steady and firm. It might ease in time, perhaps even unravel altogether. Or it might calcify, and she would learn how to exist in her body alongside it. She *must*, for this parting was what their stories had always been inching toward, building in stops and starts—a steamer ticket bought in secret, a goodbye written in the dark, a place that made her think, *I want to stay.*

Who might Sofía be now without Adelina at her nexus? Where might she go when her narrative no longer bent to someone else's north? The thought left her dizzy, almost nauseated with possibility.

The smokestacks gusted ashen streams into the endless blue above, and with a jerk, the steamer was off. Adelina pressed closer to the railing and Sofía followed instinctively, moving to the farmost edge of the boardwalk, close enough to feel the spray of salt water on her cheeks as the waves slapped the hull. Neither raised their hand in farewell, knowing better than to seal this moment with such a conclusive gesture.

It was a long while before Sofía surrendered her vigil.

The steamer was already a dark silhouette against the mirror-bright sea when she lowered herself to a seat at the end of the boardwalk. Her legs dangled over the water, swaying idly to and fro as the ship faded farther into the mist and the next chapter of her story crystallized more sharply into reality.

A moment later, she heard the creak of wood behind her, followed by the soft pad of familiar footsteps.

"You've just missed her," Sofía said to Sol, knowing it was her brother without having to turn. "Though I suspect that might have been intentional."

Sol settled beside her, and though he said nothing, his silence bore a language of its own. She read the weariness in his inarticulation, the regret that could only be expressed through an absence of words.

"It's better this way," he confessed once his silence had said its piece. "Adi can't look me in the eye, and I—I can barely stand to be in the same room as her. How could I? *My* freedom is *her* grief, what is there between us now aside from this crushing blame?"

"Is that what you've told yourself, that Adelina faults you for her papá's fate? Oh, Sol . . . if anything, she's punishing herself for not seeing the truth of him sooner, for ever assuming a life by our master's side would be kinder than a life out in his fields."

"And when she learns of my part in it all, will she not begrudge me then? Sweet sister, you think me some blameless bystander. Would you, still, knowing it was me they first came to with his name? That I did not hesitate when they asked, *should he be next?* and when his life was put to a vote, it was my hand that shot up first."

Sofía closed her eyes, thinking back to her brother's words the morning before the fall of Carnaval. *I was unrecognizable* . . . He'd been hurting and lost yet had chosen to spare her that version of himself, the ugliness she could not squeeze into her picture-perfect paradigm of him. How lonely that must have been for her brother. How lonely it had made them both.

"Have you not considered, Sol, that she might have made that very same choice? Beaten you to the vote, I'd wager, were I the betting sort."

"Then it's good you're not one to gamble," he said. "It's blatantly clear she mourns him."

"*And* she loathes him. A heart, I'm coming to understand, may house as many contradictions as it does arteries and veins. Figuratively speaking, of course."

He looked at her askance, a glint of mischief in his eyes. "My, you really are a changed woman . . . Today, it's similes. Tomorrow, epic poetry."

Sofía gave his arm a light whack. "Gods, I'd forgotten you could be obnoxious. Must be all that nostalgia—an upside of not speaking for five years, I suppose."

She'd meant it in jest, but his mood turned somber, and worry that he would shut her out again twisted in her belly. She was racking her brain for some way she could put it all to rights again when he spoke. "I missed you terribly," he said, as though he felt the ache of it still. "I missed us. This."

"Sol . . ."

"You have to know, you have to believe I never meant to hurt you. This whole time, I thought I was doing what was best for you and—"

"Sol." Her hand settled gently over his wrist. "Do you think, hmm . . ." She scoured her mind for the words, not entirely sure what she wished to ask him. "Would you tell me about, well . . . everything? I want to know about your life here. Your friends, the unruly ones, how did you meet them? Did it take you long to learn Taike'ri? Your tattoos, did they hurt? What does this one mean? The painter with the sizable nose, when did you start courting him? He seems kind. Is he kind?"

At Sol's stunned expression, Sofía rolled her eyes. "Please, I saw the way you two were dancing. Now, I may not partake in courtship behaviors, but I'm not entirely ignorant of them either."

Her brother scratched the back of his neck, looking bashful. "I, um, I'm not sure what this . . . I mean, what we . . . Eyduan and I . . ." He heaved a sigh. "We were out of time, and then we weren't, and so now . . ."

"Now comes the hard part."

As the hours wore on, Sol indulged her every question, regaling her with all she'd missed, and as she listened, interrupting only occasionally to comment, she found herself reaching—out of habit—for the pendant on her neck. Each time she did, her fingers felt only the empty hollow of her throat where an inriri had nested for years. The necklace was lost to her now, entombed beneath rockfall perhaps, or sunken deep into the waters where her life ended and began.

Catching the motion, Sol paused midsentence to say, "There's hope for it yet—we're still finding things buried in the rubble. Every minute it seems we dig out something someone thought was gone for good. That said . . ." He reached into his satchel and produced a slim wooden box. "It occurred to me I could fashion you a new one, make something that was uniquely *you*. Woodpeckers are more my thing, anyway. So I tinkered with some cedar. Then pine. I even briefly dabbled with this gorgeous piece of blue mahoe—"

"Personally, I see myself as more of an oak. Plain, but reliable. Sturdy."

He held up a finger. "Hush, I'm telling a story."

"You were listing out timber."

"I was setting the scene, but since you clearly have no appreciation for my narrative artistry, let's skip right on to the end—there I am, just me, the river, and my canoe, when I spot this branch, silver as the Mother's waters. And, gods, the moment I hold it . . . I *know*. I know what it wants to become."

The lid of the box opened then to reveal a pen, carved with the most exquisite detail.

"Sol . . ." Sofía inhaled sharply. "Is this—"

"The Mother's ceiba, yes."

Reverently, Sofía traced her way down the image sculpted into the barrel. One wing, then another, folding flush over the lithe body of the pen, the tips arching slightly, delicately, above a cap ending in tail feathers. The raised texture gave way to smooth etching as it moved into the lower half of the barrel—a practicality that, no doubt, was for her sake—and as her touch glided over the oval of an eye, the curve of a throat, the pieces began to coalesce into a distinct figure.

The pen was a hummingbird, the barrel its body and the nib of guanín its beak. She tested its weight—well-balanced, not too heavy—and its grip too was solid, a perfect fit for her fingers.

"Every artist needs their tools." Sol nudged her shoulder with his. "It was you who gave me my first chisel, and now, I'm giving you your first pen."

"First . . . ?" Sofía stared at her brother uncomprehendingly; her brain so saturated with emotion she could hardly begin to make heads or tails of his words.

He swept his arms out grandly. "You've been reborn, Kán-Kán. Given a divine fresh start no less."

"Ah." It all fell into place. The origin story was a favorite among Coaybay's children, who adored watching Tínima swoop around the audience as they recounted the tale of the primordial hummingbird, remade by a god into a creature of two worlds: the cosmic and the earth, the world of the living and the dead.

Looking at her pen, Sofía felt an instant kinship. A fondness deepened by memories of bygone days, when she'd chase the little birdlings between tobacco flowers.

"It's . . ." Her voice caught. "It's perfect."

She squeezed the pen in one hand, reached for Sol's with the other, and with her eyes, she held the shadow of the ship sailing ever deeper into the mist.

"Stay with me awhile?"

Instead of answering, Sol closed his fingers more firmly over hers in a gesture that once meant *forever, if you need me to*, and now meant *as long as I'm able*. The rope that'd bound them for years after the womb had served its purpose. Kept them tethered when they were the only family the other knew.

All they could do now was trust that when they did let go, something other than fate or survival would bring them back together. That in the times between, she might leave him a cloud from her storm and take a bit of his sunlight with her, trading her shade for his warmth until their seasons aligned again.

Until then . . .

Until then, she would dare to hold as if all they'd ever know was temperate weather.

AFTER

AMID THE GILDED SEA, there is an island in the shape of a beast. Among sailors, it is known as Deadman's Coffin, for it is said no crew makes it through its waters alive. Others refer to it as Isla Fantasma. A ghost, visible only to those seeking somewhere to disappear.

To the locals, it is no less a legend.

Soraya, they call it, the island of spirits and gods. The vessel of the Mother, from whose womb the world was born. Shelter she gives to those who need it, and in return, her children tithe to her their art and dance and song. She grows stronger with every hammock they weave, every plant they crop, every cazabe bread baked crisp over the flames.

Once, the zemí's words were known, but now, it is through the earth she speaks. Her children know her moods by the leaves she sheds, the fields she fills with coffee and corn, the springs she fills with fresh, sweet water.

To some, she is the wrath and the storm. To others, she is the safe harbor. Should you seek in her a home, fear not when you pass through the mist, for she shall know your inten—

"Chronicler."

Sofia glanced up from her journal, her pen nib poised over the page. Kaona stood before her, the afternoon sun crowning her sable hair in gold.

"Here," she said, handing Sofia a sealed envelope. "This came for you this morning."

From the treetops erupted a chorus of sharp screeches and whistles, drawing both their gazes upward.

The parrots' emerald down blended seamlessly among the foliage. It was only the thin streaks of red above their beaks that set them apart from the landscape. There were at least twenty parrots there, pecking at the pods of tamarind fruit dangling from the branches.

"Never seen so many iguaca in one place," Kaona remarked.

"They're nesting!" Fátima piped in cheerily from behind Sofía. She was sitting on a mossy log next to Yuna, their resident ornithologist, with a sketchpad balanced across her knees, her stick of charcoal flying across the page. "There are loads of eggs up in these trees, at least two tucked into every hollow. Plain-looking things though, so don't go getting too excited."

"She expected them to be green," Sofía explained.

"At least spotted! Any sort of pigment, really . . . Scrawls, blotches, squiggles . . . *oooh*, maybe even a texture. Like emu eggs!"

"*Oye*, focus now. You're distracting Yuna."

"Yes, boss."

With a click of her tongue, Sofía turned her attention back to Kaona. "You're hand-delivering missives now?" She accepted the envelope. "It's barely been two moons since your abdication. Don't tell me you're that bored already."

The former Cacika nudged her chin toward the letter, ignoring the question. "What news has Kachi?"

Sighing, Sofía slid her nail under the seal, reached inside the envelope, and unfolded the letter. "Ah, some good tidings . . . Sol's found the entrance to the Jagua cave."

"He followed the petroglyphs then?"

"Per your exact instructions. He's been, let's see . . . gone a week since the writing of this letter, and considering how many provisions he left with is unlikely to be back anytime soon."

"It is no quick task, making vessels worthy of the zemís." Kaona's manner was rough as ever, but there was a maternal sort of pride under all those prickly layers. "And Eyduan?"

"Where else, if not by his side? I imagine he's painted the entire cave in murals by now. The letter does say he 'took an unconscionable amount of pigments with him.'" His and her brother's mediums might have been different, but their devotion to their art was the same—second only to their devotion to each other. A fact Sofía found equal parts nauseating and endearing.

When Sol left their little island, bound for the place he swore never to return to, she rested easy knowing Eyduan would be right there with him, the two of them taking back their birthright with every thrust of a blade, every brushstroke. Remaking the land into the home they'd once longed for.

Live, and find another way to fight. Those were the words Sofía had told Kaona once atop a rooftop. Since then, many others had found their way too—through story, poetry, and laws, through Carnavales that spanned the breadth of entire barrios and pueblos, filling the streets with bright colors and infectious beats, tales of coquís and lizard-snakes, creation caves and opi'a who dance until morning. And when the fighting got too hard, when their weary souls needed a reprieve, they always had the island to return to.

"Those boys' art can move the living," Kaona said, her tone contemplative, "but is it enough to wake the spirits?"

"It happened here," Sofía said. "Who's to say, with a little nudging, that another land might not awaken elsewhere?"

Kaona cocked an eyebrow. "A few years ago, *you* would have."

"A few years ago, I'd have blamed all this on potent hallucinogens. Fairly sure I did, in fact." She was pinning the letter between the pages of her journal for safekeeping, when a slip of paper fluttered out. A clipping from *La Gaceta*, and on it, a grainy photograph of a place Sofía had not seen in a long, long time.

Hacienda Esperanza Becomes School for Freedpersons, read the article.

The land, the manor . . . she'd given it all back. "You fiend," Sofía muttered under her breath, fighting back a laugh. "Doña Elena must be fuming . . ." Not to mention, every other hacendado in the whole of Etérea. An act like that was not just bold, it was political. Bridges would have been burned, feathers ruffled, and Adelina labeled a firebrand—which, no doubt, would have pleased her immensely.

With a wistful smile, Sofía tucked the slip away to read some other time. "Tell me. Why are you really here, Kaona?"

Her obsidian eyes squinted against the light, settling somewhere beyond the treetops. Breathing deeply, she said, "I'm going for a swim."

"Oh" was all Sofía managed. "And Anan—the Cacika, does she know . . . ?"

"I told her last night," she said, and for a moment after, there was only silence. "If your work can spare you, will you brave the waters with me, Chronicler?"

Sofía closed her journal over her lap. "Let me gather my things."

WAVES LAPPED GENTLY against the sides of the canoe, carrying them farther from shore.

Kaona brushed her fingers along the symbols etched into the wood. Two-tailed spirals, representing the waters that connected the earth and heavens, the overlapping nature of beginnings and ends.

"This canoe is the first I've built in over two centuries . . ." It was of exquisite craftsmanship, every detail labored over lovingly. "Back in my tribe, before all . . . this, I was a canoe maker."

"Tínima once told me you built the ones that brought your people here, that it was you who made it possible for them to escape." Sofía opened her journal to a blank page. At the top, she marked the date in the crisp black ink of her hummingbird pen. "Is that why you were appointed Cacika?"

"It was certainly part of the reason, but not all." Kaona took the naje and swept it across the water, paddling without hurry. "My mother was Cacika, her name well-known among the coastal tribes. By the time we took refuge here, there were so few of us left, and no leader among us. If anyone was to rise to the role, it seemed fitting that it should be her daughter."

"Was it not what you wanted?"

"Wanted? Gods no, but it was what was needed," she admitted. "I was never destined to ascend to chiefdom, nor did I care to. In my youth, I dreamt of adventure . . . imagined my fate was bound to the seas. One day, I thought, I would sail the world on a vessel of my own making. The finest anyone had ever seen." Her face softened at the memory. "My cousin, they were the one the tribe had chosen to take my bibi's place. There was truly no one better suited to lead. A kinder, more selfless spirit you would not find elsewhere."

Sofía listened and transcribed as Kaona spoke, without redactions or amendments, for such were the duties of a Chronicler. She was there to preserve and record, not editorialize. Too long already had her people's stories been mistold. She would not make that same mistake.

"That soft-hearted fool, they died protecting us from the arijua," she said. "I had no time to grieve them—there was too much loss those days. Hardly a moon went by without someone being taken from us." The ire that once had honed Kaona's every word into a blade had lost some of its sharpness. It was not blunted, exactly, but neither did it define her. She had learned in the years since Carnaval's fall how to hold her anger without letting it consume her. "I was never meant to lead, much less fight. It was my bibi who was the leader. My wife, the warrior. They gave their blood to protect those of us who were too weak, too cowardly, to protect ourselves."

Sofía glanced up from her journal. "I'd argue neither word applies to you."

"And you'd be wrong, Chronicler. I was a different person then," she said. "Our son, he was captured during a raid the summer of his sixth year. Yuisa, she went after him, and I . . . I stayed behind. Told myself I'd only get in the way. What was my fishing spear to her bow and arrow? Sure, I could spear a shark as well as any man, but what chance did I stand against enemy steel?"

None at all. The Taike'ri's weapons were no match for the invading forces'.

"She was taken," said Sofía. Kaona's silence was admission enough. "And your boy?"

"Chained to a ship heading east . . . Never saw him again." The naje stilled in her grip. "My wife, I freed the only way I could. Bloodflower seeds, slipped through a gap on the wall where they kept her."

For a while, there were no more words between them. Just the scratch of Sofia's pen and the gentle swish of the waves. It was a beautiful day for sailing, the waters fair and the sky a gradient of dusk blue fading to brilliant orange. The ever-present mist around Soraya gave way for them, peeling back to reveal a crystalline sea, and a thriving reef beneath it. Fish swam among the algae and coral, boasting scales in every hue.

Without looking up from the reef, Sofia asked, "How did you and Yuisa meet?"

"Oh, there was never a meeting, we just . . . *were*. She and I were raised side by side." The transformation in Kaona was instantaneous, the mere mention of those brighter days lit up her very being. "We were born in the dry season, days apart, under the stars of the One-Legged Hunter. For as long as I'd drawn breath, she had been by my side. I suppose that is why I did not fall in love with her . . . I grew into it, as I grew into my bones. It felt natural, inevitable even." She chuckled. "Not for Yuisa. She loved another, a boy from the mountains who once a season came to our tribe to trade. They were wed when she came of age, and two harvests passed before I saw her again. She returned to the tribe newly widowed and heavy with child."

"And you were there for her." It was hard to reconcile this version of Kaona—a loving wife and mother—with the woman who had once cared only for vengeance.

"Every step of the way."

The burden weighing on her lightened the more she recounted of their lives together. There had been so much beauty there, not just in the years before the invasion, but in the moments in between their struggle for survival. Several times, Sofia had to remind herself to write. To not lose herself in those stories.

The former Cacika was partway through another, when something caught her attention.

"... Kaona?"

She was staring out into the mist, head angled like she was listening for something, waiting for a voice to call out from it. "Can you feel it?"

Sofía peered into the gray. "Feel what?"

"The Mother's hold, stretching thin." Kaona lifted a hand to the mist, and it woke to her touch, circling the length of her arm, its movements serpentine. "We are at the boundary of her power."

If Sofía focused, drew her attention inward, she did feel it, the cord that bound her life to the island pulling taut, willing her back to the safety of its shores.

"It is one thing to bring a body back from death," said Kaona, "but to bond to it a spirit that has already brushed the sands of Coaybay . . . that is something else entirely."

Despite all she had witnessed, Sofía still was not sure she believed in spirits, or gods for that matter. Not as most defined them, anyhow. *Reason* was her creed, and always would be, and perhaps that would someday lead her to the divine, to a pantheon and an afterlife. To believing—as many others did—that a god lived inside the land. Not that the land itself was a god.

Until then, the natural world was the only faith she subscribed to.

"It's true then," Sofía said, thinking of the words a diviner foretold years ago . . . *What is your search worth? What will you become?* "I can never leave the island." It was its power that kept her life from draining out of her body. Kaona had warned her, of course, but it was a different matter entirely to experience it: the sudden weakness in her muscles, the dullness of her thoughts, the voice that urged her to *turn back, turn back*. Were she to cross the mist, her tether to this world would be broken, she was sure of it now.

"Do you resent it, being confined to this island . . . ?"

Sofía considered the question. "Not today," she replied honestly. "Today, I have all I need here."

"And what of tomorrow?"

"Hmm." She tapped her knuckles lightly against her journal. "I don't have an answer to that. Do you reckon there'll be a great many tomorrows?"

"However many you'll let the Mother keep you for is my guess. It was the same for the others who returned from Maketaori's land with me that night. They lived, until they chose not to."

Sofia nodded slowly, digesting the information. She had known it, on some level. Seen the signs on her unchanging skin, the illnesses her system purged before they ever got ahold of her. "And how will I know when I'm ready to . . . move onward?"

Kaona smiled crookedly. "When you stop asking yourself that question." She leaned over to clasp Sofia's shoulder. "Time can be a mercy, child, as it can be a ruin. Consume it like you would uikú—just enough to warm you. Take it from me," she said, "the more you reach for that cup, the more dangerous it becomes."

And with that ominous warning, she stood. The canoe rocked with the motion, but she balanced her weight across the vessel expertly, with one foot propped against the bow seat, and another on the thwart.

The mist curled in tendrils around her, like arms clinging to her in an embrace. Begging her to s*tay, stay, stay*. Here, where she'd be comforted. Protected. "Mother," Kaona's eyes welled, her irises like pools at midnight. "You have to let me go now. It's time for me to come home."

At her words, the mist shivered and shrank like a creature wounded.

"My bibi, my wife, my boy . . . I have kept them waiting for too long already. Let me come home to them. Please, Mother." She extended her fingers out into the gray. "I was not ready the night I met you, but I am now."

Tentatively, the mist reached back, brushing along the tears on her cheeks.

Kaona, leaning into the island's ghostly touch, whispered, "Thank you. For all you've given me, thank you . . ." To Sofia, she said without turning, "Keep the fire warm, ituno. The world shall know of us one day."

Sofía dipped her head, sealing the promise.

As she lifted her gaze, Kaona slipped into the water. She went without a goodbye, drifting farther into the waves, toward the island that was once her home. And as she swam, she sang. Of spirits, and bats, and the lands where the dead dance into the night. Little by little, the mist closed around her, and her lullaby became a sigh in the wind.

Taikaraya, taikaraya . . . yarari . . .

Taiguey, taiguey . . . nanichi . . .

Sofía listened until the last echo of the last note faded, and with it, what remained of the day. And there, under silver and shadow, in the company of a god and a ghost, she lifted her pen, and wrote.

★ ★ ★ ★ ★

AUTHOR NOTE

WHILE A WORK of fiction, *Beasts of Carnaval* is grounded in the historical realities and events of the colonized Caribbean. It draws inspiration from the culture, beliefs, and history of the Taíno—the largest group of indigenous people that, among other places, inhabited what is now known as Cuba, Jamaica, Haiti, the Dominican Republic, the Virgin Islands, and my home of Puerto Rico.

This story has meant *so* much to me personally, and I'm immensely honored I get to share it with readers. At its core, this is a story about joy, art, and cultural reclamation as a form of rebellion, and how choosing to honor the stories, ways, and words of our ancestors is an act of liberation. Which is not to say there is one right or wrong way to fight against systems of oppression. The unfortunate truth is that for a people colonized, every path to liberation demands a price.

In this novel, I specifically wanted to explore the role of carnavales in Caribbean resistance, the roots of which trace back to a pre-emancipation ritual called Cannes Brulees that first occurred on the sugar plantations of Trinidad and Tobago. Enslaved people of African and Indigenous descent resisted their oppressors by setting fire to sugarcane—a valuable colonial commodity—and through a celebration that involved music making, performance, and oral tradition.

Since then, Carnaval continued to evolve across the Caribbean and beyond as a form of nonviolent resistance, a way of fighting back colonial forces that aim to separate, dehumanize, and disempower by embracing the opposite: community, culture, and remembrance. If you're interested in learning more, a good place to start is Northeastern University's archive *Caribbean Carnival Exhibit: An Act of Opposition.*

We also see early traces of Carnaval dating back to the first years of Spanish colonization, when the Taínos rebelled against their oppressors by continuing to play their ball games and hold their areyto ceremonies. This thread has been carried through to the present-day Caribbean, where celebrations, art, music, and dance remain a core part of our collective culture.

In bringing the world of the Taike'ri to life, I leaned on works such as Sebastián Robiou Lamarche's *Mitología y religión de los Taínos*, a comprehensive look at the Taíno belief system and cosmology (it's available in English as well!), and José Juan Arrom's edition of *Relación acerca de las antigüedades de los indios*, one of the first (and sadly, only) original ethnographic works we have about the Taíno. For the Taíno language, much of which was lost during the period of the conquest, my go-to resources were "*Vocabulario indo-antillano*" by historian Cayetano Coll y Toste and Javier Hernández's *Primario básico del Taíno-Borikenaíki*, which provides a foundation for the restoration of the Taíno language. I also want to give a special mention to Lucia Faria's "The Power & Limits of Language," which dives into the politics of language and its role in identity reclamation and nation making.

The overall world of Etérea has been adapted from mid-1870s Puerto Rico shortly following the abolition of slavery, almost a decade after the end of slavery in the United States. Considering this is a fictional world, some elements and events have been intentionally reimagined—notably, the timeline of Spanish colonization. In Etérea, Hisperian colonizers would have arrived roughly eighty years later than Spanish colonizers, and a few key events would have unfolded differently as a consequence. In this alternate history, Taike'ri descendants remain as the main enslaved population for centuries, whereas the Taíno population was nearly decimated by disease, violence, and exploitation, and soon replaced by enslaved people from Africa.

AUTHOR NOTE

Some historical narratives claim the Taíno became "extinct," with some records indicating there were fewer than five hundred Taínos remaining by 1548. The reality is much more complicated, resulting from a combination of mestizaje, Taínos taking refuge in remote areas, forced cultural assimilation, and a phenomenon termed "paper genocide," in which a group of people are forcibly erased through the intentional destruction or alteration of documents and records related to them. For example, even though Taíno slavery was *officially* abolished in 1542, a Spaniard could reclassify an enslaved Taíno as African in order to continue exploiting their labor.

All these factors contributed to the myth of extinction, a sense that the Taíno people are in the past—that *we* are in the past. Though I was aware of this part of my heritage growing up, like Sofía, I struggled with knowing how much of that identity I was "allowed" to claim as a person of triracial ancestry. If this part of Sofía's story spoke to you in any way, I truly and sincerely hope you know you are enough.

If you're interested in learning more, you can check out my website for further reading suggestions and a full list of the resources referenced here. Thank you so much for visiting this world with me.

ACKNOWLEDGMENTS

I AM SO deeply grateful to everyone who sailed off toward the unknown with me. I couldn't have braved these waters alone.

First, an enormous thank-you to Allegra Martschenko, agent extraordinaire and current record holder for fastest email responses (I can only assume). You saw to the heart of this story and believed in it when my own confidence wavered. I may be able to write a book, but I seriously lack the imagination to envision a better business partner than you.

To Dina Davis, wow! I feel so incredibly fortunate to have you as my editor. Thank you for giving *Beasts of Carnaval* a home, for challenging me to dig deeper into this story, and for championing it every step of the way. It's been such an absolute honor working with you. You deserve a lifetime supply of pasteles. (It's highly likely one or more of my family members will make this happen. Stay tuned.)

To Spencer, my partner, best friend, and first reader, for patiently listening to the first seed of this story and every revision since. Thank you for encouraging me and keeping me well-fed through all the long nights, self-doubts, and endless rewrites. I'm so, *so* grateful to have you in my life. Te amo.

Thank you also to the incredible Laini Taylor for her support, guidance, and playful writing workshops. Not only do your stories occupy a whole shelf in my heart, but through them I have also found the most magical community of writers. A hundred thousand thank-yous to the Muses that make up this lovely community: A.Y Chao, Amy Zed, Ariana, Ashley, Bee, Brooke,

ACKNOWLEDGMENTS

Camille Le Baron, Clare Edge, Elaine, Eric, Georgia Summers, Joanna Roddy, Kae, Kim DeRose, Lauren, Laurence, Lucy, Mara Rutherford, Margaret, Riv, Séverine, Shana Targosz, Shveta Thakrar, Sonja Howard, and everyone who has offered me advice, support, and celebrated new publishing milestones with me. A special thanks to Leah List for the many cowriting sessions as well as for being an overall incredible person and friend. I would have missed so many deadlines if not for you.

Thank you to my family. My mom and my brother, who nurtured my love of stories; my abuelita Sofia, who let me use her name; my abuelo Rati, who is largely responsible for my peculiar sense of humor—*ninoninonino*—and to my own sister in heart and best friend of nearly twenty years—Kat, my childhood was so much brighter with you in it.

To the incredible team at MIRA and HarperCollins that made this book possible. Publisher Loriana Sacilotto. Associate publisher Amy Jones. VP of publicity Heather Connor. The editorial team's Margaret Marbury, Nicole Brebner, April Osborn, Evan Yeong, and Fiona Smallman. Managing editorial's Katie-Lynn Golakovich and Stephanie Choo. Proofreading manager Tamara Shifman. Copyediting manager Gina Macdonald. The typesetting team, including Bill Rowcliffe and Sara Watson. My publicist, Kamille Carreras Pereira. The marketing team, including Ana Luxton, Lindsey Reeder, Randy Chan, Ashley MacDonald, Diane Lavoie, Rachel Haller, Pamela Osti, Puja Lad, Alex McCabe, Ambur Hostyn, Riffat Ali, Brianna Wodabek, Ciara Loader, Daphne Guima, and Jaimie Nackan. The art team, including creative director Erin Craig, art director/designer Elita Sidiropoulou, and illustrator Valentino Lasso—thank you for the glorious cover! The subrights team, including Reka Rubin, Christine Tsai, and Nora Rawn. The sales team, including Bailey Thomas and Melissa Brooks. Galleys and cover manager Denise Thomson. Audio producer Jennifer Lopes and the fabulous audio narrator Inés del Castillo. Sensitivity/DEIB readers Sossity Chiricuzi and Isabelle Felix, thank you for all your thoughtful feedback—this book is stronger because of you.

ACKNOWLEDGMENTS

To everyone else who worked on and believed in this story, thank you from the bottom of my heart, and to you, dearest reader, I'm so honored and grateful you chose to visit el Carnaval de Bestias with me.